A Chronicle of Horrors

AN ANTHOLOGY

DREAD HOUSE PUBLISHING

A CHRONICLE OF HORRORS

Paperback ISBN 979-8-218-89185-5

Contents

1860s

Trottelheim

A.C. Hessenauer

Laila was over it. She was over the drive, over the trip, and quite frankly, she was starting to feel over Jace.

He gripped the steering wheel in one hand, the crumpled map in the other, rustling in the silence of the car as he squinted down at it. As he struggled with the thin creased paper folding in on itself, Laila reached over and grabbed it, practically ripping it out of his hands. "Dammit, Jace, give it to me."

She spread the map, holding it upright, angled towards him. He reached out, pointing, eyes darting between the map and the road. Either it was Laila's imagination, or the fog was getting worse. The VW Golf's headlights did little to cut through the dense soup surrounding them.

"We should be right around here somewhere. I'm positive," Jace said, eyes back on the road.

Laila lowered the map. She stared at the spot he had indicated; an empty stretch of road, in the middle of nowhere Germany.

There was nothing marked on the map. Although even if there had been, she might have struggled to read it. And Jace; he was hopeless. She knew that was why he refused to stop to ask for directions. Also, because, as she was starting to realize, he was a bit of a macho idiot.

He had laughed at the Lingoodle prompts. At the little Owl icon, scolding him. His favorite had been when the owl "died" from his lack of practicing German. He'd shown her the image of the owl lying on the lid of a crypt, with black 'X' marks for eyes.

Laila had paid for the premium subscription and practiced every single day. Not that she was fluent; far from it. But to Jace, the whole thing had been a joke, apparently.

Laila grit her teeth. "I don't understand why we didn't just stop and ask for directions in that last town."

Jace rolled his eyes. "Babe, we have GPS, and it was still freaking working at that point."

"Was it?" Laila asked. She was fairly certain the little cloud symbol had a line through it, even back then.

Laila returned to the map. There was no point in arguing with him. The time to turn back had long since passed.

Jace leaned over the steering wheel. "Look!"

A crooked wooden sign, leaning drunkenly read, '*Trottelheim*'. She ran the pronunciation over her tongue, mouthing it silently. "*Fool's Home ...*" she murmured. It looked hand-carved. She turned to Jace. "Did you see that? The sign said the town's called Trottelheim. That translates to Fool's Home. I've never heard of it ..."

Jace didn't look at her. He just nodded and hummed a little in his throat, "Mmhmm."

She hated when he did that. Pretended he was listening to her. Why was he constantly patronizing her? She swore that half the time he treated her like an annoying child.

Her cheeks blazed. "Did you hear me? I said the sign says the village is called *'Trottelheim.'*" Her gaze fell to the map. "But there's nothing here; no town on the map." Jace didn't respond.

They were heading uphill now. Jace ground the gears with a curse, gravity pressing her back in her seat. The fog was getting thinner. Maybe it was the elevation. Or it was finally starting to clear.

They crested the hill, and a building loomed into view, sporting wooden siding. Laila leaned over Jace as they passed, and she caught his self-assured grin. "Don't you dare say I told you so."

His grin only widened, as he chuckled, both dimples showing.

"Do me a favor, and pull over before I scream."

Jace laughed again, but the Golf veered over to the right, and slowed, coming to a stop in front of a somewhat dilapidated-looking house.

Laila sighed as they ground to a halt. Grateful not to be moving, she closed her eyes for a moment. "I'm going to find a restroom. And *you* are going to stop and ask the first person you see for directions. Got it?" She pressed the map against his chest, and he took it, his lips pressed in a thin line.

He mumbled something in response.

"What?"

"Sure thing," he said more loudly, his tone long-suffering.

Laila unclicked her seatbelt and climbed out, slamming the door behind her. There had to be a shop, maybe a little bakery, that would have a public restroom. The crunch of Jace's boots on the road behind drifted to her as she walked, and she felt a sense of satisfaction at each stomping step of her own that took her farther away from him.

Laila turned, gazing in all directions. It could hardly be called a village. There were only a few scattered buildings. A larger building loomed ahead, with a pointed roof.

"Jace—" She turned to him, pausing. A young woman stood across the street, a wicker basket slung over one arm. She froze, staring back at Laila. She wore a long black dress, and an old-fashioned bonnet on her head, her hair tucked underneath. Her mouth gaped open, her eyes traveling up and down Laila's body. Laila watched as her gaze shifted to Jace, and she began to back away slowly.

"Wait!" Laila called out. The woman's eyes went wide, and she ran, disappearing into the fog. "What the hell?"

Jace stood staring after her. "Where in the heck are we?"

"Where?" Laila spat back at him. "I think you mean *when*. What century is this?" she sputtered, her gaze on the odd thatched roof on the building across the street.

Jace scoffed, "Oh, come on. What—you think we drove into some sort of ... German version of the bermuda triangle? This isn't the goddamn twilight zone." He waved a hand after the woman. "This is probably all part of some sort of festival." He trailed off at the expression on Laila's face, as she stared back up the road.

Jace turned. A small crowd of people stood there. All men. Several older men, a few who looked to be about their age, in that indeterminate middle of life, and a young boy. One of them held an actual pitchfork.

They stood some distance from the Golf, as though they were afraid to get any closer. An older man turned, his eyes locking onto Laila's. The fear and icy hostility reflected there made Laila's blood run hot.

Jace turned abruptly and made a beeline for her. "Come on." He grabbed her arm. "Let's head for that building; it looks like a church."

Laila muttered, "Ouch." But she followed him, glancing backward.

They reached the church, and Jace swiftly scaled the stairs. Laila paused, her steps faltering. Bundles of corn stalks were tied to the railings with woven ribbons, bunches of flowers tucked into the folds.

She frowned. "I dunno Jace. I'm not so sure this is a church ..."

Jace eyed her briefly from the doorway, a look of barely concealed derision on his face, before he turned and was swallowed instantly by darkness.

Laila glanced back up the street. The strange men still stood there, staring at her now, instead of the Golf. She turned and followed Jace inside.

They made their way haltingly. Laila held one hand out in front of her, swinging it back and forth, as she waited for her eyes to adjust. Her hand hit something hard, and she grasped onto it; the side of a wooden pew, followed by another.

She followed Jace's footsteps, echoing hollowly up ahead. "Hello?" he called out tentatively. "Is someone there?"

A faint rustling, followed by a thump, from somewhere to their left. Laila jumped at the noise.

A light bloomed ahead of her, off to the right. Laila oriented towards it. Jace's face, bathed in orange, as he leaned forward, studying something on the wall. He held up his lighter, leaning closer, his brows furrowed.

Laila moved to his side, peering at the painting. The hand-painted artwork covered the entire wall, as far as her eyes could make out in the flickering flame.

The image directly before them depicted two young men, facing each other, separated by a thick line. They stood in identical poses. Their outfits and their features were identical as well. A second figure loomed behind the man on the right. Long black legs, knees bent oddly backward, a rounded face, with a slight snout, and two pointed horns poking out of its forehead. A wicked grin was half-hidden below the snout.

The lighter flickered out and died just as Laila opened her mouth to speak. Jace murmured a curse, moving away from her, and his thumb struck the wheel, once, twice, three times, before the flame took once more.

In the flickering light, Laila could make out something hanging against the back wall of the church. She moved closer to Jace, sliding her arm through his, her hand gripping his bicep a little too tightly. Her mind settled on the rough outline of a man wearing a crown. Two eyes that shone faintly in the dark. They must be painted white.

Laila leaned forward, squinting, taking in shaggy black hair in matted curls, curving, twisting horns, and below, stark white eyes, rolled back in its head. Mad eyes. The eyes of a wild thing that had died in agony.

Some sort of goat, she realized with a sharp stab of panic. Its limbs were splayed, tied with rope. It wore a crown, not made of thorns, but twigs. More of the flowers from out front were scattered on an altar beneath it. Its hooves were filthy. An awful stench wafted over her.

There, in the center of the altar, wrapped in a swath of white fabric, lay something bloody; the blood soaking through the fabric so dark, it was nearly black. Laila recoiled, pulling Jace's arm.

"Oh God," he murmured, releasing a gagging, choking sound.

Laila stared into those dead white eyes, dread rising in her chest, as overhead, bells began to toll. A mournful, awful sound, as though they were calling out to the devil himself.

The creak of floorboards behind them was just barely audible. A man stood there, pitchfork in hand. A slow smile spread over his lips. *"Wilkommen in Trottelheim. Wir haben Sie erwartet."*

"Oh my God," Laila gasped, hot tears of fear springing to her eyes, her nails digging into Jace's arm. She looked up at him in horror, and he stared cluelessly back at her.

"What?" Jace shrugged. "What'd he say?"

"You have got to be kidding me! You idiot!" Laila snapped.

Jace's eyes widened, perhaps in surprise, more than fear, as the pent-up rage that had been building in her chest, threatening to spill for days—no, make that weeks—make that *months*—broke loose like water from a dam.

"He said, *'Welcome to Trottelheim; we've been waiting for you!',*" Laila shrieked. "I sent you all those goddamn streak-freezes for nothing!"

"W–what?" Jace murmured, taking a step back.

"*Lingoodle*, you piece of shit!" The tendons in Laila's arms, her neck, stretched taut. "We wouldn't be here right now, lost in a fucking M. Night Shyamalan movie if you had just practiced German like you were supposed to!"

Jace continued to stare at her, his expression a mixture of horror and bewilderment.

"*Fuck!*" Laila added one final expletive for emphasis. She grabbed Jace once more by the arm and dragged him away from the motionless man with the pitchfork, behind a curtain of dark fabric that stood to the left of the grotesque effigy.

Jace stumbled after her, his hot breath heavy on her neck as they fumbled through the dark corridor.

"Why is it so freaking dark in here?"

"Electricity hasn't been invented yet, you absolute dullard," Laila shot back at him. "We need to get out of here; circle around and get back to the car."

"Just what do you think is happening right now?" Jace asked, the ire rising in his voice. "That goat-thing ... whatever it was, back there, was fucking disgusting. Messed up ... but nothing's happened, Laila. We need to calm down, not lose our heads."

Laila snorted in response.

"This is so typical."

Laila stopped dead, turning to Jace in the darkened hallway. "Excuse me?" she said with exquisite slowness.

"What?" Jace held his arms out to his sides. "You always blow things out of proportion. You always overreact."

"Yeah?" Laila sneered. "If underreacting was an Olympic Sport, you'd win the fucking gold medal, wouldn't you?"

"You used to like that about me, you know," Jace said quietly.

Laila's features softened slightly in the dark, before her eyes narrowed and her jaw tightened once more. "Yeah, well ... guess that makes me an idiot too." She turned away from him. "Let's go. We're wasting time."

Laila expected to emerge into the dim light of a foggy day at any moment. She pictured herself squinting. The light would be too bright after the pitch-black interior. The building they had entered had only been so large, and most of it was taken up by the room containing the altar. Yet, they continued to stumble forward in the dark. After a while, she recognized the faint strain in her calves for what it was.

"Christ, we're walking on a slope, aren't we?" she said to Jace, her contempt for him overshadowed by the bubble of panic in her chest. "We're heading underground."

There was a long pause before Jace answered. "No." He shook his head, a rustle of movement in the dark, as he glanced back the way they had come. "Are we?"

Laila placed her hand against the wall to her left, cool to the touch and slightly damp. "We are, Jace, I can tell. This corridor is taking us deeper underground. Maybe we should turn around. Go back."

The bell still tolled in the distance, the sound echoing mournfully. But now, in addition to the clanging of the bell, faint voices drifted to Laila's ears along with the shuffling of footsteps. She pictured the man with the pitchfork, waiting for them in the opening of the corridor, or perhaps just behind that curtain. Had he rallied the men inspecting the Golf? Were they coming after them?

"Maybe this is another exit," Jace said thoughtfully. "That has to be it. We might be underground now, but maybe it leads to a back entrance. We can circle around and head back to the car."

Laila doubted this tunnel was built solely as an alternative exit, but she didn't have the energy to argue, and the last thing she wanted was to run into that band of strange men in this dark tunnel.

"Fine, let's keep going then." She picked up the pace, Jace trailing behind her.

Laila sensed more than saw the walls of the tunnel widening, falling away on either side. They were in a larger, more open space. The air, which had been dank and unmoving, thick and still, contained a hint of freshness, a bit of movement. Laila breathed in deeply. Jace had been right, for once. There was an opening here, somewhere up ahead. The tunnel must branch to the surface.

"Where's your lighter?" Laila turned to him. "I think there's an opening somewhere off this main corridor."

A hand clamped over her mouth, and she let out a muffled cry.

"Laila?" Jace called to her, and Laila felt a brief twist of odd satisfaction at the concern in his voice.

She realized too late that the roughness she felt against her lips was due to a rag pressed tightly over her mouth and nose. She held her breath for as long as possible, struggling to break free, before breathing in helplessly. The acrid chemicals stung her nose, bringing tears to her eyes. Her eyes rolled back in her head as her equilibrium swung and she tipped into darkness.

Laila woke to the cool breeze kissing her skin and sighed in relief. She was outside. She had made it. Her eyelashes fluttered as she struggled to maintain consciousness, floating deliciously in her delirium.

She slid her legs beneath the sheets, and when the skin between her thighs rubbed together, her eyes snapped open. She had been wearing jeans, hadn't she? She stared at the ceiling overhead, dark beams of wood. White curtains billowed to her left.

Laila managed to sit, her head swimming slightly with the movement. The room she found herself in was sparse. A simple wooden chair, back ramrod straight, sat against the far wall, beside a closed door. A small wooden chest of drawers, with a plain white ceramic washbasin and pitcher resting on top sat against the other wall. A wooden bedside table sat beside the narrow, uncomfortable cot on which she lay. A single unlit taper set in a rounded dish, sporting a thumbhole on the side; its walls sloped to catch dripping wax.

Laila felt as though she had awoken in a museum exhibit. She pictured the tiny rooms full of antiques, staged in the Henry Ford Museum back home.

How she had loved to stroll past them, peering in at the quaint old-timey furniture. She had remarked over every detail to Jace, exclaimed over how small people must have been back then. How austere their lifestyles. How she had longed, in an odd way, for the simplicity. How she had envied them that. She had pictured their lives devoid of things like tiktok, and electricity and somehow more full of meaning.

Jace had no interest, of course. He had groaned when she begged him to go to the Henry Ford with her that day. He said he had no interest in the past. Same thing with the art museum. And just last week, he'd been bored in the library in Vienna. How could you be bored in such a place? Surrounded by stories and folklore and history? Laila found it all fascinating, quaint, and picturesque.

But there was nothing quaint about the mattress she lay on. It felt as though it were full of straw; sharp ends poked and prodded at her. The white nightdress she found herself wearing was stiff and scratchy.

She gazed around the stark room with a frown. What on earth did people do once it got dark each night? Did they sleep fourteen hours a day, just to avoid the dullness of life? Laila shook herself. Focus. She needed to focus. Where was she? Why had those mystery hands clamped over her nose and mouth, only to drag her to an old-fashioned homestead and dress her in a cotton nightgown?

Laila groaned and forced herself out of bed; the frame creaked in response as she unburdened it of her weight.

She staggered a bit, her legs weak and shaky beneath her. She felt more awake now. Sharper. Jace. She needed to find Jace.

A faint light shone around the door, a glow that seemed to grow, swell, and then fade against the floorboards.

The creaking of the door sent yet another volley of icy fingers of dread down her spine, even though she knew she was the source of the noise.

The door swung outward, revealing a single room beyond. A fire flickered in an antique-looking black stove across from the doorway to her small room, with a kitchen area to the right and a small, humble-looking wooden table. Laila spied flames dancing through the thin slats in the stove's grate;

a little door with a knob handle kept the flames enclosed within. A wood-stove, her brain added, as an afterthought. That's what it was called—a woodstove. A long black cylinder rose behind it, disappearing into the ceiling, rushing the smoke and ash overhead to be released into the night sky. She gazed through the hazy, thin curtains that covered a pair of small windows to her left. It was fully dark now.

Laila turned to her right, and a startled little gasp left her throat involuntarily. A man stood there with his back to her.

Broad shoulders under rough-spun wool fabric; he sported a brown jacket, layered over darker pants. His arms hung at his sides. No pitchfork or other weapon visible. He wore a rounded black hat with a broad rim.

Laila's gaze flickered to the wall before him, and her breath caught in her throat once more. The man was staring into a small mirror that hung on the wall, its glass cracked along the bottom of the frame, silver backing dusty and faded. The man tilted his head to the side, raised one arm, and grabbed the rim of his hat. He tipped it, once, twice, as though he were practicing the movement. His features were shadowed, beneath the hat, but Laila recognized those cheekbones. The slope of his nose.

"Jace?" Laila's voice was laced with apprehension and uncertainty. Jace froze, his features hidden by the shadows beneath the hat, one hand still raised, caught in the motion of reaching to grasp the brim once more.

He turned towards her. "Laila," he breathed in a rush of air, "thank God you're awake! I was starting to worry. Are you okay? How are you feeling?" He moved towards her, footsteps hollow against the creaking floorboards. The fire popped and crackled, causing her to jump, as he reached for her.

Jace paused, his gaze roving over her features, taking in her hunched shoulders and the fear in her eyes. "It's just me, Laila, it's okay." He swept the hat off his head, brushed his hand through his hair, and swept it off his forehead, laughing.

Laila's shoulders dropped, and she took in a deep inhalation of air, allowing it to stream steadily through her lips on the exhale. "God, Jace. Where the fuck are we? What do these people want with us?" She held her arms out to her sides, peering down at the plain cotton nightdress, taking in the bit of lace and the ties at her throat. "I mean ... what the fuck is this?"

Jace shook his head, his brow creased as he studied her. His eyes seemed to linger briefly on her chest, her nipples peaked against the scratchy, stiff fabric in the chilly air. She squirmed internally, a flush rising to her cheeks. *It's only Jace. What the fuck is wrong with you?*

"I don't know," he said thoughtfully after a moment. "But I'm not going to let anything happen to you. Don't worry."

Laila shivered and wrapped both arms around her chest, running her hands up and down her bare arms.

"Are you cold?" Jace frowned at the goosebumps that rose on her arms and moved swiftly to the woodstove. He grabbed something resembling an oven mitt from a hook on the wall nearby and pulled the little slatted door open. Selecting chunks of firewood, he shoved them inside. Orange sparks flew out, and he grunted slightly as a particularly large one landed on the exposed skin of his wrist. He shook his hand and continued to feed the flames until they crackled and roared within. Laila frowned a little watching him.

Jace shut the stove door and turned to Laila. He paused, glancing around the room, then dashed over to pick up a rocking chair. He moved it closer; a few feet away from the stove, setting it on the edge of the woven rug that lay there. "Here. Sit here; you'll be warm in no time."

Laila moved slowly over towards the fire. She sat in the wooden rocker, leaning back, and clutching the armrests.

She turned as Jace left the room, his footsteps retreating further into the house, down a dark hallway. "Jace?" she called after him, a momentary burst of panic flooding her chest.

But he was already back. He carried a bundle in his arms. Laila's mind flashed to the altar—the black blood, soaking through the tiny shroud. Just a blanket, Laila realized numbly, as he spread it over her, covering her lap and chest, tucking it in gently beneath the armrests.

"There." He moved to take a seat on a low stool across from her. "You'll be snug as a bug in a rug now." Laila's frown deepened as she stared at him. His smile came easily to his lips, his eyes were clear, open, and honest. He grinned at her and shrugged. "What?"

"Nothing," she mumbled, her focus shifting to the crackling wood behind the grate. They sat in silence.

Laila cleared her throat. "How long have you been awake?"

"Awake?"

"Yes. How long have you been awake? How long was I sleeping?" Presumably, he had awoken just as she had. In an unfamiliar bed, in another room of the old house. Dressed in unfamiliar clothes. "Why would they do this? Drug us? Knock us out ... just to, what? Change our outfits? Dress us up like them?" Laila forced herself to try to calm down, her heartbeat accelerating to an uncomfortable speed in her chest. "What do they want from us?"

Her voice sounded small. Weak, to her own ears. She stared at Jace, waiting, as though he would have the answers. As though he could protect her. Save her. Could he fight? She tried to picture it. She studied the stark room around them, searching for anything that could be used as a weapon. The night sky, glimpsed through the shifting curtains, was pitch black. They were here, by the fire ... the light would be visible for what? A mile around? More? Was the fog still there? Did it lie thickly, offering some protection from prying eyes? What did it matter? They had put them here, in this house. They knew exactly where to find them. She pictured Jace, throwing fists against the man with the pitchfork. There was only one of him, against how many of them? And besides; it was Jace.

Laila glared over at him, with his glamor muscles and his fancy protein shakes, his stupid HIT gym membership he'd paid for and never used after the first two months. Her cheeks burned slightly as he caught her studying him, and she looked away.

Laila stared into the fire as Jace shrugged. "I wasn't awake for long before you woke up. I don't know why they did this. Who knows what their motives are? But there are worse ways to wake up, surely, than tucked in a warm bed."

"There you go again." Laila's fists clenched beneath the blanket, and it slid down her chest, pooling in her lap. "Minimizing my feelings, as always." She let out a sharp huff of air and locked eyes with him. "You know, I'm starting to think this whole thing was a mistake."

Jace studied her, taking in the rise and fall of her chest. "I do that a lot, don't I?" he said slowly. He shook his head as he turned to stare into the fire. "Men are foolish creatures, aren't we?"

His tone was so flat, that it made Laila pause, her spine stiffening slightly. She watched him closely as he stared into the flickering flames beyond the grate.

"Not a lick of sense among us. Too blind to see beyond our own noses." He swiveled back to her on the stool, and something in the directness of his stare, the set of his shoulders, caught her off guard. "I'm sorry, Laila. I'm sorry for how I've treated you. I should have done better. I *will* do better. I promise you."

Laila's eyes widened imperceptibly, and she sat frozen, unsure how to respond.

Thump.

Faint movement. Where was it coming from? Was it outside? Inside the house? Laila's ears strained, her head cocked to one side.

"You deserve better, Laila," Jace went on, his eyes never leaving hers. "You shouldn't have to settle for a lesser man." He studied her features in the firelight. "You're very beautiful, you know."

Laila's brow creased, her cheeks flushing at his words. Why was her heart beating faster? It was only Jace. So he'd learned a new trick. Decided to try and pose as the penitent, gentlemanly type. Perhaps he'd finally gotten it through his thick skull that she was close to done with him.

"Did you hear that, just now?"

"Hear what?" Jace's voice was laced with concern. None of the typical flippancy she'd come to expect from him.

"I heard something, just then. It was faint. I couldn't tell if it was coming from outside or inside the house."

Jace stilled, seemed to listen. Laila joined him. The wind whispered and moaned, lifting the curtains slightly.

"I can't hear anything now," Jace said after a pause.

Laila fell silent for a moment, listening. Nothing but the wind howling outside. She sighed loudly, crossing her arms over her chest. "At first I thought it was just the trip, that was the mistake. Taking the trip together."

"Hmm?" Jace's brows crinkled, the noise a hum on his lips.

"At first I thought the trip was a mistake, but then I realized; it's you and I. We're the mistake." Laila didn't bother hiding the derision she felt for him in her tone. She let the words fall from her lips in a tumble. "And you're right, men are fools. You, especially. You are vapid. Vane. Lazy. Selfish." She leaned forward as she spoke. "You preen around like some ... some stupid peacock. You are so full of yourself. Did you think I didn't notice? At the restaurant in Vienna? The bar in Munich? You were flirting, shamelessly, with those waitresses, right in front of me!" Laila's eyes smarted. "Did you think I was too stupid to notice, or just too weak to say anything?"

She stood, flinging the blanket to the floor. "I've had it, Jace. I'm done. I—" she stammered, glancing around the room. There was nowhere for her to go. Nowhere to storm off to, but the small bedroom, or the dark corridor that led further into the house. She eyed the wooden deadbolt against the back of the front door. No way was she leaving the house. Besides, why should she be the one to have to leave?

"I want you to go," she finished, planting her right foot down and squaring her shoulders. She felt ridiculous in the white frilly, floor-length nightgown, the night air cold against her bare arms. "I want you to leave. We're done, you and I. Over." She folded her arms over her chest and glared at him.

"Go ..." he said slowly. "You want me to go?" He gestured around them. "Where am I going, exactly?" He stood, as though he would move towards her. Laila leaned back, arms tightening. Jace paused, eyed her cautiously. "I'm not going to mistreat you, Laila. Not anymore. I'm sorry. I wish ..." he trailed off. "I wish I could show you how I feel, make you understand ..." He scanned the room, as though the answer to his troubles lay somewhere in the vicinity, his eyes flickering back and forth. He met her gaze once more. "Give me one more night. Tonight. To prove it to you. To prove to you I'm going to be different. I promise you, you won't regret it." He held his hand out to her, as though he were waiting for her to accept his offer—to step forward and take it.

Once again, she took in the set of his broad shoulders beneath that rough brown jacket. The ridiculous hat on his head made him look oddly dashing—like he was some hero in an old western. He meant it, she realized. The idiot actually meant it. He believed his own lie. He thought he would be different. Better. For her.

Her shoulders slumped, and she folded in on herself. Like the air going out of a sail. She felt the momentum of her anger, her built-up frustration, which had been glowing red hot only a moment ago, cooling, withering, and dying within her, settling into an icy chill.

Jace let his hand fall to his side, still watching her. "Are you hungry?" he asked gently. "I could make us something to eat."

Since when did Jace offer to cook for her?

Thump. Thump.

It had been unmistakable that time. A knocking, or a rapping. But where was it coming from? She felt certain now it was coming from somewhere within the house. They listened, ears straining in the silence.

Thump. Thump. Thump.

There. Purposeful. Stronger. Laila thought for a moment. Then she lifted her eyes towards the ceiling.

"Did you explore the rest of the house?" she asked calmly, as Jace followed her gaze. "Is there an upstairs?"

"Yes," Jace answered. "But there was no one up there. There's no one else in the house. We're alone. I checked."

Laila nodded. Of course he had. Of course Jace had made his way through the dark house, alone, with only the moonlight to guide him, to make sure they were safe.

"Did you use your lighter?" she asked him nonchalantly.

"My lighter?"

"To help you see?"

A flash of recognition in his eyes. "Oh, yes, I did. When I checked the closets," he cleared his throat, "but the moonlight was good enough, for the most part."

Laila nodded slowly. The sound came again then, as they stood there, staring at each other. Faint. *Thump. Thump. Thump.*

"Would you–" The words caught in her throat, "Would you check again? For me?" She added that last bit, a hopeful uplift in her tone. "I'm afraid there's someone upstairs."

Jace's lips stretched in a smile, and he nodded once, gripping the brim of his hat and tipping it towards her. "Of course. I'd be happy to." He looked her dead in the eyes. "I'd do anything for you."

Laila felt a little thrill run down her spine, followed by a quick, throbbing stab between her thighs.

Jace smiled, and his smile was slow and easy, as though he knew the effect he had on her. "I'll be right back," he said, and he took off down the dark hallway.

Laila waited. She listened as his footsteps retreated. She waited until a distant creaking from somewhere up above drifted to her, and then she spun towards the wall to her right.

The mirror Jace had stood in front of hung there, and in the back corner of the room, just past it, was a small door set in the wall. Laila ran to it now, raised on the balls of her feet. Her nightgown swished and swayed, catching between her legs. She lifted it higher, holding it aloft with both hands as she went.

When she reached the little door, she paused, listening, ears straining. Was he upstairs now? Or had he only pretended to scale the distant staircase to placate her?

But no—there it was, a soft creak of the floorboards more directly overhead. As silently as she was able, she grasped the doorknob and pushed it open.

It swung inward, mercifully on noiseless hinges. Laila stared into the wall of black that met her with dismay. *Dammit.* She'd forgotten; she

19

would find no light switch on the wall to flick on. She turned back to the room and paused, panicking for a heartbeat, before she remembered.

Laila ran once more, skirt lifted, back into the little bedroom. She grabbed the candle beside the bed and crept gingerly back to the wood-stove. She paused there once more, listening. There was a faint but steady shifting of wood—movement, overhead, somewhere off behind her. She grabbed the handmade mitt and pulled open the little metal door. Laila shoved the wick end of the candle into the flickering flames, holding it nearly horizontal.

The candle caught quickly, and she removed it, wax already melting, dripping down over the back of her hand in thin lines. She hissed slightly at the heat, but left it there to cool and crack as she moved swiftly back towards the little wooden door.

Thump. Thump. Thump.

No. No, not now. *Not right now.* Somehow, he had bought her ruse that she'd detected the sound as coming from overhead. The thumping might bring him back downstairs at any moment.

Laila paused only a second before plunging forward into the darkness.

The light from the lone taper lit the space dimly. She gripped her nightgown in one hand, lifting it up and away from her bare feet.

The floor was made of earth; tightly packed soil beneath her toes. The cool air of the dry space kissed her calves and wormed its way up between her thighs. Goosebumps rose, the chill of this space in stark contrast to the heat of the woodstove in the cozy front room.

Laila raised the candle higher, away from her, lifting it as she spun in a slow circle. Shelves. Shelves full of jars. Sacks of coarse cross-hatched material.

A cellar. Laila took in the space as she moved forward, shining the candlelight into the dark corners of the room. The roof narrowed, angled downwards as she moved forward. The far wall was nearly half the height of the one she had entered through.

There was nowhere to hide. Nowhere big enough to hide a person, at least. Perhaps the noise had come from outside the house after all.

The candlelight fell into the far corner, and Laila froze. She stared at the flat wooden boards set into the ground. Curved handles of black iron rose in the middle.

Thump. Thump. Thump.

Lyla eyed the stretch of rope securing the handles warily. She moved closer, set the candle down on the smooth dirt floor, and began to untie the knot with suddenly clumsy fingers.

Fuck. Fuck. Fuck fuckitty-fuck.

She strained as she did so, her eyes wide, heart pounding, listening for his footsteps in the distance. But either they had stopped, or they were too faint, too far removed, to reach her at this distance.

The final knot in the rope loosened and gave, and she flung the short stretch of rope to the side.

Laila lifted the wooden door on the left. It was heavier than she had expected, and she set it down gingerly, trying to move as silently as possible.

"Hello?" a voice called up to her, thin and reedy, laced with fear.

Laila cursed under her breath and spun, reaching for the candle. She gripped it in a trembling hand, sliding her thumb through the smooth ceramic hole as she held it out over the dark yawning tunnel that fell away below.

The walls were earthen, darker, richer soil than the ground beneath her feet. The tunnel dropped straight down, and for a moment, Laila thought the candlelight would be too weak to reach the bottom. But she lowered her arm further and crouched low, careful to keep her balance.

Jace's face peered up at her from the darkness of the pit, and an ice-cold sluice of fear washed down her spine. She stiffened and twisted, certain that the man who wasn't Jace would be standing there behind her. But the doorway leading from the cellar back into the front room was empty.

"Laila!" Jace called up to her, a note of panic in his voice. Laila turned back to the pit, lowering the candle once more. She stared down at Jace, caught, like a rat in a trap, and watched as his features crumbled and broke.

"Oh, Laila! Thank God! You have to get me out of here. There's no ladder. No way out." He turned in a circle, moving his hands over the wall. He strayed slightly out of the candlelight and swiftly stepped back into it. "I've been trapped down here for ages, in the pitch black. I felt all over. I couldn't find a way out. There's no way out." His voice trembled and a low sob left his throat. *"Fuck.* I thought I was going to starve to death down here, until they decided they wanted me for some other fucking deranged ritual." He paused, his eyes finding hers once more, "Laila, help me. Find something. A rope—anything. You have to get me out of here."

Deranged ritual ... Her heart, pounding jaggedly in her chest, had migrated its way up to her throat and lodged there, like some living, writhing thing, wholly separate from herself. She thought it might choke her, as she stared down at Jace's upturned face.

Laila cleared her throat. "I'm fine, by the way. Thank you for asking," she said numbly.

Jace seemed to freeze at her words. His already wide, panicked eyes grew wider. "Good," he stammered, flashing her a wobbly smile. He swiped at the sweat on his brow as he blinked up at her. "Good. I'm glad. Glad to hear it."

"Yes," Laila called back down to him, "I'm sure you are."

Jace only stared up at her.

"What was the name of the village, Jace?"

"What? The name of the village?" Jace frowned, his eyes flickering back and forth as he tried to remember. "Which one?"

"The one we're trapped in right now. Do you remember me reading you the name on the sign?" Laila's lips pressed into a thin line. "Maybe you weren't listening?"

"What? I–I was driving, Laila. Through the fog. I was distracted," a flash of annoyance washed over his features, "trying to make sure we didn't crash, or go off the road in the fog." He wiped his hand over his face. "God, Laila ... give me a fucking break. Will you focus, for once? Can you go find a ladder? Or a rope? Give me a fucking hand, would ya?"

Laila stared down at him, her heart beat a steady tattoo now, having returned to her chest. "Say please, Jace."

Jace stared up at her, his face going slack momentarily. Then his features hardened, his eyes narrowing. "*Please.* Laila." When she didn't move, his gaze narrowed further. "Please. Please help me get the *fuck* out of this *fucking* pit."

Laila smiled down at him then, benevolently. "Of course I will, Jace. But, *auf Deutsch*, would you?"

"What?" Jace sputtered, his features contorting once more in barely concealed anger.

"Say it again. Say please. But in German, this time."

Jace stared slack-jawed at her placid expression. "Are you insane?"

"I'm waiting, Jace."

She stiffened slightly as Jace let out a string of expletives below her. She turned her head, angling one ear back towards the opening to the cellar.

"You crazy fucking bitch! Get me out of here. Fuck your stupid *German-fucking-owl,* and get me out of here!"

Footsteps sounded in the main room. A shadow passed between Laila and the fire from the woodstove.

Laila didn't react when he stepped into the cellar doorway. Silhouetted from behind, he was a solid shadow, his shoulders spanning the width of the small door, and he had to stoop slightly to enter. The round-brimmed hat on his head sat at an angle. She couldn't see his face, but Laila knew his eyes were on her.

She turned back to Jace, down in the pit, before setting the candle down. Laila grasped the wooden door with both hands and lifted it, grunting slightly.

Jace let out a shriek below. "Laila! No! For the love of God, don't close it! Laila! *LAILA!*"

His voice was muffled slightly as the door slammed shut. Laila stood, brushing her palms against each other and then on her nightgown. She turned to the man in the doorway and said calmly, "One night." She stood with her back straight, her shoulders down. "You have one night, to prove you're different."

She ducked down, and scooped up the candle. The ceramic was cold, smooth, and comforting against her skin. She slid her thumb into the holder. It fit like it was made for her.

Laila grabbed a handful of her dress and moved forward, relishing the feel of the hard-packed dirt beneath her toes. She felt like a lady from some old-fashioned, gothic novel, as the man before her stepped to the side and bowed slightly. He straightened, and Laila took in the faint smile on his lips as she passed.

She sat in her chair by the fire.

The man who wasn't Jace lifted the blanket from where it lay on the floor and draped it over her lap.

He took his place once more on the low stool and leaned forward, resting his forearms on his knees.

"What now? Are you hungry? Shall I make you dinner?"

Laila thought for a moment, studying his familiar features. He was handsome, all right. Jace had always been attractive. That had never been the issue.

Thump. Thump. Thump. Thump. Muffled screams drifted through the silence. The wind picked up, white curtains billowing into the room. The breeze carried the crisp scent of fall—of rain, storm clouds, decay, and new beginnings.

Laila blew out the candle she still held in one hand. "Hmm," she mused. "I think I'd like you to tell me a story instead."

The man wearing Jace's face straightened, a wide grin breaking out over his features. "Now that I can do; I love a good story."

Laila smiled back at him and watched as he turned and stoked the fire in the woodstove with a long, sharp poker.

"Would you like me to tell you a story in English, *order auf Deutsch*?"

Laila laughed. A real, deep belly laugh.

The man's smile widened.

"English, *bitte*. Please," Laila said, a faint smile on her lips. "For now," she added softly. "I'm still learning."

Their eyes met meaningfully for a brief second, then he cleared his throat and began, *"Once upon a time ..."*

Laila blinked, closing her eyes as she drew in a deep breath. The firelight flicked alternating shadows against her eyelids, its heat suddenly too warm on her face.

When she opened her eyes once more, she was alone in the room. The wind blew, rattling the panes and the house creaked and groaned.

She frowned, surveying the familiar space. Everything was as it should be—where it should be—but something felt off. Something was missing.

It came to her slowly, as her brain fumbled and whirred away, *remember, remember* ... like a name once known so well and now forgotten, it was there, but blurry, wiped away by time. Time. How long had she been sitting here, listening to his deep voice rumble away, spinning horrors out of the air? One night. She'd given him one night.

Laila listened now to the relative silence, the creaking and popping as wood expanded and contracted, and the fire crackling away in the wood-stove.

It was quiet. So quiet. Nothing stirred in the house, and she knew with deep certainty he wasn't here. He'd gone away; left her alone for perhaps the first time in a long time.

Laila stood on weak, wobbly legs, and surveyed the room. The mirror on the far wall. That was where she'd first seen him. Yes. His hat pulled low over his face, as he practiced being charming. Who—it came to her now in a flash. Jace. It had been Jace, standing there, only not. And not-Jace had been kinder, warmer. Not-Jace had *seen* her, in a way that Jace never really did, no matter how badly she wanted him to.

It was too quiet, she realized, with a dull ache in her chest. The knocking. That constant ... *Thump ... thump ... thump ...* had grown slower, fainter, weaker. And at some point, she no longer could recall when, it had stopped altogether.

Laila moved to the table, and grabbed the candle, the single taper already lit. Sliding her thumb into the cool groove that fit her like a glove, she made her way to the little cellar door. The door swung open on rusty hinges, long un-used. The cool dry earth felt anciently familiar beneath her toes.

The rope that had once tied the handles of the little wooden doors set into the floor lay discarded to the side, just where she had left it. *How long ago was that? How long?*

She had sat as though transfixed, under a spell. Each story had been more grim, more gruesome than the last, and yet ... and yet she couldn't look away, leaning closer, to hear every word, her breath caught in her throat, her eyes locked onto his, his voice echoing and rumbling, bouncing around in her chest, wrapping around her heart, until it beat in time with his words. One night. She had given him only one night. But he had never stopped, had he? He had kept going and going, until—

When Laila lifted the wooden door, the boards creaked and groaned, coming apart slightly at the seam. She tossed it with all her strength and peered into the darkness below.

"Jace?" she called out, but her voice came out raspy and low, more like a whisper. She cleared her throat, working muscles long dormant, as though they had forgotten how to move in concert. "Jace?" she called again, stronger, this time, then remembered the candle.

Laila lifted the candle, lowering it down into the pit. She choked on her own breath, her own saliva, as the quavering circle of light hit the bottom.

Jace, or what was left of him, sat sprawled against the wall of the earthen tunnel. His hands, once large in hers, were now white, narrow bone, fingers splayed and palms open, pointing skyward, towards a horizon he would never see.

Laila sobbed, the words half-formed on her lips, *"No, no ... how? But how?"* She whispered the refrain like an incantation, repeatedly, and with each uttering, her heart slowed, her blood cooled, and she became still.

Laila sat there, her features smoothing, then going slack.

She stood. She didn't bother to close the door to the pit, nor to the cellar.

She carried the candle aloft, lifting the skirt of her stiff white nightgown in one hand as she marched like a wraith back to the warmth of the fire.

She was there, waiting for him, when he re-entered the house.

While Laila had never seen anything beyond the room with the woodstove, and the bedroom she had woken in, she felt his presence somewhere in the dark recesses at her back. She knew when he reappeared. She knew before she heard his footsteps on the floorboards. How had she not heard it before? How obvious it was to her now.

The *clomp, clomp, clomp,* of cloven hooves reverberated through the house. She could feel the vibrations beneath her as they rattled through the stiff-backed chair.

She had tucked the blanket around her once more, as though she had never left her place. But he would know. Whether she had left the door open or closed, he would have known.

She waited for him to speak first. He stood in the doorway behind her. She didn't turn. She watched him, regardless, in the mirror on the wall. When he removed the hat this time, she caught a glimpse of his tousled hair, and the short, rough, twisting horns that sprouted there. Her gut twisted with some emotion she'd rather not name.

His smile was easy, as he moved around her chair, and took his seat once more on the low stool beside the woodstove. He grabbed the poker, and pulling open the little door, shifted the logs as sparks flew, winking in and out of existence in what felt like an instant, but might have been an age.

"Do you need anything?" he asked, his tone measured and calm. He was always so calm. At the sound of his graveled tones, the muscles in her arms went slack against the chair. The tension she was holding in her core relaxed.

When he turned to her, Laila was smiling, the slightly smug smile of something feline and feral, that's been soothed by violence and blood-shed into a semblance of peace.

"Just you," she said smoothly, and although the words came out before she thought them, when she heard them, they felt just right.

Not-Jace grinned, and the world settled. "How about another story, then?"

A.C. Hessenauer

A.C. Hessenauer describes herself as a writer of horror with gothic romance & weird girl lit vibes. A.C. has self-published five novels and one novella, including *Dread House*, *Jumpers*, and *MANIMAL*. A.C.'s first traditionally published novel, *Going to the Six*, is set to be released in 2026 by Cemetery Dance. When she's not participating in macabre ceremonies dedicated to the eldritch horrors out in the woods, A.C. enjoys spending time with her family: her husband, two sons, and border collie named Maximus. She loves a good horror movie, and of course, getting swallowed whole by a good book. www.dreadhousepublishing.com

1870s
THE TOURNAMENT OF SHADOWS

Garrett Boatman

In my dreams and waking hours, I feel the call of that awful place. Sitting in my study, book in hand; walking the cobbled streets; lying in bed, unable to sleep, remembering. Perhaps if I go back and do not find the gates, I can return to this colorless yet blessedly mundane existence and endure my remaining days with some semblance of grateful sanity. I have a great resiliency, as my years of service and numerous adventures attest, but I feel I shall go mad not knowing if what I experienced was real or a product of my fevered brain.

I cannot promise I will return. The way is long and fraught with danger. I barely made it back before. And though I do not mean for this to be farewell, I cannot deny it may well be. I will say only that you are all in my heart. Though I have been home four months, I have withheld the true nature of my last mission. Partly because I did not want to trouble your sleep and partly because I was certain you would deem me Bedlam-bound were I to reveal the true nature of my adventure.

True? Who can say what is true and what is not? Since my return from India, I walk these sunlit streets and see only darkness. Not the dark of English night with its streetlamps and roof of moon and stars, but the utter blackness of the pit. The very aether vibrates with howls and laughter bestial and grotesque, and beyond the mocking voices a brooding silence vast as the gloom of eternity.

But as I treasure the affection you hold for me and would not burden you with the vexation of not knowing the reason for my sudden departure, I am resolved to set down the details of my late commission. As you know, the Corps of Guides is entrusted with the security of the North West Frontier against domestic rebellion and foreign incursions. What you did not know is that I have spent much of my time on special assignments in the buffering states between Russia and British India gathering intelligence for the War Office. My latest mission was to accompany the British Emissary to Kabul, ostensibly to strengthen relations with the Amir of Afghanistan, Sher Ali Khan. In actuality, I was charged to look into Russian incursions into Afghanistan by way of Bokhara. The Russian bear is forever loitering on the borderlands, and any such incursion would be considered a *casus belli*.

Normally, I enjoy the "Great Game," as our newspapers call the series of moves and countermoves for influence over the borderlands between the Russian frontier and British India, what the Russians term the "Tournament of Shadows." Nothing, short of a plunge into the thick of battle, can compete with the thrill of seeing new lands, of gaining knowledge for knowledge's sake, of matching wits against a cunning foe. But this time the game was cut short. My Russian counterpart, Captain Ivanoff, was already in attendance when I arrived at the Amir's palace. Suffice it to say our mission failed, my men were massacred, and I barely escaped.

My retreat over the Khyber Pass back to Peshawar being cut off, I was forced to flee north across the hard, brown hills of Afghanistan into the Hindu Kush: over five hundred miles of some of the world's most rugged terrain. I dared not stop to rest: Captain Ivanoff and a certain fierce Pathan warrior, who, with his long-barreled *jezail*, could hit his mark at four hundred yards, were hot on my heels. Each time I crossed open country, my back burned with anticipation of the marksman's bullet.

For three days my little *Kirgiz* horse carried me deep into the Kush before its gallant heart gave out and I continued on foot. Nearing evening on the fourth day, the great upthrusting, cloud-cloaked peaks rearing stark against the purpling sky, I found myself in a narrow gorge that dead-ended in a cliff-face. But no wall of grey stone rose above me as I approached. Instead, the sunset cast a ruddy glow on the towering bronze doors set flush into the rock.

Soaring ten times the height of a man, the gates were decorated profusely with bas-reliefs that defied description. Being familiar with the Greco-Roman and Assyrian entablatures of the British Museum, I would have expected representations of battles and mythological beings, of gods and heroes. Instead, I gazed upon monsters that made human-headed Assyrian lions look like something you'd find at the Zoological Gardens: here a tentacled grotesque devoured legions of naked men and women, there a winged creature with three snake-like heads spewed fire over a city of gravity defying towers, and there humans poured like a cataract into a fiery pit from which a terrible teeth-filled maw rose to receive them.

A colossal pyramid dominated the center of the tableau. Beset with row upon row of windows, as if the great structure contained a thousand levels and might house a million people, the pyramid appeared a habitation rather than a tomb. At each of the gate's four corners, what appeared to be mountains with monstrous faces gazed hideously and steadfastly upon the central pyramid.

But as riveting and mysterious as these marvels were, the two giant statues that warded the gates were even more imposing. One possessed an enormous ass-like head with gigantic ears and peered down into the gorge with an expression of eternal watchfulness. The effigy held a staff in one hand, an ankh in the other. This was the Egyptian god Set, destroyer of souls. The female statue opposite had four arms. Fearsome, with lolling tongue and glaring eyes, she held a skull-topped staff in one hand, a sickle in another, a trident, and a severed head. A necklace of human skulls hung to her navel. A girdle of severed arms, hands hanging down, circled her waist. This was Kali, the Hindu goddess of death.

The hackles rose on the back of my neck as I gazed up at these two harbingers of ultimate annihilation, not only of the body but of the spirit. I shrugged the gloom off: if I had learned anything in my brief existence, it was you can't avoid your fate but must face it head on. I had, however, little time for philosophical thought; my foe would overtake me at any moment and I had nowhere to run.

Unless…

I approached the gates. I put my shoulder against the cold bronze and pushed.

A bullet pinged off the bronze inches from my face. My company had arrived.

I pushed harder. The gates gave. I shoved through the narrow space. I glanced back; the sunset illuminated the narrow gorge, but the light did not penetrate beyond the gates. It was as if the darkness swallowed the rays. My adversaries, I saw dimly through the murky atmosphere, had dismounted and followed me through the gates, the big Pathan in the lead, the tall Russian in close pursuit, sabre in hand. The gates closed. I'd assumed I'd entered a tomb, but this place was immense. Were it not for the ruddy glare of fires burning across the dismal nightscape, I would have been blind, stumbling over rocky terrain as difficult as anything in the Kush. Whether they were bonfires or volcanic fire-pits, I knew not, only that I was grateful for their light as I zigzagged from outcropping to outcropping to throw off the Pathan's aim.

Again, a shot ricocheted off a rock by my cheek. I reflected it would take the Pathan some seconds to reload, and, though I knew by reputation Ivanoff's swordsmanship was almost equal to my own, I spun and charged my rivals. Ivanoff's cruel smile broadened and the Pathan's bearded frown deepened as we closed.

Suddenly, a great shadow fell upon the Pathan. The attack brought me to my heels. Looming several feet taller than the Afghan warrior, the giant was distinctively human if massively simian in appearance. It was also utterly naked. The red shine of the fire-light gleamed off corded muscle as the creature dashed gun and blade from the Pathan's grasp and broke the warrior's thick neck as if it were a child's. The giant hurled the corpse aside and turned to face me.

I crouched, blade ready to come in beneath those massive arms. But my rival struck first. Lunging from behind, Ivanoff pierced the giant's kidney and jumped free as the creature turned, its howl rending the silence.

Taking advantage of the distraction, I rammed my sabre through its back, hoping to find heart or lungs. Falling, its momentum carried it toward my rival. Surely Ivanoff would have been crushed had he not leapt a full six feet back, landing like a cat. The giant collapsed at his feet. Even as it bled out, the monster flailed. Ivanoff dispatched it with a strike to its throat.

For a moment, we stood panting and watched it die. Then, remembering our rivalry, we rounded on each other, sabres ready. Ivanoff grinned. Lowering his weapon, he said, "Under the circumstances, I suggest we join swords until—" he waved his blade at the corpse "—we resolve our current dilemma."

I concurred with his wisdom and lowered my sabre. I looked around for the Pathan's gun but it was lost in the damnable dark. For the first time, I looked up.

Night's ramparts rose into the invisible firmament. Moonless and starless, with no gauge to demark the limits of profundity, the roof of creation might be thousands of feet above or infinitely distant. The gloom of eternity bore down on my senses, oppressing me with a claustrophobic sensation, as if we had journeyed to the center of the earth rather than tread upon its surface.

A horrible baying as of hounds rose out of the night, and I wondered what other creatures the Pathan's gun and the giant's roars had roused. We had to get moving, but which way? The night land stretched around me, a country of crags and valleys littered with fires as far as the eye could see. There was nothing to show that the gate through which we'd entered ever existed. To our left a narrow defile led down into a valley where a sinuous ribbon of fire glowed as if through a rift in the earth.

A while later we stumbled onto a road. And such a road! It was wide and paved with what appeared to be asphalt but glittered as if mixed with crushed glass. I commented that it was as good a road as any of London's new asphalt byways. With no carriages or omnibuses to wear it down, it looked capable of lasting centuries if not millennia.

As we walked, I asked Ivanoff why he'd pursued me into the night land. The soldier replied: "I come across such a wonder in the midst of the wilderness, how could I not? Wouldn't you?"

We shared a laugh over this. In many ways, we were alike, in our love of travel and adventure and assimilating different cultures. I admitted, even if I had not been pursued, my curiosity would have gotten the better of me.

"And the Pathan's aim?" I asked.

"Your fame as a swordsman precedes you. I would not have you dispatched before I tried your blade."

I confessed he flattered me and promised to cross sabres with him when we found our way back to the world.

No sooner had I spoken than a sharp pain stabbed my skull. My head jerked as if I had been slapped.

"What's the matter?" I heard Ivanoff dimly, as if my head were submersed under water.

With the pain, an image flashed in my mind's eye. It vanished too soon to make out specific features, only that it was of a woman. I got the impression of great beauty. Her lips moved but I heard nothing over the roar in my head. Then she—or whatever perception had arrested my attention—passed. "It is nothing. I thought I saw ..."

Ivanoff's expression was, if not compassionate, at least curious. "Saw what?"

I waved him off. "Nothing."

Sometime later I called a halt to our progress. A green mist had sprung up along the road, limiting our vision. I saw nothing but sensed a presence ahead. Then, staring fixedly, I perceived what looked like grey shadows, as if ghostly beings ten-feet tall and shrouded to their feet moved silently along the road. I shuddered.

It took me a moment to recognize the alien emotion that swept through me—if emotion it was and not some side effect of fatigue. I felt a quickening of my pulse and a lightheadedness, much like the faintness one gets when dehydrated on a long trek under the blistering Indian sun.

In truth I *was* dehydrated, damnably so; my swollen tongue cleaved to the roof of my mouth and my parched throat felt as though stuffed with cartridge wadding. But thirst was not the cause of this peculiar sensation, nor was fatigue, though my muscles—nay, the very bones of my limbs and skull—ached. Nor was it a totally new sensation but something I'd experienced in my boyhood, when, for no logical reason, I had been reluctant to venture into our father's cellar, which, as you know, was and is a dark and musty place. And so it dawned on me that the strange and unwanted sensation that crept over my flesh like an army of fleas and thrilled my spine like a galvanic charge was fear—good old-fashioned, primitive *fear*. A sensation I had considered cast aside like the baby teeth I had shed for my grownup ones.

The phantoms seemed made of mist, and though I had never known mist to hurt anyone, I had developed a soldier's sense regarding what was dangerous and what was not; and my tingling nerves advised me it was best we did not encounter these mist-men. Ivanoff obviously shared my apprehension, for as I rubbed the gooseflesh from my arms, he did so himself.

We dropped into a shallow ravine, and using the low moss-bushes that grew beside the road for cover, we made a wide compass of those wrath-like, soul-chilling beings.

At one point, I was startled by something scuttling in the dirt. A great, yard-long scorpion barred my path. The tip of its stinger glistened with venom. Ivanoff stabbed it and flicked it into the dark. By the dull-grey phosphorescence of the lichen growing on the boulders, I saw amusement in his black eyes. I had flinched and he had not. I tendered him a nod of thanks and crept on.

Back on the road some hours later, I felt a strange excitement as if something wonderful lay just ahead and I couldn't wait to see it.

"You feel that?" The Russian was smiling, not his cruel Cossack smirk, but looking for all the world like a boy on his way to the fair.

"Like a loadstone, pulling me," I said.

He nodded. We both quickened our step.

Soon, I saw in the red glare of the fire-pits a house upon a low hill. Light poured from its windows, as if a grand ball were being prepared; but the windows were uncased and the light cold and uninviting. Yet I felt an attraction, as if some psychic magnetism drew me toward the wide-open door. The utter silence emanating from the house should have warned me that the place was evil; but, even as my skin crawled, my footsteps carried me nearer. I seemed to have lost all conscious thought and was moving like an automaton, when the pain I experienced earlier suddenly stabbed my brain and, again, I saw the woman.

She was beautiful. Nay, more than beautiful. There was an other-worldly ethereality about her that radiated a glory I've not seen in mortal woman. For the life of me, I cannot recall if her eyes were blue or brown or green or grey, or if those tresses that framed her fine-cheekboned face be blonde or brunette or her complexion fair or dark. She came to me not in the vivid colors of a portrait in the Tate but as a vision in the night. I would say *ghostly* but that is not right. Words fail me even as my memory does. *Glory* works, for her beauty stunned my senses. The shock of beholding her blasted from my befuddled brain all desire to enter that tempting portal. Wrenched from the exquisite pull of the ocean of silence that lay beyond the gaping door, I woke, as if I'd slept and a pistol shot had gone off beside my ear. Gazing spellbound at the vision before me, I immediately comprehended the danger Ivanoff and I were in. Indeed, the Cossack was some yards ahead, his hand stretched toward the house.

Hurry, I heard her say. The voice was melodic, the accent one I couldn't place. She spoke inside my head, and the single word conveyed more than the sense of dire urgency. I understood the house was, indeed, evil, and that there was more at stake for those that entered than the peril of their bodies.

"Ivanoff!" I shouted into the Russian's face. His gaze sought the house; his rapturous smile did not falter. I dropped the point of my sabre over my left shoulder and cracked him squarely in the forehead with the pommel. He dropped instantly. Sheathing my weapon, I shouldered the man and marched away in the direction of our saviour's voice.

As I strode, the woman and I conversed: a silent exchange that took place in my mind. Her name was Miralee. She was the daughter of the Chief Monstruwacan, whose duty it was to watch and record the movements of the monsters that beset the Last Redoubt, as she termed the great citadel that housed the last millions of humanity. In brief, she explained that the world into which Ivanoff and I had stumbled lay millions of years into our future, a time when the sun had lost all power to light and the earth was dying. In her distant past, scientists had made an incalculable error. Seeking to create a miniature galaxy whose energy they might use to power their cities and prolong mankind's existence, they opened a rift disturbing the unmeasurable Outward Powers, and had allowed to pass the Barrier of Life creatures and Forces that fed not on the flesh but on the spirit.

I understood how far science and technology had come in the last thousand years of our own time, but creating galaxies? Opening portals in the aether? I shook my head in incomprehension. I felt as a cave man must were he transported into Victoria Station.

The evil that had come through the rift took many forms; the House of Silence, as she named that ghastly place we had just quitted, was the most powerful. No one who entered its portals ever returned. *The danger is not for your body alone,* she said. *In the night land, death of the body is considered a kindness.*

A kindness? What do you mean?

I speak of the spirit. There is that in human kind which is immortal ... unless the house or some creature from the other side take it. We multitudes of the Redoubt know the difference between when a spirit, freed from the clay, ascends the aether, and when one that shrieks in horror is swallowed by the Silence.

As we talked, I was aware of a murmur in the night, as of many people talking far off, so that no individual word could be discerned but that the collective voices sounded like the dull roar of a cataract. Merilee explained that this was the voice of the Peoples, who were anxious for our safety.

Ivanoff came to and I set him down. "What happened?" he asked, rubbing his brow.

"You took a knock on the head."

"I am looking forward to our duello," was the captain's sardonic reply. He really was a capital fellow. I imagine, were we not on opposite sides of the Game, we would have gotten along splendidly.

He asked where we were headed and I filled him in on what Miralee had told me. He shuddered when I described the peril of the House. To his credit, he did not consider me *Bedlam-bound*, but fell in beside me as I followed Miralee's directions to mankind's last refuge.

At one point, the low thunder of a great laughter stopped us in our tracks. All the hairs on my head and arms bristled with the eeriness of the sound. The heart-shaking voice rolled through the night and was answered by a furious howling of hounds and a vast roaring of giants.

Hurry, Miralee said. *The House has awakened the land. If you do not make it to the Redoubt ...* She left understood the fate that awaited us if we did not reach safety. Tired as I was, the howling and roaring of monsters spurred me on. I ran. Offering no objection, Ivanoff kept pace.

All about, the aether throbbed with danger, as if unseen Powers followed our progress with malicious interest. I felt like an insect squirming under the gaze of some vast, malign intelligence.

Guided by Miralee, we ran uphill toward a narrow cleft in the rock. On either side, back-lit by the fire-pits, I saw great loping hounds, as big as horses. I drew my sabre. Perhaps it would be useless, but I felt better with its grip in my fist.

They are herding you, Miralee said. I suspected as much; otherwise, we would be fighting for our lives.

Reaching the summit, I looked upon a sight that stopped me cold and stole my breath. Below stretched a broad plain whereon fires burned as if the earth was rent with volcanic fissures. Mountains ringed the plain, their peaks lost in the eternal dusk. In the center, miles wide at its base and soaring twice as many miles into the aether, rose a vast and mighty pyramid of grey metal. Three hundred thousand embrasures on the facing side shone their light upon the plain. Millions watched our progress and sent out their well-wishes. Their outpouring warmed my heart.

A mighty sense of déjà vu swept over me. Here was the pyramid I'd seen on the outer gates. And if that representation had been impressive, this—the last bastion of humanity's surviving millions—this soaring, sky-piercing monument to man's ingenuity—was an undertaking that made Britain's steamships and railways seem infinitely puny.

A moat of startlingly white light surrounding the pyramid kept the monsters at bay and protected the Redoubt from Evil Powers. At a distance from the Electric Circle, rose what looked like a squat hill, but I knew at a glance it was no such thing but a living mountain of malicious intent. Its shoulders were humped like two small hills and its great head, shaggy with moss and boulders, jutted toward the pyramid. Before the beast, a glowing dome rose from the ground over which it stared with eternal watchfulness upon the pyramid.

This is the Watcher of the South, Miralee said. *There are four that came from the corners of the earth in the Darkening Time, but the Southern Watcher is the largest. There seems to be a Force opposing the Watchers, for as they neared the Pyramid, the domes rose out of the ground, staying them. For an eternity they have trained their cold stare upon our home. They are emissaries of the House, or of whatever Force lies beyond the house in the realm beyond the rift ... In time, when the Earth-Current fails, the Dome and the Circle will extinguish and the Watcher and the other Beasts and Monsters will advance and the Redoubt will perish.*

The hounds bayed on every side. Sleek shadows flowed in the dark. We began our descent. If I expected a welcoming party from the pyramid to greet us, I was disappointed. Miralee informed me there would be no such party. The Millions would do what they could, but to risk the destruction of their spirits was madness.

As we advanced, keeping well away from the hideous bulk of the Watcher, I saw that the hounds flanking us were not the only obstacle to our winning the Redoubt. Many dozens more of the four-legged brutes along with a score of giants were lined up this side of the Circle. Behind this hideous assemblage, a causeway arched over the moat of light and beyond this an iron gate, its two massive panels broad enough to admit an army. The gates were closed, but a smaller gate in one panel stood open, as if the populace had no fear of the monsters passing over but through which we could pass, if we could run that gauntlet of living horror.

Ivanoff and I exchanged glances. He raised his sabre in salute. "See you on the other side, Englishman," he said, and charged.

The thrill of battle swept through me as I sprinted beside him as if we were in a footrace and not rushing to certain death.

As we closed with the night army, I saw behind the hounds and giants, as if they were generals directing troops, monstrous black mounds that quivered and swayed, glistening like great slicks of oil.

Beware these, Miralee warned. *They, too, are destroyers of spirits.*

The hounds broke ranks. The earth shook with the thunder of their charge. When they were nearly upon us, the tide parted, enveloping us on either side. Then they turned and attacked. I smote the nearest snarling beast across the head. My blade deflected off its skull and split its face but failed to slay it. To my horror, its bristling quill-like hairs dripped venom. As it sprang I ducked and ran my blade across its throat. It fell, quivering as it bled out. Then I was in the thick of it, my blade slashing left and right. Claws raked my arm and shoulder. I hoped these were not venomous.

I felt rather than heard the anguish of sympathy poured down from the embrasures of that tremendous Redoubt. The spiritual noise of the People's emotion uplifted my spirit and lo! I felt my arm grow stronger as their collective will empowered me, and my aching wrist ached no more, and my blade flashed and spun in the light from the moat and pyramid and cleft meat and bone on every side so that the press fell back as if astonished.

A thunderous roar went up into the night, and out from the mob of giants, the largest lumbered forward, his great legs sweeping hounds aside as he waded into battle. Ivanoff was panting and bleeding but managed a grim nod before turning to the giant. He darted in, rolled between the giant's legs, and slashed at the tendons behind the knee. Faltering, the giant swept a hand behind him, caught the Cossack's coat, and flung him to the ground.

Still game, Ivanoff slashed the giant's arm. The blade bit deep into the hairy flesh, but the massive bone stopped its passage. Roaring, the giant stomped him. I flinched at the noise of breaking bones.

I launched myself at the giant, but the brute swatted my sabre from my hand and hurled me into a boulder. The world spun. Fighting darkness, I forced myself to my feet and made to renew my attack. What I saw stopped me.

Out of the night, another giant had appeared. This one looked nothing like the others. Easily forty-feet tall, the strange and wondrous being shone as if made of pale mist.

Miralee warned this, too, was one of the eldritch abominations that came through the rift—like the House and the Mounds, a devourer of spirits.

The abomination's mouth stretched impossibly wide, revealing row upon row of serrated teeth. Its great clawed hands reached for Ivanoff. Cossack rage contorted the captain's face as he slashed weakly at the wrath ... to no effect.

Broken, bleeding, Ivanoff looked at me with an expression of pain, horror, resignation, and—if I am not entirely mistaken—melancholy Russian humour. He tossed his sabre to me and said, "Do it."

The weapon pinwheeled hilt over blade. I caught it and, with no time to lose, ducked under those gargantuan arms, severed the captain's head from his body, and rolled beyond the phantom's grasp. Any other stroke would have prolonged death and suffered the Russian's spirit to oblivion.

I stood, surrounded. The hounds, emboldened by the wraith's presence and the diminishing of their opposition, circled closer. The giants advanced. The black mounds still barred the causeway, and, to my horror, two more of the wraiths emerged from the night to join their sibling. In the distance, the Watcher, indifferent to the conflict, maintained its silent and eternal vigil, its unwavering gaze bent upon the pyramid. Time was on its side. My survival or death was nothing to the mountain of living watchfulness. In the end, earth's fires would die and the creature would feast on the Millions' souls.

I grasped the leather-wrapped grip of the fine Russian blade and gritted my teeth.

Miralee?

I felt such a flood of passion pour from her that I looked to the pyramid longing to see her face—and saw *her*, all of *her*, as she might appear in a dream ... shapely, sad, achingly lovely. Her ghost-like fingers touched my cheek. I reached for her, but she was gone.

The aether trembled with the unity of sympathy the Millions poured out for my beleaguered state. The giants halted their advance. The hounds ceased howling and backed away. And from the utmost pinnacle of the People's home a strange blue light shot downwards and struck the plain behind me. I turned to see what miracle had stayed my executioners—and saw the gates through which I had entered the night land.

Farewell, my hero. Go! I heard Miralee say.

Ere I could reply, I felt myself hurled through the air towards those towering gates. My momentum must have slammed the gates open and carried me through, for I awoke sometime later as the morning sun rose over the mountains of the Kush.

Two horses stood nearby, nervously flicking their tails. I rose, Ivanoff's sabre still clutched in my hand. Facing the mountain, I saw only a cliff of naked grey rock.

Of the gates and its silent warders there was no sign.

Being back these four months, I feel as if I were a ghost.

I thought seeing the Horse Guard drill at Kensington, walking the sun-lit paths of Regent's Park, snuggling up to a good book and a better brandy in the family study, I would see my obsessions for what they are—nightmares brought on by fatigue of the body and mind. But rather than dissipate like morning mist before a warming sun, my mind-fog has grown denser. I see the monstrosities of the night land and hear, every day more clearly, Her voice. Calling me. Entreating me to return.

I can no longer refuse. To have saved myself and left her there to face the world's end is unbearable. Besides, I no longer feel I can live without her. No matter what far-flung future that benighted land, I must try to find it and bring her back to this world of sun and moon and stars. And if that is not possible, to abide with her there and offer what protection is in my power against the abominations of the night.

The young man seated at the desk set the sheets aside. His mother sat stiffly on the study's horse-hair sofa. She had not spoken during his reading of his brother's letter but had stared fixedly into the hearth fire. Now she looked at him and spoke.

"And what of Edith?"

"He called the engagement off before he left. Her father is considering suing."

"Is he mad, after all?"

"Perhaps, but he did bring back the sabre." His gaze went to the empty space above the mantle where his brother had hung the weapon he'd brought back from India. With its brass knuckle-bow and quillon, and its scabbard sheathed in niello-inlaid silver, it was a handsome example of the bladesmith's art, not a museum piece but designed for battle.

"Pshaw! Anyone coming back from service could buy one of those at a bazaar."

The young man shrugged. "Still, I like to think it will stand him in good stead and be a talisman for his safety."

"Humph," was his mother's reply, but her eyes glistened with hope.

Garrett Boatman

Garrett Boatman is the author of the Paperback from Hell Stage Fright (Onyx 1988, reprint Valancourt Books 2020), the 1890s Victorian hooligan nights novella Floaters, and the epic horror trilogy Night's Plutonian Shore, The Clocks of Midnight, and The Mirror of Eternity. His collection, A Prisoner of Dreamland and Other Oneiric Terrors, was published in 2024 by Weird House Publishing. His southern gothic (*hoodoo swamp horror*) novella, Bloody Bones, inspired by his granny's bedtime stories, is out from Cemetery Dance. Golden Dog is publishing Czech editions of Stage Fright and Floaters. His stories have appeared in The Valancourt

Book of Horror Stories, Penumbra, and Weird House Magazine among others. An active member of HWA, SFWA, and the British Fantasy Society, Garrett lives with his wife and rescue mutt in coastal North Carolina. https://www.garrettboatmanauthor.com/

1880s

Heavy Dreams

Megan M Davies-Ostrom

On a Friday afternoon like this—lectures done, office hours and marking complete, and dinner still hours distant—I like nothing more than to lock the door, kick off my shoes, and take a well-deserved nap on the leather couch usually reserved for nervous students. The mellow afternoon sun warms my tiny, ground-floor office, turning dust motes into drifting stars that settle on the overstuffed bookshelves and scattered papers like glittering snow. Lowly lecturers such as myself are, by tradition, relegated to spaces no one else wants, and my matchbox office is no exception. The walls have cracks, the ceiling sags, and the beautiful lead-glass windows overlooking the Fellow's Garden make for drafts in winter and a furnace in summer. I love it, all the same. I worked hard for these meagre luxuries, applied myself to my studies and pushed my way into the most august of academic circles by sheer, stubborn determination. And a skill for making myself useful; one can't forget that. After years of pouring over ancient texts late into the night and putting myself forward for every odd-job and expedition the university had to offer, no matter how dreary, I think I can say I've earned my Friday afternoon naps.

Good thing too, because I'm particularly tired today, my lids borne down like weighted curtains, my body weak and languid beneath the heavy folds of exhaustion.

Perhaps it is a lack of sleep that pulls me so determinedly toward the soft embrace of my couch. I slept poorly last night, plagued by strange dreams, and was woken just before dawn by a clattering, wailing commotion in the back lane. Cats or feral dogs, I suspect. Or drunks—a lecturer's salary does not stretch so far as to allow for fancy accommodations, and the rooming house in which I rent the third-floor resides in a less-than-fashionable quarter. My neighbours are nice enough people when the sun is up, but nighttime brings drunken brawls and caterwauling domestic disputes the likes of which I hesitate to describe in polite company. Jeffries—a roguish young lecturer in Paleontology who rents rooms on the second floor and always knows everything before anyone else—thinks the clamour out back can be laid at the monstrous paws of whatever wild animal escaped its shipping container and caused such a fracas at the station the day before last. The box car in which the animal was being transported, he informed me, was practically ripped asunder, and the southbound line had to be closed to clear wreckage off the track, leaving London-bound passengers stranded indefinitely. The streets were far busier than usual as I made my way home Wednesday evening, and it took my horse drawn tram over an hour to get from Regent Street to Newmarket Road. According to Jeffries—and the headlines and shocking illustrations in the evening wheezes—the beast is still at large, and officials have advised caution. For my money, the thought of a lion or tiger knocking over our bins is a gas. Odds are it was Bertram, the jocular day labourer from the basement flat next door, careening home three-sheets-to-the-wind after his nightly visit to the tavern.

It could also be hunger that leaves me so fatigued. Our landlady is away, visiting her mother in Ipswich, and the girl who's been standing in didn't show up this morning. After such a rude and early awakening, I could have used a good hot breakfast to fortify my nerves, but when I came downstairs at my usual hour, the table was bare and the girl nowhere to be found, with not even so much as a note to explain her absence. I checked the kitchen, scullery, and cellar with no luck, and a full search of the house turned up only Jeffries and our fellow boarders, all equally hungry and confused.

Jeffries and I even peeked into the back alley on the off chance she was putting things to rights out there, but found nothing save the crumpled bins, a scratched-up back door, and a foul pile of offal on the steps. Jeffries was convinced the marks and sad mess were indisputable proof the missing creature had paid us a visit, and terrified our fellow boarders with stories of the monstrous skeletons he digs from the cliffs by Dorset. For my part, despite years of studying all manner of ancient and fanciful things, I prefer to let Occam's razor guide my thoughts. I'll speak to Bertram this evening, or, preferably, his wife; a much more moderate and serious-minded soul. For all Bertram's jokey charms, hauling waste out of the bins and hacking at our door is a step too far.

To make a long tale short, I've had scant nourishment today. Left to my own devices, I—like most youngish people of the academic persuasion—am poorly equipped to sustain myself in any civilized manner, so once it became clear the girl was well and truly absent and there would be no breakfast forthcoming, Jeffries and I caught a tram to campus and broke our fast in the faculty lounge. Lacking the sack lunch the girl was also meant to prepare, I was forced to reprise my foraging ways a few hours later. Our rent includes meals, and while dining halls abound, unlike Jeffries, whose parents send a weekly stipend, I can scarce afford to spend on what I've already bought. Two meals in a row cobbled together from left-over sandwiches and stale biscuits are hardly enough to feed a man, but at least the tea was hot and plentiful.

Or maybe it is excitement wearing me down.

Dr. Allenby, my former advisor and closest friend, wrote to me a little over a month ago. His letter was hectic—nothing like his usual neat hand—and filled with exuberance and superlatives. He wouldn't say much; only that our expedition last summer, an incredible journey that started with an old book in a forgotten library and ended in an ancient city far beneath the surface of the earth, had born sudden and unexpected fruit. The rest, he said, was too unbelievable to commit to paper, but he had something incredible to show me. He promised to come as soon as he could prepare his find for travel; by the end of this week, at the latest. I'd hoped to see him earlier—my friend is typically punctual to a fault, if not ahead-of-schedule—but he should definitely be here this evening, and I cannot wait to see what he has discovered. He may even be waiting for me by the time the six o'clock tram delivers me home, and my nerves are afire with anticipation.

For now, however, the couch beckons; its sun-warmed cushions an answer to the lassitude creeping through my veins. I slide off my shoes, lay my head upon my arm, and listen with closed eyes and a smile to the students chattering in the garden beyond my windows. The weight upon me is soft and warm, and I slip sideways in a breath.

Half-sleep; the playground of the mind. My drifting thoughts are filled with the wonders and horrors of last summer's expedition. An ancient city, home to a race lost and buried in some great, forgotten cataclysm, and the temple at its centre; oh, how we shuddered as our lanterns lit its crumbling façade, illuminating for the first time in aeons those prehistoric carvings. The great worm X'tchomal, god of sleep and hunger, adorned every surface; his coiled, segmented body, his great gaping mouth, filled with row after row of teeth, forever ravenous.

It was Dr. Allenby who discovered the hidden library and the book, but the hours of study and translation required to plumb its secrets were all mine, repaid with a place on the expedition and later, with the recommendations that secured me this position. I would have done it for nothing; but Allenby, despite his titles and wealth, is a paragon of decency. He would never short-change his diligent postgrad.

We travelled north, first by train, then boat, then ski and sled, and when we reached the correct coordinates, our hired guides dug a tunnel through the ice. Below lay caves, long and dark, and beyond those twisted passages, we found a mammoth cavern and in it, a ruined, empty city. It was everything I imagined and more; the find of a century, both our academic dreams come true.

We stayed a week in those dark, echoing halls, exploring, studying, documenting. Our sketches, notes, and artifacts—including three beautiful crystal sculptures meant, I can only imagine, to represent the eggs of the great worm—are with Dr. Allenby. His laboratory and preparation rooms at Aberdeen are perfect for storing our finds, and his tenure affords him time to devote to their study. I have no such liberty, as he well knows. For him to ask for a meeting mid-term like this, knowing my schedule and fixed income, he must have found something remarkable. I only wish he had arrived as early as he said he might. The suspense is killing me.

Further still I slip, immobilized like a swaddled child by insistent exhaustion.

Now, truly, I dream.

My office is gone. The colossal halls through which I stride are familiar, but oh-so changed from how I saw them last. Towering walls, cyclopean statues; it's the lost city—it can be no other—but I am seeing it as it was, rather than how we found it, restored to its former glory. Gone is the dark and the weak, flickering light of our lanterns. Gone is the grime, decay, and ruin. Now, the walls are clean and whole. Sun streams through high arched windows, throwing lines of light and shadow across stone floors. Warm wood, bright fabric, gold, silver, and gems polished smooth and brilliant; furniture and ornaments sit where Allenby and I sifted ancient dust. There are books too—room after room of them—and workshops filled with beakers and scales, and a huge observatory with two telescopes, one aimed to the stars and the other into a deep, man-made borehole, toward the centre of the earth.

Walking though these halls, observing these things, I see it now; what we missed with our lanterns, maps, and notebooks, what we didn't understand. This wasn't a city, it was a university, like my beloved Cambridge, a place for learned men to gather and study, a place to explore the mysteries of the world. And the building at its heart, with the carvings? Not a temple, but a laboratory, dedicated to their greatest undertaking; the excavation—and revivification—of the fossilized remains of a titanic, prehistoric worm they dubbed X'tchomal. Allenby and I mistook antediluvian science for religion; a common enough mistake, in our field. I can't wait to tell him what I've learned.

It is wondrous—so wondrous—and yet ... something is wrong. Something is happening.

From the laboratory, a crack like thunder, like a great chain snapping, and the floor bucks beneath my feet. The stone throbs, and the lines of light on the walls dance and spin as if I were walking through a kaleidoscope. The familiar sounds of academia—footsteps, ruffling pages, the droning murmur of a lecture—have gone high and hectic like a fairground organ. They bounce and whirl and turn to screams. So many screams.

I am cut loose from my moorings, dizzy and spinning.

And exhausted, even in this strange and vivid dream, pulled down and down and down by lethargy I cannot shake.

I want to sleep, cannot help but sleep. I slide to the floor as the city churns around me, limbs numb, cheek pressed to cool stone.

Cool stone or warm leather? No, I am on my couch. I can feel the soft cushions and hear the voices in the garden. I make to rise, but the weight is suffocating. I cannot move.

Lying in the great stone hallway, I am frantic. Lassitude holds me fast, but I must get up. From distant halls comes the sound of many feet—people running, fleeing—but here there is only clinging somnolence. The city shudders like a dying thing, and still I cannot move. Worse, I hear a new sound, thick and heavy, sliding across the stone toward me. It cuts through the kaleidoscope of echoes; a susurrus, a leathery whisper that resonates in my bones. Its smooth advance is punctuated by small bumps—*thump-thump ... thump-thump ... thump-thump*—as it navigates the stoops and doorways. Every now and then it pauses and, with a terrible slurping, and chewing, devours something in its path before starting forward again.

My heart beats a terrible countdown. If this is a university, where are the bells? Where are the students, librarians, and professors; anyone who can pull me up to safety?

I know the answer; can feel it in the vibration of that slow approach and hear it in those wet, throaty gulps. Those who once studied here are like me, trapped beneath this groggy weight, helpless as death slithers ever closer. It's coming. It's coming and it's coming and it's almost here. I'm too tired to move, and there is no one left to help me.

I wake with a start, and find myself back on my couch.

It was all in my mind, thank God, only a fantasy, and I gasp in heady relief, but ...

I cannot rise. The heavy dreams hold me still.

And it's coming. The voices in the garden outside my windows have turned to screams, and I can hear it, slithering down the hall. *Thump-thump ... thump-thump ... thump-thump.* It's almost here.

And now, with a cold weight in my stomach, I understand what has happened.

To those ancient natural philosophers and their ruined city. To Dr. Allenby, who did indeed arrive early with his deadly prize, on Wednesday evening's ill-fated south-bound train. And to my landlord's girl as well, in the alley behind the house.

Not sculptures, those artifacts we retrieved, but eggs. Ancient eggs, brought to the surface and shown the sun for the first time after millennia of darkness. What might hatch, from such a vessel? I know that answer too. Like those who came before, Allenby and I dug too deep, reached too far, and in our ignorance and arrogance, we unearthed something we couldn't control.

Prehistoric beast or ancient god? It matters not, because it's coming all the same, carrying sleep, hunger, and death in its great coils.

Smothered by a sluggish fatigue that will not let me go, I shudder to think of my part in bringing this horror to the world. I shudder and wait for that segmented body and that many-toothed maw to find me.

X'tchomal has come again.

Megan M. Davies-Ostrom

Megan M. Davies-Ostrom is a Canadian author with a penchant for horror and dark speculative fiction. Her short stories have appeared in Fantasy Magazine, Cosmic Horror Monthly, and anthologies such as Dark Waters and Bodies Full of Burning, and her debut novel is coming out with Bad Hand Press in 2026. She lives in Ontario with her husband, daughter, and two (strange) cats. When not writing or carrying-out the duties of her civil-servant alter-ego, she enjoys hiking, reading, and playing board games. Discover other works by Megan at: https://mdaviesostrom.com/

1890s

THE VERITY OF FLESH

Jonathan Daniel

London, 1893

Horace Alcott had been deep in thought, his pen poised above the paper, when the knock came at his door. Initially he didn't hear the rapping, so absolute was his focus. The paper was going to be the best treatise that he'd penned in the last two years. His theory on the technique for achieving lifelike qualities in the ocular orbs was sure to be a theory for but a brief moment. Once others in the community, especially that blowhard Michaelson, understood the practical application Alcott was certain it would become common practice.

Then he would be back at the top of the field. He reread the previous sentence. 'Death is a lie told by entropy. The soul may depart, but the form remains. And in that form lies a truth—if only we're clever enough to coax it back to the surface.' He smiled, reacquiring the train of thought, and touched the pen to the paper.

The pounding came once more, slightly more insistent this time and Alcott frowned. Where was that infernal girl? Surely she heard the commotion and knew that his work was too important to be disturbed. Then he remembered. He'd sent Harriett home early, despite the girl's protests about preparing his dinner. But with Martha at her sister's house for the next week and the girls remaining at school over the break, Alcott had seized the opportunity for a rare night of solitude. In the parlor off the entrance sat an unlit cigar alongside his decanter and a chipped cut crystal glass waiting for a spot of bourbon. He'd been looking forward to the sweet liquor, something he'd grown deeply fond of ever since finishing the job for the man from Kentucky and receiving a case of whiskey as part of his payment. The cigar, one of his vices that Martha detested, was another—

A third round of knocking, most tenacious, rattled the door. In his cramped workshop at the rear of the house, Alcott believed he could feel the vibrations through the wooden floor. He let out a deep exasperated sigh and placed his pen on the desk, the train of thought he'd held onto now blasted apart. Scowling, he exited his work room and approached the door, his fingers curling around the knob as yet another barrage assaulted the wood. He pulled the door open, a verbal thrashing rising to his tongue. Yet as his gaze fell on the interloper, the words shriveled and died.

At first glance, the man on his doorstep appeared to be a cadaver. It was only when the man's gaunt face turned slightly to focus on Alcott that the illusion of death was broken. The man wore a plain black suit, a black derby, and a stiff, starched white shirt. A simple long black tie peered from beneath his waistcoat. But it was the man's skin that held Alcott's rapt attention. The dermis was so white as to be almost bloodless. His eyes were a startling juxtaposition to the man's pallor, the orbs the deep color of jade.

A large crate constructed from rough, dark wood, sat behind the man. *Must weigh over seven stone,* Alcott thought. *There's no way he could have carried it by himself.* Yet no servants could be seen lingering near the road. In fact, the street was devoid of even a carriage or horse-drawn wagon.

"I do apologize for intruding on your evening." The man's voice was warm honey. Alcott thought perhaps there was a hint of an accent there. Liverpool? Or somewhere more exotic? The man didn't look Spanish or Italian, yet his voice lacked the subtle harshness of the Slavic tongue.

Alcott, realizing he'd been staring gobsmacked for some time, managed a mumbling mixed with the clearing of his throat. "Not at all." The sound of his own voice, suddenly almost apologetic to the person who had interrupted his work, brought yet another round of clarity to his mind. He sharpened his tone. "I was in the middle of some very important work, however. How can I be of service?" He let the last word linger, his eyebrows raised in an unasked question of the man's identity.

A quick smile curled the man's lips and he extended a hand, a pearl white envelope pinched between the index and second fingers. Alcott blinked at it. He'd not seen the man move to retrieve the item.

"My name is of no consequence. Truly," he added, seeing the darkening expression of mistrust creep into Alcott's features. "I am merely a messenger, bound in service to a much higher master. Please." He extended the sheaf further, and Alcott took it.

Alcott took the parcel and turned it over. "And who, exactly, would your master be?" The heavy vellum bore no return address—only a crimson wax seal stamped with a simple 'K'.

"I am here on behalf of Kepler & Sons."

The envelope vibrated in Alcott's trembling fingers. He glanced sharply at the man. "I think you should leave. I've no time for—"

"My employers learned that you were the one who completed the job for Lord Kenswick. The reconstruction you did on Liora after what that madman did to her was absolutely masterful. My employers are most impressed."

"How did—" Alcott began, but clamped his mouth shut. He'd never told anyone about the work he'd done over the course of that weekend. Not even Martha. She would have been appalled at his acceptance of the task. Even the money promised wouldn't have swayed her; she would have reminded him that her parents could be called upon to help with financial troubles. But that was a Pandora's Box Alcott wasn't willing to open. So he'd taken the job and only told her he was attending a series of lectures over the course of a weekend at St. Bartholomew's. Yet the fact that the firm of Kepler &Sons had knowledge of it was somehow not surprising. Once more his eyes drifted to the large crate.

The man, seeing Alcott's attention shift, made a half turn to regard the box. "Ah, yes." He turned back to Alcott. "That is why I am here. Inside that envelope you will find a set of instructions and the first payment for your services."

"Services? What does the crate contain?" Alcott thought briefly of Liora Kenswick, how what had remained of her could have fit inside a much smaller box. He shuddered at the memory.

The man's pallid, wormy lips twitched in a grin. "I'm afraid I'm not privy to that information. All you need to know is contained within the envelope. They said you're to begin at once."

"Begin what, exactly? I'm sorry, I don't understand." A fearful tingling had started to worm its way along Alcott's spine and was now seeping deeper into his extremities. As bad as the work he'd done for Lord

Kenswick had been, there was something considerably wrong about this man and that crate. His hand tightened on the door, eager to push it closed. He thrust the envelope towards the ghostly man. "I'm not interested. Please convey my apologies to Mr. Kepler, but I'm not available for any new projects." It wasn't a complete lie, he had placed the pursuit of new work on hold while he penned his latest paper. But the presence of the messenger from Kepler & Sons was intriguing. It had been some time since anyone of stature sought his expertise. Most commissions now came from collectors with more coin than discernment.

The man remained motionless. His eyes flicked to the envelope then back to Alcott's. "You are to begin at once," he said once more. This time, however, his words were edged with a silvery menace.

Something creaked from deep within the house, and Alcott whipped around, heart thrumming. The last thing he needed was Martha or one of the girls to come home early to find a representative of Kepler & Sons along with a strange and, if he had to be honest with himself, disturbing, crate at their door. The house was silent, as it had been all evening. When he turned back, the man in the black suit was no longer on his doorstep. In the soft pools of light thrown by the two gas pole mounted lamps, the cobbled lane of Seddon Street was empty, the other houses dark, their occupants slumbering.

At Alcott's feet, the crate was like a silent, ugly tumor growing out of the stonework of his doorstep. Stuffing the envelope into a pocket, he bent forward and gripped the rough wood. A pulse of revulsion shot through him at the touch of the coarse material, there and gone in an instant. He gave the crate a shake, appreciating the heft. It had weight but could be moved, though not easily.

Pulling the envelope from his pocket he thumbed through the sheaf of bills. The total sum brought his eyebrows up and sent his heart into a canter high in his chest. His daily work brought in a meager salary: enough to pay for Harriett, the groceries and Martha's personal pursuits, but even then it required a stretching of every single pence he earned. To his distaste, Martha's parents, not wanting their granddaughters to become destitute or—God forbid—be forced into a similar practice as their father, insisted they pay for the girls' tuition.

But this amount ... If this was the first payment as the man had suggested, Alcott would have the means to sever that previously iron-clad tether.

Tucked behind the pound notes was a folded slip of paper.

Mr. Alcott,

Your reputation, though unjustly diminished of late, has not gone unnoticed among those who value mastery. We find ourselves in need of your particular expertise for a project of considerable delicacy and discretion.

The nature of the specimen is ... uncommon. We are confident that you will find the work both challenging and enlightening.

Remuneration will be generous, but more importantly, we offer an opportunity to work with something singular. A commission worthy of your legacy.

You are to begin reconstruction immediately upon receipt. Standard materials and preservative agents are at your discretion. The object is to remain in your care and under no external observation. This crate is the first of six. Each must be set before the next arrives. Additional segments will follow every two days. Do not attempt to alter or interpret their origin.

You are trusted because your reputation is well known and favorable to us. Additionally, you refrain from asking questions, Mr. Alcott. Do not change that. Further compensation will arrive with each subsequent segment.

K&S

Alcott read the missive twice more before tucking it and the money back into his pocket. He regarded the crate.

They knew his name.

Not the press. Not the taxidermy guilds or the city inspectors who had spoken of stripping his license and muttered behind clipboards. Not even his in-laws who, alongside those fools at the museum, called his work *morbid curiosities.* No, someone *real* knew him. Someone who saw his work for what it was — not grotesquerie, not spectacle, but preservation. Preservation of verity — of *life,* frozen at its peak, caught in that final breath before death stole the illusion from the flesh. People who understood the art.

His hand drifted to his chest, his fingertips pressing against the cloth and feeling the yielding bulge of the letter and money beneath. This was an opportunity he could not pass up.

It took him a half hour of grunting effort to maneuver the crate into the house and to the small workshop near the garden. Once there he hurried to fetch a prybar and hammer. Finding a thin seam between wooden slats, he worked the flat blade in. The wood gave obstinately with a splintery crack. Alcott peeled back the lid and immediately recoiled, one hand flying to his mouth as he staggered away. As an anatomical taxidermist, he'd encountered many specimens in various states of decay; such was often the nature of death and its aftereffects. The destruction visited upon Liora Kenswick specifically was inhuman. For weeks, Alcott feared he wouldn't be able to clear the sights and smells from his memory. The poor girl had been baking in the sun on the banks of Regent's Canal for some time before she'd been discovered.

The smell that surged out of the crate like a living creature was beyond anything he'd ever experienced. Alcott spun on his heel and barely made it to the slop pail he kept tucked away next to the tin lined sink before retching the last dregs of the meager sandwich he'd made for dinner.

His legs shaking, Alcott dragged in a breath. Almost instantly his throat clamped shut against the foul air and once more his stomach rolled. He stood, swaying, for a few moments before his body relented and allowed him a measure of control. Heart thudding, he approached the crate. The object inside was covered with a thick layer of straw. He noted with revulsion that much of the protective chaff was blackened, slicked with some offensive substance. He snagged a pair of forceps from a nearby table and carefully removed the grass.

What lay beneath defied his mind, refused his eyes in their attempt to discern form. It was a large piece of tissue, roughly two feet by four feet. How big beyond that he couldn't tell for all the slimy straw packed about it. The flesh was thick and leathery, a mottled brown that appeared as if dappled with shadows from a thick canopy of trees. Alcott reached a tentative hand towards it and, before his fingertips connected, paused. A measurable warmth emanated from the specimen.

What in God's name is this?

He cleared a suitable space on his primary work table. Donning thick leather gloves he pulled the specimen from its nesting place. He grimaced at the sensation of its heat seeping through the protective mitts. The thing was considerably heavy, perhaps not quite the seven stone he'd imagined, but close. Sweat dotted his body from the effort of moving the mass the three feet to the table. When it was settled and sufficient light directed upon it, he circled the table, trying to get the measure of the thing. There were no limbs, no neck or head. The piece appeared to be a large section of an even more massive torso. The leathery skin protruded in places, small ridges where deeper bones extended upward.

"What am I to do with you?" he muttered. Removing the gloves he went to the strange alien flower form of the phonograph in one corner of the room, a gift from Martha's parents. Until receiving it, Horace had never fully realized how much more enjoyable his work was with the strains of song filling the room. He worked the mechanism and soon the first notes of *The Last Chord* drifted out of the massive horn.

He retrieved his tools and bent over the specimen. The scalpel's keen edge touched the thick flesh and, using a skinning hook to hold the meat back, he began his work. The musculature gave way begrudgingly. Alcott frowned. Usually flesh yielded almost eagerly. With this specimen he found the need to exert more pressure on the blade, occasionally working it like a saw in order to clear a path forward. He hummed along with the song as he cut and probed, digging his way deeper.

The anatomy of the creature was unlike anything he'd ever seen. Alcott had preserved things from lions to lamprey, from a harbor seal to, of course, human beings. Never in his time had he ever witnessed a physique such as this. There were muscles, certainly, but running within them lay a strange webbing of veins. Yet unlike veins of any living creature he knew, these, when viewed at different angles, shimmered as if possessed of some strange luminescence.

Several inches down he reached the first bone and there he stopped, his brow furrowing in confusion. The material was dark gray, and, when touched by the tip of the scalpel, emitted an almost wooden, hollow *thunk*.

Angling the scalpel, Alcott probed deeper.

The haunting melody from the phonograph faded to a soft drone.

A sharp noise, the slamming of a door, snapped him out of his concentration. Alcott sat up, blinking stupidly as his surroundings came back into focus. A dull ache spread across his lower back and he arced, bent and twisted to relieve the pain. He glanced at the specimen, saw the levels of dissection he'd reached, the matter he'd separated from the primary unit. Inwardly he gave a tired smile; the work had been so engaging, he couldn't clearly remember all of it.

Footsteps along the hallway beyond his workshop door drew his attention. They stopped on the other side of the door. "Morning, Mr. Alcott. Would you be needing anything? Coffee? Tea? Shall I prepare breakfast?" Harriett. Alcott stared at the closed door, his mind scrambling to make sense of things. The hell was the servant doing here? He'd sent her home early. And what was this talk of coffee and breakfast? Was she drunk? Opening the door he found the small, mousy figure of Harriett standing, hands clasped before her. Behind her lay the hall that led to the sitting room. The glow of sunlight filled the doorway and spilled into the hall.

"It's morning?" Alcott mumbled. His throat was thick and rough, the words forced past a thick, dry tongue.

"Aye." Harriett's face screwed up in concern. "Were you working all night, sir?"

Alcott stepped into the hall, closed and locked the door. Pocketing the key he stepped past the Irishwoman. "I'm going to bed. See that you make no disturbance, please." The servant's head bobbed in acknowledgement and Alcott climbed the steps to the second floor where his bed awaited.

He awoke to find himself still dressed and laying at an odd angle across the mattress. His tongue was heavy against his palate, and his head swam. Fragments of dreams slipped away like fish darting into the protective darkness of the depths, leaving him only with an unsettling vibration through his limbs. The dreams had been quite disturbing, he knew that much.

As he climbed off the bed a series of bursts of pain flared from his joints, forcing a gasp out of his throat. He remained bent forward, hands resting on the mattress until the wave receded. He took another slow breath and stood upright, tense against the anticipation of yet another bodily protest. When none came he stepped back and began the process of changing clothes. The aches remained, though. Such things were a well known friend in his line of work. Bending and holding positions whilst maneuvering the body of his specimen often bore such discomforts. But still, the soreness upon waking was considerably more intense than any previous.

Once he'd pulled on a fresh set of clothes and splashed sufficient water on his face, he descended to the first floor to find Harriett dutifully cleaning the floors of the sitting room. Alcott's eyes strayed to the front door, remembering the courier and his strange delivery. Another would be coming soon, if the author of the letter was to be believed.

Ignoring the gnawing hunger burning in his gut, Alcott bypassed the kitchen and slipped inside his workshop. The foul odor remained, clinging to the very air like stubborn cigar smoke, yet today there was something slightly more agreeable about it. An undercurrent of sweet cut through the putridity. Alcott lit the candles and approached the worktable. The specimen sat on the surface like some horrible tumor, tools scattered about it like worshippers bowing in reverence to a lunatic god.

Alcott's hand froze inches above his scalpel. Something was wrong. The flesh he'd worked for hours on was a bloodless mass of torn and sliced meat. "What?" While the specimen did show signs of his efforts, it wasn't nearly as cut or as disorganized as it had been when he'd gone to bed only a few hours ago.

Parts that he recalled specifically removing or leaving flayed open were once more attached to the whole. There were no visible seams denoting the passage of his blade. Alcott ran a hand along the rough, pebble-like texture where he distinctly remembered making a cut. The skin dimpled at his touch, as if hollow beneath. Yet even then, the mass felt different than it had the day before. It was as if the structure of the thing had shifted into a new configuration after his work had been completed for the day. With some effort he turned the piece a few degrees to survey the far side.

"Dear God."

He knew that he had fallen into some sort of fugue state during the night, his hands working automatically, but even so he distinctly remembered the area he stared at as being a single, flat stretch of flesh. Now the flesh bulged several centimeters. The crown of the protrusion contained four smaller lumps, evenly spaced apart in a semicircle.

A dreamy smile spread across his face. What on earth was this thing? From where had those madmen at Kepler and Sons procured it? A fluttering of excitement rippled in his chest. What would the next piece be? What secrets would it reveal? What would this thing, this foreign mystery reveal itself to be?

Alcott lowered himself to his stool, picked up his tools and, humming happily, bent to his task.

2

Alcott took delivery of two more crates over the next several days. He couldn't say how many had passed—three? Five? Days and nights were a blur, a hazy scene of bloodless flesh, the gleam of lamplight off instruments and bizarre dreams the details of which he could never recount upon waking.

Each new box was identical to the first in size and composition, but their contents were markedly different. The first contained what, after hours of study, appeared to be a lower section of torso. The second revealed six limbs, arranged in the putrid straw like contraband muskets.

As he withdrew the limbs—each more strange than the last, containing multiple hinge points—the palm of his left hand was nicked by a fragment of exposed bone jutting from what he believed to be a shoulder joint. The cut was deep, much more severe than he would have imagined and required a small detour of duties whilst he stitched himself.

To his great satisfaction, the thing was starting to come together. The process of determining its unique structure had been a long and laborious one, but now he believed he could see its true shape. The specimen was revealing itself to him, in the slow and steady manner in which all broken things eventually must. Even Liora Kenswick had, and she had been a frightful mess. Alcott had been challenged to bring all his considerable talents to bear on that particular project. Naturally the speculation amongst those in the manor had been that the Ripper, after a period of blessed quiet and inactivity, had claimed yet another victim. That fearful rumor had been given fuel due to the lack of suspects in the poor girl's demise. That, and the state of her remains.

After almost a week of nonstop work, Alcott had called the undertaking complete. Lord Kenswick and his wife had openly wept at the sight of their beloved daughter restored. Alcott's work had been so flawless, so masterful that one would have thought the twelve year old to simply be asleep.

But this. This project was shaping to be not only his most challenging but a true masterpiece. His work had, for a couple of days, come in fits and starts but now was speeding along. Aided, he believed, by the fact that he'd formally dismissed Harriett after the second crate's delivery. Too often he'd been disturbed by the sounds of the girl's footsteps outside his door. More than once, during breaks wherein he would attend to nature, or grab a quick biscuit from the larder, he'd returned to find Harriett loitering only steps from his workshop door. The girl had insisted she was simply dusting or cleaning the baseboards, but Alcott knew better. It was clear she was trying to sneak a look inside at his project. Or worse, interfere in some way.

He stepped from the kitchen, a warm cup of tea clasped in one hand, and paused near the front door. Briefly he considered stepping outside. As per usual in London, it was raining. Still, he could do with a draft of fresh air. Against the door lay a pile of envelopes in a scattered heap along the carpet. More were mounded against the wall, gathered there after the last time he'd opened the door. Alcott's eyes drifted over the unopened post, catching snippets of both Martha's handwriting as well as the even, practiced letters of Elizabeth and Jane. A tickling instinct pulled at him, and he took a single step in the direction of the mail. Immediately he was overcome with a swaying nausea. His skin flushed and sweat broke out along his forehead, between his shoulderblades and down his chest.

What am I doing? I haven't the time for frivolities such as the post. I am committed to a task for Kepler and Sons. I must see that complete.

The image of the specimen as he'd left it flared in his mind. He could see it laid upon the table, patiently awaiting his return. Another cold lurch spasmed in his guts. What if while he was wasting time preparing tea and staring at the useless letters and, undoubtedly, bills, someone had stolen into the workshop and was, at this very moment, absconding with the specimen?

What if they were destroying it?

Alcott dropped his mug, spun and raced to his workshop. The moment the door closed behind him, a sense of peace settled over his mind, a soothing balm on a raw and burning wound. The swirling sickness in his stomach abated. Alcott passed a hand across his brow, palming sweat away. His hand continued down his face, fingers tugging his cheeks and turning his lips in a frown. Pain quickly flared within his mouth. The warm metallic taste of blood trickled along this tongue and Alcott ran the muscle along his teeth. More pain spiked through his gums. He would have to get to the dentist at some point. Probably the doctor as well. The discomfort in his joints had been increasing as of late, most likely a result of the hours spent hunched over the table. More and more frequently he'd taken to sleeping at his desk, the thought of forcing himself upstairs almost too much to bear.

But so much progress was being made. And the specimen was doing its part, aiding his efforts. Each morning he awoke to find signs of the flesh made whole. His work was always done meticulously such that the stitches were often difficult to spot. It was a point of personal pride. Even with such meticulous care, he found the cuts and stitching healed and smoothed over. Once he'd attached three of the limbs the body had shown evidence of more new growths, including one that he was almost certain sought to be a neck.

He started the phonograph, once more allowing the notes of *The Last Chord* to surround him with their melancholic lilting. Horace lowered himself to the stool and, mumbling softly to himself, bent once more to his work.

Horace had only the faintest acknowledgement that it was the sabbath. Normally, Sundays were reserved for church followed by a relaxing afternoon at the conclusion of which Harriett would present a splendid roast. But Harriett was gone, and the penultimate crate had arrived late the previous evening, the rapping on the front door heralding its delivery startling him awake. He'd been surprised to find that he'd fallen asleep with one hand buried to the wrist inside the specimen. With the last of his waning energy, Alcott dragged the container into the front hall before promptly falling back asleep on the chaise in the adjoining room.

By the time he'd awakened, it was half twelve and his back and hips were screaming protests at the awkward sleeping arrangements. As he sat up, some small objects beneath his shoe ground roughly against the floor. Four teeth, ridges slimed with blood, lay like a child's scattered marbles.

Alcott stared at them, dumbfounded. His tongue slid over the cavities in his gum sending shards of pleasurable discomfort stabbing through his jaw.

Pulling his attention from the discarded teeth he focused on the heavy wooden crate partially visible around the opening to the hall. He needed to attend to it, and soon. It wouldn't do to leave the next piece or pieces just sitting there.

As if to drive home his concern, a series of muffled thumps sounded from overhead. He tensed, eyes darting to the dark pool at the top of the stairs leading to the second floor. He'd heard the noises before, dismissing them as figments of his overexerted mind. But now, sitting on the lounge as he was, it was clear the noises weren't fabricated. Someone was up there.

Someone from Kepler and Sons, come to take the project from me.

The thought was fierce and absolute, resonating deep within him like the tolling of a church bell and a clammy chill spread across his body. Were they dissatisfied with his progress? How could that be? He'd not even received all the crates as of yet. With the previous deliveries there hadn't been any mention of dissatisfaction or regret. And Kepler & Sons certainly was the type of organization that wouldn't be sly about their displeasure.

Which left only one possibility. There was another agency, another interested party who wanted the specimen and were actively trying to infiltrate his home with the intent of spiriting it away.

Alcott shot to his feet and took two steps towards the stairs when the light streaming through the unblocked windows behind the lounge caught his attention. When had the curtains been opened? Surely he'd not done that. Why would he? To open the curtains invited passersby to peer in and observe what he was working on. Surely Harriett hadn't returned; he'd made it very clear that her services were no longer needed. A memory crashed into his mind, he and Martha arguing over the retention of the

Irishwoman. He squinted in puzzlement. No, that had been a dream, he was sure of it. It couldn't possibly have been real, Martha was still at her sister's house and would be for at least another week. Yet the nagging, pulling feeling of the dream, its vividness, its *realness* bothered him.

No, he reasoned, it had to be evidence that miscreants were stealing into his home searching for the specimen. Galvanized with the surety, Alcott hurried to the front door, his movements lumbering and pained—the aches in his joints and back were increasing. His fingers felt for the locks, twisting them, ensuring they were all in place. He touched the small brass lever of the mail slot, pressing it firmly shut, wishing that there was a way to bar even that. The contact brought another thought and he glanced at the floor. The piles of post were gone. The letters lay in a series of neat piles on a small table along one wall of the hallway.

Bastards think they're clever. Alcott smiled grimly, but another sound from upstairs, this time the raspy, whispering sound of something dragging across the floor, pulled his attention from the letters. Moving as fast as his shuffling, limping gait allowed, Alcott climbed the steps to the second floor landing.

The corridor from which branched three bedrooms and the single water closet—something he was still getting accustomed to the idea of—was empty, the small table upon which a kerosene lantern sat, unmolested, beside a framed photograph of the girls. He stood motionless, straining to hear more sounds of the intruders.

What if they're in the very walls? A voice in the corner of his mind inquired. His fists clenched, bright pops of pain sparking through his wrists at the movement, and he strode quickly to the primary bedroom.

The room was empty. The window overlooking the street was solidly shut and he reaffirmed the security of its latch. As he stepped back, his eyes caught something peculiar. Frowning, he bent closer. A smear of blood marred the glass. It curved down to the sill where a few more drops stood out against the white painted wood. Now that he saw the blood, he noticed more of it: a few splatters across the dark wood of the floor, a trail leading to the chifforobe.

One of the bastards must have hurt himself, Alcott thought with grim satisfaction. *Serves the weasel right. And* when *I find him and his associates, I will see them buried and forgotten in a potter's field.*

A ghastly, broken-toothed grin split his face as he pictured the thieves' bodies buried beneath fetid soil. Alcott moved to the next bedroom—Elizabeth's—and confirmed the security of her window as his feet crunched over the shattered remains of the girl's favorite teacup scattered next to the bed. The pieces lay in tacky pools of blood like small insects trapped in sap. Furrows were etched into the blood, extending for a few feet across the floor as if something had been dragged. He hesitated, foot wavering over the ceramic remains. Elizabeth was a very neat girl, everything in its place and so forth. So why was her teacup in her bedroom? Had she left it there and Harriett simply missed it or ignored it? It's possible, he thought darkly. *When it comes down to it, you can't trust the Irish to do a job properly.* But surely not, he corrected. Yet the alternative made even less sense. Could the girl be home? Her sister as well? If so, how had he missed them? Of course he'd been working a lot, but even so, they'd never been shy about rapping on the door to his shop when they wanted his attention.

Before he could give the question more attention, his eyes drifted to the window's open sash. Panic blossomed bright and sour and he reached the offending casement and slammed it shut. The latch clicked into place with a satisfying *clack*, and Alcott stood back. He tugged on his vest, straightening the garment and gave the window a satisfied nod before moving on to the next room.

Once all means of ingress were secure, and more importantly, there were no further sounds of movement within the walls or any other room of the house, Alcott stumbled downstairs and began the laborious process of dragging the fifth crate to his workshop. His thoughts swirled: What piece could be in the box? Did he hear someone call his name? Oh wait until Martha sees the final piece! Did he ensure all the windows upstairs were firmly secured? And what of the kitchen door that led to the garden? But by George this crate is heavy, what could possibly be in it?

Once he wrestled the box into his workshop and closed the door, all thoughts quieted. His mind stilled. The thing on the table was bigger, *much* bigger. It was *helping* now. The creature had a complete torso. Each of its limbs ended in six digits with strange, forked nails protruding from the tips. To his amazement, what he was quite certain was the budding protrusion of a leathery wing sprouted from one side of the thing's back. His head cocked, a curious expression overtaking him. He didn't recall making those connections there, by the thing's knee. Nor those over there. Was that a second mouth on its chest? What a strange and wonderful specimen!

"Well, old boy, are you ready to finish this?" he asked, giving the body a gentle rub and a pat. He chuckled. "Oh, I've no doubt you are." Tittering, Alcott cracked open the wooden crate and began to work.

The final crate arrived on a miserable rainy day. Alcott wasted no time wrestling it into the house: even the leaden skies and gray sheets of rain sent shards of pain into his eyes. He grunted, his breath ragged gasps as he pulled the final crate into the workshop. Against his back, his shirt was a sodden bloody rag from the dozens of stinging splits in his skin. Over the last day, more fissures had erupted along his arms, his neck and legs leaving his skin in a constant buzzing, burning agony. The floors of the house were streaked from foul fluids that marked his path in thin, stinking trails.

His groin was a single, blood swollen purple mass that thumped painfully against his thighs with every step.

It was glorious.

His foot thumped against something and he turned, his body locked in an awkward hunch, to see what had gotten in his way. "Ah, you pesky thing," he admonished the object. The words spilled past toothless gums and came out slurred and mushy. He'd almost forgotten about the other specimens in the room, the other projects he'd completed. He'd been so focused on the main piece, his masterpiece, that he'd hardly noticed how crowded the shop had gotten. A sour giggle fell out of his throat as he adjusted the item to make room.

So many projects, so little time.

The primary specimen was almost fully complete and he took a moment to bask in its glory. In all his years, Alcott had reconstructed quite a number of truly amazing specimens, Liora Kenswick most significantly, but never had anything so magnificent as this come across his table. Its shape defied comprehension, such was its beautiful complexity. The limbs, the wings, its slender forked tails, all were stunning in their purity. But it was probably the thing's face that was the most wondrous. The entire head of the creature loomed at the end of a slender and powerful neck that stretched at least four times the length of an average human's neck. The face atop that neck was the single most beautiful thing Alcott had ever seen. There was some work yet to be done, naturally, but still. . .

He blinked and turned to the crate. The final crate. It appeared no different than any of its predecessors, although he could have sworn it had moved a bit more easily. Perhaps the final pieces were considerably smaller yet fragile, packed in extra padding; that would certainly explain the size of the container.

Horace opened the crate and carefully withdrew the straw. The filler piled upon the floor, the mound growing larger and larger with each double handful extracted, and still he came across no new parts. A sharp ember of panic flared in his guts, spreading to his chest as he redoubled his efforts, straw flying wildly about the room.

His fingers scraped the rough wooden bottom of the crate and closed on nothing more substantial than a few loose strands of hay. Alcott stood upright, his chest heaving from both the exertion and his near panic. He eyed the discarded packing material. Had he inadvertently tossed the contents out alongside the straw? Surely not. Kepler & Sons weren't comprised of fools who wouldn't give the specimen the proper protections. Even something as small as a glass jar. So, no, he had to have missed it somewhere in the box. He bent over the wide opening and peered into the dark corners of the crate. Behind him, the specimen loomed, its empty eyed stare a piercing weight against his back. It was as if the poor creature were begging him, beseeching, *"Where is the rest of me?"*

Yet the crate remained empty.

Something warm swelled inside Alcott, a creeping pressure that spread to fill every hollow in his body. He braced himself for the onslaught of rage, of frustration at not being provided the correct materials with which to complete this masterpiece. But the pressure didn't bring a screaming tide of anger. Instead, it washed against his extremities, lapping at them the way a placid lake pulses against the shore, cleaning the mud from the stones to reveal the truth beneath.

He understood. Knowledge, the acceptance of truth, swelled in him. His fingers trembled at the understanding. The tremors swelled, joined by a deep, bubbling laughter that burst out of him and crashed against the walls and other specimens throughout the workshop.

"Of course!" he screamed between gales. "Of course!"

With frenzied movements, Alcott's fingers tore at his clothing. Bloody cotton and wool split, sending buttons flying in a spray to clatter against the floor. He kicked free of his boots, then in a frantic almost spastic series of movements, pulled his legs free of his pants. Completely nude, Alcott stared not at his own cracked, bleeding body, the skin beneath the smears of blood discolored by a mottling of bruises. His eyes never drifted to the protrusions that had formed along his waist and abdomen without his knowledge or memory. Instead he fixed his hard gaze at the empty crate.

The crate that held the final piece. The absolute, rapturous truth.

Bloody spittle slid between his remaining teeth and trailed off his chin. How could he have gotten so lucky? How could fortune such as this have befallen him? A lifetime spent in search of the verity of life through his work, of pursuing that one perfect blend of the fragility of existence with the immutable, unmovable eternity of death.

Turning to his workbench, Alcott's fingers twitched over the instruments as if preparing to play a pianist's concerto. He plucked the scalpel up and brought it against the soft meat of his left breast.

The blade's bite was a cold caress. The removal of the patch of flesh a fluttering that reminded him of the first time he saw. . . The memory ended like a short dead-end alleyway. Alcott's brow furrowed briefly, but the irritation of not being able to remember what it was he'd been trying to see, of *who* it was, fading like small ripples from a tiny stone tossed into the water. He knew it had been a person, someone of great significance to him at one point. But it didn't matter, not really. Not when he was so close to this triumph. This accomplishment. Destiny.

Another strip of flesh came free. Alcott placed it gently on the table atop the first, then repositioned the scalpel. He focused his eyes on the specimen as he worked, blissful in the knowledge that what he was doing was going to be seen by the world as the single greatest accomplishment of the nineteenth century.

The scalpel worked slowly.

Methodically.

Reverently.

When he was finished, he gently placed the scalpel next to the significant mound of blood slicked flesh and, sighing against the sensation of movement, reached for his sewing implements. The strips of tissue fit as expected in the larger, incomplete body of the specimen. He chuckled at himself as he tugged the dark thread through the leathery skin of the creature. How had he not seen from the beginning that he had to complete his work in this manner? It was glaringly obvious in hindsight. All the uneven spacing between parts, the angles that never lined up quite right. They were simply awaiting the final piece.

Pieces, he corrected.

The last of the cuttings tugged snugly into place beneath one of the wings and Alcott took a single step back. His foot skidded on something wet along the floor. In the back of his mind he made a note to clean the workshop later.

"One final piece," he mumbled and drew close to the specimen. With some effort he climbed atop the bench. His skin and flesh burned with the fire of need, of excitement, of anticipation. It consumed his body, the sensation so great it was almost painful. Yet once he slid his upper torso into the opening in the creature's lower abdomen, once the cloying darkness was fully around him, the pain went away.

Alcott stood inside the carcass and closed his eyes under the enormous sense of tranquility that settled over him. Everything fit perfectly. He suspected he always knew it would. Somehow, even in the earliest days of this project, he knew that it would be an immaculate union. The leathery skin of the creature settled against his own exposed flesh. His limbs and the protrusions along his torso slipped into the extensions of the creature, aligning precisely.

His head filled the space atop the creature's neck with only a momentary sting of discomfort as his neck stretched along the extraordinary length. Once in position, Alcott peered through the sockets and giggled, the sound muffled by the material before him. As his mirth overtook him, as his rapturous joy swelled, the flesh about him bent and shifted, loosened and softened. The strains of laughter deepened, grew wetter, more clotted as if his vocal cords were restructuring themselves.

Alcott's thoughts expanded and shifted. Ideas formed, were torn apart and reconstructed before being obliterated and born anew. New lines of concepts, new instinctual considerations threaded through the universe of his mind, pulling him first one way then spinning him and thrusting him into six different directions at once. He gave himself to the swirling river gleefully, and was delighted when the room before his very eyes changed. Everything remained as it was, but he saw it from a new perspective. He took in each object, evaluated it for not only its potential for food but as a possible threat. The other specimens scattered through the small room were observed and understood to be his possessions. Others would want them, but they were *his*. He would eat some, plant his seed in others so that his offspring would burst forth from the dead flesh.

The world would be his. It would be glorious.

The door to Horace Alcott's home opened with a gentle squeal of hinges in need of a light oiling. A pale man with a cadaverous face peered unblinking into the shadowy expanse of the foyer. His dark suit was a black inkblot against the deep night, as was the one belonging to the man behind him.

"Empty?" asked the follower.

The man in the doorway nodded. "Naturally." He stepped across the threshold. "This way, I believe."

The men stepped through the empty house, with no evidence of their presence. Their footsteps fell silent on the hardwood floor as they approached the closed door at the end of the hall. The smell that seeped through the barrier told them all they needed to know. Pausing at the door, the first man looked to his partner and gave a subtle nod.

The workshop was a cavernous maw of black. Moving with ease through the darkness, the two men found and lit lanterns, adjusting the wick height to allow the illumination to fill the space. Their focus on the things gathered in the space, the men drifted towards the center of the room and stood beside one another.

Surrounding the work table were four forms, each bent and twisted into strange angles. Heads sat on crooked necks that had been broken, extended and reformed. The girls' limbs had been resized, cut and rejoined to fit some other logic. The wife's face, serene and glassy, was framed in a crown of teeth. The men observed the corpses with clinical detachment.

"Who's the last one?"

"Housekeeper. That one is his wife." The man's head inclined slightly. "Daughters."

"Interesting."

Their eyes rose to the massive shape atop the bench, a leviathan of flesh and claw pressing over its helpless charges. They studied its form, the appendages, the talons, the wings. The first man pulled a notebook from an inside pocket and opened it. Holding a pencil in one hand, poised above the paper, he said, "This one did it on his own."

The second man took a hesitant step closer, peering at the creature. One of the thing's eyes twitched, a wet shimmer in the dark, ragged flesh as it focused on him. "Interesting."

The pencil made a series of quiet scratches. The man closed the notebook with a soft *thump* and returned it to his pocket.

"Shall we box it up?"

Jonathan Daniel

Jonathan Daniel lives in Birmingham, Alabama with his wife and hyper Boston Terrier, Buster (the Hellhound). He is the author of *Blood Night*, *Feast of the Unclean* and *The Uninvited*. When not writing about nightmarish things, he enjoys cooking, reading, brewing beer and trying to watch every horror movie made in the 80's. www.byjonathandaniel.com

1900s

BELLS IN THE FIELD

George Woodruff

Monday, October 1, 1900

A small, chubby finger extended out and gently flicked across the face of a hammer-finished bell.

The girl gasped in delight, jumping slightly in surprise at the ring being much prettier, and much louder than she expected. Scarlet winced in sudden pain as the hand resting at her shoulder turned into a pinching vice. She tried to shrug off her mother's hand, but even through the many layers to brace against the cold morning air, the woman's grip was certain.

"*Letti,*" her mother admonished in a hiss Scarlet was sure was actually half smoke— her mother's scorn red-hot to match her daughter's cheeks.

The others surrounding them on either side formed a black ring around the hole in the ground, averting their gaze in awkward unison. Older women with gray veils and matching plain mourning dresses shook their heads, though some smiled through pursed lips. A tall man holding an umbrella over his wife politely coughed to stifle his own laugh.

Scarlet's curiosity knew no bounds, and her own sister's funeral was no exception to endless inquiry and exploration. Her mother relaxed her grip but left her hand at the ready should it be needed to guide her inquisitive child again.

"It's pretty," Scarlet said, pointing to the bell.

This was all Laura Murphy could take, her eyes brimming with tears that streamed freely as she stared at the trinket, its origin both beautiful and terrible. She wept openly, but not forgetting herself, neither turned to her husband nor did she release her unruly daughter.

Scarlet looked at the bell, still able to hear its bright note in her mind as she stared quizzically at the thin, carved wooden arm that held it. A penny nail through its center affixed the arm to a rod run into the ground. Tied to the end opposite the bell was a length of brown leather lace, darkened by the rain that had started at first light, running down into that deep, dark hole.

Sunday, October 7, 1900

"What kind of monster—" her father began, his words came awkwardly, like tripping.

Laura scowled behind his back, the stink of whiskey trailing behind him.

Scarlet stood in shock at her sister Amy's grave. The mound of dirt had settled completely, as if it had always been there, and she had a thought for a moment that it looked like the earth was hugging her big sister more tightly now. But she found this image most unpleasant and tried immediately to push it away.

"It was in the paper, just last month, there's been a series of these *desecrations*," her mother said bitterly.

The family stood in silence together imagining the presence of their fourth, now below.

Scarlet looked and could not find the small hole where only a week ago to the day, a length of leather lace that was now gone ran up to the funny wooden gallows that stood empty and silent, her sister's bell also missing.

Saturday, November 3, 1900

A stout man stood hunched, hammering at his workbench by lantern light. The early winter evening had claimed the sunlight hours ago, along with any trace of warmth left in the air. He blew out a breath that swirled before him, cold mist floating over the diminutive anvil he stood over, holding an equally small hammer in his hand.

Outside, the sign that read simply, 'Tinsmith' glowed as the streetlight over it was lit. Stanley Müller was too modest a man to put his name on the sign over his shop. Despite his stern upbringing telling him a man should be proud of his accomplishments, he opted for the trade name instead. He knew his mother, a ghost of thirty years now, would have scoffed at his abandoning his native tongue, but it was hard to imagine the townsfolk of Natch, Rhode Island using *Blechschmied* in easy conversation.

The lamplighter walked his way back down the light pole to the ground, looking in through the shop window to Stanley and gave a wave before continuing on his route.

Stanley returned the wave then resumed his work. Each strike thudded with a dull resolve as his work continued to take shape, the small, repetitive movement barely helping to keep him warm. The tinsmith's eyes crinkled as he thought that in this cold season it would be a welcome change to do heavier work that necessitated a forge, but that also meant more money, and, on this small island town, might be short lived. For now, he was content to stick to the tradition he brought with him half a century ago that made the lion's share of his business; simple chalices for parents to give to their children receiving first communion. After that, they would be stored at home. Many chose to use them for other childhood holy rites, but traditionally most of the townsfolk would bring them out a final time for their wedding. Happy couples returned sometime after to Müller's shop to have the vessel and base sawn apart. The base, being mostly hollow, was returned to the couple to serve as a candlestick holder, and the top end stored safely once more, as nearly all followed the more solemn practice of its final use.

It was sad work, each transformation rendered in the shop. Stanley had come to terms with the fact that the eventual recycling of each of his works signified a passing of time in his own life.

Reaching for a rawhide hammer, he tamped the final touches on a new chalice. They were never bespoke, much to the dismay of some of the wealthier newcomers to Natch, who were keen to request japanned work, or details like fine filigree or family crests. He would have none of it. Part of what made this special was the sameness of it all, something they all could recognize in the identical tin pieces in one another's homes.

Stanley stepped away from his work bench, pinching the bridge of his nose, his eyes blurred with fatigue. He lit his pipe and admired the row of the day's work. An assortment of his trademark chalices to put on the store shelves sat alongside a set of napkin rings Mrs. Carter would be by for in the morning, as well as a lunchbox Stanley repaired for her husband. They gleamed brilliantly with the other things in the shop, reflecting and amplifying the light from gas mantles evenly spaced across the wall.

A clang of tools crashing in the next room made him stand stock still, listening. He reached for a nearby graver, making a fist over its round handle, the pointed end protruding lethally between his fingers as he crept into the room.

"Merciful Christ, girl, what are you doing?" he blustered, the fright he'd been given rapidly fading at the sight of a young girl picking up tools from the floor of his shop.

"I'm sorry, Mr. Müller, I really am," Scarlet began, looking up at the man in wilting embarrassment. "I came in to look and I tried to reach." She pointed to the shelf far above her head.

Stanley looked back at her, flushed. "It's alright dear, and my apologies for yelling," he said. He offered his hand and helped Scarlet to her feet. "I didn't realize I had company here so late. Have a seat." He pulled up a stool to the workbench and patted the worn wood seat.

Scarlet climbed up and smoothed out her skirts, looking at the tools hanging from the wall. She watched as Mr. Müller brought down the small crate she had so foolishly tried to reach for herself. Seeing him strain to lower it made her realize she hadn't considered the weight of what might be inside and she was grateful to have knocked over some tools instead of dropping a wooden box on her head and leaving her parents with a second Murphy daughter to visit on Sundays after church.

Stanley lowered the crate to the bench with a heaving breath. "What'n the hell were you thinking trying to grab this then?" he asked her.

"I don't know," she replied.

"You don't know?" he posited.

"It's the only thing in here I couldn't see." She shrugged, "I wanted to know what it was."

Nodding, Stanley drew the pencil from his work apron and set to sharpening it with a knife he produced from his hip that Scarlet was certain was at least a foot long and appeared to be sharp enough to cut through stone. After finishing and sheathing the blade, he held out the pencil to Scarlet. "Do you write?"

"Yes," she lied. Then added, "I'm still learning."

"Well we're going to fix the mystery of this box for any other inquisitive children to avoid heads being squashed like pumpkins, hmm?" He raised an eyebrow to her and smiled.

Taking the pencil from him, Scarlet asked what to write, and he walked her through the label one letter at a time.

"S-c-h-r-o-t-t?" she asked, "what's that Mr. Müller?"

"Scrap. From my work, in my old tongue," he said, sweeping at the pencil shavings on the table as he spoke to her.

"Is your tongue any older than the rest of you?" she asked, puzzled.

The man laughed. "No, I suppose not. May I have my pencil please?"

She handed it back to him. "Then why not just write 'scrap' on the box?"

Stanley gave her a mischievous wink when he told her, "I suppose it's no fun removing all of the mystery, now is it?" With that, he lifted the box and returned it to its place on the shelf overhead.

Scarlet laughed at that and pointed to other items in the shop, strange tools, other experimental pieces half-constructed, asking all manner of questions.

Across the street, John Murphy watched his daughter through the window, his cheeks flushed as he drew his coat closed against the flurry of snow that had already begun to collect on his shoulders. His eyes narrowed looking at the man that had the audacity to mentor his daughter. To make *his* daughter laugh. He had never trusted the German and was convinced his silent demeanor was a façade to hide something he left behind in his homeland. The fact that everybody had adopted his stupid traditions of cups and candlesticks and bells that clearly were a ruse to relieve gullible families of their coin only infuriated him more. He stood fuming, other passersby unconsciously avoiding the man boiling silently just outside the streetlight's halo.

Unnoticed by his daughter or Stanley Müller, John walked into the night toward the Black Stag.

<u>Friday, July 5, 1901</u>

Scarlet made a regular practice of stopping by the tinsmith's shop since that night. She liked the way it smelled— a mixture of metal and wood and pipe tobacco. Some days she would stop by to walk around and look at the shelves she had perused a hundred times, leaving after a few minutes with a friendly farewell. Other times she would ask to use the extra workspace to study and do her homework.

Scarlet walked the neatly stocked rows of the back of the shop once more, the opposite wall covered in all manner of snips, gravers, pliers, and other tools she had learned the names of as she returned each week. She watched Mr. Müller work sometimes for an hour or more, standing quiet as he turned sheets of raw tin into any number of items seemingly by magic. On the days she arrived later, she helped sweep, and asked if she could keep the smaller bits of refuse too small to be useful. After a few weeks of this, Scarlet showed up after school and proudly handed Stanley a gift: a wadded ball of the collected scrap. A strand of ribbon Scarlet would use to tie her hair with ran through the middle. He looked at her, not understanding.

"It's so nobody else scares you late at night," she said proudly. "I smashed it together so you can put it over your door." She pointed at the front door as she explained and Stanley noted the small strips of linen dotted red tied around two of her fingers. They mounted the gift that day and Scarlet was delighted at the distinct thud that announced any incoming patrons.

Recently, Mr. Müller had occasionally let her help with some of his commissioned pieces, showing her how to carve small details in the metal he shaped. She took to it quickly, and eventually he offered her a small pittance for her assistance in some of the more detailed work his hands refused to do without protest. He would mark the materials for her, then let her trace over them, which she did faster than he ever could have even in his youth, though he'd never admit it.

Stanley smiled, drawing from a freshly lit pipe, watching Scarlet finish her work. He thought absently how strange it would be to formally take on a female apprentice, much less one so young— oh, how this small town would gossip!

"What is it, Mr. Müller?" Scarlet asked, blowing away small wisps of metal shavings to inspect her work.

"Nothing, just thinking. Are you finished?"

"Almost. What are you thinking?" she replied, looking back once more at her work.

He paused, then decided the hell with it, why not.

"Would you like me to show you how to make a bell?"

Scarlet nodded, smiling. She returned the tool she held to its place on the wall then set down the salt and pepper holder on the table next to the polishing cloth for Mr. Müller to inspect. She slid off the stool and looked up at him. "Today?" she asked.

"No," he replied, setting his pipe on the table and fishing in his pocket. He withdrew a pair of coins and held them out to her. "For your efforts, miss. Thank you again." He picked up the shaker rack, looking at it but not truly concerned with Scarlet's work. By this time she had proven more than proficient with the work he gave her and the inspection was a formality to ensure she didn't become too confident in her skills never being questioned.

They had had this debate before but she still felt compelled each time to say something. "You really don't have to pay me, Mr. Müller, it's fun to learn, and I like it here. I'm happy to help and not be a bother just stopping in and buzzing about like some housefly."

He looked at her, appreciating the good manners she displayed every time he saw her.

"You could never be a bother, Letti. We'll start next time you visit— " he started, cut off by the voice that started as the door opened behind him.

"Scarlet, what are you doing here?"

Behind John Murphy the setting sun peeked between buildings across the street, casting him in blinding backlight. He remained in the entry, an expressionless shadow.

"Daddy!" Scarlet said, turning toward him, slipping the coins into her belt unseen. "I was just— "

"Leaving." John finished for her. "No need to bother Mr. Müller further, I'm sure he has plenty of work to do."

Scarlet hung her head, turning to Stanley, but too embarrassed to look at him. "G'bye Mr. Müller," she whispered.

The two left in silence, a whoosh of hot summer air blowing in as John threw the door closed behind him. The tin ball thumped down against the door frame like an axe, leaving Stanley alone in the quiet shop.

Thursday, August 1, 1901

John Murphy set his glass down on the bar and turned to the men on either side of him. "What do you know about our resident tinsmith?" he asked.

On his left, Percy Cunningham sat nursing an ale that remained suspiciously full despite his eyes being rimmed red, even in the low-lit tavern.

At his right, Albert Grant, the town barber, rolled a cigarette and considered his friend's question.

Murphy looked back across the bar to the owner of the Black Stag, William Black, and held up two fingers, summoning two bottles of heavy ale. He kept one and slid the other to Grant. "What about you, Bill?" He sipped his drink, locking eyes with the barkeep in interest.

Black looked at the three men seated before him. A full house, the evening was just getting to its peak, dinners served and patrons full and ready to clear the tables and make room to dance. The crowd was a roar and William was all too happy to have the conversation he felt coming again be buried to most possible eavesdroppers.

"One *year*, Bill. A year next month since all this business started and nobody has been brought up to answer for it. Mysterious deaths, those damned bells everybody insists on hanging still, despite not a one actually saving anybody, and the *sho*ck and frenzied *gos*sip grow each time one goes missing." John took a long swallow, finishing off his drink and tapped the bar for another as he went on. "And then we have *Herr* Müller," he sneered, "who is all too happy to *tin*ker away, the smithy turning out more for us, at a *mo*dest cost of course." His speech had started to slur, and William served yet another round to the man with a look of disapproval that did not go unnoticed by the group.

The barkeep finally spoke his mind, knowing at once it was falling on deaf ears. "John, now listen to me. That man does just as honest work as the rest of us. You don't bear any ill will against Grant here for the townsfolk returning to his shop to have their hair cut, do you? Or you don't mean to accuse Percy of any shady dealings just because he keeps the cemetery?"

Murphy could see where this was going and hated William for it. He stood from his seat.

"John, be sensible here. Take a room for the night, don't let Laura see you like this. You—"

"I'll not be told how to mind my family, *Will*iam." John stepped to the hooks at the wall, taking his coat and hat, donning them violently. He stepped back to the bar to drop a handful of coin, letting the pieces scatter and fall. "Good night to you all, *gentlemen*," he remarked in a drunken growl before turning heel and shuffling his way back home.

<u>Wednesday, January 1, 1902</u>

Scarlet sat reading *The Tale of Peter Rabbit* sitting on Amy's bed. Being brand new, it was her current favorite of her modest collection of books. She kept the small card her mother tucked inside to mark her place, though it was rare she didn't finish reading it front to back in a sitting. It was inscribed by Laura only, who wrote simply, "To our little rabbit. Love, Mom". Scarlet hadn't questioned why her father didn't sign as well.

She read aloud, doing voices for the characters, looking occasionally up toward the window over the headboard. She was getting to her favorite part when her father spoke.

"Why do you read that so often, Letti? You've read it aloud everyday since Christmas," he said.

"That was only a week ago daddy!" Scarlet giggled at her father's exasperation over such a new activity.

"But don't you tire of it? Reading the same story each day? And it's such a youngish book, something for small children." He couldn't hide his confusion over why his daughter was so infatuated with a silly talking rabbit.

Scarlet asked her father earnestly, "Am I not a child still?"

He looked back at her, saying nothing.

"The important thing," Laura Murphy said, ending their conversation after growing tired of her husband's obtuseness, "is that you always re-member there is danger in adventure. Poor Peter does his best, doesn't he? But in the end, I think the point of the story is that staying close to home is the best way to remain safe."

Scarlet jumped to her feet on the bed, earning an immediate flash of warning from her mother. She quickly dropped down, sitting, sliding off the bed to stand on the floor in a pose of defiance.

"But what of the world?" Scarlet pleaded, "*I* thought the point was that mommy loves you always, even if you make mistakes?"

In a rare moment of surprise, Laura paused, looking at her daughter in admiration, stopping her own thought of teaching, thankful her girl still held a glimmer of the innocence she knew would not last many more years.

Scarlet looked to her mother still. "Is the safety of home a fair trade for knowing what else is beyond our small town?"

Laura rose, recomposed and wooden once more.

"Wash up, darling, we'll have supper shortly."

<u>Wednesday, March 5, 1902</u>

I would stare at the lighthouse at Castle Hill, imagining what life was like there. The waters of our town were relatively calm, but at night I would picture that lighthouse being the only thing keeping us safe, that if it were to break down, the things that scratch loud enough to cut through the howling winds would finally close the gap the rings the three towers in the East Passage afforded us ...

"What are you doing?" The voice over Scarlet's shoulder was hardly more than a whisper, tense as piano wire. The girl twitched, her pen scratching over and off the paper, nearly knocking the blotter off the small secretary's desk she sat at in the front room. Scarlet's school books were neatly stacked on the desk, her homework arranged on top of the concealed paper she hurriedly tried to cover.

"Mom!" Scarlet squeaked, eyes wide as clock faces.

"What is this nonsense?" Laura took the paper and examined it. "What things do you hear scratching? I haven't heard anything?"

"Mom, it's a story, make believe. Like to tell at Christmastime?" She looked to her modest collection of books above the desk and regretted it instantly.

Laura crossed the room to inspect the shelf. Tucked behind the small number of books Scarlet owned was a battered volume so badly worn all that could be read on the binding was, 'Wollstonecraft'. She shook her head in disapproval, but to Scarlet's surprise, left the book in its place. Laura turned to her daughter once more.

"Stop daydreaming out the window and get back to your studies."

"When am I ever going to need to know the names of all 45 capital cities in the United States? Daddy said we'll live here forever, all I should need to know is Providence," she said with a *hmph*.

Hearing his name while passing through the hallway, John made his best effort to sneak back to the study and avoid being caught in this conversation.

"Speaking of daddy, look what I got him for his birthday."

John paused at that. The soft scuff of the desk drawer sliding open preceded the sound of its contents being shifted around. He surmised his daughter must have hidden away whatever it was to the back of the drawer.

"Letti," Laura whispered, "how did you afford this? Please don't tell me this came from where I think it did."

Feeling the blood begin to collect and redden his face, John waited still.

"I know, mom, but I wish daddy'd give him a chance!" Scarlet sighed. "Just look at how nice it is, I even put his initials on it!"

"*You* put his initials on it?" her mother asked.

Scarlet paused in panic, quickly recovering. "Of course, like on the order slip. Just like you did last year for the bread box?"

Laura nodded and smiled, handing her daughter back the monogrammed snuff box. Her smile faded when she saw her husband, now standing in the room with them.

"Oh, Daddy, you weren't supposed to see!" Scarlet cried.

When he didn't say anything she took his gift and held it out to him. "Well, I know it's tomorrow, but happy birthday anyway!" She beamed in what he assumed to be the basic child's joy of giving a gift, but beneath that enthusiasm was more than he knew— pride, recognizing her own parents' inability to discern who had made the box.

"Thank you, Scarlet," John replied, "this is a very fine gift." He questioned it no more, simply placing the snuff box in the breast pocket of his coat, pinching and denting it horribly between his fingers before hugging his daughter.

Monday, November 24, 1902

"It's him, I'm certain of it." John said, staring at the ceiling and into the worried face of Albert Grant, who stood over him, straight razor in hand.

"John, I want you to stop and consider what it is you're saying," the barber replied before setting to work. Near closing time, John was the last customer of the day.

"I know how to prove it," John started.

Albert pulled the blade away as he spoke, his face flush with frustration. "I said *consider* what you're saying, not keep on saying it, man. May I continue?"

John frowned, nodded, returning to his thoughts.

"If I might offer something for you to stew over, John, why do you begrudge that man so? He's been nothing but kind to everyone, and often donates his wares to the church." Albert worked the blade like an artist, long strokes along the throat, rapid shaping movements at the jaw, swiping mug soap on a cloth draped over his arm without looking away as he continued. "I've had Müller to my home for supper on more than one occasion." To which John grunted in mute reply. "He was polite, brought good wine to the meal, and kept interesting conversation. He's lived here longer than I have for mercy's sake!" Albert wiped away the remaining streaks of white lather from John's face more roughly than he intended and turned to set the blade down.

"I've been reviewing the papers— there's a pattern," John said, ignoring his friend. "The bastard makes his move under total cover, he's waiting for the new moon. That gives us five days."

"Us?" Albert looked into the eyes of the first person to greet him when his family moved to Natch, scarcely recognizing the man that looked back at him. John and his family had been kind to the Grants, and Albert worried now for his friend's sanity, but also couldn't be sure if that scrutiny might shift elsewhere if he continued to insist on Müller's innocence.

Unsure of what more to say, he simply listened to John Murphy's plan. In truth, it was simple, and in Albert's mind, maybe the best outcome for everyone involved, though it would surely not end well for John once Laura became wise to what her husband was up to. The barber resolved the consequences were none of his concern, that John was set on making this bed, and so too he would have to lie in it.

Saturday, November 30, 1902

Laura Murphy and her daughter stood next to a mound of freshly dug earth.

Scarlet didn't have the heart to touch the bell that now hung over the hole her father lay in. She was sad to know how that bell would sound having rung one like it already.

Services for the funeral of John Murphy proceeded in standard fashion through the gloom of morning, and the denizens of Natch drifted off in a slow wave of black, leaving only a handful of birds in the nearby trees, and the sexton, Percy Cunningham, to finish burying one of his closest friends.

That evening, Albert sat in the now silent Black Stag at a table below one of the high windows, the light of a single candle threw all manor of crawling shadows over the beams that ran the lengths of the thatch roof tavern. William sat opposite him and poured a glass for each of them, saying nothing.

They continued like that, sitting in comfortable silence, sipping liquid fire, waiting as more men gradually arrived, let in the back door by William's wife.

Each of the newcomers took a seat, instructed not to speak for fear of raising an alert there were intruders in the tavern that had closed for the funeral and remained so out of respect. By midnight, there were a dozen of William's most trusted friends sitting together in the frigid room, tensions rising in wait.

William rose and climbed the ladder inside that ran up to the street-facing window and peered through, down the lane to the shop with the "Tinsmith" sign over its door. He made about half a dozen trips up and down the ladder over the last hour, trading with Albert as they watched for

Stanley to make his move. The two men met at the bottom, exchanging a brief report.

"Anything?" Albert asked.

"All quiet," Black replied. "But he's there alright. Saw him step out to sweep the front step a bit ago."

Albert nodded, pulling his gloves on to brace against the chill that crept through the glass to touch whoever stood at the top of the ladder.

William made a pass around the room, thanking the men for coming, asking after some of their families, generally ensuring nobody became disinterested in their plan and decided to head back for the warmth of their homes. He felt good about their numbers, and prayed they would prove unnecessary. If John had been right, if the tinsmith was the perpetrator, William was fairly certain it would hardly take a dozen of them to detain a man that typically required the aid of a cane for walks outside of his shop. His feelings of preparedness were dashed in a word when Albert breathed out once in a yip, then repeated doubly loud from up high, nearly falling as he turned to yell,

"**Fire!**"

On the deserted grounds outside the chapel, Percy wiped the sweat from his brow and took a long drink from the well pump, the frigid water shocking his senses. The work was slow going without his assistant, but he had already removed half the earth he had filled into the grave earlier that day.

"Soon, friend. Enjoy your rest while you can, you'll have hell to pay tomorrow." He laughed aloud in wonder at what the day might bring, then stopped, jerking his head at the sound of the town alarm bell.

He stood still, listening to the bell clang over and over, wondering what could be the matter. A few minutes later, in the pitch dark of this moonless night, he saw the glow begin to bloom from inside the town streets.

"My god," he said, dropping his shovel to the ground and taking off at a full run.

In total darkness, John Murphy chewed on the venison jerky that had been placed in his burial suit. After draining the contents of the flask Percy loaned him earlier, he was grateful Albert had the good sense to suggest boring a hole in the bottom of the pine box should John need to relieve himself.

He'd had an excellent nap, the cold, the dark, and the whiskey all making for the ideal time to doze off. But now time began to evade him and the ticking of his pocket watch seemed deafening, taunting him with a face he could not read. The air had become stifling over what he approximated to be the last hour, and he grew increasingly anxious as he began to hear the scraping of the shovel close by.

He tried to gauge the time by the digging, counting the distant sound of the shovel cutting through earth, equating some thirty or so of the motions to five minutes passing. As the night wore on, there were longer breaks between, and he was proud of his friend for doing such grueling work on his own.

Worry over his wife and daughter's fury at his deception had clawed at him since hatching this plan, but he knew in his heart this was what had to be done to put an end to the madness that had plagued his town for far too long.

John couldn't be sure exactly how much time had passed since the digging stopped, but his concern was mounting as his burial suit took on an unbearably snug fit, sweat making the garments stick to him with no space to remove them.

He closed his eyes and waited for the exhumation to resume, praying to feel the night air on his face soon.

Percy heard the screams of the crowd gathered on the street through town, and finally reached the smoldering remains of what was Stanley Müller's shop.

A charred skeleton sat at the bench, slumped to one side, holding Stanley's pipe. Its jaw had cracked on one side, giving it the appearance of being in the throes of laughter, as swirling steam and smoke that lingered in the shop drifted up through the incinerated space where the roof had been. A line of people that lived inside town held buckets, and stood exhausted and dejected despite having saved the bordering shops from being consumed as well.

Approaching William, who had taken point on the efforts to fight the fire, Percy called out, "What the hell happened?"

William looked at him grimly and nodded at the laughing remains of the old German who had helped Natch grow over the decades.

"It's over," he said.

Sunday, November 30, 1902

Percy and Albert trudged back to the cemetery, soot-streaked faces making them nearly invisible in the dead of night.

"No, that can't be," Percy said in flat shock.

All of the dirt that had been pulled away mere hours before the fire now lay neatly replaced, filling the grave completely.

"I thought you said he was nearly out?" Albert asked.

Percy quickened his pace to the plot, distracted momentarily at the sight of the fixture that held John's bell— now vacant. His foot hooked into a sunken grave marker and he went headlong into the white slab next to Murphy's plot.

Albert winced at the dull sound of the impact, dropping down to help Percy to his feet.

Shrugging off the gesture out of combined embarrassment and panic, Percy staggered upright once more, snatched his shovel from the ground, and nearly threw it, thrown off by the unexpected change in weight. He looked in horror to find the handle broken a foot from the blade end of the tool, rendering it all but useless.

Percy fell to his knees and clawed at the earth.

"Help me, dammit!" he shouted to his friend. "This wasn't supposed to go on so long. How in the hell did this hole get filled back?" He looked to Albert frantically, still digging with his cupped hands. "He was almost out, man! He was almost out!"

Albert ran from the grave to the back of the chapel. Unfamiliar with the grounds, he staggered as his shin slammed into one headstone, then nearly lost his footing as Percy did on another. He tore open the tool shed door, groping blindly— and found it to be as empty as the night sky.

After an hour of digging their hands bloody and raw, they were forced to break, retreating to find tools.

By the time they broke open the casket lid, there was diffused light from a new dawn, and looking upon the body of their friend, Albert and Percy saw they had not been alone in their efforts. John lay twisted, his suit ripped apart, his gory fingers now stiff claws, shredded to the bone– splintered fragments of fingernails and bone protruded from the soft wood.

"His clothes," Albert started in wonder.

"He must have gone mad in panic," Percy said, his voice low in pained regret.

They stood there together, looking in at the hole that held the twisted body, and shattered remains of his coffin, stunned by the night's events.

Neither could have said who moved first, but both very slowly and without further conversation began to move the dirt back over their friend, not speaking a word until the deed was done.

They parted ways at the street, the first rays of the new day trying to push past a sky full of gray clouds.

William was finishing preparing to open the Black Stag for midday meal service when Albert and Percy walked through the front door. The plan the four men had made days before was to reconvene at the Stag once the German had been arrested in the night, making a joint presentation to the constable. Seeing the look on their faces, and the absence of John Murphy in their party, he reached for three glasses and began to pour as they approached, bracing himself for the worst.

Friday, December 31, 1909

Dense fog fills the entirety of Scarlet's vision, only the very tips of the tallest trees stretching like hands, reaching for somebody to pull them out.

She walks easily despite the lack of visibility, never missing a Sunday to visit her family. Thinking of the events of the past week to share with her sister and parents, she trips over a protruding rock, skinning her knee deeply on another as she lands. The spill leaves a bright red bloody imprint over the lichen rash that covers the rock.

Scarlet stands, grimacing at the pain and doing her best to tamp down the fiery temper that threatens to boil over at such a careless mistake. She sweeps her hair away in a rough movement, then brushes off the dirt and pebbles from the skin showing through her torn stockings, smearing the blood that readily pools once more. She walks on, her hands outstretched before her waist. Her feet move gingerly, feeling for more obstacles to avoid falling once more.

A twinkle, like butterfly wings made of gold lace— the sound of bells in the distance. First one, then dozens, *hundreds* ringing together, a mad, metallic cacophony that in a single beat snap from complete chaos to a single, unified, unending chime in chorus. The effect is instantly dizzying and Scarlet feels certain now she is no longer alone.

The sound becomes exponentially more intense as she continues onward, regardless of what direction she moves in. As suddenly as she had lost her sight entering the fog, it returns as she steps through and into a small clearing with tall grass coated in rime. In an instant, the fog blows away in a swirl outward from the clearing and the twinkling ceases.

The cemetery, her intended destination, lies far down below where she stands now, the top of a steep hill overlooking the burial grounds, with a view clear past the nearby fog over Natch and the throat of the passage surrounding them. Taking in her surroundings, she catches her scream at the bottom of her throat, eyes widened to the point of threatening to burst at the sight before her.

Bells hang over ancient headstones, all suspended in mid-air as if being held and rung by the shades that call this place home. They are carved from rock, then taking a beat, she sees that they have likely been hewn on site. Most of the headstones have a savage bite taken from a corner or edge, and sharp refuse from crafting them litters each of the monuments marking the bones that lay beneath; like beds of teeth.

Deep in the fog-shrouded trees that shelter the grounds, a snap of a branch. A bird some ten meters away from it takes flight, breaking through the fog and tree cover, then silence.

She strains to listen, closing her eyes until the panic is too great, imagining some lurking figure rushing toward her. Scarlet pushes away the occasional twinkle of a bell, knowing full well her mind is filling in the nothingness her ears are receiving, knowing what she wants to hear. She shivers then, shaking off that thought. She most certainly does *not* want to hear that sound again.

Scarlet knows when she opens her eyes it will be there, within arms reach, whatever malevolent force it is that mocks her senses now, that stole so much from her family, her town.

Her lids flit open, the cloud diffused sun failing miserably to dispel the mist below, but nothing stands before her. Her mind is still at odds as it tries to decide whether or not the soft clatter of bells she hears in the distance is real, carrying farther away down below. The sound bends madly from hundreds of feet to her right, then twice as far to her left, the noises spinning, twisting in all directions, as if riding the wind itself before trailing off, leaving her alone once more.

George Woodruff

George is a fledgling author and recovering band geek. His works have appeared on the *Horror Hill* and *Creepy* podcasts. When he's not writing, he provides narration through his audio services business, Full Throttle Sound, and has been featured on *The HP Lovecraft Literary Podcast, Strange Studies of Strange Stories, Tales to Terrify,* and *Chilling Tales for Dark Nights: Evil Idol 2025.* He lives with his wife, daughter, and canine familiar. https://fullthrottlesound.com/gw-author-page/

1920s

REST EASY IN THE SPEAKEASY

Cassandra O'Sullivan Sachar

Mrs. Edna McKay looked too pale. After placing a dab of rouge on the apple of each wrinkled cheek, I reassessed. Better. Though far from shaving the years off the old gal, the cotton stuffed in her face combined with my sub-par attempts at cosmetology made her appear livelier than when I wheeled her in here the previous night.

A loud thump, followed by a raucous burst of laughter, disrupted my contemplation, and a curse wormed its way from between my lips before I could censor myself. Though my client took no offense at this breach of etiquette, I attempted to comport myself with dignity. Father always said that I must act a certain way, especially to be taken seriously as a businesswoman.

Smiling, I imagined his pride that I managed to keep the funeral home—his legacy—afloat. It was far from easy due to the old-fashioned attitudes many held toward unmarried women. Father urged me to strike out and find a husband when I finished high school, but I insisted on attending embalming school instead. Since Mother perished during childbirth, I grew up in my sole parent's shadow and wanted nothing more than to follow in his footsteps, shepherding families through the grieving process and providing their loved ones with thoughtful send-offs.

Suddenly, a crash resonated from down below, so loud that the lipstick nearly danced off poor Edna's thin lips and onto her sagging chin. Always on alert, I stopped my hand before destroying my careful work. I could not have that, especially with the viewing the next morning.

This is what I must do, I reminded myself. Although Father was well-known and respected in our small town, my femininity failed to garner the same gravitas, and my client list withered before my eyes like their beloved deceased at the rival funeral home. When the dapper, expensively attired man who called himself Joey the Jaw stepped into my parlor one afternoon and made me his offer, I had no choice but to accept—that or lose my business.

I held my breath and prayed that this night would stay on the tame side, that there would be no reason the police were summoned to my simple dwelling to raid the gathering assembled downstairs. Though I would have preferred to remain on the correct side of the law, it was that very establishment which put me in such a predicament: the Volstead Act. If the drunken revelry in my cellar was any indication of behavior across the country, it seemed highly unlikely that the legislation was achieving the desired effect of curbing alcohol consumption.

My role in this arrangement was to carry on as usual, pretending there was no debauchery beneath me. I was not to descend the staircase of my very own residence after 8:00 p.m. Friday through Sunday evenings, and I was not to breathe a word to anyone of these goings-on. In exchange, I received a handsome sum in cash once a week that assisted in keeping my business open and electricity running. Though Father and I only joined the modern world a few years prior, I had become accustomed to this convenience as much as to the running water through my pipes, and I would have loathed a return to candlelight.

As long as everyone left before daylight—which Joey assured me would always be the case—I could maintain my legal business with my head held high, turning a blind eye and deaf ear to the depravity in my cellar. Joey never explained exactly what he planned to do with the space, but I had read enough in the papers to put the pieces together.

Though my curiosity was piqued by the unique music and jovial chatter filtering through the floorboards, I had no interest in participating in such illicit behavior. The cellar, emptied of my paint cans and filing cabinets, now likely held bottles of moonshine and gin. I kept the door locked from my side, just as they did on theirs, and tried to refrain from peering outside at the fanciful costumes on the stream of revelers who paraded across my backyard.

It was strange to think of "their" side in my own ancestral home and business. Considering I had only met Joey and did not have knowledge of his associates, I was unaware of whom "they" might be. This might have been beneficial if the police questioned me; though I knew little of organized crime other than what I had read in the newspaper, Father raised no fool. I vowed to keep my mouth shut and mind my own business.

Humming a church hymn to myself, I strived to block out the infernal racket below, but that proved ineffective. After a short time, I caught myself tapping my toes along with the rhythm. When a clear, sweet voice joined the melody, I couldn't help but smile, for Violet sounded like an angel.

Violet didn't sing every night, but her presence helped make the uncomfortable arrangement worth it. The first time I heard knocking coming from my cellar door, I ignored it, expecting some drunken louse had somehow managed to escape beyond Joey the Jaw's watchful gaze, but then I heard a murmur: "Please, open up."

I continued to disregard it, hoping it would go away so I could return to reorganizing the chemicals in my cabinet, but the voice persisted.

"I need a break from downstairs. A safe place to rest," she pleaded.

A safe place. Based on the youthful pitch, I surmised the voice's owner to be little more than a teenager. Who was I to deny refuge to a young woman? Still, I hesitated to open the lock, positioning myself against my side of the door, my ear straining for further communication.

"I know you're there. *Please.*" She took on a frantic tone, and I relented.

Indeed, the woman who practically collapsed into my dining room-cum-mortuary appeared as if a fragile bird. In addition to her bare, skinny arms and stocking-clad, toothpick legs, her short, feathered dress completed the comparison, suggesting a swan. She caught herself mid-stumble and stood up, extending her hand to me. "I'm Violet," she said. "The singer I'm sure you've been hearing."

"Margaret," I replied, feeling her soft skin grazing my rough, larger hand, dry as usual from embalming chemicals. "I own this establishment. The above-ground one," I clarified, lest she think I was referring to the cesspool beneath us.

"You own all *this*?" she asked, her eyes imbibing my property. "I didn't know a woman could have so much. It's not your husband's? Or your family's?"

"I'm not married," I said. After having passed the so-called old-maid marker of thirty years old, society dictated I should feel ashamed of this fact, but I had no inclination to find some beastly man with whom to share my business—and my bed. "My father died a few years ago, so all this is mine."

A rush of gratitude warmed me that no body graced my cooling table at the moment. The girl would likely be terrified, but I had finished my preparations of young Harrison Bauman hours ago. The poor child, small as he was due to his tender age and the devastation of tuberculosis, had taken less time to prepare than I had originally anticipated, so he was already in the reception room laid out in his coffin. Still, though Violet was a stranger, my stomach clenched in anticipation of her judgment at the morbid surroundings: the black-and-white tiled flooring; the glass cabinet full of chemicals; the workstation with the tray of gleaming embalming tools and instruments; the stark, white walls contrasting with the ornate, textured wallpaper decorating the other rooms.

Of most concern, of course, was the lingering smell of formaldehyde, a stench that permeated the air and crept into other areas of the house. I would have preferred to have kept the mortuary in the cellar as my father once had, but his declining health and bad back made it too difficult to move the bodies up and down the cellar stairs. How Joey and his men managed to bring a piano down there, I could not fathom, though I heard its resonant chords almost every night, proving its existence with my ears if not my eyes.

I appreciated the ease with which I could wheel in a stretcher, not to mention that this move upstairs provided me with an area ready to be occupied when Joey arrived with his offer.

Violet sniffed the air, and I winced, but she surprised me by laughing. "Oh, I don't mind that one bit. I grew up on a pig farm. This nose *knows* some smells."

"Why don't you join me in the parlor?" I asked, wanting to distance her from the grislier reminders of my profession. "I'll make us some tea, and we can sit down, if you have time." I glanced toward the door from which she arrived, that portal to a different world. I still didn't know what troubled her, why she had appeared asking for help, but she now seemed quite at ease.

"That would be lovely," she replied formally, her regal words at odds with her smoky eyes, painted lips, and naked flesh, making me wonder if she were mocking me. I was struck by the differences in our appearance: Violet, small and bright versus my larger, unadorned form. We were certainly unlikely companions.

Though I ushered her into the parlor and urged her to take a seat, she followed me into the small kitchen and flitted about trying to help as I heated the kettle and gathered the tea service.

"This is beautiful. I love it," she declared, holding up a delicate porcelain cup that had belonged to my mother.

My face warmed. Accustomed to dining alone, I had never even used this tea set, so I only nodded in acknowledgement and grabbed the cream from the icebox.

We eased into the wingback chairs flanking the table, my hastily constructed tea party before us, and Violet tucked into some cookies left over from a service the day before. It was one of my few perks of my profession, as the bereaved family members often left abruptly after the last guest departed, leaving the remnants of whatever feast they provided. Though I discarded many mysterious casseroles over the years, I enjoyed the occasional sweet treat, though never so late at night.

I sipped my tea in silence for several minutes as Violet slurped hers and chomped away. Judging by her emaciated appearance and voracious appetite, I began to wonder when the poor girl had last eaten. Her clothing and shoes looked fairly expensive, though. As many questions as I had of my elusive guest, I bit my tongue and waited.

"Thank you. For everything. For letting me in and fixing all this." Violet swept her hand—the nails of which were lacquered ruby red—across the remains on the table. "Joey doesn't always let me eat, so I'm plumb famished, and singing makes me build up an appetite."

My blood ran cold. "Joey the Jaw is your ... employer?"

She nodded, but her red lips, now smeared, turned downward. "I guess you could say he's my fella, as well. I don't love him, don't even like him, to be honest, but he sends my family money so long as I show up and sing with the band. I don't mind the singing—used to do it back at my church. But I don't love some of the other things that go on down there. Or behind closed doors."

As if in response, a trumpet blasted from below, three times.

Violet's eyes widened. "That's my cue. Stan told me he'd signal when I had to come down again to sing. He helped distract Joey so I could come up here for a break. He told me you're a nice lady."

The word "lady" sounded severe and made me feel depressingly ancient, but my brain stuttered as I tried to place the name. "Do I know him?"

A smile touched her lips, and she said, "Yes. He's your milk man! He grew up on a farm, too. He reminds me of my little brother. He tries to help when Joey gets in one of his *moods*." The happiness receding just as quickly as it arrived, her face darkened.

Based on my few interactions with Joey, the inspiration behind his nickname eluded me. I was unsure whether it referred to the fact that he liked to talk or something more nefarious. His actual jaw looked perfectly normal. Regardless, I wasn't surprised by her choice of words. Though he seemed polite enough and certainly elegant in his finery, an air he carried suggested that there was no room to say no to him, that my funeral home would host the illegal speakeasy whether I agreed or not. He didn't show me a pistol or threaten me in any manner, yet I couldn't help but wonder what he would have done had I gone with my gut instinct—and the more moral choice—to defy him rather than allow my business to metamorphose into a den of iniquity.

"I see," I replied, which wasn't entirely true, but a response seemed necessary. "Have you considered leaving him? He doesn't seem like a man with whom you enjoy spending time."

Violet knitted her fingers together as a tear escaped from one kohl-lined eye. "I think about leaving every day," she whispered, even though we were alone. "But he said he'd kill me if I left him, and then he'd come after my family. Look what he did last week when I showed up two minutes late." She pulled up her short dress even higher, exposing a smooth, creamy thigh blemished with a fading, greenish bruise.

Blanching, I averted my eyes, not only from my shock at her bare flesh—such a contrast to the cold, mottled skin of the bodies I prepared—but at the mark of violence.

"It's worse on my stomach. It hurt to sing that night, but he only punches me where no one can see. He says a roughed-up dame will drive the crowds away." Violet's hand lingered on her leg, and she let out a sigh before covering up again. She slumped back in her chair.

Though I have heard of men beating their women, even the mothers of their children, I had led a rather solitary existence since Father passed. There were times when days stretched on and I exchanged but a few words with fellow living beings as I went about my errands and made arrangements. My most constant companions, the dead, did not confess their worries, all of which had evaporated once their time on earth finished.

But this young woman, this kind and talented songstress, had chosen me as her confessor. I was under no delusion that Joey the Jaw was a proper or pious man, understanding as I did that he was a bootlegger. Despite my acceptance of *this* fact, I could not condone his treatment of Violet.

I said not a word, but my fingers trembled with rage on the coffee table next to my teacup. Violet placed her hand over mine in a gesture of comfort that seemed diametrically opposed to the situation.

"I'm fine," she said, her quaking voice betraying her. "I can handle him. I'm sorry to have brought this trouble to you. It's not your problem." She stood up.

"No," I murmured, motioning for her to sit back down. "I'm glad you came. I want to help."

The words spilled forth from my lips before I could stop them. Though far from destitute, I held neither the money nor the connections to go head-to-head with a mobster like Joey.

But Violet's dark eyes met mine with such naked hope, such ferocity, that I couldn't bear to let her down.

The staccato blast of the trumpet—another signal from Stan—shattered the moment.

"I need to go," Violet said, and her small form slipped away from the parlor and back down the stairs, ghostlike.

As I cleared our late-night tea, I wondered if she was here at all or merely some hallucination brought on by sleep deprivation and exposure to strong chemicals. But the marks of her red lipstick on my teacup, along with the lilting sounds emanating from my cellar soon after her disappearance, evidenced that Violet was very much real.

The memory of her bruised thigh seared into my brain, serving as proof of Joey's diabolical nature. Though I had never considered myself a heroine by any stretch of my imagination, and I had fostered no meaningful relationships in my life apart from Father, I knew that I was the one who must stand up to Joey the Jaw.

Time passed, as it does, the days filled with work and quiet, the nights alive with thrumming music and shouting voices. Once, I heard what sounded like a gunshot outside my window, but I saw nothing amiss in the morning and preferred to believe it was a car backfiring.

Violet began visiting me almost nightly, stealing upstairs for a quick chat or cup of tea. I looked forward to her visits, those light moments in my monotonous days. But as frequently as her painted lips curved into a smile while recounting her childhood adventures on the farm, as quickly as her delicate laugh tinkled like a chandelier, she would fall into despair before steeling herself to head back down to the realm of her tormentor. Even the heavy powder she wore could not cover the marks encircling her neck or the cigarette burn on her upper arm. I dared not envisage the marks of brutality I could not see.

I knew that my dalliance with that mobster needed to end. As much as I had excused my own complicity in the illegality, telling myself that these customers were likely safer drinking alcohol in my cellar than making their own moonshine without knowledge of how to do so properly at home, I could not allow Joey's violence against young, innocent Violet to continue.

I had often been told that I was a severe woman. Though this sedate manner suited my profession, as mourners would scarcely trust a giggling schoolgirl with the demands of funeral arrangements, I learned that certain men find this characteristic unlikable.

"You could smile more," Joey told me one afternoon as he delivered my envelope of cash. "I'll bet ya have some good gams under that dress. You borrow it from your grandma or something? You're past your prime, but ya might look good if ya dolled yourself up a bit more. I told my wife the same thing. She don't make no effort. I don't know what it is with you older broads. But I might let ya come downstairs for a night out. I put some extra in there for ya this week. Maybe go to the beauty salon downtown and get fixed up, ya know?" He punctuated this stream of filth with a lascivious wink.

"Thank you for the rent," I said. Though my skin crawled with revulsion and contempt, I pretended the whole transaction was above board and that he was merely my tenant.

Closing the door behind him, willing myself not to slam it into his hulking frame, I seethed with resentment. *Past my prime?* This man was at least fifteen years older than I. While I should have been shocked at his cavalier admission of adultery and animalistic nature, I felt beyond that point. My feelings of disgust were useless; they did nothing to help young Violet escape from his evil clutches.

In my spare time, I began devising a plan to help her. Most of my ideas—some borrowed from novels—were convoluted at best. Though it would have been simple enough to purchase a train ticket and send Violet out of town, that wouldn't keep her family safe, and Joey would likely exact his revenge on them.

Violet didn't need to leave town, *Joey* did. Should I have called the police or even gone straight to the feds? Surely that would have put some fear into him and whatever organization he was part of. But what if he or one of his collaborators knew I had ratted him out? Was I willing to risk the consequences that would potentially befall me? Woefully ignorant of the letter of the law, I could not jeopardize my own livelihood or even freedom. No—best not to invite undue scrutiny!

Then again, perhaps I could make him *think* there was a threat. If Joey heard word that the police planned to raid the speakeasy, surely he would leave town for greener pastures. Small towns like Blackthorn, Pennsylvania, couldn't possibly hold the allure of a larger metropolis, especially with the many financial opportunities the Volstead Act had created for criminals like Joey.

Night after night, when Violet made her way up to me, I bore witness to her spirit diminishing, her skin becoming an even ghastlier shade of pale. She grew quieter, more withdrawn. Even though she was an entertainer by profession, she seemed to wish that *I* entertain *her*. She asked me to tell her about some of the novels I read, and I did, filling her ears with whimsical stories. She told me she had left school earlier than she desired to help her parents on the farm. Since she was now able to provide them with money, she no longer needed to toil away. However, she had traded one form of servitude for another, and this was far more dangerous.

If I didn't find a solution to get her away from Joey the Jaw, or at least get him away from her, I feared he would kill her.

In the weeks of our acquaintance, Violet's visits had mostly occurred just after midnight, when the band took a break between sets. Expecting her, I had made sure to clean up my mortuary room, making it as unassuming as a doctor's office, so as not to alarm her. Most people did not care to know what happened to bodies post-mortem. The placement of the cellar door was far from ideal, but I was always quick to usher her from the area where I completed what some might consider gruesome work.

On this night, however, as it was just past 8:00 p.m., I was still elbows deep in the cadaver of Mr. Ronald Jacobson. His body, nude except for a modesty cloth, lay on my cooling table, a trocar inserted in his abdomen to remove the fluids. The embalming machine—a new arrival I could afford due to the very circumstances in which I now wished to extricate myself—suctioned away, the slurps and whooshes adding a somber yet soothing note to the upbeat tune creeping from the cellar.

Absorbed in my work, I didn't notice when the song abruptly stopped, but the fast and frantic knock on the door ripped me from my concentration.

Apron on, trocar in hand, the deceased on full display, I wasn't ready for a visit from the woman I now considered a dear friend. Normally, I would have run to answer that knock, but I hesitated, right in the middle of my process.

The door flew open, my lock unable to withstand the brute force of the mobster, and both Violet and Joey the Jaw spilled into the room.

By this point in my career as a mortician, the sights, sounds, and smells of death had ceased to bother me. This was part of my role, just as a schoolteacher must correct spelling exams or a farmer must clean out a pigsty.

Shock and disgust registered on the faces of my unexpected visitors, their eyes wide and lips curled. But their expressions quickly changed, Violet's giving into fear, Joey's to rage.

"*This* is why you're sneaking off?" Joey yelled, his face reddening. "To watch this here lady do weird stuff to a corpse? That's twisted, doll. You don't go anywhere without I tell ya to go."

Violet had risen to her feet, but Joey's closed fist shot out and punched her in the face, sending her crumpling back to the floor.

"Don't touch her!" I screamed, my voice shrill and foreign-sounding to my own ears.

Like a tiger hunting new prey, Joey swung his head around, his eyes narrowing. "Now *you* wanna tell me how to treat my girl? Lady, you do what I tell ya. And I tell ya to mind your own goddamn business!"

He lunged toward me then, his meaty hands already curled into fists, his massive frame seeming to block out everything else from my sight.

Unthinking, mind blighted by fear, heart pounding in my chest, I raised my right hand—the one still holding the trocar.

Joey the Jaw pressed on, impaling himself on the sharp end of the long, cylindrical metal instrument. Eyebrows rising into two sharp peaks, his lips stretched back in horror as it pierced through his woolen suit and into his skin, but his momentum was too much to stop.

I held the trocar steady only for the moment of initial contact, feeling it slice into his chest, but I let go and scampered to the side as the large man came crashing forward.

The gore-coated tip poking through his back, Joey the Jaw lay still.

The racket continued from downstairs, but the room seemed suddenly quiet apart from the steady sucking of the embalming machine to which the trocar was still attached.

From her position on the floor, Violet rose to her feet and closed the cellar door.

I shut off the machine. We locked eyes, and I nodded.

On a rainy Monday morning a few days later, I watched the final shovelfuls of dirt completely cover Mr. Jacobson's gravesite. I let out a deep breath.

It was done. Long after the gravediggers had left the previous afternoon, after the cars full of speakeasy guests had driven off in a huff when the cellar door refused to open—the only key to the lock back in my pocket where it belonged—Violet and I dug a few feet deeper.

Despite her diminutive size, she was accustomed to farmwork. With the two of us shoveling together under the light of the gibbous moon, we carved out Joey's final resting place and slid his corpse into the hole before covering it once again. Unlike the reverent way in which I casketed most bodies, we tossed that vile man into the ground like a bag of trash.

Before the first flickers of dawn's morning light, I bathed and lay down for some rest before Mr. Jacobson's funeral. Though the bags under my eyes might have given testament to my late night, I did not appear out of place amongst the mourners.

Little did they know of the eternal companion over whom their dearly departed would rest for eternity. Desperate times called for desperate measures.

I had never been a violent woman. Any guilt I felt from the dreadful act was assuaged when I thought of the damage the bastard had inflicted on poor Violet's body.

Violet was free. Over the weeks of our blossoming friendship, we had spoken of her plans for the future. She confided her wish to attend secretarial school to elevate her circumstances, and the wad of cash we extracted from Joey's pocket—her severance pay, as I thought of it—would help her achieve the goal.

I smiled to myself while viewing the bouquet of violets left by one of the mourners. While I didn't know if she and I would cross paths again, as her secretarial school required her to move to another town across the state, I knew one thing: I would plant violets in the spring to flourish as he rotted, just as I hoped Violet herself would in her life without Joey.

Cassandra O'Sullivan Sachar

Cassandra O'Sullivan Sachar is a writer, English professor, and Bram Stoker Award-nominated editor. She enjoys traveling the world when not at home in Pennsylvania channeling her fears and experiences into spooky stories. Learn more at https://cassandraosullivansachar.com/

1930s
The Great Depression

Tyler Downs

As he and two other men swayed in the rattling truck bed, Joe watched the silhouette of Oklahoma City shrink in the distance.

Every other mile, they drove past deserted farmhouses with collapsed porches and crops that'd grown infertile. A rusty weathervane on one of the roofs started spinning like a top in the rising wind, gaining speed, and next thing he knew, they were driving through the dark heart of a dust storm. The wind howled. Pebbles clanked off the truck like hail, and Joe shut his eyes as swirling dirt pelted him in the face. He yanked the fabric of his shirt up over his head to protect himself. It didn't help much, but at least he could breathe without topsoil turning to mud in his mouth. The other men coughed and cursed. One of them followed his lead, lifting the lapel of his coat as a shield. The other dropped prone in the truck bed.

Joe couldn't rightfully say how long it took to drive through the storm; longer than he would've liked. But they eventually emerged on the other side of it, from darkness to sunlight. He spat a mouthful of dust-tinged saliva off the side of the truck. His hair was caked in dirt, and his lungs were itchy, but compared to the thought of returning home empty-handed to a malnourished daughter and the disappointment in his wife's eyes, this was nothing.

The truck eased to a brake-squealing stop. As the other two men climbed out of the truck, Joe surveyed the farmhouse before them. It was a modest one-story home that looked similar to the other places they drove past on the ride out. Bleak. Run-down. Most of the windows were cracked or broken. A crow was perched on the roof, cawing above a front door that hung off its hinges and swayed in the breeze. The Great Depression didn't discriminate. City-folk. Farmers. They all got a taste.

Joe was last off the truck.

By the time the driver opened the door to exit the vehicle, the youngest of their trio was there waiting to help her down.

"Such a gentleman." The old woman grasped him for support, gingerly stepping down from the truck. She was tiny; roughly five feet tall and frail, with coarse white hair that was tied back in a ponytail. Joe figured she must've been in her sixties or seventies. She unraveled the shawl from around her face and frowned at the sight of them. "If I knew a storm was brewing, I would've let you boys squeeze up front with me. The dust has a habit of popping up when you least expect it."

"It wasn't so bad," said the man who'd helped her. Joe and the third man were still busy brushing dirt off their clothes.

"Good." She sized them up. "Well, ever since my husband Earl got sick, I've got a strict rule against letting nameless strangers into my home. The last thing I need is a group of young men taking advantage of me." She smiled, then pointed a crooked finger at the talkative one. "Out with it."

He arched his brow. "Pardon?"

"Your name, honey. If you don't mind."

"Oh ... Floyd, ma'am." He removed his cap and flattened it to his chest. He was of average height and build, wearing a pair of dusty overalls. "Floyd Henderson. It's a pleasure."

"Floyd." She nodded, then pointed at the biggest of the trio. "And you?"

The man standing beside Joe was built like a sasquatch. His leather jacket strained to contain his broad shoulders and arms, and he had a nasty scar running down the side of his face. "Name's Hank."

She turned her attention to Joe. "And last but not least?"

"Joe."

"Well then. Floyd, Hank, Joe ... I'm Edna. Edna Fleming. Now that we're properly acquainted, let me show you what work needs done. Then I'll get to whipping up a batch of my famous sweet tea." She turned and headed for the house, moving with a labored gait, her ankle-length sundress billowing in the breeze. Once she reached the base of the porch, Floyd took her arm and aided her up the creaky steps while she gripped the handrail for support. Joe and Hank exchanged a look. Then they followed Edna into her home.

The interior of Edna's place was nicer than he thought it'd be. Spacious. Both her kitchen and living room were decently maintained and visible from the entrance, thanks to the open floor plan.

"Nice place ya' got here, Miss Fleming," Floyd observed.

"Why, thank you, Floyd." Edna stopped and faced the men in the kitchen. "Are you boys okay with getting paid after the work is done? Is that how it usually goes? I've never done this before, but I thought it was time I got some help before this place becomes incurable."

Hank's voice was nearly as gruff as he looked. "Actually, if you've got the money nearby, you can pay us now—"

"Paying us afterward is fine," Joe said.

Hank clenched his jaw, but let it be.

Joe had clocked Hank from the moment he laid eyes on him. Certain men had an aura. An energy. And due to a short stint in prison and a decade of factory work, Joe had developed a sixth sense for parsing out the unsavory types with broken moral compasses. Bad men were inevitable, but few things were more dangerous than a bad man who was desperate and broke. When Edna parked outside the warehouse earlier, seeking odd-jobbers to help with home repairs, he saw the way Hank's eyes lit up—like a hungry wolf sizing up a wounded lamb. The thought of letting this sweet old lady get robbed or worse didn't sit right with Joe, so the moment Hank volunteered, he did as well.

Edna smiled warmly at Joe. "That's very kind. Thank you."

Joe nodded.

"So ..." Floyd glanced around. "What work did you need done?"

Edna gestured for them to follow as she moseyed to the other side of the kitchen. She gripped the handle of a door and tugged it open. Within, a dark stairwell led down into an even darker basement.

"I've got a furnace down there that won't quit acting up, no matter how nicely I ask. Earl always said he'd fix it. But now that his health's taken a turn for the worse, that ain't happening anytime soon, and I'm sick of needing five quilts just to avoid freezing to death at night."

Floyd hesitated, peering down the stairs. "Ya' got a lantern or some candles we can use?"

"Oh, silly me. Of course, sweetie." Edna wandered into the living room. It took a few tries for her to strike a match with her shaky hands, but once she got the lantern burning, she returned to them and handed it to Floyd. "The furnace will be down on your right. Can't miss it. There should be a big toolbox full of Earl's old stuff on the workbench, too. But I'm a shout away if you need anything. Do you boys like lemon in your sweet tea?"

"Yes, ma'am." Floyd smiled, then paused and glanced at the others. "...That is, if you fellas approve?"

"Lemon's fine," Hank said, giving Floyd a push from behind. "Go on, lantern boy. Lead the way."

Floyd began descending the creaky stairs, holding the lantern out in front of him as he went. Hank followed close behind. Joe, however, paused when he noticed a thin stream of dirt pouring through a hole in the kitchen wall, the same way water might spew from a crack in a dam. It had formed a growing pile of dust on the floor.

"Want us to fix that, too?"

"Oh, that's nothing." Edna waved it off. "Happens from time to time whenever a storm hits."

Joe eyed her curiously. It didn't seem like 'nothing' to him, but it wasn't his business. He made his way downstairs to join the others. By the time he reached the base of the stairs, Floyd's glowing lantern provided just enough light for him to see where he was going. Joe looked to the right and spotted both men. The lantern's glow cast their shadows against the far wall, where the furnace was said to be. They were already searching the area.

Floyd twisted to look back at Joe. "She said the furnace was on the right side of the basement, right?"

"Dumb old bitch probably doesn't know right from left anymore," Hank said.

Joe surveyed the rest of the basement, figuring Edna just got her wires crossed. The space was mostly barren. Cement walls. Cement floors. A leaky pipe. The smell of mildew. An old rocking chair in the corner was coated in cobwebs. He spotted the workbench she mentioned, and there was Earl's toolbox, right beside a big rusty wrench.

Joe returned to the base of the stairs and peered up the stairwell. "Miss Fleming," he called out. "We aren't seeing the furnace. You said it was to the right?"

Edna stood at the top of the stairs, staring down at him. She had some kind of device in her hands, and when she pressed a button on it, a set of prison bars loudly sprang into view, filling the basement doorframe.

"What was that?" Floyd asked.

But Joe was already rushing up the stairs. When he reached the top of the steps, he surveyed the crisscrossing prison bars that barricaded the door. It looked like the door of a jail cell. He grabbed hold of the iron bars and shoved on them, but they didn't budge.

"... Miss Fleming? What the hell are you doing?"

She stood silently, watching him through the bars.

"Hey!" Hank hollered from the bottom of the stairs. "What's going on? ... *What the*—" He thundered up the stairs and shoved Joe aside to get a better look. He grabbed the iron bars and shook them hard, strong enough to make the hinges rattle, but they remained sturdy. He kicked them, seething. "Let us the fuck out!"

"Guys?" Floyd called from downstairs. "What's happening?"

"*Now-now*, boys ... That's no way to address an old woman. Where'd all those sweet manners of yours go?"

"I'll show you manners ..." Hank lunged at her, jamming a meaty arm through the bars, but his shoulder collided with iron before he could reach her.

Edna frowned. "That isn't very nice." She backed away into the kitchen and collected a pair of lemons from the pantry. "I'll wait," she said, picking up a knife off the counter. She started calmly slicing a lemon into thin pieces atop a wooden cutting board. "You boys just let me know once you've finished your bellyaching and you're ready to listen."

"I swear to God," Hank fumed. "If you don't open this—"

Joe cut in. "What do you want?"

Edna glanced their way and smiled. "Don't worry. I'll let you out eventually. Well ... one of you, at least. If you behave yourselves."

"One of us?" Joe asked.

"Mhmm." She nodded. "Whoever's left standing when it's all said and done. You'll be free to go."

"What the fuck are you talking about?" Hank glared at her.

Edna kept slicing lemons. "There aren't any rules. My Earl's never liked rules. You three are welcome to starve or die of dehydration down there if you like. There's no shame in that. Kinda' boring, but it'd be an honorable death. A moral one. And it'd be a first for me, admittedly. I've never seen a group of men make it that long."

"Did ... did she lock us down here?" Floyd asked.

Joe looked over his shoulder. Floyd was now standing halfway up the steps behind them, clutching the lantern. His face was pale.

Edna resumed. "No food or water has a way of turning even the most agreeable men into beasts. So, you three can wait until that mania rears its head and rips the facade of decency from your desperate fingers, or you can bypass all the foreplay, and get straight to bumping uglies." She glanced at them and waggled her brows.

"What is this?" Joe asked. "Some kind of human cockfighting?"

"Cockfighting. A battle royale. Natural selection. Call it whatever you want, honey, but it's very simple; no one leaves that basement until only one of you is left standing."

Joe glanced over at Hank.

Hank stared off in a daze.

Joe didn't like the look on his face.

"Well," Edna said. "No need to stay here chatting with lil' ole' me. Go on." She shooed them away with her hand. "You boys have the whole basement to yourselves. I'll be up here waiting with a fresh pitcher of tea for whoever makes it out alive."

Hank grabbed the iron bars and shook them again with all his might. But once he seemed sure the bars wouldn't budge, he stormed off down the stairs, shoving Floyd aside as he passed him.

After collecting himself, Floyd moved up the stairs to eye the prison bars more closely. "Is she serious?"

"Sure seems that way," Joe said.

"Miss Fleming ..." Floyd spoke to her. "Ma'am, why are you doing this? I don't understand. Will you please let us out? I ... I've got a mother and sister at home who need me."

Edna hummed to herself and ignored him, turning the stove top on.

"Please?" Floyd tried again. "My uncle owns a factory. If you can get word to him, I know he'd be willing to pay for my release."

Edna never lifted her eyes off her kitchen duties. "Sorry, Floyd. There's only one way this ends. I've got nothing else to say on the matter."

A loud clatter from below tore Joe's attention away.

Floyd turned as well.

Edna grinned. "You two might wanna get down there. The big fella doesn't seem like much of a team player."

Joe snatched the lantern from Floyd and hurried down the stairs. His mind was racing. One half of his brain was still struggling to process the situation they were in, and the other half was already preparing for a fight to the death. Edna was right; Hank didn't seem like the sensible type. By the time Joe reached the bottom of the stairs, Hank was over by the workbench, noisily rifling through Earl's old toolbox.

"What are you doing?" Joe asked.

Hank turned without a word, clutching a big iron wrench in his hand. Joe locked eyes with him and braced himself. This was it. Do or die. They'd fight, here and now, and whoever won would deal with Floyd afterward.

"C'mon then," Joe said, tightening his grip on the lantern. It wasn't an ideal weapon, but it'd have to do. His pulse spiked. He reared back with the lantern, poised to hit Hank with it, but then realized the big guy had already bee-lined past him.

Hank rushed back up the stairs.

Joe exchanged a confused look with Floyd. They turned and peered up the stairwell, watching as Hank started beating on the iron bars with the wrench like a steel mill worker. Loud, metallic clanks echoed down throughout the basement, along with the distant sound of Edna humming to herself upstairs.

Hank hollered down at them, mid-whack. "Y'all gonna come help or what?"

52 hours later.

They had spent most of the first day working on the door together. Hank hammered at it with his wrench. Joe used a screwdriver to chip away at the spots where the iron was embedded into the concrete frame. Floyd searched the basement for anything useful, and they swapped roles whenever one of them got tired. Edna must've gone out or was perhaps biding her time in another room. There was no clock or access to sunlight, so as the hours blurred by, it was impossible to tell how long they'd been down there. Maybe a day. Maybe several. Every now and then, one of them would doze off while leaning against the wall, only to jerk awake shortly after and shake off the exhaustion. They didn't have the time or trust for sleep.

Joe had experienced severe dehydration before. The ravenous thirst was constant, but he was more concerned with the increasingly frequent migraines and dizzy spells. After another long stint of work, the trio reluctantly took a break. They sat sweaty and exhausted in the dark basement, huddled around the lantern, dazed by their predicament.

Joe had experienced severe dehydration before. The ravenous thirst was a constant, but he was more concerned with the increasingly frequent migraines and dizzy spells. After another long stint of work, the trio reluctantly took a break. They sat sweaty and exhausted in the dark basement, huddled around the lantern, dazed by their predicament.

"Maybe we can dig," Floyd said, out of breath. "There must be a weak spot in one of these walls, right? We can dig our way up to the surface."

Hank wiped sweat off his face with his shirt, never taking his eyes off the lantern's glow.

"Yeah. Good idea," Joe lied, rubbing at his blistered hands. "We'll just rest a little while longer first."

Joe had already accepted the fact that they weren't escaping. Whoever installed the prison door at the top of the stairs knew what they were doing. They'd searched high and low through every nook and cranny of the basement to no avail. At first, he tried convincing himself that there was still time to stumble on a last-minute miracle, or perhaps crazy old Edna might finally come to her senses. But with every minute that passed, they inched closer to the point of no return. Without food or water, there was only so much physical exertion they could expend, and by now, they'd already burned through most of it.

For the last hour, Joe had been cataloging all the weapons the basement had to offer and plotting out the most efficient way to kill Hank and Floyd. Since Hank was the biggest threat, he planned to get Floyd alone and talk him into teaming up. Two on one made for better odds. If they succeeded, he was confident in his ability to deal with Floyd once the dust settled. But he knew Hank was likely mulling over similar thoughts by now, and if he wasn't, he would be soon. Edna was right. In life, survival was king.

Hank stood, brushing dirt off his pants. "Y'all got your second wind yet? I think that door's bound to budge soon."

"I'm ready," Floyd said.

Joe nodded. "Go on ahead. I liked Floyd's idea. We'll take a closer look at these walls first and check for any weak spots, then we'll meet you up there."

Hank gave Joe a look. "Suit yourself."

Joe waited until he heard Hank's boots thumping up the steps, then he glanced over his shoulder at the stairwell to make sure the coast was clear. "Alright," he whispered, swiveling his attention back to Floyd. "I hate to say it, but we're gonna need to start making some tough decisions—"

He froze.

It took him a moment to process what he was seeing. Floyd stood in front of him, clutching a pistol, aiming it directly at Joe's face.

"... What are you doing?" Joe asked, even though the answer seemed obvious.

"I've got people who depend on me, Joe. I can't afford to die down here."

He had to give Floyd credit. There was no cowardice in his voice, nor any tremble in his grip on the gun. He'd clearly underestimated him. "We all have people who need us, Floyd, but we can make it out of here together if we just keep our wits about us."

Floyd smirked. "Oh, please. You were just about to talk me into going after Hank."

"Well, why wouldn't I? It's the smart play. He's clearly the most dangerous."

"Not from where I'm standing."

"Where'd ya get the gun?"

Floyd nodded over towards the workbench. "Behind the toolbox. I found it while you two idiots were upstairs begging that crazy old witch to let you go."

"Well, you'd better be a good shot. Hank's gonna hear, and I'm betting it'll take more than a few bullets to bring down a man his size."

"I'll take my chances. Sorry about this, Joe. It's nothing personal."

And just like that, Floyd pulled the trigger.

Click.

... Click ...

... Click-click-click.

They locked eyes.

Joe lunged at Floyd, grabbing the gun and wrenching the weapon free from his grip before the younger man was able to stop him. He popped open the cylinder of the six-shooter and saw it was empty. "Didn't check to make sure it was loaded first?"

"Joe ..." Floyd stammered, backpedaling. "I ... I'm sorry ..."

Joe saw red.

He charged, tackling Floyd to the ground. He had a good size advantage on the boy, so he was able to pin and mount him without much trouble. Joe grabbed a heavy brick off the floor and smashed it down against Floyd's face. Floyd's arm went limp, flopping to the ground. His panicked eyes became dazed and distant, then even more vacant as Joe brought the brick down again. Joe caved in the boy's cheekbone first. Then the side of his forehead. Floyd gurgled incoherently as Joe brought the brick down a third time, then a fourth. The groans and sputters eventually went silent, and all that remained was the steady sound of brick striking wet meat; over, and over, and over.

Once he was sure the job was done, Joe dropped the brick and assessed the aftermath. He panted heavily. His hands were soaked in blood. Floyd's face looked like a smashed pumpkin, oozing red guts and clumps of bone matter. It took Joe a moment to register the sound of footsteps rushing down the stairwell. He spun to look over his shoulder. Hank stood there.

No words were necessary.

They both knew this was coming.

Hank rushed towards him. Joe scrambled back to his feet, but before he could, the bigger man tackled him to the ground. They rolled end-over-end a few times. Joe planned on using their momentum to ensure he ended up on top, but before he could, he found himself being bear-hugged from behind. His eyes bulged as he felt Hank's big, hairy arm lock into place around his neck. The muscles in Hank's forearm tightened and squeezed Joe's throat like a boa constrictor, leaving Joe alarmed at how rapidly his airway was cut off.

Joe thrashed and bucked on the floor like a bronco. He flailed his arms around wildly, striking at whatever parts of Hank he could reach. But hitting Hank felt like hitting a brick wall. Joe's face burned hot. His lungs ached. He tried to gasp, but no air came. He blindly groped around on the floor for something. Anything. Then he found his screwdriver from earlier and grabbed hold of it.

He stabbed Hank in the leg. Jerking the screwdriver free, he stabbed Hank's arm, and blindly stabbed at the area where he believed Hank's head and neck were. Some blows landed, getting stuck in the meat. Some didn't. But as the seconds dragged on, every flail of his arm became weaker and less controlled. The blood vessels in his face seared hotter. His chest felt ready to burst. He swung the screwdriver again and again. He felt dizzy. Weak. Then his arm limply flopped to the floor. His vision flickered in, then out, then in, then—

It all went black.

Hank had planned on letting the two men tire themselves out a bit more before making his move, but when he rushed downstairs and found Joe straddling Floyd's lifeless body, it was do or die.

He grunted as he hobbled towards the base of the stairs. Joe had done some damage with the screwdriver, and the effects of the injuries were multiplied after days without food or water. There were bloody puncture wounds along each of his arms, his right thigh, and he was pretty sure there was a hole in his throat. Hank stopped and yelled up the stairwell.

"Lady! It's over."

While he waited, he pressed his fingers against his neck and grimaced at the sight of how much blood stained his hand.

"Hey!" he yelled again.

Edna's dark silhouette finally appeared at the top of the stairs, behind the prison bars. "So, you're the last one left?"

"I am."

"Can't say I'm surprised. Show me the others."

"Come down and look for yourself."

Edna laughed. "You think I was born yesterday? Either show your evidence or you're welcome to stay down there and rot."

Hank sighed and hobbled over towards the bodies. He grabbed the leg of Floyd's pants and dragged his lifeless body across the basement, leaving behind a red streak of blood and brain matter along the cement floor. Then he came back and grabbed Joe by the shirt collar, dragging him over as well. He flopped their bodies side by side at the base of the stairs.

"I ain't carrying them up the stairs," he panted.

She watched from above. "And they're both dead?"

"Dead as doornails."

"Promise? Cross your heart and hope to die?"

He smirked. "Yes."

Edna studied the scene for a good while before responding. "Good on you, Hank. Congratulations. I can't tell you how much we appreciate you helping us out."

"Sure. Just hurry up and get me out of here."

She leaned against the iron bars. "Killing folks the old-fashioned way isn't easy for people our age. Poison worked for a while. The men would be so thirsty after a day of hard work, they would've chugged down a cold glass of anything I gave 'em. But it started making Earl sick, so ..." She frowned. "He prefers his meals unseasoned now."

"Lady. If you don't open that fucking door right now ..." Hank started up the stairs, but after a few steps, he realized how lightheaded he was. He braced himself against the wall and took a shaky breath.

"As you wish."

Edna flipped a switch on the wall.

A second later, Hank heard rumbling behind him; the sound of shifting concrete. There must have been a hidden exit in the basement. It made sense that Edna wouldn't want to put herself in danger. He clasped the side of his neck and tried to keep his blood from spilling out as he shuffled back down the steps. A section of the basement wall was sliding open, revealing a doorway. Wherever the mystery door led looked dark, but he didn't have any better options. Hank hobbled toward it.

Halfway there, he paused.

A figure emerged from the darkness, slowly crawling out of the doorway and into the dimly lit basement. It took Hank a moment to realize it was an old, naked man; nothing but wrinkled skin and rickety bones. This must be the infamous Earl he'd heard so much about. The man didn't appear to have functioning legs. He army-crawled across the floor, and every time he went to drag himself forward with his forearms, his bones *clicked* like rusty wind-up toys. Each breath Earl emitted was a raspy wheeze, and dust steamed off his body like floating pollen clouds. When Earl lifted his face, his eyes were oyster gray and cloudy. Vacant. He looked blind as a bat. He sniffed hard at the air a few times. Then he moaned and started crawling towards Hank, slow as molasses, dragging his limp old legs behind him.

Hank watched in disgust.

Poor bastard.

He was able to sidestep the old man easily enough, and he continued towards the door. Hank made it a few more shaky steps before his vision blurred and his legs turned to jelly. The wall he tried to brace himself against wasn't there. He collapsed, sputtering blood from his cold lips. He promised himself he wouldn't die down here, but his wounds had allowed his remaining energy to spill out over the floor. As Hank lay there in a puddle of his own blood and eyed the doorway Earl had come through, a part of him accepted that it wasn't a proper exit, anyway. They were never meant to leave. Edna made it sound like this game of hers was nothing new, and letting survivors run free would have surely brought retribution to her doorstep.

He glanced back at the others.

Earl had crawled over to Joe and Floyd's corpses. Once the old man reached them, he extended his arm and placed his hand on Floyd's chest. Then he bowed his head, as if in prayer. Perhaps he was a religious man. Maybe Earl was just another one of Edna's prisoners, hidden away down here, suffering like the rest of them.

But then he heard it.

There was a noise, like crinkling paper, and it got more intense as Floyd's body began to *shrivel*. His skin got tighter over his muscles, and he rapidly lost weight, deflating, like a juicy grape that was time-lapsing into a dehydrated raisin. It happened fast. And after all the moisture had been siphoned from Floyd's body, his limbs started snapping, collapsing inwards on themselves. His eyeballs got so dry that they cracked and shattered. In a matter of seconds, Earl had used his touch to transform Floyd into a dried-out mummy who looked like he'd been rotting for centuries.

Earl reached out and touched Joe next. And just like Floyd, all the moisture was rapidly vacuumed through Joe's skin, and his body deflated and shriveled up until he was nothing more than a petrified husk of a man.

Then Earl began hammering his fist down against their dry, brittle bodies, and with every swing of his arm, their figures broke apart like gingerbread houses. Joe's gaunt face turned into a caved-in crater. Floyd's chest became a gaping pit. And Earl kept hammering away at them, breaking their bodies down more and more with each blow, smashing them to bits, until all that was left was a pile of dust and dehydrated extremities. A pruned leg. A few curled fingers. Half a skull.

Hank prayed that his dying mind was playing tricks on him. His pulse was slow, but it still managed to quicken when the old man dropped his face into a pile of corpse-dust and began snorting like a wheezing pig. Earl took a wild sniff, raised his head to cough and sniffle and clear his throat, then put his face back in the dust and snorted again. Loudly. Over and over. Treating their remains like human cocaine.

Hank used what fleeting strength he had left to roll onto his belly and crawl towards the door. It didn't matter where the doorway led at this point—he needed to get away from whatever this abomination was. He dragged himself across the floor, bit by bit, leaking blood. The snorting stopped. He didn't dare look back.

Footsteps approached.

Before he realized it, a pair of old, veiny feet were in front of him, blocking his path. Hank weakly raised his head and peered upwards. Earl stood before him, staring down at him, still old but rejuvenated. There was no expression on the old man's face. No words. Nothing. Earl squatted down on spry legs, placed his hand on Hank's shoulder, and Hank gasped right before he felt all the moisture in his body being summoned to the surface, like iron to a magnet.

Upstairs, Edna sat at her kitchen table with a glass of sweet tea. She was flipping through the pages of a photo album, and had stopped on a picture of her and Earl, back when they were young and happy. Earl was caked in dirt after a long day of work on the farm, hugging her from behind, and she was laughing while trying to squirm away. Even now, she could feel his arms around her and smell the fragrance that clung to him like a never-ending cologne; leather and motor oil.

Familiar sounds arose from the basement.

Snorting.

Earl's manic moans.

Edna traced her dirty fingernail along the outline of her husband's face in the photograph. She couldn't help but think about the boys downstairs and imagine all the smiling faces that filled their photo albums.

It made her sad.

At the end of the day, she knew she wasn't much different than them. When the world got mean, they all had to venture into dark places to find a sliver of light. Some folks were able to leave and go home afterward. Others were forced to stay behind. But what fueled them was universal.

People did what they had to for the ones they loved.

And for those like Edna Fleming and the three young men downstairs, the depression never ended.

Tyler Downs

Tyler Downs is a long-time writer and avid reader who's new to the author scene. He loves writing weird, dark stories that give his imagination a place to run wild, and his only hope is that a few of you out there enjoy reading them. He currently resides in Maryland and yes, he loves crabs. His debut short story collection, *Fifteen Eyes*, was released in August of 2025, and he has two novels planned for early 2026. www.tylerdowns.org

1940s

THE CLEANSING

Besu Tadesse

Brody "Silverfish" Samuel–Fish, as they would call him—quickly greeted the pastor after Sunday church service before rushing home to prepare for the night's festivities with his second oldest son, Joseph. Fish wanted to stay home to get ahead of his plans, but everyone would have noticed their absence. Their Southern backwater town was small—so much that it didn't even appear on several maps that were issued that year. They were invisible to the outside world, but Fish and his family were as famous as President Roosevelt to their two hundred and seventy-three neighbors. After a service about the purity of "their" kind and "their" values as "the true reflection of God's words", the congregation lined up to greet the pastor and catch up on their lives. For Fish, it was a beautiful and respectable song and dance. Communion never brought him joy or connection. His happiness came from the "cleansing." The hunting of the undesirables.

Everyone in the town knew about the cleansings. It was how the men in the town felt alive. It was something for the women to speak about at their social functions. It was part of the fabric of their lifestyle. They knew they would be safe from retribution—Sheriff Bailey was the law of that town, stymied by due process and uncaring in how it was administered. The sheriff knew the gap between what should be done and what he wanted to do. He could, and did, turn a blind eye to what Fish and his brood conducted. Fish knew he cleansed the town to Bailey's liking when he would come home and find a small box with a cigar and a little star written on a sheet of paper using the sheriff's signature red ink pen. A silent commendation for a job well done.

As he walked home, Fish talked about the changes going on in the country. Or rather, he berated his family about how they needed to be vigilant lest Negroes and Yankees come in and take over everything. Joseph hung on every one of his father's words, while Claire, his wife, rolled her eyes. Not that she disagreed, it was just that she had heard his rants several times before. Eva, their eight-year-old daughter, tugged on her mother's dress and whispered about how she missed her older brother, Jacob, who was travelling home from Oklahoma after a series of droughts destroyed his business. Claire politely nodded quietly as her husband continued his tirade for the next twenty minutes. She walked Eva into their house and prepared dinner, kissing Fish on the cheek and reminding him to get the car extra clean before he went out. She planned to go into town for supplies the next day and didn't want to look uncouth. After Claire and Eva went into the house, Fish went to his garage with Joseph and began their preparations.

Not long after they returned home, Rangles came over with his eldest son, Bryan. Bryan and Joseph had been in the same school class for ten years, and Rangles was one of Fish's close disciples and friends. Rangles wholeheartedly believed in the vision. Bryan was less committed but equally as devoted to his relationship with his father as Joseph was with his. The Rangles men walked in with large chains, two lengths of rope, and a set of freshly sharpened hatchets.

"You ready, Fish? We brought a bit extra, just in case."

"Thanks, Rangles. What did you think of the service today?"

"Wasn't there. We're not as famous as you, so we didn't bother. We took the time to get ready. Figured we could beat you here."

"Sorry to disappoint you," Fish said with his gravelly voice. "Did you at least go for Easter services?"

"When was that?"

"Jesus, Rangles, it was two weeks ago."

"Really? I guess I missed that too," Rangles chuckled.

Fish didn't find it amusing. "Well, it's good you got here quick. Better to get out there sooner rather than later. I don't quite know what we're going to see out there."

"Not a problem," Rangles said. "Where the hell is Dale? We need that horse."

"I'm here," Dale Bader said slowly, his tall, languishing frame looming over the group. The others jumped back in surprise. "I brought my big one, Lucky. Figured we'd want to be ready for anything. Is that good?" Dale nodded toward his towering horse.

Fish smiled. "More than good, friend. Glad to see you. Just waiting on one more."

"You mean Tommy? He's not coming."

"Not coming? Why?" Rangles asked.

"I dunno. I just saw him on the way here. He said he talked to his wife about it. She said it didn't feel right, so she made him promise to come straight home after he got some food."

"Jesus Christ," Fish quipped, "that woman is going to be the death of him. Always talking that 'cosmic' nonsense."

"Yeah, it's not Christian," Joseph said.

Fish exclaimed, "That's right! It's not Christian."

Rangles and his son nodded in agreement.

Dale nodded. "That's fair, but that's not my concern. A man's going to do what he needs to do, even if it means making peace with his woman. We'll get him out next time."

"Whatever you say, Dale," Fish said, waving his hand in dismissal. "Get Lucky hitched on the post and we can hook him up to the Buick when we're done cleaning."

"Ah, yes," Rangles replied, "the good ol' Hoover Wagon."

Dale hitched Lucky onto the large post just outside the garage then joined the others in washing and polishing Fish's 1936 Ford Model 68. Automobiles were rare in those parts, and the Samuels owning one made them all the more popular. Fish and Joseph had saved as much as they could from odd jobs over the years, supplemented by looting the dead bodies that they left after their "cleansing" outings. It was the fanciest thing they owned or would ever own. But fuel was too expensive, so they needed to hitch a horse to it if they wanted to get anywhere further than a few miles away. And they would never be seen dragging around the body of that beautiful specimen without purifying it first.

Fish smirked while he worked. "A good cleansing of our home requires an even better cleansing of ourselves."

The men drew several buckets of water from the well before washing the car using sponges, rags, and a heaping amount of detergent. Tires, headlights, windows, even the door handles needed to be pristine. The ritual not only cleaned the car to a glistening shine—it also confirmed their self-proclaimed righteousness. How awful could a group of men be when they took such diligent care of their belongings? How could their actions be rotten and vile if they felt closer to each other and to God when they did them? Their justifications were reinforced by their community and by each other, reaffirmed through their own beliefs and sweat. It didn't matter that they cursed or skipped church or cheated on their wives. No one asked too many questions about the bloody hatchets or rusted chains. If the car was shiny enough, it would blind the people from Fish and his crew's own deeds. And maybe, blind them from their own.

Once they were done, the Samuels grabbed their shotguns and jumped in the freshly cleaned Ford, along with the Rangles men and their tools. Dale unhitched Lucky from the post and hitched him to the hood of the Ford then put Lucky's saddle in the car before jumping onto the hood itself. Once everything was secured, the men were on the road in no time. They told old stories of their life growing up and sang lewd songs about women and booze as they headed for the creek. They talked about what they were planning to do later that night. The Rangles boys were going to have a nice dinner. Bryan would call it an early night while Daddy Rangles came up with a scheme to see old man Miller's wife near one of the abandoned mills for an evening tryst. Rangles was a sleaze, so laying with his elderly neighbor's inappropriately young wife was nothing for him. Fish said that he was going to have a night with family, but Joseph put that to rest when he talked about the new girl working at the general store that asked him over. Everyone began hollering and patting him on the back.

It took thirty minutes to get to Indian Head Creek when the car functioned as intended. Nearly one hour when the horse was leading the way. The men in the lynch mob had received word that a Negro man was taking residence in an abandoned shed within an especially wooded enclave near the creek. The plan was to get as close as they could with the car then walk down the wooded hill until they came upon the shed. There were five of them; even if the Negro man had a gun, it wouldn't be enough to stop them.

They reached the designated area near the creek. Dale hopped off the hood and hitched Lucky to a tree while the other four men hopped out and began exchanging weaponry. Everyone received a hatchet while the elder fathers secured the shotguns for themselves. Dale took a hatchet in each hand and secured a third to his belt—he took pride in his expert marksmanship with them. They also brought along various non-lethal tools—rope, twine, and blankets, all carried in large burlap sacks.

Their walking paths intertwined as they crept through dry trees and behind rotted, moss-covered logs to avoid a potential ambush. Aided by the croaking of the bullfrogs, their loud echoes bounced against the trees, filling the woods enough to cover the sound of their steps. A soft chorus of buzzing insects joined the bullfrog orchestra, emerging more persistently as they stalked.

Dale's eyes darted across the fields. "Cicadas are out a couple of years early," he said to himself as he felt the crunch of a few unfortunate ones under his shoes.

As the creek gently trickled along its nooks and curves during their descent, everyone swiped at the air and against their own skin. Joseph looked at Bryan scratching his neck and hair harder than the others. "Hey Brian, are the flies getting to you too?"

Bryan's expression was crooked as he scratched harder at his head. "Nah, I think my lice is starting to act up again."

The men grimaced, especially Fish. "Rangles, tell your boy to get that fixed!" In their town, you never told another man's son what to do when they came of age, but you did have the right to tell their father, even if the son was around. *Especially* when the son was around.

Rangles agreed. "Seriously, boy, go wash yourself off. At least try not to get it on us."

Bryan sucked his teeth, bent down, and started throwing creek water onto his head. As he started feverishly trying to wash out the critters from his hair, Joseph noticed the creek changing color.

"You seein' this?"

"What, boy? What are you talking about? Why are you talking?" his father whispered aggressively. "We gotta stay quiet."

"Yeah, I know, but … why is the creek red?"

The men looked down and saw the water reddening, starting from a few paces behind where they were positioned. "That looks like red clay coming down the creek."

"Yeah … but why isn't the creek red back there?"

Samuel looked, and saw only clear water further back. "Boy, don't worry about it. You just need to get focused."

"Alright." Joseph felt uneasy as Bryan stood up with red streaks of water pouring from his scalp. And regardless of his effort, the lice remained.

They continued until they reached a clearing where the creek dumped into Foster Lake. The sun gently bathed the area in a brilliance that the group of men could not appreciate. They were too focused on the dead goat slumped in front of the dilapidated shed. Flies and maggots surrounded the mouth and open rib cavity of the goat carcass, and the rotten stench overwhelmed their senses.

Joseph covered his mouth and nose. "Ugh, this smells like hell."

"Yeah, no shit," his father replied. "Worse than your mother's stew. This ain't good."

Rangles asked, "How long do you think it's been out here?"

Dale looked from a distance. "Based on the decay, it's probably been a couple of weeks."

"How do you know that?"

Dale looked Rangles in his eyes. "Because I read, man. You should try it."

Rangles wanted to strangle Dale for trying to embarrass him, but he knew that they needed to be ready for anything. He would deal with Dale later. "Son, what do you think?"

Bryan was too busy scratching to care about the question. With each swipe, they could hear the dryness of his skin against his overly long fingernails. He scratched his dirty blonde hair furiously. The others backed away from him and groaned in disgust, except for Dale, who remained stoic. They were now concerned, given how close to each other they had been all afternoon. Bryan shrugged and continued scratching. Joseph shook his head in disappointment as they walked around the goat and into the shed.

The inside of the shed was beyond shabby. The darkened walls were rotten and broken with splinters and sharp jagged boards sticking out. The windows were stained by nature—bird droppings, sludge, and other sticky substances. The air reeked of excrement and burned the men's noses. There were no furnishings, save a single bed containing the aforementioned Negro that they were looking for. He was emaciated and covered in boils, and the skin on his feet had crusted over. His hair and beard were patchy, and his clothes were tattered and stained with all manner of fluids. He was sweating and struggling to breathe.

"Looks like we hit the jackpot," Fish sneered.

"This is what I'm talking about," Rangles said.

"Yeah, Dad," Bryan said, "and it doesn't look like anyone else is around. This is perfect."

Joseph stepped back and looked around. "I don't know. Something doesn't feel right."

Fish ignored his son's pessimism. "I think it's time to cleanse this place."

Dale stepped forward but nearly fell through a gaping hole in the floor. They looked down and saw little red insects running across the grass under the shed.

"What are those? Ladybugs?" Bryan asked.

"Nah," Dale replied, "those are chiggers. Berry bugs. Not sure why there are so many."

Fish and Rangles chuckled to themselves.

Dale looked at them with confusion. "What's got you giggling? Do you want to share with everyone here?"

"It's just funny," Fish said.

"Yeah, it's chiggers under a–"

"Can I help you gentlemen with something?"

Everyone gasped in astonishment as the emaciated Negro man spoke with a weak and raspy voice. He leaned his head forward in order to get a good look at the white men in front of him, a disheveled mess of denim overalls and work-worn hands. He stared at each man up and down, and he was unimpressed. "It appears that you gentlemen were looking for me?"

Fish Samuel composed himself and answered ahead of his slack-jawed brethren. "Looks that way. We came for you."

The emaciated man laughed. "Are you sure about that?"

Joseph felt a chill in his skin, and his eyes widened. "Fellas, I don't think this is the person we were looking for."

His father snapped, turning his head only slightly to respond. "What do you mean?"

Joseph gulped in fear. There were too many unusual occurrences happening around the cabin. It all felt too familiar. He was having second thoughts about their mission. "Well, I know we heard there was someone out here. But look at him. He's got bumps that are leakin' all over the place, and he's thin as a skeleton. He's basically dead, so why are we getting info about someone that's damn near a corpse?"

Fish looked at the others and said, "Hold on, fellas. I need to talk to my son outside." He then nodded his head at Joseph, signaling him towards the door. Joseph reluctantly followed him.

They moved outside, far removed from the front door and the dead goat. Joseph hoped that the incessant croaking would help protect against the verbal lashing he was about to receive.

"Boy, have you lost your mind?"

"Dad, I can explain–"

"I don't want to hear it, son." Fish stepped closer to Joseph, nearly nose to nose with ever-increasing color in his cheeks. "We are not here to judge whether that beast is fit to live. We are here to *cleanse*. This is what is expected of us."

"I'm not saying we're going to leave. I'm just saying we should take a minute. Doesn't this seem ... kinda easy for us? Especially with him just lying there waiting for us?"

Fish Samuel's face reddened. "I'm not going to argue with you here. *This* is what we came for. You've been through this enough to know what it's all about. Now if you're gonna quit on me, then *quit*. You can walk your scared little pigtails back to the house and explain to your mother and the sheriff and the *whole town* what happened. Because I'm not gonna be there to help you!"

Joseph swallowed his emotions as he stared at his father. The last time he cried was when he was eleven, the same day he earned the scar on his upper lip. Fish made sure to give him something else to cry about. Ever since then, he knew it was better to respect his father and do his duty. But before they could argue anymore, Joseph was hit over the head with a cold, hard projectile from the sky.

"What the hell was that?" He jerked his head around. He darted his eyes up and down, side to side, trying to find the source.

Fish looked at his son. "What was what?"

Joseph touched the affected spot and turned quickly to see what had happened. He looked at the ground, at the sky, and every place in between, hoping to find the culprit. "Why is it so cold? Is that ice?"

Fish turned his son around and looked at the spot he was touching. "I don't see anything."

"Dad, check again." He could feel a small bump forming.

Fish sucked his teeth and open hand smacked his son in the same spot. "Get it together."

They walked back into the shed. Joseph rubbed his head even harder from the pain.

"Everything okay, guys?" Rangles asked.

"Just fine," Fish spilled. "We're ready."

The sick man replied, "I ask again … are you sure about that?"

"You're startin' to test my patience, boy," Rangles said, stepping toward the sick man before remembering that he didn't want to catch whatever he had.

"Gentlemen, I ask you … do you know not what you are doing?" The men stopped and contemplated the question, not knowing how to answer "yes" or "no" to such a question. "I can see that you are unsure of what to say. I will ask a different way. Do you know who I am?"

"You mean besides being a monkey on the wrong side of town?" Bryan said, jumping into the conversation ahead of the others. "That's all we need to know."

The sick man struggled through heavy lungs. "I think you can be a bit more curious, young Rangles."

The men of the lynch mob stepped back in astonishment. All except Bryan, too stunned to move. "What did you just say?"

"Bryan Rangles ... that's your name, correct?"

Bryan clenched his fist. "How the fuck did you know that?" He pulled himself back from reacting further. He needed to keep his cool for the cleansing ritual.

The man continued. "I know it is a bit uncomfortable to hear that, young Bryan. I assure you that your father Jameson didn't share your information with me."

Only the closest people in his life would have the honor of using Rangles' first name. Even then, saying his name the wrong way could get a fist to the chin.

The man continued enumerating, raising his hand with a weak pointer finger for each man. "And of course, Dale Bader. Joseph Samuel. And the leader of your little group ... Brody Samuel. Do they all call you 'Silverfish', or will 'Fish' suffice?"

Fish was red in the face again. "How in God's name did you get our names? Tell us before I cut you right now!"

The sickly man winked and smiled. "Lucky told me."

Dale was livid. He didn't have any children, so his horses filled that void. He would not allow anyone to speak about Lucky as if he knew him. Dale walked over to the man and attempted to hit him, but Fish and Rangles pulled him back. Dale was screaming and cursing to let him go, but the older men restrained him.

"Dale, you gotta relax. He might give you some kind of disease."

Dale wasn't having it. "Who the *fuck* does he think he is? How does he know about us? Who told you about Lucky? Who told you?"

Fish tried to reel him back to reality. "Listen to Rangles, man. That boy could get you sick. It's not worth it. Let's be smart."

After a few performative tugs and swipes from their clutches, Dale calmed down. The man in front of them would be gone soon, so there was no need to risk his own life over someone so frail. "Fine. Let's just get this over with."

"Sounds good," Fish said. "Dale, can you take Joseph and Bryan to go find a strong enough branch?" He then nodded toward the sick man, whose skin seemed to have become increasingly more leathery and sore. "Rangles and I can figure a way to get this boy out of here without killing everyone."

Everyone nodded and went to their tasks. While Dale took the younger men to find a branch that would support the man's swinging weight, Fish and Rangles grabbed the blankets out of the burlap sacks and tied them together with twine. They then put on a set of gloves to protect themselves from the sick man as they shifted and rolled his body onto the tied blankets under him. The man winced and moaned in agony as he rolled over each boil, each scratch, each gaping wound that pulled at his exposed skin.

The man spoke again, softly but firmly. "Do you think you're doing something special? That you're doing something righteous?"

Fish responded first. "'Course we do. Anything we can do to rid the world of you people is enough for me."

"Enough for us," Rangles echoed.

The sick man hacked a moist cough through a smirk. "That's funny to me."

Fish loosened his grip, dropping the man to the floor while Rangles held onto his portion of the blankets. "What the hell does that mean, you son of a bitch?"

The man lay on the ground moaning in agony for a few seconds before launching into a full-blown guttural cough, wheezing nearly every other breath. Rangles watched as Fish's cheeks turned visibly maroon—the sick Negro man turning more ashen and purple with each convulsion. Finally, the man got a hold of himself, calming his breathing and allowing his muscles to loosen before he continued. "Silverfish, I know that you think you've had all the answers all your life. When you're the oldest in a house full of children, I can see why you would think so."

Fish responded with a kick to the sick man's ribs and two swift punches to his face. He could feel each of the man's bones shift and crack under his knuckles. Rangles pulled him back before he killed him, tumbling both of them to the ground.

Rangles knew it was true. Fish was, in fact, the eldest of eight children. He adored his father until his passing, inheriting his father's anger against the world along with his own resentment at becoming the "man of the house" at twelve years old. And he did tend to push his will on everyone. Rangles couldn't believe this man could break down his friend of so many years. His mouth was agape as they sorted themselves.

Rangles held his friend tightly. "Come on, man. We need to keep him in one piece for the ceremony."

"Fuck that bastard! I'm gonna kill him now!" Fish continued kicking and tensing his arms to pull away.

Fish almost loosened Rangles's grip before he realized what he had done. His fists contacted some of the man's leaks and fluids, putting his own health and the health of his family and comrades at risk. He remained tense as Rangles tightened his grip, just in case Fish changed his mind.

The man continued his goading through the swelling in his mouth. "It doesn't matter what you do to me. It won't be long before we stop seeing each other in the realm of the living. So do what you will. But mark my words—we're not *all* going to escape alive."

Fish and Rangles chuckled to themselves. First restrained, then hysterically. The sick man had finally come to his senses. They all knew that there was nothing he could do to change his fate. He was too weak to fight them. Either he would die by his sickness or by their hands, but everyone knew his time was short.

After a hearty laugh, Fish and Rangles stood up on their feet and collected themselves before repositioning the blankets to carry the man out of the shed and into the open forest. As they dragged his emaciated, bump-ridden body, they observed their sons and Dale next to a thick tree, tugging against a large branch with a length of rope. They pulled with enough strength to test if it would break under their man's weight. With how much the sick man had wasted away, they were confident that it would do the trick. Once the man's body was finally out of the shed, Bryan went back in to loot any valuables that may have been hidden.

The sick man continued to wince and moan as his body dragged against the ground, the blankets providing little relief from the sharp rocks and splintered wood strewn against the ground. Most of the boils had since burst, oozing into the blanket and dragging across the earth. One larger stone in particular cut the back of his head, leaving a thin trail of blood leading from the doorway. He struggled to stay conscious as the members of the lynch mob discussed how they would go about their ritual. Fish, Rangles, and their sons talked about what scriptures they would recite as Dale prepared the noose. They agreed that they weren't going to do anything fancy, just the standard fare:

Psalm Chapter 23, Verses 1 through 6.

Psalm. Chapter 51. Verses 1 through 4.

First Corinthians. Chapter 15, Verses 24 through 26.

A protracted version of The Lord's Prayer, followed by a quick sprinkle of holy water on the sick man and themselves before he was to be hoisted by his neck.

Joseph wondered why the entire ritual was so important, so necessary for what they came to do. The man was dead anyway, so why spend the time? They were miles from their home, and they were wasting precious time that he could have been spending with his fling for the night. Fish had always stressed that they were the civilized ones, that what separated them from the "human animals" were their traditions and rituals. The savages, as he put it, didn't have what the white man had—they weren't inclined to conquer or build, only to take from others and give it away. Joseph grew up around indoctrination his entire life, but it was only recently that he had been questioning his beliefs. He saw the shiftless, ignorant people in his town practicing every vice in the Good Book. Not more than anyone else, but certainly not less either. He still thought that the others were beneath him, as his father believed, but he started to wonder why they were even risking their eternal souls to prove a point.

He would never tell his father. Fish Samuel was too strong in the town and in Joseph's life. He was too much of a coward to fight against the tide. But he knew that his future wasn't in their small town. It was only a matter of time before he would leave, like his brother did, and remake his life. Joseph still loved and admired his father, but his future was clearly somewhere else. He just needed to get through the rituals, the traditions, the killing and the nonsense, until it was the right moment.

Bryan slapped his friend across the face. Joseph realized he must have zoned out. Bryan knew he was prone to letting his mind float into the clouds, so this was nothing new for him. "Hey man, you alright?"

Joseph moved his jaw, a cursory check to make sure Bryan didn't jostle him too much. "Yeah, man. Sorry, I had a moment."

"No worries, man. Just need to get this monkey ready for the cleansing. He didn't even have anything nice in the shed."

Bryan and Joseph placed the noose loosely around the sick man's neck as Fish produced a dusty, beaten Bible from his overalls. Rangles tied the man's wrists together then did the same to his ankles. Dale stood back, casually peeling an apple and watching the others prepare the man's body. Normally, he would have been responsible for shaving the man's body hair with one of his many blades, but the boils on the skin made him think otherwise.

The man's clothes were completely torn, barely able to keep his appendages and privates covered while many of the boils leaked. Despite the humidity, his skin was even more ashen and his lips and face even crustier than moments before. The wheezing had subsided, but his breathing remained labored. He rolled his eyes toward the older men. "Would you like me to say a little bit about you boys?"

Fish stepped up. "Nope. I don't know how you found out about us, but I stopped caring in the shed. Whatever you heard before we got here, it's no use to us. You'll be gone before we have time to care. And whoever told you, we'll find 'em and do the same thing we're gonna do to you. Except it's gonna be *way* worse." There was a darkness that entered his voice, a streak of vengeance and hatred that floated just under the surface of Fish Samuel's thin layer of Southern respectability. He was showing his true self when it least mattered.

Rangles jumped in. "Boy, I don't know what you were thinking. Trying to make us do something to you before we finished our work. You must have lost your cotton-pickin' mind."

The man coughed heavily, then his eyes rolled completely back in his head, showing only the whites. While the others tried to understand what was happening, the sick man launched into a frenzied oral history of each man.

Dale Bader. Only son to Gene and Evelyn. Bullied as a kid. Couldn't buy a friend to save his life. Only had a few books in the house. Spent his time learning about things on the radio and through whatever person stopped through town. Really good at using tools, small weapons, and taking care of animals.

Jameson Rangles, son of Elijah and Jolene. Oldest of four. A regular life with regular problems. Not much of a looker. Quite fortunate to have the life he has.

Bryan Rangles. Oldest of three. He takes after his father. Not good looking. Not a leader. Just a regular man that needs to be made to feel special by someone much more capable.

Joseph Samuel. Second of three. Loves his father, wants to make him happy, but tired of the life that they live. Hopes to escape one day and find his own path.

It was here that Fish looked at his son with confusion and slight disdain, hoping that what he heard wasn't true.

Brody Samuel. Silverfish. Oldest of seven. Grew up in chaos. Never knew a moment's peace since he was three days old. Father Moe was a drunk, Mother Lorraine was two steps away from going to the asylum.

The man turned to Fish, still with his eyes rolled back, and speaking to him with a raspy and brittle tone.

"Three children died because you were supposed to be watching them. But it wasn't your fault, Fish. You weren't supposed to have that kind of responsibility. You were too young to understand how—"

Before he could complete what he was going to say, Fish kicked the man again in the ribs. "You shut up! You don't know *anything* about that!" He continued kicking swiftly over and over again, flailing his arms and yelling expletives until the others pulled him back. In his rage, Fish felt a couple of ribs crack. He was ready to end the man's life right there.

The sick man coughed and wheezed through the pain, trying to compose himself after the onslaught. Blood was pouring from his mouth and skin, and he nearly fainted from the onslaught. He stayed in the fetal position until the men could restrain Fish. The men of the lynch mob sat in the dirt, wrestling Fish until he relaxed. He stared at his son with confusion and slight contempt, wondering if the sick man was telling the truth. Had his son cared for him so much? Was he really so fed up with living there that he would take the same risks that his older brother took? Those thoughts were pushed away by the near-reveal of the full weight of his own trauma. Fish had accidentally kept a lantern lit when he was younger, a lantern that set ablaze a small pile of hay that engulfed the barn that several of his siblings were sleeping in. Three dead bodies recovered—his siblings—with a friend missing to that day. He knew that he would get a beating from his father if he admitted to the oversight. But he was only eleven years old, he had no business watching over the others. It weighed on him, until he came up with the idea to blame the colored boys in the next town over. His family took care of the situation, and he convinced himself that the incident was resolved.

But how did the sick man know about it? How did *this* filthy, pitiful man in *this* shed in *this* forest outside of town know about them?

Fish Samuel didn't care anymore. None of them did. What thin veneer of respectability existed was gone. The sick man knew too much about them, and bearing witness to them was too great a risk to their cleansing ritual; to their very way of life. The elder Rangles, seeing his friend in distress, did the only thing that he could do to placate him. He grabbed the noose and tightened the knot, hoping to end the ritual early and stop the madness. Bryan and Dale jumped up next to make sure ropes were secured around the extremities. They wanted no mistakes or upheaval, just a quick jerk of the rope and a chance to get home before the sun went down. Fish and Joseph sat still and breathed heavily before they stood. Neither of them looked at the other or acknowledged what had just happened. They merely brushed it off and went to work.

Neck, wrists, ankles. The ropes were finally secured. "You think that's good, Fish?"

Fish looked at the work his friend did. "Not bad, Rangles. I think we can get this one done and be back in time for all of us to fuck our ladies before the moon comes up."

At that moment, their skin went cold and the light began to fade around them. As they looked up, the sky was nearly dark. A golden ring against a black disk appeared over them—a solar eclipse. As the moon completed its position between the sun and the Earth, the rancid odor of goat and sick man disappeared, leaving only cool, crisp air rushing into the forest. Everyone except for Joseph looked directly at the eclipse, drawn to its glory as they held fast while the sun's corona burned their retinas. Bryan was the first to scream out, followed by his father. Dale released a deep and painful moan while falling to his knees. Fish held out as long as he could, but he was unable to pull away, frying his vision as well. Not long after that, Rangles collapsed on the ground, writhing and unable to control his limbs. Bryan and Dale were not far behind, convulsing the same way, kicking leaves and dust into the air while they bled from every opening and howled.

Joseph was frozen in shock. He had never seen such a gruesome scene. He watched as his father succumbed to the burning and the pain, dropping to the ground as the foam around his mouth blended with blood. Fish was surprisingly silent as he twitched and seized, adding even more to Joseph's horror.

He ran to his father to hold him up, foolishly thinking this was going to change his fate. But the damage was done, and Fish continued to seize with little fanfare. This wasn't something that was supposed to happen to them. Suffering happened to others.

He turned around to see the sick man, still shifting on the ground with the noose around his neck. With nothing else to do, Joseph ran to the rope and yanked over and over until it became taut. Then with one quick pull, he would lift the sick man into the air by his neck and it would be over. Whatever was happening to his father and his friends must be tied to that man. He gripped the rope tightly and pulled. He expected resistance but found himself yanking an empty knot. Joseph tumbled into the dirt and slammed into a pile of sticks, scratching his face, neck, and chest. Lifting himself on his elbows, he looked up to see the once sick man looming over him.

No longer riddled with boils and bodily fluids, the man stood straight and healthy. His skin glistened a dark walnut color and his tattered clothes were replaced with a fine blanket—four layers of bright, white cotton draped around his body like a toga. The lining shimmered with silver and gold threaded subtly throughout the fabric. He was still slender, but his muscles were dense and strong. The scraggly hair was gone, trimmed down to the stubble, and his fingernails and toenails sparkled with what appeared to be gold dust.

Joseph was mesmerized. He fell to his knees to bask in the gilded brilliance, overcome by the sudden change from the lowly man that he nearly lynched to something otherworldly. While the others felt the burning, melting sensation of the sun, Joseph tingled as cool air washed over his skin.

He didn't notice that the bodies of his father and their friends continued to shatter and disintegrate, bones breaking and organs rupturing until they were nothing more than gelatinous mush. The man smiled at Joseph, and he smiled back.

"Thank you for finding me, Joseph. You have been useful in cleansing the world further."

As his mouth agape with a silly grin, Joseph could utter only a single question. "Who are you?"

The gilded man simply replied, "I am."

As the moon finally shifted away and the eclipse ended, Joseph blinked, overwhelmed with the glory before him. When he opened his eyes, the man was gone.

As quickly as the man disappeared, Joseph's senses flooded back. He spun around to see only piles of flesh and bone remaining, muscles still twitching uncontrollably in places from what was left of their nervous systems. He ran to his father's remains and shouted for him to wake, but his face was caved in. There was no saving him or any of the others. With no other options, Joseph grabbed one of the shotguns and a hatchet and ran back up the hill to the car. After several minutes, he finally made it back to the road, where Lucky patiently waited for the group to come back. Joseph opened the car door and grabbed the saddle, secured it onto a confused but calm Lucky, unhitched the horse, then rode back to town as fast as he could. Lucky was hesitant at first, but he instinctively knew something was wrong. Twenty-one minutes later, they were back to Joseph's house, arriving before the sun went down. He tied Lucky to a post and ran inside the house frantically.

"Mom! Eva! Help!" he yelled over and over. But his mother was seated in the living room with Eva's head buried in her lap. Both were sobbing. "Mom, what's going on?"

Claire looked at her son. "Joseph?" She then reached out and dangled a paper note from her trembling fingertips.

He snatched the paper out of his mother's hand and unfolded it. He only had to read the few words that stuck out.

'Regret to inform ... Jacob Samuel ... unfortunate accident ...'

Jacob Samuel. Eldest son of Brody and Claire Samuel. Dead.

Joseph's hand shook as he gripped the paper. He fell to his knees for the second time that day. Held back tears for the second time that day. He knew that he needed the strength to tell his mother and sister that they not only lost a son and brother, but also a husband and father.

On that day—April 7, 1940—the stories of Dale Bader, Jameson Rangles, Bryan Rangles, Jacob Samuel, and Brody "Silverfish" Samuel came to an end. Their deaths were as gruesome as their lives were petty and meaningless. For those that survived them, especially Joseph, there was a chance at salvation. They only needed to have the courage to take the next step or meet the same fate.

Whichever path they would choose, one way or another, they hoped to be cleansed.

Besu Tadesse

An author based in Maryland, Besu Tadesse loves to write horror and speculative fiction. He has published two books – The Ghosts of Poplar Valley, a paranormal horror novella about our history's echoes into the present, and Broken Persons, a short story collection that deal with broad themes of grief, trauma, and speculation on the future. His short stories have been included in the horror anthologies, Devour the Rich!, Arsenic and Grandma's Refrigerator – Horror Told in Colours, and Dark and Dreary – A Basement Horror Anthology, as well as the upcoming anthology With Teeth and others. He also works as a gaming writer and reviewer for Uncomfortably Dark. Besu is working on his first full-length novel. You can find him on all social media platforms under the handle @stickybearartist.

1950s

CRIES THAT ECHO STILL

Zach Lamb

The first time Carolyn heard the baby cry wasn't at the bridge. It was Sunday morning in church, as her father riled up the congregation with that morning's hellfire; he saved the brimstone for Sunday nights. She sat against the bathroom wall in the downstairs Fellowship Hall, deciding what to do. Her father's voice boomed through the air vent above her head. She focused on the peeling wallpaper. The coral hibiscus and pastel blue paper had been hung that spring to liven the place up, but the curled edges already matched the rest of the building. The guaranteed damnation of the sinner rained down, followed by a raucous chorus of amens from the crowd sitting on warped pews.

Carolyn had known she was pregnant, but not how far along. The town hadn't been the only ones fooled by the baggy clothes, apparently.

Stomach cramps had started the previous night. She'd thought she'd been hungry. When a widening bloom of moisture and pain spread across her lap, she realized her mistake. She slid from the wooden pew, where she sat with the rest of the teenagers in the back of the sanctuary. The emotion in her father's voice rose as she pushed through the sanctuary door. She'd have to deal with that later, but she had larger issues.

She thought she'd be able to pass off discovering the child on the church steps, abandoned by a mother who couldn't care for it. But now, sitting in the bathroom alone, staring at the unmoving child, she knew that wouldn't be possible. She crept to the kitchen in the empty Fellowship Hall and took two white tablecloths from the cupboard. She placed the child in the center of one and used the second to clean up the blood and remaining evidence. Blood smeared on bright white tiles and left an ugly brown swirl. She'd have to mop it up later and hoped nobody noticed until she had time to clean it. When she finished, she placed the ruined tablecloth on the child and wrapped the other around everything and bound it.

On the way to the back door, she stopped at her father's office. Pain radiated through her lower body, and she ran a hand over the cross that adorned the door and prayed a sinner's prayer of forgiveness for what she'd done and what she was about to do. Her final request was to lessen her pain. She didn't ask for it to be taken away because she didn't believe she deserved complete forgiveness, only that she wasn't left with more than she could bear.

It had rained earlier and would continue that afternoon and help with what she had to do. She crossed the green grass to the graveyard. Her insides bounced and felt like they would drop from her body and spread over the ground, leaving her to bleed to death. She clutched the tablecloth to her stomach and lowered her head. She continued to the back of the graveyard and stepped into the wooded area that worked as a barrier between the consecrated and the wild.

Her father would never allow the burial of an unbaptized child out of wedlock, but she didn't believe anybody should be left out. Especially if it hadn't been their fault. Now that her plans had been changed, she wondered if it would have been better if she'd gone into town and had it taken care of by one of those back alley doctors her father always railed against. She didn't even know if they existed or if they were just part of her father's rhetoric.

Carolyn wiped the tears from her eyes, ducked into the forest and laid the bundle behind a tree. She would come back later and give her a proper burial where it was least likely to be noticed, but still hallowed. She had to hurry. It had already been too long since she'd left. She said one more prayer and turned. Movement from the corner of her eye got her attention, and the breath caught in her throat. Had it moved? That couldn't be possible, could it? She didn't have time. There would already be questions about where she'd gone. Carolyn turned and fled the forest.

She eased the door to the sanctuary open. Not a single head turned, but her father made eye contact and held it without skipping a beat.

"Some of you are going to bust hell wide open when you get there."

Carolyn faltered as she made her way back to her seat. He always seemed to know what she was up to. She couldn't get away with anything. Beads of sweat ran down her face, and she wiped her clammy hands on her dress as she moved down the aisle. Fire burned through her lower body, and she prayed the extra pad and wads of toilet paper wouldn't leak or that she would not pass out from the pain. Agnis gave her a worried look punctuated with widened eyes. Agnis didn't know about her pregnancy; nobody did, but she knew how Carolyn's father would react to her going MIA in the middle of his sermon. Carolyn gave her a subtle shake of her head and sat down gently on the knotty pew, twisted from water damage when the river flooded its banks in '53.

It had been four years, and they'd only repaired the lower level. They had the money to fix the pews, but her father said he wanted to keep the sanctuary original to maintain spiritual continuity with the past. Carolyn believed he kept them so parishioners wouldn't fall asleep in the middle of service.

Carolyn tried to drown out her father's words with her thoughts before he made her feel horrible and she ended up confessing her sins at the altar for all to hear. She drew her focus to the backdrop behind him. The kids' Sunday school class would put on their seasonal play that night. A large hand-painted sheet depicting Noah's Ark hung behind him, but off-centered enough to look like the great ship would be scuttled on the piano.

Carolyn remained lost in thought until a cold hand slithered up her arm. She jumped to her feet; hands pointed to the sky. A sharp laugh rang out from her best friend Lottie, followed by a chorus of laughter from the other girls.

"Why are you so jumpy? Looks like the holy ghost got into you," Lottie said.

Carolyn looked at the empty pulpit and then at the lines of parishioners as they filed out of the sanctuary. They'd all shake her father's hand one by one and head to their regular Sunday lunch gathering places.

"That's not funny," she said. "I was lost in thought."

"Reciting scripture, I'm sure."

Carolyn rolled her eyes and followed the rest of the girls outside. It irritated her that even her best friend treated her like the goody two shoes preacher's daughter. If Lottie only knew, she'd find another target. She might not even want to be friends anymore.

Carolyn pushed past her friend and went to wait for her father at his car. She hated the Dodge Coronet. It shuddered when her father shifted the three-speed transmission. At first, she thought it had been his driving, but after he let her drive it down an old dirt road last month, she realized it was the car. The paint was already faded to a dull black when it had been donated to the church in '55 by a traveling salesman "getting out of the game," as he explained it. Carolyn thought it was more like he didn't know how to play the game. That had been two years ago, and they'd never seen the man again.

Her father didn't speak as he approached. He gave her a stern look, then opened the door and slid behind the wheel. She moved to apologize, but he slammed the door before any words escaped her mouth. She climbed into the backseat. She would ride up front with him, but when she knew she'd upset him, it was better to ride in the back of the sedan. It gave her enough distance that his wrath would be weakened by his yelling toward the windshield, and he could only stare at her with his hateful eyes for short bursts in the rearview mirror. They drove to Melanie's Diner in silence. The grinding of her father's shifting the only sound.

Carolyn stepped into the diner and walked straight to their booth while her father moved slower, shaking every outstretched hand as he passed. This ritual bothered her because he'd already shaken most of these same hands less than thirty minutes prior. They ate at Melanie's for lunch every Sunday. The food wasn't anything special compared to the other local diners. Her father would never admit it, but they always went there because they always held a booth for them no matter how busy the place happened to be, and they hadn't paid for their meal once. Carolyn wasn't sure if the diner footed the bill or if a different parishioner paid each week. They'd always keep up appearances by approaching the register after each meal only to be waved off. Her father would give a slight nod to the diner staff, then a nod and tip of his hat to the rest of the customers, and they'd leave. When they got in the car, he'd always say he hoped they weren't trying to buy their salvation, though he never refused the charity.

All hands shook, her father joined her at the table. A waitress brought over their drinks. A glass of water for him and a Coke with an extra pump of cherry flavoring for her.

"Mama's meatloaf and a cheeseburger, only mustard and a side of fries will be up shortly," the waitress said.

They didn't have to order their own food either. Everybody already knew their order. Carolyn fidgeted with her hands while her father stared at something above her head. She didn't know how to approach the subject, but she needed to go out tonight for the burial. Her dry lips parted, and she prepared to speak when he interrupted.

"Where did you go?"

"I … uh … I wasn't feeling well and went to the restroom."

He stared into her eyes.

"Don't you lie to me, girl. I won't stand for it. You will honor your father."

She looked around the room searching for the words or some semblance of help.

"Look at me when I'm talking to you. If you're going to lie, you can do it to my face."

"I'm not lying. I promise. It must have been something I ate. I got sick in the sanctuary and left before I vomited. I didn't make it all the way to the restroom and had to clean up. I swear."

"Don't you swear to me. I'm glad you had sense enough to clean up and not leave it for somebody else. Are you sure a greasy cheeseburger is what you should be eating right now?"

"I'm sorry. I'm feeling much better now."

The waitress sat their food on the table and made herself scarce. She was a nice woman and attentive waitress, but she'd learned it was best not to hang around too long.

Carolyn squeezed ketchup onto her plate and stirred it with a fry. A group of teenagers sat in the booth behind her father. His top lip twitched as the group spoke loudly. Even when one calmed them down, they were above the preacher's desired level, which rivaled a library. He gripped his fork tight enough for his knuckles to go white. Carolyn didn't recognize the teenagers, but jumped in before he turned around and embarrassed them and her.

"I know it's last minute, but can I stay at Lottie's tonight? We have a school project that we need to finish."

"Why is this the first I'm hearing about this project?" he said.

The lie had slipped from her mouth before she'd had time to think it through. She cleared her throat before speaking again.

"We've been working on it and didn't realize the due date was tomorrow. We thought we had more time."

Not telling him the truth terrified her. It was wrong, and she felt bad about it, but she was also afraid of what he would do if he ever found out. She didn't know any other way. He wouldn't let her go out long enough on a school night for her to take care of her situation, and even if he did, she couldn't come back covered in dirt.

"I suppose I can't say no when it comes to your schooling. But you better not let me find out that you two were out gallivanting around town. Especially with any boys."

She relaxed because he'd gone along with it, but only a little. There was still enough malice in his words that she thought somebody overhearing their conversation would believe he was disciplining her.

"Thank you. We won't be doing any of that."

They continued to eat in silence. Carolyn went over the plan in her head when the teenager's conversation floated over to their table.

"I can't believe ya'll went to Crybaby Bridge. I would never," one girl said.

"Yeah, Darline would rather be playing a little backseat bingo," a guy added with an exaggerated laugh.

A loud smack rang out.

"Cut the gas, Mike," a deeper voice said.

Whoever said that had to be the group's leader because they all shut up until one meek voice spoke.

"What's Crybaby Bridge?"

"What kind of square hasn't heard of Crybaby Bridge?"

"Mike! Come on, man, cut it out," the deep voice roared again.

Carolyn saw her father wince and hoped he wouldn't turn around or want to leave. She'd never heard the story before.

"Anyway, the story goes that the bridge is haunted. This doll, she was in confinement, and hid it from everybody. She couldn't tell her family because they would send her away, so she went to the bridge and dropped the baby over the side."

Carolyn's breath caught in her throat, and she felt her face growing red as blood rushed to it. She hoped her father didn't notice.

"Blasphemy," her father said.

His eyes shot in her direction, and she didn't release the breath until he shook his head and looked away. The story the boy told was horrible for the baby and the mother, who thought that had been her only choice.

"That's so sad," Darlene said.

"Yeah, it gets better. The girl couldn't take the guilt, or whatever, and she hanged herself off the bridge. When you go out there at night, you can hear the baby crying and the girl moaning while she searches for it."

"Did you guys hear anything?"

The clank of her father's fork against his plate caused the entire restaurant to stop. Nobody said anything. The minister stood, wiped his mouth and dropped the napkin on his plate.

"We're going," he said to Carolyn.

She wasn't finished with her lunch, but knew better than to protest. He didn't look at anyone as he walked to the front of the diner. Carolyn ran to catch up and slowed when she thought he would stop at the register. But he didn't stop. He continued through the door without putting on any airs that he would need to pay for their meal.

When they climbed into the car, Carolyn eased herself into the front seat. Aftershocks of pain spread through her body as she sat. Neither of them spoke. Carolyn, because she feared what he would say, and her father, because he was mad. The silence continued as they started down the road.

After a few minutes, her father asked, "Did you know those kids?"

"No, Daddy."

"Good. You wouldn't anymore if you had. Nothing they said was true, and they shame their families talking like that in public. They shouldn't be telling those stories in their homes either. Murder and suicide are not sins that should be talked about. If the stories were true, that young lady would be in hell for eternity. That's nothing to be celebrated."

Carolyn didn't think they were celebrating anything. There were just stories kids told to have something to do. They weren't a big deal, but there was no way she'd ever say that to her father. A chill ran through her body at the thought. Carolyn watched out the window as they drove past their house and went back to the church. Her father got out of the car and went straight to his office, locking himself inside.

Carolyn lay on the back pew in the sanctuary, watching the sun filter through the stained-glass. She thought about sneaking out to the graveyard, but couldn't risk him taking a break and coming to look for her. Instead, she stayed on the pew, going over her plan with her hands clasped to her lava churning gut. As she plotted, thoughts of the unwed mother, feeling like she had no other choice but to drown her child and then hang herself, took over. She thought about the similarities in her own situation and shuddered at the thought of slipping a rope around her neck. She would never risk eternal damnation, she told herself over and over until she drifted off to a fitful sleep.

She awoke with a start, throwing her hands on the back of the pew. Her bent legs shot out in front of her. A chorus of laughter erupted, and she turned to find Lottie and the back row girls waiting to sit for Sunday night service. Her body ached as she sat up and wiped the sweat from her face. The girls continued to giggle as they found their seats.

Her father's sermon, aided by the scene at lunch, continued with the same hellfire gusto he'd had that morning. Now, armed with anger, he railed against the fornicator and all their actions to cover their sins. Carolyn knew the story about Crybaby Bridge had sparked this sermon, but she couldn't help but feel like he was up there calling her out. She slid down in the pew, thinking about the girl on the bridge. Carolyn prayed for both of their souls. They were victims of the harsh world created by people like her father. Surely, that would be taken into account, and God would not throw the unwed mother in hell?

Carolyn filed out of the church with the rest of the congregants. She walked stiffly down the steps and hugged her father goodbye.

He leaned down and whispered in her ear, "I hope you're doing the right thing tonight. I'll see you tomorrow after school."

"I am," she said. "See you tomorrow."

She walked to the side of the church, made sure nobody had followed or seen her, then slipped into the groundskeeper's shed. It took her only a moment to find the shovel. Could she go through with this? What would she say if she got caught? There was no time to think about the consequences. She had to act.

The graveyard was silent and dark. She hurried through the grounds. A sharp, grating racket pierced the night air, and she froze in terror. She looked around to see she had hit a gravestone with the shovel blade. Her heart continued to race as she waited to see if anybody came to investigate the noise. A few voices carried from the parking lot, but didn't seem to be headed her way, and she continued.

When she reached the back of the cemetery, she could barely see anything. She dug the hole before retrieving the tablecloths from the woods, that way she could come up with some excuse for what she was doing if somebody caught her, though she had no idea what that would be, and prayed it wouldn't come to that. She slammed the shovel blade into the ground.

The dirt was easy to shovel, but her arms throbbed and matched the burning she felt below. After forty-five minutes, she stopped and headed for the woods. Lightning strikes of pain shot through her rubber arms as she made her way to the hidden tablecloths. Her body protested further exertion, but she knew she wouldn't want to start up again if she didn't continue.

The wrapped tablecloth was where she'd left it. Her body shuddered, and she gently picked up the tablecloths by the knot, then cradled the weight against her as she made her way back to the hole.

Tears ran from her eyes as she laid her baby to rest. She looked to the sky and prayed.

"Please, Lord, take my baby. She is innocent of her mother's sin and never asked for any of this. I know I have no right to ask, but please let her know why I can't join her, if that is your judgement when my time comes."

Tremors of grief shook her body as she gathered the first shovelful of dirt. The thick material had shifted so one tiny eye and nose poked out. She fell to her knees and reached for the baby. Her fingers hovered inches from the face when the eyes blinked. The scream building inside her chest couldn't be held any longer and echoed through the forest. She covered her mouth and searched the empty graveyard.

Confident she was still alone, Carolyn reached into the hole again, but there was no movement this time. She decided her tired mind had been playing tricks, and she stood again. Taking the shovel, she thrust it into the mound of dirt and tossed it over the baby's face before she *saw* anything else.

The back door creaked as she let herself into the church. All she wanted to do was lie down and sleep away the exhaustion and pain. As she walked down the darkened hallway, she knew she couldn't go home tonight, but she didn't want to stay here either. The church had always been a warm, welcoming place, and now, being alone in the dark after what she'd done, she didn't want to be here either.

She went to her father's office and dialed the phone. Lottie picked up on the third ring.

"Hello."

"Hey, Lottie. It's Carolyn."

"Hey. What are you up to?"

Carolyn paused. Lottie was her best friend, but she wasn't sure going to her house was the best decision. It's where she told her father she'd be, and it would be the safest place if he decided to verify her whereabouts, which he'd never done before. She'd never given him a reason not to trust her.

"Nothing. I was just bored and wanted to see if maybe I could stay with you tonight?"

"Yeah, let me ask my folks," Lottie said and banged the phone down. She returned a few minutes later and said, "Okay, everything is fine with them. It didn't even take convincing. I think they like you more than me sometimes."

"If they only knew," Carolyn said.

Lottie laughed so loud Carolyn had to pull the phone from her ear.

"That's a good one. I'll swing by your house in a few."

"No, wait. I'm not there."

"Ahh, maybe you do have some secrets. Where are you?"

"The church."

"Never mind. You're their favorite daughter again. See you in a minute."

Carolyn hung up the phone and went to the front of the church. She hoped nobody would drive by and see her and Lottie, and wished she'd told her somewhere down the street. After a few minutes of hiding in the shadows, a car approached and turned into the parking lot.

Her mouth dropped. Lottie was driving her father's brand-new red Corvette with the top down. He'd been the talk of the church since he'd driven off the lot. They weren't a rich family. However, Lottie's mother had gone back to teaching because she wanted something to do, and they had more disposable income. Carolyn's father thought it was a prideful waste, but didn't hold it against them and still let her be friends with Lottie. When somebody asked him what he thought about it, his reply had been, "Who am I to judge the frivolous nature of man?" as he removed his black robe.

Lottie pulled up and yelled, "Let's go. I gotta have this back in two hours."

"I can't believe your dad let you drive his car," Carolyn said.

"This is the second time. You didn't sound right on the phone, and I thought you could do with some cruising with the top down to clear your mind, if you didn't want to talk about it."

Carolyn stomped her feet on the concrete to knock any loose dirt from her shoes and slid into the comfortable seat. She wished she'd known Lottie was bringing her dad's car so she could have changed clothes or something. She hoped her dirty clothes wouldn't hurt anything. There was no time to reconsider because Lottie hit the gas and they left the parking lot.

After a few minutes of silence, Lottie spoke.

"So, is everything okay with you? I love having you over, but it's not like you to call out of the blue like this. Did you and your dad get into it?"

Carolyn didn't know how much she should tell Lottie. She trusted her more than anybody, but didn't want to involve her.

"I'm fine. Just been down lately and needed a friend."

Lottie smiled, though Carolyn didn't know if her friend believed her.

"Well, here I am. After your dad's sermon tonight, I was worried. He's always intense, but that felt like a Sunday morning sinner purge. After finding you asleep in the sanctuary, I was going to ask, but you disappeared after service."

"Sorry about that. It wasn't nothin' I did. We went to lunch, and some teenagers started talking about Crybaby Bridge, and he stormed out and wrote that sermon."

The sudden deceleration from Lottie removing her foot from the gas pedal jerked Carolyn forward.

"What's wrong?" she asked.

Lottie looked over at her and pushed the accelerator again.

"What were they saying?"

"You've heard of it?"

Lottie raised an eyebrow and alternated between watching Carolyn and the road.

"You're kidding, right?"

"No."

"I thought everybody had heard about Crybaby Bridge."

Carolyn sat back in her seat. Of course, she'd be one of the few who had never heard about it.

"Guess I'm not into the local legends. They were saying an unwed mother threw her baby from the bridge and then hanged herself. And if you go out there, you can hear the baby and mother crying."

"Seriously? That didn't happen."

Carolyn's tense body relaxed. She knew the story couldn't be true, but it felt better to hear somebody else say it.

"I didn't think so."

"No. What really happened is a farmer's wife got pregnant. They already had seven kids they couldn't afford, so the wife drowned the baby in the river. The mother was so overcome with grief she threw herself from the bridge. If you stop on the bridge at night, you can hear the baby crying and sometimes hear the mother searching for her lost child."

Her body went rigid again. She'd hoped there hadn't been a story. The one Lottie told her was just as sad as the other. She wasn't sure which one was true, but the first one from the boy in the diner felt more realistic.

"It doesn't matter which story is real, if either is. It's horrible that people were in a position where that had been the only way to solve their problems."

"Hey! I got an idea. Let's go to the bridge right now."

"No, we don't need to do that."

Carolyn didn't know what to do. There's no way she wanted to go to the bridge at night. She didn't completely believe either story, but she didn't want to find out that one of them was actually true.

Lottie slowed down, completed a three point turn and headed in the opposite direction. Carolyn knew there was no stopping her once she got an idea in her head. She was along for the ride now, whether she liked it or not.

Fifteen minutes later, Lottie stopped the car with the bridge barely visible in the early evening. Riding in the convertible had been nice with the breeze, but now that they were no longer moving, the heat hit her again.

Carolyn squinted to make out the dark, covered bridge. Aided by the night, the bottom seemed to sag toward the rippling water below. Carolyn's chest grew tight.

"There it is," Lottie said. "Not much to it, is there?"

Carolyn shook her head but didn't agree.

The car rolled forward, and Carolyn's mouth went dry. A choir of cicadas sang, drawing them toward the bridge like sirens leading a ship to its doom. Lottie let off the gas and let the car coast to a stop. The headlights cut through the darkened maw, illuminating the first half of the bridge. Three open windows on either side of the structure let in greying light from outside.

Carolyn stared up at the dark husk above her head. It looked like the pointed mouth of a bird of prey, preparing to chomp down on the car. She dug her fingers into the armrest as the car rolled forward.

A loud burst of static erupted from the radio. Both girls screamed and covered their ears. The static dropped in pitch, then rose again as if a ghostly hand rolled the radio dial. Carolyn reached for the radio, and the static cleared. Buddy Holly's voice belted out his new single "That'll be the Day." The sudden change caused her to cry out and yank her hand back from the radio. Lottie reached over and turned the radio off. Cricket song pierced the deafening silence that followed.

"Maybe this was a bad idea," Carolyn said.

"Maybe. But we're already here, and going forward is the fastest way back to my house."

Carolyn didn't like Lottie's response, but she was right, and they needed to get to Lottie's house.

"Okay, but drive across as fast as you can."

"Sure," Lottie said and laughed.

Carolyn closed her eyes as they crossed the bridge and hoped that would make it seem faster. There was a slight bump when the tires rolled onto the bridge, and she clinched her eyes tighter. After what seemed like only a few seconds, the car stopped. Carolyn didn't open her eyes. They couldn't already be on the other side of the bridge.

"I never wanted to do this."

"Do what?" Carolyn asked and opened her eyes.

Darkness surrounded her. Carolyn looked around frantically for any shape she could recognize. Until she saw gray mist float softly in the moonlight through one of the propped-open windows. They were still on the bridge. A cold hand grasped her elbow, and Carolyn screamed. The echoes reverberated down the length of the bridge, then came back to them like it had bounced off a wall, blocking their exit.

"Hey. Hey! Calm down. Everything's okay. You're okay!" Lottie yelled.

"Then why aren't we on the other side of the bridge!"

"Because I stopped in the middle. We're already out here, so we might as well see if the stories are true. The only thing I've heard so far is you freaking out though."

Carolyn had never struck out at anybody in her life, but she felt the urge to punch her friend. She was tiring of her excuse for all her actions being *"we're already here, so we might as well do it."* That didn't make any sense. That horrible advice had been the reason Carolyn ended up in the Fellowship Hall bathroom this morning. It felt so long ago now.

"Relax. And what did you mean when you said, 'Do what?'"

Carolyn took a deep breath.

"It sounded like you said, 'I never wanted to do this,' or something like that."

"I didn't say anything."

"But I heard some—"

The wail of a baby cut her off. It sounded like it had come from below the bridge. From the water. A chill cruised through her upper body, crossing the knotted bridge of her spine and rolling down to her toes.

"Oh, hell. Did you hear that? Come on, let's see if we can see anything," Lottie said and opened the door.

Before she could step out, the baby cried again. This time it sounded like it was coming from the trunk of the car.

"Lottie, let's go. I'm scared."

"Me too," Lottie said and then pulled the knob to turn on the headlights.

Light flooded the bridge except for a dark blob in front of the car. The sudden illumination made everything blurry. Carolyn rubbed her eyes to help them focus. She wasn't sure if it helped or only made them water more. She fought the brightness, and a waterlogged voice spoke.

"I never wanted to do this. I need my baby. Give her to me."

The baby continued its muffled wail, and the shadow before them dropped its veil, revealing a beautiful young woman. That's not what Carolyn had expected, and her body relaxed. Another cry from the trunk caused the woman to move toward the car.

"I said give me my baby," the woman yelled. Her soft features turned hard as she stared at the car. Black goo poured from her hairline, covering her face. The once-straight nose cracked and bent with a sharp crook. Bags formed below her eyes, and age lines marred the once smooth face. The crone lurched toward the driver's side of the car and dragged her long fingernails across the paint, screeching to bare metal like they'd been scratched across a chalkboard.

Carolyn tensed and shuddered through the noise and covered her ears again. The damage to the car upset Lottie more, and she didn't take the time to protect her ears. She put the car in gear and sped to the end of the bridge, where a blanket of darkness greeted them.

A baby screamed and dragged her from unconsciousness. She tried to look around to get her bearings, but saw only darkness. Carolyn put her hands on the ground to push herself up, and as soon as skin met wood, she knew she'd somehow ended up back on the bridge.

Alone.

Her head swam as baby cries bounced in her mind and down the covered bridge walls. The swirling effect gave her vertigo, and she bent over and puked.

She stood and wiped her mouth with the back of her hand. She had to find Lottie, but didn't know which way to go. There didn't seem to be an exit at either end of the bridge. After a few minutes, she moved in the direction she happened to be facing.

A woman stood at the window. The woman didn't make any indication that she knew Carolyn was on the bridge with her. She wore a black dress and petticoat from the antebellum time period. A dirty white bonnet covered her dark hair. The woman let out a ghostly wail, and Carolyn's arms broke out in gooseflesh.

"I don't want this. But what am I to do, Lord? We can't feed another mouth, and my husband has commanded that I get rid of this one."

The woman cried out to an apathetic Old Testament God, and Carolyn thought of her father and his sermons. Her heart went out to the girl, and she approached loud enough not to startle the mother.

The woman turned to face Carolyn and asked, "What?"

"I didn't say anything," Carolyn said.

"I'll be there directly. Please give me more time," the woman said.

She wasn't talking to Carolyn, but there wasn't anybody else on the dark bridge with them. At least nobody that Carolyn could see.

The woman continued to look in Carolyn's direction without seeing her. Tears rolled down her face, cutting streaks through the dirt on her pretty face. She wiped the tears from her face, and Carolyn recognized the woman.

It was Lottie.

Carolyn moved toward Lottie and her friend flinched.

"I hear you. Let me alone. I'll do it on my own time!" she yelled, agitated with somebody who Carolyn could only guess to be her husband.

The woman turned back to the window and raised the bundle in her arms.

"No! Lottie, don't do it," Carolyn yelled and ran to stop her.

Her heart thudded in her chest as she ran. She reached out to stop the woman, but her hands went through the woman's body and she fell. Carolyn landed on the hard surface and turned in time to see the woman push the bundle out the window. The baby didn't make a sound until it splashed into the water below. The woman cried into her hands, then turned away from Carolyn and screamed into the void.

"There! Are you happy now! I've killed our baby. Look what you made me do."

The woman went back to the window and hefted herself onto the sill. She pulled the bonnet from her head and let it fall to the ground.

Carolyn jumped to her feet. She didn't know how to reach Lottie. Her hands went through her body when she tried to touch her, and she couldn't hear anything Carolyn said. She moved toward the window and Lottie pushed herself off.

When she splashed into the water, the darkness spun and a chorus of babies wailed in a cacophony of agony. Cries rained down on her, swirling in a tidal wave of anguish. Everything went black.

Carolyn awoke to a baby and young mother crying. She sat up and moved to the same window Lottie had jumped from. A girl, small in stature, stood at the window, trying to hush the baby to no avail. The girl looked in her direction, and Carolyn realized she was staring at herself wearing a dress her father would never approve of. Blood ran down between her legs and pooled in her soaked socks.

"Please. You have to be quiet. Somebody will hear. I don't know what to do," the girl said.

A swelling of guilt built in the pit of Carolyn's stomach. The poor girl was all alone. If she was like Carolyn, she didn't have a mother to teach her how to handle a child and had an overbearing father who would never understand mistakes that his daughter made. She thought of reaching out or attempting to speak to the girl, but knew it would be futile. The woman resembling Lottie hadn't heard a thing before she jumped, and Carolyn's hand had passed straight through her. Instead, Carolyn thought about the look on her own baby's face as she covered it with dirt in that shallow grave. The baby's blank eyes pleaded with her, but neither dared to make a sound.

Sobs wracked both girls' bodies, and they fell to their knees. Carolyn watched the other girl through blurry eyes. What could she do? What could either of them do? If they had come clean, they would've been sent away from everything they ever knew. None of the girls who Carolyn knew that had been sent away had ever returned. Why should they both be damned? Why should any of them?

"I don't know what to do! I can't think straight," the girl screamed in defiance of the blank wall in front of her. She staggered to her feet and moved toward the open window and before Carolyn realized what she was doing, the girl dropped the baby into the rushing water.

"No!" both girls screamed in unison.

The girl looked over the side of the bridge. Sobs ravaged her body so hard that Carolyn thought the girl was having a seizure. Her small voice floated through the closed in space, creating no echoes.

"I'm sorry. I didn't know what else to do. None of this is fair. You didn't deserve this."

Carolyn tried to hug the girl even though she knew it wouldn't work. It made her feel a little better that she at least tried. Her arms cut through her like a cloud of mist.

The girl walked off into the darkness. Carolyn couldn't see her any longer, but she heard her crying and whispering to herself. After a few minutes a thump startled her and the girl's murmurs headed back to the window, dragging something.

Carolyn rubbed her cold arms. She didn't know what to do. Nothing but darkness surrounded her. All exits were closed. The last time everything changed on its own, but that only happened after the girl … jumped from the bridge.

The girl reappeared, dragging a rope the diameter of a finger. She tied the rope around a support beam and threw a loop around her neck, not giving herself time to second guess, she climbed on the windowsill and sat with her feet dangling out. She turned and locked eyes with Carolyn.

"I'm sorry," she said, and then pushed out the window.

Carolyn heard the girl's neck break like a tree branch caught in a tumultuous storm. The sound traveled through her entire body, leaving her spent and woozy. She crept to the window and thought about looking over when she noticed the bonnet left on the ground from the girl who looked like Lottie. She bent down to pick it up when a shrieking wail came from the darkness. Her mind went blank as electric waves of fear flooded her body and her hand trembled with each new surge.

She peered into the darkness and a wavy white figure materialized. It was the waterlogged woman they had first seen when the baby was in the trunk. Dark water poured from her sleeves and slip, creating a puddle at her feet that gave the appearance of her walking on water.

"I found my baby. Your friend had her the whole time. You didn't believe me!" the woman yelled, holding a soaked bundle to her chest.

Carolyn gasped as the lady's spectral face came into view.

"It wasn't us. I promise. Where's Lottie?"

The woman laughed.

"I took care of her. There's no need to worry about her anymore."

Panic gripped Carolyn's chest so tight she felt like her heart would explode.

"No!"

The woman nodded and walked toward her.

"I did. But I'm going to give you a chance your friend didn't allow me to offer."

Carolyn furrowed her brows. What chance was she talking about? The woman approached her and extended her arms, presenting the bundle to Carolyn.

"Here. You take this baby and care for her like none of the others would."

The woman beckoned Carolyn with a crooked finger. Carolyn was confused. She didn't trust the woman, but this might be the only way for her to get off the bridge alive. The blanket rocked in the outstretched hand.

Carolyn hesitated, but took the bundle and brought it to her own chest. A cry emanated from the blanket and she tried to soothe the child. The crying grew louder and Carolyn sensed something was wrong. She pulled at the fabric where the child's head should be and found nothing.

The woman unleashed a loud cackle and jerked the blanket back. Carolyn moved to catch the falling child, but there was nothing there. The woman laughed louder.

"You already know what it's like to lose one. Did you really think I'd give you another? It's all your fault it's dead. You did it. You and your kind deserve to carry the burden of shame."

The woman screamed. Dust fell from the rafters above.

"You will know what it's like to live with that shame. You don't get to hide. They will all know what you are, and what you did."

Carolyn didn't know what the woman was talking about. She'd felt shame. The only thing she hid was the proof.

The woman lunged at Carolyn and caught her by the arm. She tried to pull away, but the woman possessed supernatural strength.

"You won't get rid of this baby," the woman said.

The pressure on her arm stung. The woman ripped her own dress down the middle, exposing a pale baby bump. She drove one long fingernail into the clammy skin below her sternum and sliced down to her waist. Black blood oozed from the wound and landed on the ground in clotted splats. She drove her hand inside the wound and screeched so loud Carolyn though her ears would bleed. Blood poured from the slit and the woman pulled her hand out and lifted Carolyn's dress.

Carolyn tried to fight the woman off, but she released her arm and grabbed Carolyn by the throat, cutting off her air supply and will to fight. She lifted Carolyn's dress above her waist. Carolyn couldn't see, but a searing, hot pain erupted from her belly. Blood ran down her legs and she went lightheaded. She shook her head to keep from passing out. The thought crossed her mind that it might be better if she went to sleep and didn't wake up.

The woman squeezed her throat and forced her head down so she had to watch. She reached back into her own belly and pulled out a half-formed child. A baby cried in the distance because this one could not cry for itself. She held the child upside down by its feet so Carolyn could see. Its skin was a translucent pink, covering a network of blue veins.

The woman lowered the child and Carolyn's abdomen erupted in flames again. Before she passed out, she understood what the woman had done. She'd put the baby inside Carolyn so she'd have to follow through this time.

Neither Lottie nor the car were at the bridge when she woke. It was still dark when she walked back to town and as she reached the old filling station, the sun had already started its ascent. She dropped a dime in the payphone and spun Lottie's number on the rotary dial. A groggy voice answered on the fourth ring.

"Hello?"

"Yes. May I speak with Lottie, please?"

After a few moments the voice on the other end responded.

"There's nobody by that name here. Never has been."

She must have dialed the wrong number, she told herself.

"I'm so sorry," she said and hung up before they responded.

She searched the ground and prayed that she'd find some lost change. A joyous cry escaped her mouth as she bent down to pick up a dime lying in the grass. She slipped it in the slot and dialed Lottie's house again. Two rings later, the same voice answered. This time she hung up before saying anything.

She'd dialed the right number both times, but they'd never heard of Lottie. Carolyn didn't know what to do. Lottie had disappeared over the side of the bridge and it seemed like she'd disappeared in real life too. She didn't know if she should mourn for her missing friend or if Lottie had gotten mad and left her on the bridge. Either way she was stuck. Lottie had been her cover story, but now she had none. What would she tell her father? What excuse had she given him if Lottie didn't exist anymore?

As she planned her next move, a sharp kick from inside her protruding abdomen almost made her double over. She sat down on a bench and rubbed her stomach, hoping to calm the little one. A strong breeze kicked up and coming from Crybaby Bridge, a soft cry followed by a sorrowful moan arose. It was then that Carolyn knew no matter what had changed in the present world, she would face the same generational indignity as those who came before and those who would follow. Now, more than ever, she believed both the stories she'd heard had been true, along with many others lost to time with cries that echo still.

Zach Lamb

Zach Lamb is a Fictionist who creates thriller, horror, and dark fiction stories. He is the author of The Suicide Killer. Mourning Glory, Dark Water Sacrifice and Remove the Veil. Zach has an MFA in Fiction Writing. When he's not writing, he teaches composition and literature at Columbus

State University. He lives with his wife and kids in Cataula, Georgia. Find out more at zachlambauthor.com

1970s

Mr. Snaps

V.S. Lawrence

"Well, kids, thanks for coming to play. We surely had a magical day! We learned some lessons and had some fun, but now our time here is good and done. Be kind, be helpful, and don't forget: strangers are friends we just haven't met! And friendship is for everyone, so go on out and have some fun!"

The seven-foot-tall gingerbread man posed, arms raised in the air and held the pose until the clapboard slammed down and the director yelled cut. Cigarette smoke drifted across the soundstage, curling up toward the hot studio lights.

"Good job, Jerry. That's a wrap for today."

Jerry Nolan dropped his arms and groaned, desperate to get out of the stuffy suit and light a Pall Mall. Spending hours in the god-awful thing was bad enough, but when the old costume started to wear out and smell like mildew, they upgraded to a "new and improved" version—thicker, heavier, and completely suffocating. But hey, at least it wouldn't wear out as fast as the old one. Who cares if he got heat stroke as long as they didn't have to keep paying for new oversized gingerbread costumes.

Peeling off the husk, he gulped fresh air and kicked his legs free. One of the PAs scurried over holding a flimsy paper Dixie cup of water from the cooler, cringing as Jerry yanked it away, downing it in one swig.

"J, can I have a quick word?"

The nasal, high-pitched voice of the director grated on his already frayed nerves. He didn't have the patience for the bubbly woman, not right now. Still, he slapped on a dazzling smile and turned to face her.

"How can I help, Diz?"

Diz Malloy crossed her arms and let out a dramatic sigh. "Bad news, J. The suits pulled the plug."

Jerry blinked, his brows pulling into a tight line. "They're canceling *The Gingerbread House*? What the fuck, Diz? You're putting me on. This is the top show on Saturday mornings. Kids flip for Mr. Snaps. They can't dump me!"

Diz grimaced at the profanity, but didn't bring it up for once. "That was last year. Kids today don't want giant plush mascots. They want cartoons about crime solving dogs. Their attention spans have shortened and *The Gingerbread House* is just too ... slow."

Jerry scoffed. "No. I don't believe it. That stupid hippo in bell bottoms is still around, isn't he?"

"Nope." Diz shook her head. "Hip O. Pottamus is getting the ax, too."

Disbelief settled in, and Jerry crushed the waxed paper cup in his fist, the soft rim collapsing noisily. Diz reached out, placing a consoling hand on his arm. "Sorry, J. That's the biz. Better dust off your resume. We've got just one more show then we're out."

He watched her walk away, laughing with some of the crew, feathered hair bouncing under the studio fluorescents. Actually laughing. That bitch. How could she laugh when everything was falling apart? She never loved the show—not Mr. Snaps, not Cinnamon Sam, not even little Spicy Mike. She didn't love any of the residents of *The Gingerbread House*, and it was her show as much as it was his.

Jerry stormed out of the building, throwing the crumpled cup on the ground as he left, striking a match and lighting up before he was even out the door.

"To hell with 'em," he muttered. "To hell with all of 'em."

He took a long drag and snapped at the PA who'd brought him his water, practically throwing his car keys at her. Smoke curled from his lips as he glanced back at the building just in time to see the giant heap of gingerbread suit being wheeled off to wardrobe. A pang hit him, low and sudden. As his fresh-off-the-lot '72 Mustang pulled up to the curb, he stubbed his cigarette out on the wall and marched back inside. The costumer barely had time to react before he snatched the suit from her arms. He wadded it up, stalked back to the car, and crammed it into the back seat before peeling out.

He wasn't going to let *The Gingerbread House* go down without a fight. The only question was, how was he going to stop it?

The next—and final—shooting block wasn't scheduled until the following week, and Jerry spent that time in a haze of depression. He should've been talking to his agent, landing auditions, accepting that Mr. Snaps was no more. But he did none of those things. Instead, he drank. He drank and sat on the sagging, plaid sofa, next to the empty gingerbread man suit, reminiscing about all their wonderful times in *The Gingerbread House*.

"I just ... it can't be over. I mean, I'm Mr. Snaps. Jerry? Who's that? I don't even know what to do with myself if I'm not in the house with all my pals."

Mr. Snaps' cold black eyes returned his gaze, reflecting the soft orange glow of the lamp.

Jerry tipped his bottle in its direction. "You know, that place is magic. I know, I know, I bitch about it. But there's something really great about the show. Those kids ... they just eat it up. Ha ha. They look at me, and you, like I'm—we—are a god. We *are* their god."

He drained the bottle and got up for another, jostling the coffee table and nearly spilling the overflowing ashtray all over the floor. Not that it would make a difference. The smell of smoke was already infused into every inch of the place, with a strange afternote of incense and patchouli from the nights he had a lady over for company. When he returned, he paused, squinting with one eye closed at the suit. Had it moved? It looked closer now, its head tilted slightly in his direction. He shook it off, cracked the cap, and took a long gulp.

Six days blurred by, each one dragging him deeper into the hole. And each day there was a moment when he could have sworn the Mr. Snaps costume had shifted or moved in some way. But the costume was new, the material slick, and there was a rational explanation for everything.

By the time the final day of filming rolled around, he still had no plan. Just a pounding head, spiraling thoughts, and the gingerbread suit buckled into the front seat like a passenger. It sat there, grinning in silence, while he white-knuckled the wheel and tried not to fall apart as Fleetwood Mac warbled from the warped eight-track. He wasn't just losing a job, he was losing himself.

Don't flip your wig, friend! It's not the end.

Jerry flinched. His eyes darted to the suit. That was Mr. Snaps' voice—cheerful, sing-songy, warm as a freshly baked cookie. But that didn't make sense. *He* was the voice of Mr. Snaps.

He turned back to the road, raking a hand through his greasy hair. "Man, I must still be half in the bag."

At the studio, he pulled up in front of the door and honked long and loud until a PA in platform shoes clomped across the asphalt to meet him. They reached for the passenger door, but Jerry waved them away.

"I'll take Mr. Snaps in. Just park the car. Somewhere close. As soon as this is done, I never wanna see this place again."

Careful not to drag the costume along the asphalt, Jerry carried the large heap of fabric inside to wardrobe. He placed it in one of the chairs in front of the makeup table, and took his own seat beside him. Being in the suit meant there was no need for makeup, and the area was abandoned.

Jerry stared at his reflection—red-rimmed eyes in a face he barely recognized. Then his gaze shifted to the mirror beside him. Mr. Snaps stared back. He looked at himself. Then at the suit. Back and forth. The longer he looked, the harder it was to tell where one ended and the other began. They had the same empty black eyes, same slack expression. Even their skin tones matched.

He dropped his head into his hands. What was he going to do? How could he get them to stop this? To uncancel the show?

Friends always stick together.

He raised his head slightly and looked at Mr. Snaps in the mirror again. "Yeah. Friends do stick together. Too bad none of these assholes are our friends."

No, they're not, but that's alright. You and me will win this fight!

"I don't see how. But I'll try to talk to Diz."

Don't you worry your little head. Soon enough they'll all be dead.

Jerry narrowed his eyes. "What?"

The costume stared back lifelessly, and Jerry shook his head. What was he doing talking to a goddamned costume? And did he actually think the thing was talking back? That was ridiculous.

"Hey, J. What a drag, huh?"

Phoebe, the woman who played Spicy Mike, drifted up behind him in a loose, paisley blouse that looked like it belonged at a love-in more than a kids' show. He caught the cloying smell of her clove cigarettes before he saw her reflection behind him as she placed her hands on his shoulders. He locked eyes with her in the mirror and immediately clocked the fake frown, the manufactured sympathy in her voice. He went rigid under her touch and shrugged.

"Yeah, well. Everything ends at some point."

"Far out." She moved to the costume rack and plucked her tiny gingerbread costume from it, a miniature version of Mr. Snaps but with a backwards baseball cap. "I heard Diz brought in a live audience for the finale. Should be a real gas, saying goodbye like that."

Jerry grunted and watched as she pulled the costume up. "You'd better get dressed. I think Diz wants us all on set in ten."

She waddled off, and he looked at the costume rack. Cinnamon Sam's suit was gone, which meant Phil was already on set, and all of the gumdrop costumes were gone, too. They were all waiting for Jerry, waiting for the star of the show, Mr. Snaps.

There would be no time to talk to Diz. He hadn't really been planning on it, anyway. He knew there would be no convincing her to save the show.

"She probably didn't even try to hassle the brass," he muttered, rising from the chair. He slipped into the suit. It clung to him like it remembered. A perfect fit—snug, warm, welcoming. Like sliding a hand into a glove. Although it was a new version of the suit, it was familiar. It was a part of him.

She didn't try to save us, you say? Time for them all to go away.

He found the zipper around back and tugged it up. It was stiff and he struggled for a bit before it finally slid up to the top, smooth as butter. He let the top of the costume, which comprised half his torso and head, dangle down over his chest and caught his reflection staring back, half man, half gingerbread. He grappled with the knowledge that this would be the last time he would look through the small mesh window in the gingerbread man's smile.

It doesn't have to be.

"It doesn't have to be."

He smiled and pulled the head up. Mr. Snaps smiled back.

"Hey kids! Thanks so much for being part of the super special final episode of *The Gingerbread House*!" Diz waited for the kids to cheer or react, but she was met with blank stares.

Jerry chuckled inside his suit. Diz had explained to the cast and crew about the kids, told them how much of a struggle it was to find any who actually wanted to be there, and asked the performers to keep it clean—no cussing, no off-color stuff. A bored "APPLAUSE" sign blinked uselessly above the cameras, while in the back a couple of parents smoked and sipped stale coffee from paper cups, attention elsewhere.

After failing to squeeze any energy out of the kids, the director turned to the cast.

Everything started as usual—Cinnamon Sam skipped into the house with Spicy Mike. They played with the gumdrops, all laughter and cheer, just another wonderful day in *The Gingerbread House.* And then it was his cue.

Head bowed, Mr. Snaps shuffled into the room and into the harsh glare of the klieg lights. Cinnamon Sam and Spicy Mike turned at the sound, their painted-on grins frozen in place as they stepped toward him.

"What's wrong, Mr. Snaps?"

"I'm feeling sad because we all have to move away."

"What?"

"Move away? What do you mean, Mr. Snaps?"

Mr. Snaps nodded, his big black eyes cast downward. "Yes. We're moving to a new gingerbread house far, far away. That means I won't be able to see my friends anymore." He opened his arms wide, turning to face the camera.

"I don't wanna move away!" Spicy Mike crossed his arms over his chest. "I'm not gonna!"

"But Mike, we have to."

In the script and during rehearsal, Mr. Snaps was supposed to help Spicy Mike manage his feelings, reassure him he'd make new friends, and remind him he could always keep in touch with the old ones. It wasn't really goodbye. Jerry had practiced those lines. He knew them by heart.

But standing there, boiling in the suit, tears streaming down his face while the crew smiled and acted like it was any other day—like none of this actually mattered—something inside him ... snapped.

"If you don't want to go, Spicy Mike, we don't have to."

Cinnamon Sam turned towards Mr. Snaps and Spicy Mike sputtered. "Uh ... what?"

"We never have to leave *The Gingerbread House* and all our friends." Mr. Snaps faced the assembled group of kids. "Do you want to live in *The Gingerbread House* with us and be friends forever?"

The boys and girls stared back with blank expressions, fidgeting. One picked his nose. Another leaned in to whisper to the girl beside him. Not a single hand went up.

Mr. Snaps frowned. That wasn't the right reaction. They should be smiling and jumping for joy. This was the gift of a lifetime.

"Well?" he said, arms outstretched, his voice still sweet but thin and fraying at the edges. "Come on down and we can play all day."

Diz was waving frantically, trying to get his attention, while the camera crew kept the cameras swiveling between the three characters.

"But, uh, Mr. Snaps," Cinnamon Sam tried to improvise, "nobody can stay in the same place forever. Life is full of changes, and we—"

Mr. Snaps whirled around, yanking a giant lollipop from the set, the stick splintering at the base as he ripped it free. He swung it with full force, the bright swirl a blur, and knocked Cinnamon Sam's legs out from under him. Inside the suit, Jerry's head was filled with the voice of Mr. Snaps egging him on.

Cinnamon Sam is so rude. Put an end to this traitorous dude!

Over and over, the lollipop slammed down on Cinnamon Sam. The children all screamed, scattering in terror as they called out for their mommies. But Jerry kept swinging, a blur of candy colored rage, until the other gingerbread man stopped moving completely.

He spun around to face the cameras, his icing outfit streaked with blood.

"Sometimes, there are people in our life who stop being good for us, isn't that right kids? And we need to ... *hey, where are you little shits going? Get back in here before my fists start throwing!*"

"Whoa, J, what the hell, man? This is seriously uncool." Little Spicy Mike approached Mr. Snaps, their hands up trying to calm him.

Mr. Snaps raised the lollipop high, ready to bring it down again, and Spicy Mike stumbled back, hands raised in defense. Jerry paused, but then Mr. Snaps reminded him how flippant Phoebe had been as she slipped on her gingerbread suit. She didn't care, not one little bit. With a vicious leap, Mr. Snaps lunged at Spicy Mike, slamming the lollipop down with brutal force, knocking his stupid backwards cap clean off. The tiny gingerbread man fell backwards and didn't get up again.

"Someone call security!" Diz screamed as the rest of the crew bolted for the doors. A couple of parents up front dropped their coffee cups and ran, while a middle-aged man with wicked sideburns shoved his kid toward the exit. The gumdrops huddled together, wide-eyed, but they were innocent. Mr. Snaps had no issue with them. It was the rest of them, those traitors, those crumby little cookies, that needed to pay.

Jerry peered through the smile, his own twisted into a grim reflection of his gingerbread counterpart. They truly were one as they worked together, swinging the lollipop back and forth, bashing cameramen and PAs, working towards the main goal; Diz.

"*Get back here, bitch, I'm coming for you. You have to pay for all that you do!*"

Diz screamed as two oversized gingerbread man hands clamped around her neck. With Mr. Snaps' strength surging through him, Jerry lifted her off the ground, squeezing harder, watching her face flush the color of a sugarplum. Her eyes bugged out while her mouth opened and closed like a fish out of water. When she finally stopped thrashing, Mr. Snaps released his grip, letting her drop to the floor.

The part that was still Jerry heard the distant wail of sirens, and knew he needed to go. The set was deserted now, save for the broken bodies of his former cookie comrades and the rest of the traitors. His hands, soft and round, groped blindly behind him for the zipper, but the tab eluded him, slipping through his fingers each time.

The sirens grew louder, and panic surged through him, but he couldn't get a grip. His hand flailed around behind him, searching ... there! He caught it. He yanked, gasping in the stale, recycled air of the suit. *God, it was so hot.*

The zipper budged, barely an inch, then caught. Stuck fast. He yanked again, frantic now, pulling with everything he had. But it wouldn't move. He pulled harder, desperation clawing at his chest. He was stuck, trapped in his gingerbread shell, and the police would be right on top of him any moment. He couldn't waste any more time.

Moving quickly was difficult in the heavy suit, but on thick cookie legs, he ran out the door, searching for his bright red convertible amongst all the others.

There.

And the idiot PA had left the roof down. Normally, that would've pissed him off, but today it was a blessing. If the roof had been up, he'd never have fit inside with this costume on.

Without hesitation, Mr. Snaps vaulted over the door, landing in the driver's seat with a loud thunk. His thick hands fumbled with the keys left in the ignition. If that PA was still alive, Mr. Snaps thought, he'd have to come back and deal with him.

It took some maneuvering, but at last the engine roared to life and he threw the car into drive, stomping a cookie foot down on the gas. The suit, once heavy and awkward, was starting to feel less like a prison and more like a second skin.

The wind howled through the mesh mouth, and Mr. Snaps took a deep breath. No cops in the rearview yet, but he knew they would come. Still, he was finally free. Free of *The Gingerbread House*. Free of Cinnamon Sam and that insufferable Spicy Mike.

I know I have to run, he thought. *As fast as I can. But they'll never catch me. I'm a gingerbread man.*

Reaching a cookie hand up, he adjusted the mirror, catching his icing smile in the reflection. It stretched wider as he laughed.

V.S. Lawrence

V.S. Lawrence grew up in Utah being scared of everything. Now, she puts her fears on paper, writing spooky books that feel like Scooby-Doo chase music. When not writing, she can be found buried in a horror novel, wandering aimlessly, or cuddling her dog, Rigby. She is still scared of everything. https://vslawrence-author.com/

1980s

TRICKLE-DOWN TRAUMA

T. Kulp

THE PIT

When the door opened, screams burst from the old community center. Through that doorway was the rumbling insanity I needed. It called to me. And I gave myself to it.

This was my first punk rock show.

I had just turned 18, but my parents never let me go to concerts. This one was okay because it was at a community center, ended at nine, and I didn't go alone.

Abe and Jorge went with me—then ditched me the moment we got inside. My parents thought they'd make sure I didn't wander away for drugs or hookers. But Abe and Jorge couldn't even be troubled to even talk to me nowadays.

Besides, drugs ruin your future.

And hookers didn't want broke guys getting ready for college.

But we were in DC, and according to my mom, temptation was everywhere.

Inside, drumbeat waves slammed against my lungs. Guitars roared in discordant tunes against the singer's screeching. The community center's bright fluorescent lights felt like a soup kitchen, or morgue, not a concert.

No darkness. No shadows to hide in.

I got my black X stamp and moved down the hallway lined with unmanned tables. Zines covered the tables. I gathered a few for inspiration. Their scribbled line drawing artwork was art in its primordial form, like the music, raw feeling.

Beyond the zines were tapes and records, but the bands were inside the show with everyone else. All the tables were unmanned except one.

A white-haired goddess, not much older than me, stood at the end of the hall. Her hips slowly swayed to the music, full lips mouthing the lyrics as she waited for someone to come to her. A sleeveless white shirt that read *Finger Licking Good* pulled taut across her small breasts. If her baggy graffiti covered jeans plunged any lower, I'd see her underwear ... if she wore any.

I looked away, so I didn't stare.

My eyes flicked back to her, but I didn't let them linger. Her boyfriend is probably in the show. And Jorge wasn't out here to defend me, like he did years ago.

Bands played on a small stage in the cafeteria. No show lights, only the fluorescents casting their harsh glow. People kept jumping off the stage, blurring the line between band and crowd. But the band wasn't the star here. Punk wasn't about being a rock god. It was about letting go. And I had a lot to let go tonight. My future was killing me. School, tutoring, test prep, AP homework, extracurriculars, college prep—it never stopped.

Tonight, I needed a moment to get away.

Bodies thrashed in the pit, soaring from the stage, crashing into the sea of flesh and sweat. Jorge was there. He pushed off other shirtless guys in a frenzied ecstasy, fueled by collision and feeling. His head smashed into someone else. Blood sprayed. Everyone jumped away.

Two guys at the edge of the pit ripped him from the storm. Abe followed from the far wall and the two of them found me in the doorway.

Jorge mopped the blood with his shirt, dyeing the white t-shirt deep crimson. Abe cackled, whooping and hollering about how badass that was.

"Yo, Tommy, you getting in there?" Jorge applied pressure to his battle scar.

"No way, Tommy boy gettin' in there. Might sprain a finger," Abe mocked. He rolled his eyes, whining, "Shit man, did you really bring that?" He flicked my backpack. "What, you gonna draw some shit?"

I shrugged.

"Or do homework," Jorge laughed.

I pretended to laugh along. "Just thought I'd sketch some," I said.

My eyes wandered to the goddess. I'd draw her—but that'd be creepy.

"Shit dude," Abe protested, "why you always workin'?"

Jorge agreed, "Yeah man, just get in the pit. Live a little. So worried about your future you're missing life, man."

They pushed around me to the bathroom.

The band screamed on.

Swirling, rolling, crashing, the pit called to me. It was everything I wanted to be: violent, angry, chaotic, awesome. But that storm would break me because I'm what my parents made me: weak, frail, afraid.

I took out my sketchbook and drew. Soft charcoal sticks smeared my hands as I captured the pit's chaotic storm in fast black smudges ... it was the same storm within me.

"Artist?"

I started, jumped away, snatching my sketchbook to my chest.

"Oh! Sorry." It was the goddess. She reached for my arm. God, what if she touched me? I wanted her to touch me—but was terrified of it too. "I didn't mean to startle." Her voice was smokey and as soft as her ivory skin.

"No, sorry, I was just—uh," I nodded to the show. "Just trying to capture the feel."

"Just don't capture the stink," she laughed. Her teeth glimmered. She inhaled deep. A breath caught in her throat. Then her expression soured, her eyes softening with grief.

Her beauty made the sadness tragic. Tears swelled in my throat. I pushed out a smile because if she started crying, I'd drown in her tears.

But she caught herself, plastering on a smile.

I drew in a deep sniff, faking a choke to lighten the mood. The show stank like a locker room without the bleach. But her cotton-candy smell overpowered the reek of sweat and blood. Was she chewing gum? No. Not that I saw.

A burning wave of tension grew in me, between us. She was so close. She asked, "Can I see?"

"See?"

She reached for the sketchbook. Her corpse-cold fingers grazing over mine. My hand snapped away from her icy touch, but not before she had my book. I mindlessly rubbed where she touched to bring the warmth back.

"Wow," she gasped. "You *drew* these?" She flipped the pages slowly, drinking in each sketch. "Like, wow."

I stuttered or nodded or squeaked—I didn't know which.

"Whoa, Tommy," Abe said, suddenly there, arm draped over me. "Who's your friend?"

My heart sank. I squirmed in his grip.

Abe was a tan, muscular skater boy. He could charm the skirt off a catholic schoolgirl—or so he claimed loudly and often. No girl looked at me after seeing him.

Jorge was behind us.

"I ... I didn't catch your name?" I said.

Abe and Jorge scoffed at my stupidity.

"Lidia," she said. "Tommy was showing me his drawings."

My cheeks burned. I shuffled away, but there was nowhere to hide in this light.

"Well, Lidia, we're heading back in. Want to join us?" Abe released me and extended his hand to her.

She sniffed the air in two quick pulls, drawing in the foul stench of the community center as the band raged, as the bodies slammed together, splashing sweat into the air.

Lidia shook her head. "I can't leave my table. But you all could join the band for an after party?" Her eyes met mine. "I'd like to show your artwork to James. He leads our band. You guys can talk about album covers. If you're up for it?" She smiled wide at Abe and Jorge. Her lips clicked as they pulled away from perfect, saliva slick teeth.

My heart sunk, but I buried it with a smile. She wanted them at the party. I was just a plus one.

Abe returned her smile with his goofy grin, the one that removed schoolgirl skirts. "Yeah, we can swing by, but Tommy's gotta get home for homework."

"No, no, I'm sure I can stay."

Mom and Dad were going to be pissed. But I'd tell them the show was running late.

"Well, don't let me hold you back." Lidia handed my sketchbook back. She winked at me. "Don't get too rowdy, boys."

She strutted back to her table.

Abe leaned in to me, whispering, "Like you'd even know what to do with a pussy like that. I'd hit it."

Jorge returned to the pit. Abe stood behind the wall of men keeping the pit contained.

Abe was right.

What the hell would I do at this party? There's probably going to be drugs and drinking, and what if it gets busted by the cops?

What am I doing?

Talking myself out of the most awesome night ever?

I wanted one night in my teenage life to be cool, and here it was.

I followed Lidia to look at the posters on her table. Her band's name was *Trickle Down Trauma,* and the posters were loud, bold, and on glossy paper. High quality for a DIY punk band.

"Couldn't stay away?" Her seductive tone made me stagger. Her eyes ran over me, narrowing as she bit her lip.

Words jumbled in my head, but I started talking anyway, "Oh, I'm sorry, I don't want to bother you." I cringed. She giggled. "I just—where is the party?" My face burned in the harsh lights. Why did I care? Look at her. *Wherever it is, just go!*

"It's at the Ardorf Museum on Q and 92nd. We rented the museum for the night."

"Serious?"

She tilted her head. "Familiar with it, Tommy?"

"Yeah…" Then, I couldn't hold back anymore. "I'm sorry, those guys call me Tommy, but I'm Thomas. They think it's funny to call me that." I forced a chuckle. They call me Tommy because it irritated me, and they thought it was funny.

My dad always introduced me to his construction coworkers, *Thomas; like Edison, too bright to just be a ditch digger like me.* He was always so proud of my name and what it declared—I'd have a bright future.

Lidia held out her hand. "Nice to meet you, Thomas." Her grip was tight, cold, as lifeless as her pale skin. "The party's going to love you." She tapped my sketchbook. "They haven't seen anything like you … well, since James."

I smiled and returned to the show room door. The band thrashed, the pit seized, and I kept glancing at Lidia.

She was watching me too, still singing, still swaying. Her eyes tracked my hand as it captured the storm of bodies colliding, sweat flying, souls abandoning flesh for rage, passion, ecstasy.

My eyes flicked between the pit and her hips, their swirls and sways stirring my storm. Heat battered my mind, drowning reason until I didn't care why she stared, why she bit her lip. I just gave her the show she desired—me capturing the feral fury before me.

THE PARTY

It was only a little lie.

When I called my parents, instead of mentioning the party, I focused on the band wanting to see my art. Dad agreed, but didn't like it. Still, the lie soured in my mouth.

Jorge, Abe, and I took a taxi to the museum. Traffic was quiet, we passed only a few cars in the haze of fog and streetlights.

My stomach lurched with worries. What was I going to do while Jorge and Abe hooked up with some chicks? I'll talk to James, and then what? Be the awkward guy in the corner?

Abe kept saying, "Man, I can't believe you got us into a party."

Jorge laughed, "Yeah, but it's at a museum, so that tracks. Artsy babes digging on Tommy." Jorge punched my arm too hard and barked a cheer.

When we arrived at the museum, Jorge and Abe ran ahead, but the doorman stopped them.

"Lidia invited us," I repeated what she told me to say.

He stiffened at Lidia's name. "Certainly, sir. Welcome. She is waiting inside." He opened the door.

I led the way, trying to motion for Abe to keep cool—no use. How could I blame him for being excited? This was amazing.

Everyone was young, pale, and gorgeous. Their suits made my Kmart clothes look like I rolled in off the street. The people here were laughing, drinking champagne and dark red wine. As we passed, everyone sniffed—I guess we stunk from the punk show. But I didn't recognize anyone from the community center.

The museum lights were warm and low, giving the party an air of comfortable quiet. People chatted and laughed, but volumes were low—voices politely hushed.

Waiters weaved between the sculptures with practiced grace, silver trays balanced steadily as they offered drinks and skewers of raw steak, blood pooling beneath the bright red chunks. Abe reached for one.

"Ah ah ah," Lidia called as she hurried over and playfully slapped Abe's hand. She whispered, "No sticky fingers on my friends."

Abe smiled, leaving the bloody chunks.

Lidia waved forward two women, both almost as stunning as her, and equally pale. "Abe, my friend Nina would love to show you the sculpture garden. Jorge, Jenny thought you might find the atrium to your liking."

Abe and Jorge smiled, taking their companions' arms and disappearing into the crowd swelling around us.

"Thomas," Lidia said, as she sidled up beside me. "Come with me."

She held out her hand, that cold, cold hand, and smiled wide and warm. God, I wanted to kiss her. To pull her into me and drink deep from her lips until our souls twisted together. Just like the movies. But I didn't. Her beauty was terrifying, paralyzing, but I did as beckoned and took her hand.

She pulled me through the crowd, smiling, sniffing, waving.

We stopped in the gallery with ancient Greek sculptures. I was staring behind us, meeting all the curious glares. What were they thinking?

That I didn't belong?

No, it was curiosity. Someone had a question for Lidia, but she hurried past before they could ask.

"James, it is my pleasure to present Thomas," Lidia said.

I turned to the statue of Apollo; white marble crowned in gold. A harp curled in the crook of his arm, while a serpent coiled from wrist to elbow. His lips bent in a knowing smirk, guarding a secret never to be spoken.

"Ah, the infamous Thomas," James said. He stood in front of the statue, staring up at it, before turning to me. I gasped. For a heartbeat, I thought the marble had moved. He was its echo in flesh; bronze skin taut over sculpted muscle, short curls crowning his head, sky-blue eyes distant as the heavens. His black blazer was sharp, almost mocking the ripped jeans below it, his bare chest revealed, broad and impossibly defined. He smiled, but the sadness in it made him seem older than the marble behind him.

He extended his hand.

I took it. His palm burned as hot as Lidia's was cold. He clenched tight, swallowing my frail hand in his grip.

"Our little Lidia had a lot to say about your art," James said.

Lidia curtsied.

He dismissed the surrounding people. They left quickly. "Please, sit." James motioned to a black rectangle bench.

I sat.

He held out his hand for my sketchbook.

I gave it.

Lidia straddled the bench behind me, pressing close to my shoulder. Again, her cold overwhelmed me. Her hands folded on my shoulder as she scooted closer. Her breath chilled the hairs in my ear.

"Show him the one of the girl," she whispered. "I'm jealous of her."

I nodded and tried to move away. She was so hot. So, so hot, and what the hell was I doing moving away from her? But James didn't budge. He was a wall and if I moved any further, I'd be sitting in his lap.

As if reading my mind, James said, "Lidia, dear, some space for our friend."

And she backed up a bit, swaying her hips to one side, letting her breast slide against me slowly. I sucked in a sharp breath.

"These are insanely good," James said with surprise. He flipped to another page, glanced at me, then chuckled. "You're an artist?"

"No, I'm going to college to be a teacher," I said, unable to choke off the sadness.

James laughed, "Teacher?"

He waited for an explanation, so I gave the only one I had. "It's a steady job," I said, parroting my dad.

James shook his head and said, "With work like this, you'd never go hungry. Come with me."

He stood, cradling my sketchbook as Apollo behind him cradled the harp. Lidia hopped to her feet with a delighted squeal.

People spilled into the gallery as we slipped out. They turned to watch, heads tilting, voices hushed and sharp. Their eyes clung to me—appraising, wondering why I was here.

Lidia looped her arm through mine, pulling me close. Claiming me.

We stopped at a few tables, each scene unfolding the same way: James would step forward, silence would fall, and he would open my sketchbook. Gasps, introductions, the inevitable request for a portrait.

By the third time, I realized it was all a performance, a prelude. And when James motioned me to an empty circular oak table, I knew this was the true interview. The dark wood gleamed with a golden seal; a sun encircling a harp, its edge bitten by a serpent devouring itself—an Ouroboros. On James's hand, the same seal gleamed from his golden ring.

I joined him and Lidia at the table.

Leaning in, I whispered, "James, I really appreciate this, but I'm not an artist."

Lidia laughed, hearty, broken by gasps and a cute snort that made me chuckle.

James smiled. "None of us ever think we are. Drink?"

I shook my head on reflex. Alcohol wrecks people, that's what my parents always said. They never touched the stuff, so neither did I. Lidia didn't hesitate; she took a glass of steaming red wine. I didn't know wine was served warm. James requested a Diet Coke, then again motioned to me. "They have anything you want. No shame in Straight Edge here. I'm finding it a good life."

I ordered a Coke.

"The first time I was called a musician," James shook his head, "I argued tooth and nail with that. *No, I'm just learning,*" James chuckled at the memory.

Lidia's eyes grew distant, shifting through memories, then said, "Echomedes?"

James winced at the sound, then quickly nodded. He waved low over the table, wiping away something I didn't see. Lidia nervously shifted, taking a long sip of her wine.

James returned my sketchbook. "What is your roadblock?" he asked.

"Art's just for fun. I'm going to college for a career."

Lidia chuckled, "Artist is a career. Just not the wage slave job Daddy Reagan wants you to submit to."

"Artist isn't a stable job," I, again, parroted my dad.

James nodded. "Neither is punk rock." He swept his hand toward the party. "I'm doing okay. Here, let's get this settled now. Eustice!"

At James' call, a man glided through the crowd. He glittered with gold rings and heavy gems, every step measured, his poise flawless. His smile broke wide at James' summons—prince-like, eager to be in his presence.

"Ah, precious, precious James," Eustice said and bowed to kiss James' hand. Without rising, he swiveled to Lidia, lifted her hand and kissed it, saying, "Ma Petit Princesse."

Lidia giggled and replied, "Frere mineur."

"Eustice de Malvoie, this is Thomas," James said.

"Enchante." Eustice held out his hand. I shook it, feeling his light icy touch. He drew a sharp sniff, his head cocking in a question at Lidia. She smiled, then nodded at my sketchbook. I should have washed up in the bathroom ...

"Thomas, show him," James directed.

I flipped to the girl Lidia loved. She was drawn in graphite, silver and shining on the coarse white paper.

Eustice gasped, his hand hovering over his heart.

"How much would you pay for a portrait from someone that talented?" James took a long sip.

Eustice smiled wryly, flicking his hand at James, "Ah, art's truest value cannot be in monetary measures."

A waiter drifted past with skewers of raw steak, blood sliding atop the silver tray. Eustice plucked two with practiced grace, offering one to Lidia. She winked and refused, saying, "Saving room."

The princely man turned the second skewer toward me. Before I could move, James set his glass down with a sharp clink. The sound cut through the air. Eustice froze, eyes wide, then dropped his gaze. Under James's stare, he shoved the skewer into his own mouth, then the second, chewing quickly, almost choking as he mumbled an apology for a slight I hadn't seen. My stomach gurgled in hunger. I hadn't eaten all evening.

"How much?" James repeated.

Eustice smiled and chewed. Raw juices mixed with spit glossed his lips as he ate the mouthful. Swallowing, he said, "Easily ten thousand, if said artist dealt in payment so mundane as money," Eustice said with a flourish. "But artistic genius such as this deserves only the extraordinary."

"My pictures aren't worth that ..." I said.

James laughed hard. Eustice joined him. Lidia simply smiled and patted my hand.

Ten-thousand dollars? For one portrait? How many others wanted portraits? Six? Seven?

What do teachers make a year?

What do construction workers make a year?

Right here, this could be my future. An artist. Drawing these beautiful people in these beautiful museums—or album covers, zines, my creations making a real difference in the world.

A soft chime broke through my dreams.

Lidia savored her wine, watching me watch her. Could artist be *my* career? Could I draw her? My breath caught in my chest as she slowly winked. Her eyes moved to James, but mine never left hers. I fell into those stormy blue wells, letting them mix into the hurricane in me. The possibilities of a future I was told could never be real, vibrated through me with the echo of the chimes.

"I like this one," James declared, pointing at me.

Lidia quietly squealed with delight.

The chimes rang again.

"Time for the meal," Eustice said. "Who catered the night?"

James answered, "Lidia."

Eustice raised his wine glass. "Always a delight." He excused himself, hurrying away.

"Join me for dinner?" Lidia was lighter now, her mood airy and elated, like my little cousins getting the Christmas gift they begged Santa to bring. She held out her hand. I didn't hesitate. Her chilly grip was cooling, welcoming, buzzing with excitement.

The chimes kept up their soft call as waiters walked about, tapping a mallet on a silver tube. It was soft and inviting, not disruptive—but the vibration numbed my guts like when the wrong chord lingers, making you queasy. My head spun, but Lidia kept me stable as we joined everyone in the sculpture garden.

Above us, the stars glared at the gathering, uncaring, unblinking. A sliver of moon cast its silver light over the garden's marble forms and wild hedges. Chilly breezes swept through us, but no one else shivered. Each sculpture was a knot of bodies—dancing, fucking, or devouring. Lidia's fingers laced into mine, sending my heart racing as I wondered which of those Lidia wanted from me.

In the center of the garden, Abe kissed Nina's neck with wet smacks. Her thin shoulder straps had fallen away, presenting him with her milky shoulders. He was too busy kneading Nina's breasts to notice the crowd circling him. Like the sculptures, he and her were one—but her eyes met the crowd, welcoming them to the intimate moment.

As the crowd became still, Nina smiled and lifted Abe's chin from her throat.

"What's going on?" Abe asked.

The waiters struck their chimes one last time. This chord was brighter—growing higher and higher until I couldn't hear it—but the others ... they smiled at the sound singing through their minds.

Abe looked at Nina, his brow crinkled in confusion. She closed her eyes, listening with a faint smile.

Everyone was silent.

Only Abe's breathing broke the quiet as he looked for answers.

Something was wrong here. Where was Jorge? Why were we all watching?

Nina took Abe's hands. He winced at the grip—cold, I was certain, like Lidia's. She sniffed deeply. Everyone else joined her. Delighted groans rippled over the crowd.

"What?" Abe laughed nervously.

Lidia whispered, "Don't worry, you'll be fine." Her warm breath rippled over me, igniting my excitement at what came next.

I tensed in her grip. Would I be fine?

Nina drew in a deep breath, sucking air slowly, savoring it. Abe tensed. He tried to pull away but couldn't. I squeezed Lidia's frozen hand tighter. She ran her fingers between my knuckles.

A glowing miasma leaked from Abe's mouth, golden like sunbeams through early morning fog. The cloud floated into Nina's mouth. She pulled deeper breaths as did those around me. The mist spread, flowed to the crowd. They drank deeply. Abe seized, jerking to escape, but Nina held him. A few in the crowd licked their lips, satisfied, and stepped away from the scene, letting others take their place.

Abe gasped for breath, then collapsed. Nina let him fall as she sipped the last of the mist.

But he wasn't dead.

Relief hit me—and I remembered, a few years ago, Abe handing me his skateboard after I'd shredded my knees. "Chicks dig scars," he'd laughed. "Go again." I kicked off, and he cheered, "Yeah, boy—back on that horse!"

I stepped to help him, but Lidia held me back.

Abe rolled over, his eyes locking on mine. The joker was gone—his face empty. In a flat, dead voice, he whispered, "What did you do?" His hands clawed at his skin, pressing harder, faster. "I don't feel ... anything." His cracked fingernails ripped his cheek open. He didn't stop clawing, but his expression never changed. He felt nothing. Not in his hands. Not in his soul.

Lidia tugged me back. "We should talk."

The waiters lifted Abe and carried him inside. Around us, the crowd resumed their chatter, laughing about how delightful the first course had been.

Lidia catered tonight.

She brought the food.

She brought us.

My knees gave out, but she caught me before I hit the floor. I felt her chuckle as she steadied me, guiding me back to our table.

James was waiting there.

He sipped his Diet Coke and presented me with my Coke.

The waiters took Abe to the kitchen. He shouted, not in anger but simply asking, "What did you do?" The shouting stopped abruptly.

Silence filled the kitchen. Around me the conversations continued as though nothing had happened, the guests having only paused their evening to eat Abe's ... soul.

A waiter emerged from the kitchen, his white shirt now black with blood. No one cared. They chatted about art and politics, and the economy.

The room spun.

Sweat slid down my spine.

My future—this impossible artist's life I'd just glimpsed—was gone, eaten with Abe's soul. I was going to die tonight.

"You're so pale, Thomas. Take a sip." Lidia eased my Coke towards me, her hand corpse-cold against mine. She was pale. Her lips ... so red. Wine glasses steaming around us ... full of—blood?

Vampires ...

I drank my Coke. It coiled with vomit in my throat and came up fast. Acid seared my mouth as I puked onto the tile. No chunks—just the drink.

Chunks ... oh God. The waiters weren't carrying raw steak. It was people meat. That's why Lidia stopped Abe. Why James stopped Eustice from feeding me ...

"Aww." Lidia rubbed my back, holding me close. "It's okay. It's a tough thing to see the first time."

Even now, even with bile burning my teeth, I wanted her. Wanted her icy hands, her red lips. Maybe I hadn't really seen what I thought ...

"What..." A waiter offered me water and a towel before I could finish. Another was cleaning up my mess with a mop. They knew this would happen. They were ready.

"Let's go somewhere more private?" James said. "I promise you'll be safe while we talk."

What did his promise mean to me? I didn't know these people.

"Vampires?" I groaned.

Lidia laughed as she rubbed my back. Her voice was calm, gentle, "Oh, sweetie, no. We're not like those parasites. Go with James. He'll share more." She stood, her voice turning softer, pleading. "I hope you'll consider his offer."

James lifted me from the chair. Lidia walked away, an excited hop in her step.

"Are you going to kill me?" I asked.

James shook his head. "No." He considered something then kept speaking, "I work differently than they do. I don't need to feed."

We entered an empty gallery room. Distant stars watched us through the glass ceiling. Those stars died long ago, they just hadn't realized it yet.

With no paintings, the bare walls stretched, ending in slithering shadows where light could not reach.

James' steps echoed off the wooden floor, fading as he sat on a leather couch.

"Don't throw up in here," James smiled.

The room was still spinning. The wall held me up.

They killed Abe. They ate his—his soul? And then took him to the kitchen to eat the rest. He'll be on a waiter's platter, on little sticks. And I'm next. Eighteen years of work to build a future, the hopes of my parents, all sucked away, chewed up—just like Abe.

"Freaked out?" James asked. "For now, you are not on the menu." James sat cross-legged facing me. "Your friends aren't so lucky. You have something we're missing."

What did I have?

Besides parents who taught me to be afraid of everything because everything was trying to ruin my future—oh and here's the proof. I sneak out to one party and it is full of soul sucking cannibals.

"I don't —"

"You're an artist. Just like I'm a musician. People like us make eternity worth living," James said.

"Eternity? Immortals? You said you're not like them?"

"Yes on all accounts. They've chosen to be like that. I'm, well, I didn't mean to choose this." James shrugged, as if asking, *or did I?*

"And they want me to be like them?"

"That's what Lidia is hoping. Your friends were just a bonus."

"They're not my friends. They can't stand to be around me," I corrected James. Maybe once we were friends, but I didn't really have anything in common with them anymore. If I ever did.

"We want you to fill our walls with your work." James motioned to the emptiness engulfing us. "And I," James shifted, "could use someone to be more than a patron. Business is so boring, yet, it is what they love. It is why they live."

"Are ... are you the lead vampire?"

James shifted, rolling his eyes. "They are my children, or my children's children, but we are not vampires. We are alive, not undead. I would argue we're more alive than even you. And to stay this alive, they eat flesh, they drink blood, but it is the souls of the young that satisfy their hunger. Such is the price of eternal life."

"And I ..."

"You are invited to join us," James finished my sentence. "There's a ritual for conversion. That's why my little Lidia brought you here, for their approval. For *my* approval. And I not only approve, I request your consideration of our offer."

"But you don't know me. Where's the review, the application, the acceptance criteria?" My voice cracked. "I didn't work for this."

James only shrugged. "I have seen pyramids crafted, Caesars rise and fall, Kings devoured by their subjects. I heard songs before men carved harps from wood. No application captures greatness. It reveals itself. And when it does—it cannot be ignored."

"If I say no?" I asked, eyes flicking to the hallway that led to the exit. Two men flanked the door like carved sentinels in fine suits. They weren't stationed to keep people out—they were the last thing between me and the street. Locked doors could hold a building closed; those men made sure the meals stayed put.

With the slow, casual air of someone taking out a pocket watch, James reached into his coat and produced a hammer and a chime.

"This will loosen your soul from your body, and I'll have the others eat you right now. It will crush my little Lidia," he said, voice soft, regretful. "So, I encourage careful consideration."

Saying no meant death. It meant disappointing Lidia ...

James predicted my next question, "There's no going back after the ritual. But would you want to? No one understands you like we do."

He was right. Abe or Jorge didn't know me. Neither did my parents. They wanted me to be a teacher—I hate kids. They wanted me to be safe, steady, what they wished they had. That's not me.

Is it?

My storm rumbled within, stirring and swirling with loss for all the things I've never done to prepare for a future that's ending tonight if I don't say yes. But maybe I can get out? All the exits can't be guarded. I can get home, call the police, escape this nightmare, let my autopilot future navigate the storm within me.

I should be running to find Jorge. I should be screaming for Abe. I shouldn't feel relief. No more waiting for their phone calls that never came, no more standing outside their jokes, sketchbook in hand like a dog hoping for scraps.

What kind of monster feels lighter watching a friend die?

My stomach twisted.

Abe's face flickered in my mind—laughing, handing me his skateboard—and even that memory felt distant, like someone else's life. The future was always better than today; now it had one less anchor.

"Lidia wants to receive your answer," James said. "She's in the parlor. Asked me to keep you here for a few minutes while she wrapped up a chore."

I nodded, then asked, "So, if you're not like them, what are you?"

James smiled. "A musician who asked the wrong mentor for the wrong things. I thought I was as flawless as the sun. That forever would be enough time to become myself—for others to see the real me. Instead, it was just enough time to drown in mistakes. This punk scene helps. No drugs, no drinking." He crossed his arms in an X, grinning. "Straight edge. My little rebellion against who I was ... who I still am."

I asked, "Is it working?"

"It's hard to leave the good ole days behind. The past has a way of being better than it was." He motioned for me to follow him.

I did.

We slipped through the party in silence. Waiters swept past with silver platters, blood pooling in their grooves. Abe was gone—reduced to a smear on sticks and a stain of gravy. I should have broken for him, but I didn't care.

My indifference sickened me more than the blood.

James led me into a small parlor. It was well furnished with plush velvet chairs. A soft couch invited me to lie down, take my mind off the horrible things I've seen tonight, or pluck a book from the dusty shelves lining the room, and just relax. A small fireplace snapped and popped, sending cinnamon and smoke curling through the room—sweet at first, then choking burned char.

An easel stood ready for me, facing the couch.

James shut the door as he left.

Before I could examine the bookshelves, Lidia entered through another door. She wasn't alone. A woman was with her, not an immortal. Both wore green silk robes closed loosely at the belt.

"I hope you don't mind," Lidia ran her fingers over the other woman's freckled face, twirling her curls. "Candi is going to join us."

"Is he the artist?" Candi asked, smiling, hopeful.

"He is." Lidia returned the smile, her saliva slick teeth glimmering in the firelight. Those eyes, so hungry, locked into mine as she turned to close the door.

Before it shut, the chimes began again. Their high-pitched summons called the immortals to their next meal.

Jorge ran by the door screaming, *"No!"*

I didn't call to him. Shame slithered through my guts as I stayed silent. Jorge was strong—he could fight his way out, just like in the pit, just like when he'd stand up to bullies for me and Abe. That was then. Now he barely noticed me. Now he never cared. Not like he'd help me if I was the one running out there.

I shifted towards the door, because I should. But Lidia's eyes met mine, roweling the storm, the want and cold and anger and freedom stirred deep within.

She slowly pressed the door shut with a heavy, final, click.

Lidia led Candi to the couch and said, "I want to be your first portrait." Facing Candi, Lidia slowly, reveling in the performance, pulled the woman's belt loose. She slid the robe over Candi's freckled shoulders as if unwrapping a gift.

I tried to swallow. My throat only clicked as my jaw hung open.

This wasn't real. This was a fantasy ... a temptation. *In DC, temptation is everywhere*, Mom said.

"Be a dear, lie on the floor, my sweet." Lidia guided Candi down, exposing her naked body. Hickeys blotted her breasts. Needle tracks scarred her arms and thighs. She was flesh, flawed, fragile. Real. Candi lay on the floor, shadows dragging over her uneven skin.

Then Lidia slithered free of her robe, shedding it, letting the second skin pool beside Candi. I trembled. She wasn't naked, she was revealed, nude. Beside Candi, Lidia was divine—the goddess I glimpsed at the show, glowing pale in the hearth's glimmer. Her breasts were firm, her nipples hard in the heat. In the firelight her pubic hair was blazing gold, trimmed with care as if every inch of her body had been sculpted for worship.

She lowered herself onto the couch, stretching like a queen claiming her throne. She drew Candi to her, draping the girl across her lap, guiding her freckled face to rest upon the altar of Lidia's flawless, alabaster thigh.

My breath caught. I fumbled for my charcoals, my sketchpad. How many men dreamed of this—two women, one divine, one mortal—spread before them? And here it was. My life. My future.

"Thomas," Lidia said, her voice low, "have you decided on our invitation?"

I set my page. I hadn't. I wanted to—but it was the end of everything beyond these walls.

Charcoal swept across the paper, frantic to keep pace with her beauty. Within me the storm rumbled, raging, reaching out to Lidia. Her icy blue eyes felt mine, fixing on me, inviting me, daring me closer. *Come*, they said. *Touch us. Feel her warmth, my chill, the curves of my flesh. Smear the charcoal across me until you cannot tell where I end and your creation begins. Capture me. Claim me.*

"This could be your life Thomas." Lidia sighed as she lifted Candi's face higher up her thigh.

Candi giggled, slowly drawing her tongue up Lidia's leg, all the while watching my reaction.

"And you'd have parties like this forever. Friends like Candi, forever." Lidia met the woman's eyes and smiled. Her teeth gleamed as spit stretched in webs between her lips.

Candi was Lidia's plaything, but the fantasy was cracking—the nightmare peeking through coarse splinters. My charcoal paused as I strained to see where the nightmare was taking me. The truth sent my pulse racing, my mouth filling with the metallic tang of adrenaline. Candi's fate came into focus.

I turned from the vision and kept drawing.

Lidia giggled softly, striking the chime by the couch. It rang the bright and building chord until I couldn't hear it anymore. "Well, not Candi." Lidia sucked in a sharp breath, pulling a wisp of gold mist from Candi's mouth. The dark-haired woman sighed with calm delight, relaxing into Lidia's lap. "Most like how we take everything away. All the pain, all those messy feelings rotting inside them."

I kept moving around my work, keeping the easel between them and me. Lidia stroked Candi's hair, again pulling the woman higher up her leg. She leaned down to kiss Candi, and before their lips met, Lidia took another sip from the woman who again moaned in delight.

"Why me?" I asked. "Of all the people at the show, why me?"

Lidia's face scrunched, debating, then said, "You rely on labels and dates for the quality of your food, but we have no such things. We can smell the life in you, smell how long you have because the longer you have the more you sustain us. When I saw your talent, your art, I knew it was wrong to let the world have you for so short a time."

I stopped drawing.

The charcoal tumbled out of my hand.

"I wasn't going to tell you, but you asked—and I cannot lie to someone so beautiful." Lidia pulled Candi up again, sipping more from her soul. Candi smiled, going numb sip by sip.

"I die ... I mean, young?"

Lidia nodded sadly, "I don't know how. We just know you are not long for this world. That's why everyone's been so curious about you. They knew you weren't food. They knew you were special, just like I knew."

"But ..." I couldn't finish. College. Career. Marriage. House. Kids. Retirement. A life I never started, built on my parents' fears. I'd done nothing, risked nothing, guarding a future that was never going to happen.

"Oh." Lidia shoved Candi aside, the woman sprawled on the floor, smiling blankly. "I–I didn't think it mattered. I thought you were going to say yes." Tears pooled in her eyes. "Please, don't say no. Let your future be like ours—endless, time enough to do anything, everything."

She wrapped her nude body around mine. Her cold seeped into me, numbing the storm until it stilled. Confused, I stared past her. What was the point of everything I'd done?

Her hand slid up my neck, and I quaked in her arms. She moaned—a low, delighted sound, the same Candi made for her with each sip.

She whispered close to my ear, "I want to kiss you, but can't. Even a little kiss, I might not control my hunger. God, I want you."

I pulled away from her.

She smiled then gasped at my drawing.

"Thomas." She shook her head. Tears slid down her cheeks. "Is that," her voice quivered, "is that how you see me?"

She was killing this woman in front of me. Abe was dead. Jorge was dead. And soon I'd be dead. If not at her hands, then soon. But I couldn't capture my fear, only her beauty, and the horrible beauty she saw in me.

I said, "I can't draw you how I see you. You are too ..." *Monstrous? Perfect?*

She squealed and hurried back to the couch, repositioning the limp Candi over her. Lidia took a giddy drink from the woman then licked her lips to catch any stray soul on her face.

"Please continue," Lidia invited me to pick up the charcoal.

I did.

She ran her fingers through Candi's hair and asked how she felt.

"Good," Candi sighed. "So numb. Just like you said. So quiet."

"Isn't that nice?" Lidia stroked her hair, meeting my eyes.

"Yeah," Candi whispered, breathy and light. "Yeah, no bad thoughts."

"No bad thoughts. No feeling." Lidia raised Candi's fingers to her lips and kissed them. "Just like you didn't feel that?"

Candi shook her head slowly.

Lidia held my eyes, took another finger and placed it deep in her mouth, sucking on it as she popped it from her lips. "And you didn't feel that?"

Candi shook her head.

Lidia smiled and brushed Candi's hair. She kissed Candi's fingers again, sucking on the tips to turn me on. It was working. I focused on the picture, the dark places around them. The dark lines dribbling from Lidia's mouth...

I paused.

Candi's fingertips were missing. Blood drooled down Lidia's chin, raining over her breasts as she crunched, chewing Candi's index finger.

She ... was eating her. And Candi just sighed with empty numb delight as her devourer snapped through bone.

Lidia smiled. Her teeth were a wall of razors—a shark's grin with rows and rows of spikes coiling down her throat.

She said, "Your teeth will come, but the ritual has begun. You will eat of her, and then I'll show you how to take what's left of her soul." She smiled, her perfect teeth returning as she spoke, "Then ... I owe you a kiss."

I couldn't breathe. Lidia returned to her feast. Candi let her. The wet slurping, long strands of muscle drawn from the wounds then snapping—ripping free from whatever held Candi together.

My gut clenched. My storm testing the walls holding it in me.

Lidia beckoned me to join her with a slow curling finger. Blood streaked down her breasts, around her thighs, dying her pubic hair black—and I should run. I should scream. I shouldn't want her. My body shouldn't want her, but I do. I want to fuck her—and not like in the movies where it's sweet and loving, she's an animal—a monster ... and so am I. And we'll fuck like monsters.

The storm slammed against its walls.

235

But if I take a bite, if I eat this woman, I will never stop. My future will be over. It will be tonight, again, and again, and again. My past will forevermore be my present, because this will be my life.

My feet took me to the couch. I wanted to be the storm, the pit, the anger and passion and danger. But I shouldn't—

Lidia was chewing on Candi's arm, her eyes fixed on my erection. She smiled and reached for my hand. I took her icy fingers in mine, and she pulled me gently down, handing me Candi's other arm.

"Your teeth aren't ready yet, so you'll have to work to get through her flesh." Lidia's voice was smokey and tempting. She wanted to see me struggle. To test me, to see how much I wanted her.

I shouldn't want this. But I did. So, I showed her how much. I bit.

The skin split easily. Copper blood filled my mouth, drowning my future, washing away college, family, life—and all the fucking expectations binding the storm within me.

The walls holding my storm cracked. Waves roared out.

I pulled away, staring into Lidia's eyes, pleading to go back, to take this freedom back, because it was terrifying to lose my family, to lose my future. This was all a mistake.

I couldn't let the storm out.

Another crack ruptured within me. The pressure in my mind vented—quieting the anxiety about tomorrow.

Lidia shook her head, smiling wider as she plunged her face into Candi's throat and drank. Candi reached up and petted her devourer's white hair. Blood crept through that white hair, dyeing it black where it dipped into Candi's muscle.

"We've already begun," Lidia said through slurping veins. She tilted my head back to Candi's arm. "The deed is done."

And so it was.

I cried as the damn shattered. The storm seized forth, overtaking me with the relief of a life without a future. No pressure to succeed. No applications to be accepted. I didn't have to work for tomorrow ever again because I'll never escape today.

So, I ate flesh and muscle. My storm grew, unleashed, and allowed to swell to what I was always meant to be.

The ritual ended with me inhaling the remains of Candi's soul from her lipless mouth. Her teeth scraped against mine as I sucked, feeling the freezing scraps of her soul soak into me. It tasted like cotton-candy. Sweet, nothing, strands of something more, ephemeral.

I fell back on the couch.

Candi tumbled to the floor, used up inside and out. After watching Abe die, knowing Jorge was dead, what was she to me but meat? How quickly we slip into the storm—how comforting to be enveloped by its madness.

Lidia mounted me, blood drooling from her breasts and chin, raining across my chest. She drove her hips down on my crotch, grinding with feverish need. I couldn't move—my father's hopes, the future he wanted for me, clung to driftwood in my raging storm. She smeared her gore-slick face against mine in suffocating kisses, the blood still hot on her icy flesh.

Her moans rumbled through me.

My dad's Thomas was pulled under. The driftwood sank. Never to surface again. Leaving only the storm.

I ripped Lidia's head back by her hair. She gasped in pleasure as I lapped up the strands of Candi's gore strung down her body from neck to breast to belly.

Lidia tore my clothes away. She slipped me into herself as I moaned, feeling her body's cold wet grip swallow my hard warmth. I laughed, cackled, as we fucked like the monsters we were. Savage. Relentless. The storm quieted between gasping breaths, content with our frenzy.

And all it asked of me ... was everything.

The flames shivered when the door crashed open. A figure staggered inside, chest heaving, but their frantic breaths vanished beneath my animalistic growls and Lidia's piercing cries.

"What the fuck!?" Jorge shouted.

Lidia kept moving—no pause, no glance, only her feverish grinding. Her eyes clung to mine, asking the question without words.

But the storm had already answered. She smiled. I crushed my mouth to hers, tasting her cotton-candy breath. She slid off me, giggling.

Jorge slammed his fists against the locked parlor door, sweat flying. He screamed for James to let him out. He begged. He cursed. He cried that there were monsters in here.

He was right.

Lidia sighed, delighted, and struck the chime. "I told James how they treated you at the show, how they threw you away. He thought you might want to express your," she chuckled, "dissatisfaction with being treated like that." She clung to me, her touch no longer cold. Our bodies slid over each other as Candi's remains dripped from us.

The chime thundered louder and louder, until the room itself trembled with its beauty. I shut my eyes and let it soak into the storm.

"God! Tommy—I mean ... Thomas, right? Thomas, what happened!?" Jorge whimpered.

"I took your advice." I smiled wide, feeling my new teeth split through the soft flesh in my throat just like the swirl of teeth deep within Lidia's mouth. Hunger dulled the pain. "I lived a little. And damn, it feels good."

T. Kulp

Tim writes slow-burn horror. His worlds hum with ancient whispers, familiar demons, and dying hope. He lives near Baltimore with family, two good dogs, and one villainous cat. Discover other works by Tim at timkulp.com.

1990s
PLAY ME

Brooke Montoya

Chapter 1

What's Up – 4 Non Blondes

"This day was so wack," Jessica says as she slides into the passenger seat of Stacie's car. She brushes her long, curly, dark hair out of her face, the Oklahoma humidity causing it to grow three sizes. "And my hair looks like trash."

"Nice to see you too, bitch," Stacie says, rolling her eyes at her friend. "I'm in a great mood."

"You are?" Jessica turns to look at Stacie, feeling a bit bad for being so grumpy.

"Not!" Stacie says, then proceeds to complain about a series of unfortunate mishaps throughout her day. "We need some retail therapy." Stacie turns the stereo up and reverses her bright red Chevy Cavalier out of the parking lot.

"Okay, but let's keep it cheap. I am broke until I get paid next week. JCPenney has cut back on my shift lately."

Both girls turn to look at each other in unison and scream, "THRIFT STORE!"

"Jinx," Stacie says.

The girls swing by to pick up Greg, Melissa, and Jason. The five of them have been friends since high school, and now they all attend the same shitty community college. Or what they refer to as High School Number Two. However, they still get to live at home, save money, party on weekends, and work their way through the college credits needed to land a decent job one day.

Stacie's backseat barely fits everyone, and it's doubtful that anyone found their seatbelts. Greg passes Melissa his lit cigarette. She takes a drag and passes it to Jessica to ash out the window. It's a dangerous game of pass the smoke.

"Shit, Jessica!" Melissa says, wiping ash from her eyes that blows into the backseat. Greg threads his hands through Melissa's, and she smiles at him. Jason catches the gesture out of the corner of his eye, as he turns to look out the window.

Stacie pulls the car into the parking lot of the Midtown Thrift Store, one of their favorite shopping spots for cheap treasures. The thrift store is Stacie's favorite. She loves to slowly take in all the items and think about the lives they each lived with someone else before arriving at the store. Purchasing an item is like adopting it and giving it a new life and purpose.

Everyone spills out of the small vehicle, excited to see what awaits inside. Greg always peruses the books. Jessica and Stacie sift through the clothes. Melissa typically looks in the home section for things to decorate her bedroom, and stocks up on items she wants to eventually put in her house when she gets her own place. Jason is all about music. Everyone disperses to their various spots, getting lost in the hunt to sift through trash and find the treasure.

"Look at this baby blue beauty!" Stacie says excitedly, holding up a ribbed tank top.

"That would look killer with your jeans and black lace choker," Jessica says.

"What's up with this?" Jason says, picking up a black CD with the words 'Play Me' in white, enclosed in a clear plastic case, sitting on a shelf away from all the other CDs. "Is that a band?" He examines the CD inside.

"Not one I have ever heard of," Greg says, resituating his five books so they don't tumble out of his hands. The words appear to have been written with Wite-Out.

"It's only a dollar," Jason says. "Dude, let's do it," Jason says, adding it to the two other discs he planned to purchase, and the group heads to the checkout counter.

The group piles back into the car and excitedly shares their finds. Jason pulls the CD out of his bag and shows it to the group.

"What the—" Stacie says as she turns the car's engine over. "Let's listen." She slides out the Sublime disc that had been playing and replaces the disc player with Jason's new black disc. "Play me? That reminds me of Alice in Wonderland when the food says, 'eat me' and 'drink me.'"

Greg lights a cigarette, and the group passes the smoke while Stacie prepares to play the disc. The music player eats the disc, and the number 4 appears in red on her digital dash.

"Four fucking songs?" Jason says, sounding disappointed. "Oh well, it was just a buck, I guess."

Track 1 plays *Take a Picture* by Filter.

"Oh, I love this song. I bought the Filter CD just for that track," Jessica says, bobbing her head.

"You bought an entire CD for one song?" Greg asks, looking at Jessica like that's the craziest thing he's ever heard.

"Totally, dude. Sometimes that's what makes you buy it, but then you listen to the other tracks and fall in love with those songs, too," Jason adds.

"No, usually I just pop in the disc and listen to the ones I want to hear, then swap it out for another band," Jessica clarifies. Jason laughs at Jessica and takes the cigarette from Stacie, inhaling a long drag.

"Save some for me," Melissa says, reaching toward the cigarette.

"Next song," Jason says.

Stacie hits the button, and the next song starts. Immediately, the familiar tune is recognized by the group.

"Sex and Candy!" Melissa shouts. "Who sings this again?"

"Marcy's Playground," Jason answers.

"I freakin' hate this song. It's overplayed on the radio and once you hear it, you can't get it out of your head," Stacie says.

"Sex and Candy? What in the hell does that even *mean*?" Melissa asks.

"Drugs, babe. Sex and drugs," Greg says, patting her on the head like an innocent toddler.

"Don't be condescending!" Melissa snaps at him.

Greg mouths 'I'm sorry' and kisses her on the lips.

"Next song!" Jason demands from the backseat.

'So long ago…'

"Oh yeah," Jessica says, waving her hand in the air to the tune of the Wallflowers' song, *One Headlight*.

"This is a banger," Jason says, playing the drums on the back of Jessica's seat.

"Okay, one more. What do we think it's gonna be?" Stacie asks, her finger hovering over the next button on the CD player.

"Who freakin' knows with this CD. I'm still wondering why it has an ominous 'PLAY ME' written on it," Jason says.

"Someone's probably just trying to be funny," Greg says.

Stacie hits the next button and a heavier guitar riff starts.

"Oh shit!" Greg says and starts playing the air guitar.

Melissa shoves him playfully. "You're a dork."

Alice in Chain's song *Man in the Box* plays loudly from the speakers as the group sings the chorus together. Greg reignites his air guitar as Melissa side-eyes him with a smile.

"Well, I'm not sure what to think about that," Stacie says, turning on the radio.

"Me either, but that was kind of fun," Jason says.

"Was it worth your dollar?" Stacie asks, looking at Jason in the rearview.

"Absolutely," Jason says.

Chapter 2

Take a Picture – Filter

"Jason left his damn CD in my car," Stacie says, as she pops it out of the dashboard and places it back inside its clear plastic case.

"Too bad it only has like four songs on it. Random songs at that. So weird," Jessica says.

"So lame," Stacie adds. Stacie replaces Jason's CD with Alanis Morrisette, and the girls crank the volume, singing loudly as they drive down the interstate. Their female rage surfaces closer with each guitar riff.

"God, I love her," Jessica says as the girls step out of the car and take in the view. Stacie's tennis shoes crunch on the gravel as she looks straight ahead. The spring air smells of growing flowers and allergies. It is unseasonably warm; almost summer temperatures.

Stacie places her hands on her hips surveying the scene. "Okay, so not really a mountain, more of a small hill."

"Whoever named this place Mt. Scott clearly never traveled out of Oklahoma."

"Compared to the rest of the state, this probably was like a mountain."

"Well, it's the best we've got, so let's go," Jessica says as she ties her flannel a bit tighter around her waist. The girls begin climbing the trail, slowly making their way to the flat peak at the top where they are rewarded with the ability to look out over the plains and see for miles. Their feet followed the dirt path that many before them had worn down. The trail was an easy one. A bit steep in some sections, but overall not a strenuous hike. Not like some of the trails Jessica had hiked in Colorado with her family. Those were brutal. Her dad would yell the entire time that everyone was climbing too slowly. Despite his neurotic behavior, she still loved hiking.

"Wait, stop here," Stacie says, pulling out her disposable camera. She pushes the button, and the camera clicks a picture of Jessica with trees and rocks behind her, her dark curls in a high ponytail, her cheeks flushed pink, with the perfect glow from just a bit of sweat. The girls finally get to the top and take a second to catch their breath.

"I probably need to smoke a little less," Stacie says, bending over with her hands resting on her knees.

"Let me take *your* picture now," Jessica says. Stacie takes a position just cliffside, so the camera catches the view of the city below and the puffy clouds in the sky. "That is so beautiful."

"Thanks, be-otch," Stacie says.

"Girl, I meant the view."

"Take one more," Stacie says as she glances behind her and takes one more step back, closer to the edge. "Let me pose." She bends her knee and flings out her hip for a cuter stance. "Is my stomach flat?"

Jessica rolls her eyes and places the camera up to her face to peer through the window.

"Fuck," Stacie says as she slips on the gravel and loses her footing. Her eyes widen and her hands flail as they try to find anything to grasp onto. She face plants onto the ground and lets out a yelp.

"Oh my god, are you okay? You almost fell off the edge of the fucking mountain."

The girls look at each other as the word 'mountain' lingers between them, then they bust out laughing.

"That was close," Stacie says, her heart pounding in her chest. "You'd think I had vodka in this thing," she adds, holding up her water bottle, trying to make light of what could have been a very serious situation.

"I wish you did," Jessica says.

Suddenly, a large crow swoops down near the girls, then flies up into a tree.

"Holy shit! That bird was right in your face," Stacie yelps.

"I know. Little fucker," Jessica directs her response towards the bird as she tightens her ponytail. The bird flew down from the tree and landed on the ground. "Can I take a picture of the bird who almost took off my nose?" Jessica asks Stacie, knowing her film is limited.

Stacie nods. Jessica creeps toward the bird with the camera held up to her eye. Slowly, she steps forward to get a better shot, trying not to scare it. Quickly, with no warning, the bird flies off the ground and shoves the camera hard against Jessica's face with its feet. As the bird flies away, Jessica drops the camera and stumbles forward.

"Jessica, stop!" Stacie screams, too far away to be of any help. Jessica loses her footing and falls near the edge of the mountain.It shouldn't have happened. It really doesn't make any sense that it did. But Jessica slips and rolls right off the edge of the mountain, her body tumbling to meet the rocks and branches below.

Stacie runs quickly to the edge to peer over. "Jessica!" She screams after her friend.

But Jessica's body lies mangled at the bottom, her leg contorted in an odd angle, blood already pooled around her head. Jessica wasn't moving.

The mountain was quiet except for the chirping of birds and trees rustling in the wind. But all Stacie could hear was the blood-curdling scream Jessica made as she plummeted to her death.

Stacie was numb. Confused. How could this have happened? The park ranger had said it was likely a fluke accident caused by her untied shoe, but Stacie had known better. She had seen it happen. The group gathered at

Stacie's house to mourn their friend and support one another. They cried. Shared stories. Even laughed at some of the silly memories. However, none of them could believe their friend was gone.

"Just yesterday she was bobbing her head to music in your car," Jason said to Stacie.

"She'll never get to wear the cute jeans she bought yesterday," Stacie said, sitting on her bed, looking down at her carpet, focusing on the intricate details of the course material that she had never stopped to notice before. "Oh yeah, you left your stupid CD in my car," Stacie told Jason.

"Oh cool, I wondered where I put it," Jason said.

"Wait, you said she was taking a picture of a bird when she fell?" Greg asked, standing up as the rest of the group remained sitting on Stacie's bed.

Stacie nodded, her brows creased.

"*Take a Picture*; the first song on the CD," Greg said slowly, his gaze flickering back and forth before his eyes went wide.

"Dude, shut the fuck up," Jason said. "That sounds like some *Final Destination* bullshit"

"I know. I know, but it's weird, isn't it?" Greg asked.

"It's definitely fucking weird," Melissa said. "But I think you're trying to make sense out of a tragedy that just doesn't make sense."

Tears begin streaming down Stacie's face. "That scream she made," she said. Jason leaned over and pulled her in for a hug. "What I saw didn't make sense. I just wish I had been closer to help her."

"Don't blame yourself," Melissa said, standing up to sit by Stacie and hug her on her other side. Greg joins them, and they all embrace.

"I'm just so thankful I have all of you," Stacie said.

Chapter 3

Sex and Candy – Marcy's Playground

"What do you think about what Jason was saying yesterday?" Melissa asks Greg, who is sprawled out on his black and grey comforter.

"Who knows. Can we take a break from thinking about that?" He asks as he pulls Melissa down on top of him. She rests her head on her hand and snuggles up against him. "I just want to enjoy some alone time for a bit." He gently grabs her arm to nudge her all the way on top of him.

"How can you think about making out at a time like this?" She asks.

"Because I'm always in the mood to make out with you. Besides, we have the house to ourselves, and we're in my bed, instead of being cramped in my car like we usually are. Melissa ponders this as she climbs on top of Greg, straddling him.. He's not wrong. Usually, their sex-capades take place in Greg's Mustang, where neither of them can hardly move.

She leans down and kisses him, her lips softly gliding over his. Greg is an amazing kisser. He slips Melissa's shirt over her head and tosses it on his bedroom floor amidst food wrappers and dirty clothes. His mom always bitches about how dirty his room is. But it isn't dirty; just messy.

Melissa's dark hair falls around her breasts, sitting perkily in her black lace bra, and she can already feel Greg getting excited.

"I thought we were just making out?" She says, knowing damn well he never really means that.

"We are," he whispers as he unclasps her bra, releasing her large breasts from the fabric.

Melissa slides off her jeans and lays down next to Greg. He pulls off his jeans and rolls on top of her. Just before he slides inside her, she places her hand on his chest.

"Wait," Melissa says.

"What?"

"That song, *Sex and Candy*. What if we die while we're having sex?"

Greg lets out a long, frustrated sigh. He's rock hard and ready to go, but now he has to comfort his girlfriend. "That's all just bullshit, Mel. It will be okay, I promise."

She thinks about it for a second, then relents with a whispered, "Okay."

Greg slides inside her, and the two forget about the stress, potential looming death, and their poor, dead friend, if only for half an hour.

Melissa gets dressed and runs Greg's brush through her messy hair.

"See, nothing happened," Greg says, sitting on the edge of his bed. He slides his shirt back over his head, kisses Melissa on the forehead, and then heads out of the room to the restroom.

Melissa glances at herself in the mirror for a second, making sure her hair isn't a sign to Greg's mom of what happened in his bedroom. She notices some gum sitting on the desk. Her mouth is dry, and her breath probably smells rank. She pauses, thinking about the damn song again, and reassures herself gum is not candy. She pops the gum into her mouth and tosses the foil wrapper into the trashcan.

"Babe?" she calls out to Greg.

"I'm pissing. I'm going to get some water, do you need some, too?" he calls back from the bathroom.

Suddenly, Melissa feels the gum expanding in her mouth, and slowly sliding toward the back of her throat. She tries to cough and move it back into the front of her mouth, but the sticky goo has lodged itself and wouldn't budge. Panicking, she sticks her fingers into her throat, attempting to make herself gag.

Nothing.

She tries to pull the gum out with her fingers, but it stretches and strings out of her mouth. Her throat convulses, attempting to suck in air as the bulk of the gum remains lodged in her throat.

She can't breathe.

She sees herself in the mirror; mouth gaping open, hands around her throat, eyes wide. She is choking, and she can't scream for help.

She is helpless.

She tries to walk out of the bedroom to find Greg, but she is already getting lightheaded. The room begins to spin, and she is starting to feel confused. Then, without warning, her body collapses to the ground. She falls onto her stomach, her limbs outstretched, as if reaching for someone or something that isn't there to help.

Minutes later, Greg returns with two glasses of water in his hands. He sees Melissa lying on the floor. He drops the glasses, and they shatter on the wood floor, water rushing over his feet like a burst dam.

"Melissa!" he yells, rolling her body over. Her mouth is gaping open and her eyes are wide as they stare at the ceiling.

"Melissa!" he yells again, shaking her.

Nothing.

He grabs her wrist.

No pulse.

He runs out of his room to the kitchen to dial 9-1-1.

Chapter 4

One Head Light – Wallflowers

Greg, Stacie, and Jason gather inside Stacie's room.

Same as before.

Mourning a friend.

Except this time, they are mourning *two* friends.

"What the hell is happening?" Stacie says.

"Guys. I told you," Greg says.

"Stop that shit, man," Jason says.

"*Take a Picture*. Jessica dies while taking a picture of a bird. *Sex and Candy*. Melissa dies eating a piece of gum. Jessica's death we could write off as a coincidence, but two friends in two days, that match the first two songs? I don't fucking think so."

"It just feels so far-fetched," Stacie says. "A cursed CD?"

"So is losing two friends in two days," Greg says. "We need to make sure this doesn't happen again."

"How? Burn the CD? Tell the cops? How do we battle a supernatural force that is killing off our friends?" Jason asks. "The police will think we are bat shit crazy."

"Or that we're on drugs," Stacie says. "What was the third song?"

Jason thinks for a second, trying to remember the order. Then it comes to him. "Wallflowers."

"So, nobody drives today," Stacie says.

"I have to. I drove to your house, *and* I have work tonight," Jason says.

"And I have to go over to Melissa's parents' house tonight for dinner," Greg says.

"It's one headlight. So, maybe we need to make sure we have both of our headlights working," Jason says. "Especially at night."

"Fuck, fuck, fuck," Greg says, rubbing his face with his hands.

Tears well up in Stacie's eyes. "I don't want to die," she says. Jason pulls her into him and wraps his arms around her tightly.

"I'm not going to let anything happen to you," he says.

"You don't know that! You can't promise that."

"I know, but I am going to do my damnedest to try," Jason says.

Jason pulls his keys from his pocket, and climbs inside his Chevy truck. The sun is already going down, and the idea of the cursed CD is getting to him. They have to find a solution to make this stop. Not just avoid dying. If the CD is the reason they are all dying, that is. He turns the engine over and flips on his headlights. He steps out of his truck and walks to the front to check his headlights.

"Dude, maybe I'm just losing it," he says to himself as he climbs back into the cab of his truck. He feels like an idiot for even buying into the theory about the CD, but there's no logical explanation, so why not something illogical?

As the sun begins to set, Jason pauses to appreciate the pink, purple, and orange sky that looks like a painting. He wonders if his friends are now a part of that magnificent sky looking down on him. He turns up the volume on the radio and nearly runs off the road when he hears the words, "...one headlight," coming through the speakers. Quickly, he slaps the button to turn the radio off altogether.

"Fuck that," he says, his heart pounding in his chest. He is on full alert again. No more daydreaming of the clouds, where his friends went, or whatever nonsense might keep him from staying alive.

The two-lane highway is a typical road he always takes to work. In their small town, most things are located off this stretch of road. Tonight, it is eerily empty.

What he sees next makes his blood run cold. A car is driving toward him on the other side of the road ... with only one headlight. A perdiddle, as they used to call it when they played the headlight game as kids. Jason slows down, veering his truck to the right side of the road, ensuring the car has plenty of room to pass by, and that he can react if something unusual were to happen.

The black car approaches, swerving slightly, sending Jason's heart racing even more. It passes by him with a whizz. Jason is nearly stopped on the side of the road now. He breathes a sigh of relief and steers the truck back onto the road. Too scared to turn on the radio, he lets silence fill the truck cab. The only noise is his heart still thudding in his ears, and the sound the tires make, spinning on the pavement.

Too quiet.

His thoughts run rampant. It is fully dark now, and as he comes upon a sharp curve, he sees something that stops his heart completely.

He pulls over and gets out of the truck. His heart is thumping loudly in his ears, and his thoughts are racing trying to process what he's seeing.

A white Ford pickup truck is smashed into a tree. Jason knows this truck all too well.

It's Greg.

Jason always gave him shit for driving a Ford instead of a Chevy, and he recognizes Greg's round metallic sticker that reads 'Shit Happens.'

Jason rushes up to the truck. Greg's body is wedged halfway through the windshield. His legs are dangling down the steering wheel. His head is crushed, glass speckling his face, and blood rushing down the white hood of the truck. His eyes are gaping open, as if they are staring at Jason. Jason grabs his stomach and his heart sinks. He runs to the tree line and vomits something yellow that he had consumed earlier that day. Nothing coming out of him looks recognizable, just like Greg's body. He wipes his mouth and straightens to look at Greg's truck again, as a chill runs down his body. Greg's truck hit the tree on its passenger side, crushing the front of the car. The driver's side headlight is the only working one as the single beam of light penetrates the darkness, illuminating the trees beyond.

Chapter 5

Man in the Box – Alice in Chains

"We have to stay together. That way we can make sure we both stay alive," Stacie says to Jason.

"I was with Jessica when she died. Greg was with Melissa," Stacie says. Panic is rising in her body as she reflects on the last three horrific days.

Three friends.

Three days.

"There are four songs ..." Stacie says, letting the thought go unsaid, but knowing the ugly truth that lingers between them.

Only one of them can survive.

"So, then what? It kills one of us, and it's over? It doesn't make any sense," Jason says, sitting at Stacie's kitchen table. She pours them both a cup of tea and sets Jason's mug down in front of him. He rests his head in his hands as he rubs his face. Then he releases a big sigh.

Exhaustion.

Defeat.

A bit of both.

"We just have to stay alive. Nobody has made it past the day. Maybe if we do, it breaks this curse, or whatever is causing our friends to die," Stacie says. Jason takes a sip of the tea, the steam rising around his nose. He closes his eyes, and Stacie can tell he's scared. Although he would never admit it to her.

"Stace," Jason says, looking at her from across the table. "If something happens to one of us, I want you to know that I have always really cared about you."

"I know."

"No, I mean, like *cared* about you," he says, in his best attempt. "I just can't let something happen to one of us without you knowing that."

Stacie's cheeks blush, and her heart fills up with warmth. She has always secretly liked Jason, but he has never let on that he had feelings for her, so she never told him. Stacie watches as Jason stands up and walks toward her. He stretches out his hand, and she grabs it and stands with him. She's never seen Jason act like this. So sentimental.

"I don't know what to say," Stacie says. Jason's face falls with her response. "No, no. I mean, I've *always* liked you, Jason." He looks at her, his dark brown eyes searching her words for meaning. "Like, *a lot*. I just didn't think you were into *me*."

He grabs her abruptly and pulls her into him. His hand finds the side of her face as he slowly leans down to kiss her for the first time. A long-awaited touch of the lips. Then, he pulls back and looks at her. "Of course, we get started right as it could be ending."

"Don't say that," she whispers. "We're going to survive this." She grabs the strings of his hoodie and pulls him back down, "Just in case, kiss me again."

Jason and Stacie spent the day pondering the next song. Realizing it is going in order, they know today is *Man in the Box*, which is fucking broad. That could mean anything, and nothing at all.

They searched the house looking for any type of abnormal box. Something they could fit inside that would clue them into what they needed to look out for. Eventually they decided they were safe in Stacie's house.

"Melissa died from choking on gum. We need to safe-proof the house," Stacie says.

"We can't safe proof the entire house." Jason glanced around. Stacie's room was lined with shelves that, if they came crashing down, would land on the bed, where she slept. Figurines that could break and pierce skin, potentially causing worse injuries. Her ceiling fan could cause head trauma. But a box, was nowhere in sight.

"I'm going to leave and get rid of this CD. We need to destroy it. In the meantime," Jason says, opening her closet door and glancing inside, "why don't you clean this space out and we can make a pallet in here. A safe room where a natural disaster would be the only thing that could take them out.

Stacie glanced around the closet, feeling uncertain about the plan, but better than all the potential hazards in her room, and the other unknown hazards in the rest of the house.

"Be quick," Stacie says. "I don't want to be alone." Jason pulled her into him. He wasn't just comforting her, he was also comforting himself.

He was terrified.

They'd watched some unknown force kill three of their friends over three days. How could they ensure anything would work?

Stacie begins tossing clothes, books, shoes, and other objects out of the closet while Jason makes his way to his Chevy. The CD sits beside him in the passenger seat. He checks his headlights. Both of them still work. Although that song had already killed Greg, who really knew what the rules are to this twisted game.

Everything is just a theory.

A guess.

Outside is black and the moon hangs high in the sky. He drives down the two-lane highway, which he had just been on the other night, when he found Greg's wrecked truck. He is trying not to think about the scene he stumbled upon and attempts to stay focused on getting rid of the CD and getting back to Stacie. But it's difficult. It feels like they are missing something. Something he can't put his finger on, but none of the past few day's events make any sense. When will it end? How? Why is all this happening?

As Jason drives down the dark desolate highway, he sees the road that leads to Cheever's Park, where there is a large pond. He pulls down the side road and drives all the way back toward the water. He parks the car and sits for a minute, staring at the CD sitting in the seat next to him. It looks innocent enough.

He's scared to touch it.

He picks up the killer CD and opens the plastic container. He pops the CD out of the case, rage rises inside him, and he takes the CD in his hands and snaps it in two. Then he hops out of his truck and purposefully strides to the pond. He leans back and launches the CD and case into the water like a Frisbee. The disc soars through the air and plunges into the water. Slowly, it sinks until the water is smooth as glass again. Jason breathes a sigh of relief. But unfortunately, that sigh is followed by an inhale of pure panic.

The box.

Fuck.

Just as he starts rushing back to his truck, the skies open and rain begins pouring down on him.

He reaches his truck, throws it in gear, and speeds out of the parking lot of the park. His tires spit gravel as he makes his way to the main highway, the wheel jerking and his foot revving the gas pedal to move the truck as quickly as he can. A mile down the road, he spots a payphone. He grabs a quarter from his truck ashtray and hops out quickly. Rain beats on his head and shoulders like pellets. Slipping inside the phone booth, he shuts the glass door to drown out the noise of the rain, pops the quarter into the slot and quickly dials Stacie's number.

Ring!

"Hurry up Stacie, answer the damn phone," he says, worried, anxiety rushing through his body.

Ring!

Jason looks down and notices water is starting to seep into the phone booth around his feet. "Fuck!"

He hangs up the phone before Stacie's family's answering machine picks up and wastes his quarter. Then he grabs the quarter from the change return slot and calls her again.

Ring!

Ring!

"Hello?" A winded Stacie answers.

"Stacie, stay out of the closet!" Jason warns her.

"Huh? I can barely hear you. Where are you?"

"Stay out of the closet! That's the 'box' in the warning!" Jason screams into the phone.

Suddenly, lightning strikes the payphone. A short in the electrical wiring sizzles and runs through the telephone into Jason's hand, and down through his feet. His body buzzes. The hair rises on his arms from the shock. The shock is so strong he can't let go of the receiver, as the current runs through him and into the water. His hand turns red, then black. His heart stops.

"Jason! Are you there? What is that noise? Jason?"

Stacie hangs up the phone and decides to wait for Jason to return. But his dead body slumps down to the floor of the phonebooth like a glass grave.

Chapter 6

Hold On – Wilson Phillips

Bright sunshine shines through the slat underneath the closet door. Stacie looks around and realizes she'd fallen asleep waiting for Jason, who never came back. She opens the door and stumbles over the closet's contents now strewn across the floor of her bedroom. Panic sets in wondering where Jason is and why he never came back. She grabs the keys to her Cavalier and rushes out of her room, but she is met by her parents.

The expressions on their faces are grim.

Red eyes.

Something has happened.

"No. No. No. No. No," she says, shaking her head and falling to her knees. Her mom rushes to catch her, wrapping her motherly arms around her grieving daughter. Her parents are silent. What words could they even have for a daughter whose entire friend group had died over the last four days of unspeakable tragedies?

Eventually, no more tears would fall out of Stacie's eyes. She had cried them all out. Her parents sat her on the couch and she stared off into a void. Her body sat in her living room, but her consciousness was shut down. It was in too much pain to stay inside her body. At some point her mom gave her a pill and laid her down where she slept on the couch for what felt like most of the day.

She was the only one left.

No more songs.

The CD had chosen everyone it wanted and for some reason she was still alive.

"What is this?" Stacie's mom asked. She walked in from the front porch with something in her hand. Stacie looked at her mom and as she came closer what she saw made her start trembling.

The black CD.

"'Play me?' That's weird. Is this yours?"

"No. Throw it away!" Stacie said forcefully. Her chest felt tight and her face was on fire. Jason left last night to get rid of the CD, so how did it show back up at her house? This fucking thing had powers beyond their ability to comprehend.

She just wanted it all to stop.

She wanted her friends back ... alive.

She wanted things the way they were before they found that fucking CD at the thrift store.

"It was just sitting on the front porch."

"Please. Mom. Throw it away," Stacie said, a panic rising from deep inside spewing out.

"Okay, honey. I will. You just relax and try to get some more rest."

Stacie stood and wrapped her woven blanket around her like a cocoon. Slowly, she made her way back to her room in hopes of laying down, falling asleep, and forgetting this horrible nightmare. She heard her mom's door shut and she hoped that her mom truly got rid of the CD. She wondered if she should have made sure, but she just didn't have the energy for that.

Suddenly, an electric surge bolted through her body as she stood next to her bed. She shook her head, grief filling every pore inside her. Her eyes landed on a framed photograph sitting on her nightstand. Her vision blurred as she picked up the picture, and her eyes filled with tears. Jason, Melissa, Jessica, and Greg are smiling back at her. In the picture, their arms were interwoven and they all stood in front of her house. Now frozen in a picture, that moment was one of the happiest times. Her sixteenth birthday. The day she was gifted her Cavalier. The day she got her driver's license. The day she thought they'd all be friends forever. Go to college together. Celebrate graduation, weddings, and babies.

Stacie wiped the tears streaming down her face and placed the frame back onto the table, face down. She let the woven blanket slip from her hand and fall to the floor, piling around her feet. Slowly, like her feet were moving for her, she walked in a daze to her bathroom and turned on the bathtub faucet. More tears continued to fall down her cheeks. Salty memorials for her lost friends. She watched the white ceramic tub fill with warm water and she wished the liquid would wash her memories away. Take them with it down the drain—all the late-night taco runs, the way Melissa would roll her eyes when Greg would crack a terrible joke, the way every time they heard the word major they would salute each other.

She removed all her clothes. Then, she grabbed a straight razor from the drawer and gently placed it on the ledge of the tub. She put her foot into the warm liquid and stepped in. Slowly, she lowered herself into the water until she was nearly submerged. Leaning back against the tile wall, she drew in a deep breath and felt the air filling her lungs. She placed her hand over her heart and could feel the thumping underneath her sternum. Carefully, she picked up the razor. She stretched out her right hand and sliced her wrist with the razor. She watched the blood begin to ooze in its wake. Then she switched hands and cut her other wrist. The razor plunged into the tub as blood slowly oozed from her wrists, swirling in ribbons into the water. She took one last breath as she meditated on the blood streaming from her wrists. She tried not to focus on the finality of it, but rather the process of getting to see her friends again very soon.

Chapter 7

Here We Go Again! - Portrait

Edna's Place, the local dive bar in town, is packed like a tin of biscuits tonight. All the regulars made it in tonight. Shane checks behind the bar to make sure his bartender has what she needs before retreating to his office in the back to try and sort out the inventory order again. As he settles behind his desk, his door bursts open, and Lenny, one of his bouncers, walks over and tosses a CD on his desk.

"Lenny, you gotta knock," Shane says.

"Sorry, boss," Lenny says.

"What's this?"

"Dunno. Found it sitting on the floor by the men's bathroom. I guess we can just put it in the lost 'n found and see if someone comes to pick it up."

Shane picks up the black CD to read the writing. "'Play me'," he says in a curious tone. "Why the hell would someone write that on a CD? Let's go see what the hell is on this thing."

Lenny follows Shane to the bar, and Shane stops the current music playing; some country song about divorce. Go figure.

"Booooooo!" Several of the customers yell together. Then more join in.

"Hold your horses for fuck sake. We're just checkin' something out."

Shane places the CD into the player and notices the number 4 pop up.

"Only four tracks, people, this shouldn't take long, then I will put your country bumpkin bullshit back on." He hits play, and the first song blasts loudly over the speakers.

"Okay, some Filter. I like it so far." They bar listens to the songs play, as Filter is followed by Marcy's Playground, then Wallflowers, and last, Alice in Chains.

The patrons at the bar have enjoyed the surprise of one song to the next, becoming just as curious as Shane to see what was on the CD.

When the Man in the Box is over, a collective "boooooo" rings out from the crowd again.

"Hold on, folks," Shane yells across the room, fiddling with something on the door hinge. "Let me fix this, and I will put your hick shit back on."

Several minutes pass as Shane finishes screwing in a hinge on the door that had come loose. As he makes his way back to the stereo, the CD starts playing again. The harmonica sound at the beginning of the song is immediately recognizable.

Suicide Blonde by INXS.

One of his favorite songs.

The crowd lets out a collective, "Wooooo!" An excited cheer at the sound of the music kicking back up again.

"Huh, five songs," Shane says to Lenny. "A bonus track."

"What's a bonus track?" Lenny asks.

"Don't you have any fucking CDs, Lenny? A bonus track is a surprise song at the end of a CD that you only discover if you let it play. Somebody put a bonus track on this CD."

Lenny shakes his head and asks, "Cool. Want me to add it to the lost and found?"

"Nah, I think I will keep it," Shane says and places the black CD back into the plastic case.

Brooke Montoya

Brooke is the author of spooky stories both real and created. When she's not writing she's a licensed therapist and works as the director over several addiction programs. She's also a paranormal investigator. She lives in Oklahoma with her family and two dogs. bmontoyaauthor.wixsite.com/author

2000s

GRAVE LOVE

Chase Will

W hen a door closes, a grave opens.

I'm standing in the kitchen, one hand gripping the handle of a duffle bag and the other bringing the half-emptied bottle of Tito's vodka to my quivering lips. The power in the house has been shut off for ages, and the sun's almost fully set, but I don't mind the darkness. Darkness is appropriate for what I'm about to do.

I'm your friend, a familiar voice whispers in my mind. *I'll be the best friend you've ever had!*

The memory of a voice. Familiar shivers. Years of therapy down the drain.

My girlfriend, Ila, left me this morning. No note. No text message. Just a sudden absence of her things in our two-bedroom subterranean apartment on Sixth Street. Her *Meat Curtains* band poster—gone from the office wall. Her lockbox bequeathed to her by her late grandmother—gone from the mantle over the fireplace. Her toothbrush and box of contact lenses—gone from behind the bathroom mirror. The only thing she left behind was the scent of her Victoria's Secret perfume, a scent I've associated with her presence since we met at a bar six months ago. I can't be inside the apartment right now, surrounded by the absence of these things.

And now, the voice is back. A voice I haven't heard since I was a lonely twelve-year-old boy wandering the halls of this very house.

I wasn't the perfect boyfriend. I'll be the first to admit that. I drink too much, and I've flunked out of Alcoholics Anonymous more times than I care to count. I have night terrors that kept Ila up for hours on the really bad nights, and it's always been on her to calm me down and hold me when I wake up in tears. The bar fight I was in last week, after a twig of a kid commented loudly on the whininess of trauma survivors, may have been the nail in the proverbial coffin. I've never been a violent man, and I've certainly never laid an ill finger on Ila. But I've damaged our love little by little over the course of our dating life, and the bend was bound to break.

Come upstairs, the voice beckons. *Let me get a proper look at what you've become.*

"Not yet," I mutter. I can't face him yet, not when there's the slightest bit of sobriety still in my system.

By the time the bottle's empty, it's fully dark in the house and I'm swaying unsteadily on my feet. The moonlight casts a faint shadow on the floor. For some reason, my shadow has horns.

My mind has always been poisoned. My parents knew that even before they died.

Slowly, hesitantly, I exit the kitchen and walk toward the staircase. I study the thick and undisturbed dust on the railing. Part of me was expecting handprints, or other telltale signs of unwanted visitors in the abandoned property. Part of me was expecting the voice to have taken corporeal form.

I'm waiting, Max, he says. *Friends always wait, no matter how long it takes.*

I've given up trying to block out the nameless entity's voice. I tried this morning, when it was suddenly speaking in the back of my mind, but it was to no avail. At first, I blamed Ila's unexplained departure, telling myself the long-forgotten voice from my past could just be a psychosomatic symptom of my anxiety over the presumed break-up. But the better part of me knows it's real, and he's back. It was real enough in my childhood anyway. Real enough to destroy what innocence I had.

Ila didn't leave me. She couldn't have just left. He took her, and I'm here to get her back.

I climb the stairs, laboring slightly because of my bad left hip. I took up weightlifting last summer, perhaps as a way of dealing with my quarter-life crisis. I got injured only two weeks into my planned routine. No surgery, just an occasional sharp pain to remind me of my hubris giving way to mortality.

Upstairs are three bedrooms: my parents' old room directly in front of me, their old office with an adjoining bathroom to my far left, and my old bedroom to the right. My room was the largest of the three. Some people might say I was spoiled, but my parents said it was to promote the idea of making friends and having playdates. I was a lonely child, though, prone to choosing imaginary friends over those comprised of flesh and blood. What friends I did make were quick to leave and never come back as soon as I spoke about the voice.

I walk toward my old bedroom. In a horror movie, this would perhaps be the moment lightning illuminates the hallway and scary shadows play across the walls. But the night is serene, and the creaking sound of my footsteps is the only soundtrack to my pilgrimage to where it all began.

The room is empty. Just four blank walls and a closet without a door. I stand in the center of the room, knees shaking and alcohol tying my stomach into knots. I stare at the large smiley face I'd carved into the left wall, mere hours before my parents disappeared and my life changed forever.

Hello there, friend, the smiley face says to me. *I missed you! My, how you've grown!*

"Cut the shit," I tell him, sounding much stronger than I feel right now. "Where is she? What did you do to her?"

Hmm ... I don't know what you're talking about. Did someone else leave you, Max? Did someone hurt my dear, sweet friend?

My mind flashes back to the night it all happened. I see my father standing over me in this very room, his leather belt folded in one hand as he screamed about how I'd ruined the wall. We'd only moved into the house a month prior, with plans to revitalize the old property and flip it on the market, which was vastly in the seller's favor at the time. The damage I'd done with a butterknife would cost money to fix. Money we didn't have much of.

Mom stood crying in the doorway as Dad beat my bare rear. I cried out with each lash of the belt, trying to explain between sobs that the voice was real and that *he'd* made me do it.

The beating abruptly stopped while my dad was mid-swing, and the belt fell to the floor. When I stood up, wiping tears from my eyes, both my parents were gone.

Yummy, the voice had said before eliciting a loud belch. *Nobody hurts my new friend.*

I clench my eyes shut, willing the memory away. I spent years in trauma therapy after my parents' disappearance. Doctors listened to my story. Police officers made me repeat it ad nauseum. There was no sign of foul play, so it was assumed I was just another abandoned child.

"There was no sign Ila was going to leave me," I mutter to the wall, absently wiping my mouth with the back of my sleeve. "All the time we've been together, all our long nights, she was always so supportive."

But people always deceive you, the smiley face says. *You can't always trust those you love, Maxy. You can't even trust yourself.*

"Don't call me that!" I snap, pointing a finger at the wall. "You took her. You ate her. I know you did, you bastard!"

Who, me? I'm just a wall. You'll have to ask the mirror about that.

This is getting nowhere. I don't know why I came back here after all this time. Could it be a coincidence I heard my old friend's voice again right around the time my girlfriend went missing? Highly unlikely.

Maybe she just got tired of you, the wall says. *Such a serious boy. Always asking questions you're better off not knowing the answers to. Always so worried.*

If my old friend isn't going to give me the answers willingly, I'll have to try something else. But how do you torture answers out of a wall?

I slam my fist against it, feeling the skin over my knuckles break. I leave a good sized hole right in the center of the smiley face, creating what looks like a clown's nose.

"Tell me how to get her back," I demand. "She never hurt me the way my parents did. You weren't supposed to take her."

But the wall is suddenly silent. I can feel him staring back at me, but it seems I've pissed him off. I don't care, though; I'll get what I need out of him.

I reach into my bag and pull out a baseball bat. It's the same old bat dad used to hit pop-flies to me with in the backyard, shouting at me, "Get under the damn ball!" Always a good coach, regardless of his drinking habits. Even after all the trauma of losing both my parents to the wall, I was the best player on my high school baseball team.

"Last chance," I say, winding up the bat. I don't know why I'm giving warnings to a wall.

If Ila saw me now, she'd gently take my arm and force me to lower the bat, reminding me that anger is never the best way to handle frustration.

She'd understood me because, like me, she'd had a troublesome childhood with parents that never really cared for her. Her dad had been abusive like mine, always using his fists in teachable moments rather than his words.

It was how we met, at a coffeeshop on Main Street. I was journaling at a small table, and she'd spilled her drink on my shoulder as she tripped on her way past me.

I was so stricken by her eyes—bright green, like mine—that I fumbled for words as I accepted her apology and asked if she'd like to join me. She did, and asked what I was writing. I handed her my journal, slightly embarrassed, but she didn't look at all amused or turned off as she read the half-page of bad poetry about my childhood. She actually wept a little, and she told me how my words struck a chord with her.

We talked until the coffeeshop closed, and even though a few teenagers laughed at us from across the room, we didn't stop our animated conversation. After walking her out the door, I asked if I could see her again. She said yes, and that was that—I was in love.

She isn't here right now, though, to calm me down. It's just me and the bastard wall who'd taken everything in my life, bit by bit.

Look around, Max, my friend tells me. *You'll never get your girlfriend back. You never really had her to begin with. She was never really there, was she?*

The bat, still gripped tightly in my hands, lowers slightly. "What are you talking about?"

You're a very disturbed boy, Max. All this time ... all this crippling loneliness. You needed someone to love you in a way I never could. Someone who could understand you. Someone you could touch.

I think of the morning pancakes my wife made for me only days ago. I think of the goodnight kisses, and the fanciful hopes and dreams we've shared. We were going to have children someday, kids who would have the lives we never could make for ourselves.

But there's something skewed about these memories now, like a translucent tarp has been cast over them, blocking out something.

I only take those who hurt you, my friend says. *But you've always looked out for yourself, even subconsciously. It's why you avoided showing Ila to anyone else. It's why you never took her outside your apartment.*

Suddenly, I smell her Victoria's Secret perfume, pungent and overpowering. I turn quickly, expecting to see her standing behind me.

She's not there.

But there are two shadows trailing from my feet.

You made her up, Max. You really, really wanted her to be real, but she never was. I'm sorry, but the only one who's ever really loved you is you.

"Ila?" I ask, turning in circles in search of her. "Babe, where are you?"

No one answers. But as I turn to the wall again with the bat raised, determined to get real answers and end this bullshit, I catch sight of my hands.

My fingernails are painted red, like the ones that used to stroke my arm in the middle of the night, telling me everything's going to be okay.

It's a trick. It has to be. This poisoned house has corrupted my mind somehow, and I'm seeing things that aren't there.

How unfortunate for you, Max, the wall says. *To have such an imaginative mind ... only to lose it when you need it most. It's why I called out to you again. You needed a real friend.*

"I'm going to leave," I tell him quietly. "I'm going to go down the street, get gallons of gasoline, and I'm going to burn this place down with you in it. What would happen to you then?"

The wall doesn't answer, but a cavalcade of memories leap to the forefront of my mind. I remember this morning, when I went through the apartment in a daze and threw away all the dresses I'd worn; all the parts of me that made Ila real. The only thing I'd forgotten to do was remove the nail polish.

Don't worry, Max, my friend says. *I don't care how broken you are. I don't even care that you're more cracked than I am. I'm just glad you've come home to see me. All we need is each other.*

Tears run down my cheeks, and a small, weak noise escapes my mouth. I just want Ila back. I want to feel her touch again and hear her soft voice in the night.

But she was never really there.

Our love was never real, and I'm as alone as I've ever been.

Love is just a haunted house.

Chase Will

Chase Will is from Coshocton, OH, where some of the kindest people in the world live. He loves horror movies, punk and metal music, theater, and competing in amateur powerlifting. He's written for several horror websites, including Dread Central, HorrorNews.net, Scare Tissue, and CryptTeaze.

2010s

Bloody Tide

Pamela K. Kinney

Growing up in San Diego, John Crouch remembered his mother always saying that the Pacific Ocean looked like a woman in her best dress of blue-green when the sun shone down on her. Sometimes though, the dress changed to dark gray, the waves like a skirt whipping in the wind. Mama said that was when the stormy Pacific was at her sexiest and most dangerous.

Today, the ocean looked peaceful beneath the late afternoon sun. The sunlight hitting the water sparkled like diamonds. Mama also remarked that the ocean was the right cure for you when you didn't feel well or felt down in the dumps.

Mama's right. The Pacific is the best medicine.

John rolled the motor home to a stop at their camp site a few feet from the beginning of a path that led down to the beach. He saw a boat pulling a water-skier in its wake, heading south. Farther out, a single dolphin shot out of the water, did a flip, and with a splash, vanished back beneath the waves. Seagulls screamed from above as they soared with little effort.

Yep, great medicine. Maybe this might bring his wife back to him.

Though not March 21st yet—still considered technically winter—the temperature in San Diego usually stayed in the sixties. Actually, it reached those temps back in January and February. The only cold he had experienced this winter came from his wife, since their baby son, Johnny, died exactly on January 1, 2010. An awful beginning for the new year.

Desiree never cared about anything these days, not even him or their marriage. He tried everything. Nothing helped as she lapsed more and more into depression. Nightmares plagued her every night. The pills her doctor prescribed hadn't done much good either. Finally, he took her doctor's advice about taking her on a vacation. They didn't have much money left after the baby's death and Desiree's doctor bills, plus he had only a week's worth of vacation time saved. A week down at the ocean on some land they owned at Solana Beach was all he could manage. Might be the last time they use it, as he planned to sell the land for needed cash to pay the bills.

He rolled down his window, breathed in the sea air, and turned to his wife with a grin. "The Pacific looks splendid, doesn't it? Smell that ocean air. It's invigorating."

She didn't answer him, just stared with obvious disinterest out the passenger window. A headache began to form behind John's eyes.

He exited the driver's side and stared at the water. He liked to fish, and Desiree loved to sunbathe at the beach. Most public beaches with nearby fishing piers held crowds during the summer and they both hated it. That was one of the reasons they decided to purchase this parcel of land long ago. Here he could fish right off the water and any children they had would have a beach to play on and splash in the waves. He had planned that he and Desiree would retire and build a small house or live in a trailer on the property. Johnny's death, and the inevitable sale of the land killed that idea.

Desiree did not get out, instead she climbed around her seat and into the motorhome. He wandered around to the back and rolled his motor-cycle off the trailer hitched to the motorhome and propped it upright. He took the gas grill off before unhitching the trailer. The grill sat nearby, but far enough away from the motorhome for safety. John put the propane tank onto it and a few minutes later, had the fire on the grill blazing high. After a bit, the flames lowered until the air above it shimmered from the heat.

He knew he would have to get the steaks and potatoes he'd bought at the supermarket back home. No doubt Desiree probably had gone straight to bed in the bedroom at the back of the motorhome. That was all she'd done for the past three months—sleep. But as he turned to head inside, the door burst open, and Desiree stepped out. She carried a plate with two steaks in one hand and two aluminum foil wrapped potatoes in a plastic bowl in the other. He took both from her and placed the steaks and potatoes on one side of the grill. She took the empty plate and bowl from him and carried them back inside.

He stared at the closed door for a minute. *Desiree hadn't done that since* . . . His headache eased down a notch. He smiled as he lowered the lid on the grill. Maybe, just maybe, things might be turning around at last.

He closed his eyes. *"You're right, Mama, the Pacific Ocean is a super cure.*

When dinner was cooked and the picnic table set up, Desiree brought out plates, utensils, a carton of sour cream, butter, and two cold cans of soda. Still smiling, John deposited the grilled steaks and potatoes on the plates. She sat at the table across from him and tackled her food.

As they ate, he said, "It's good to be here, isn't it?"

Silence. Except for her chewing, waves crashing on the beach, and the cry of a seagull.

He gripped his fork tighter until it almost bent in half. She must have seen that and yet, no reaction from her. His headache returned.

"Desiree. . ."

She stood, her plate of half-eaten food in hand. "Give me your plate and utensils and I'll wash up. Just toss the empty soda cans and other trash in the garbage."

He looked at her. Her eyes cut to the left. Defeated, he handed over his dish, fork, and knife.

She stopped at the door, not looking back at him. "I'm tired. Once the dishes are washed and put away, I'm going to bed. 'Night."

He threw away the trash, cleaned the grill as it had cooled completely, and then sat down in a lawn chair to sip from a bottle of cold beer he retrieved from the fridge inside. He didn't taste the liquid, his mind on other things.

The sun had gone down around six and dusk stretched its fingers across the water. A rotund moon rode the sky like a big white biscuit—the kind his mother used to make, soft and perfect for sausage gravy.

Mama had been from Virginia originally, had moved to San Diego County with his sister and him when Daddy died, as she had gotten a job at a hotel in El Cajon.

He grunted. Being born and raised in California, Desiree never made homemade biscuits or sausage gravy; said that neither was healthy. The only time he got to eat good old Southern grub since Mama died was when he found a small café that did Southern cooking down the street from his job. It left him with a guilt complex that made it hard to face his wife on those days he ate lunch there or the occasional breakfast when he left early, so he didn't do it very often. He stopped going to the restaurant after Johnny died. Biscuits and gravy didn't do much for the ache in his heart. No, he drank more to numb the pain. Like now. He took another swig of beer and swirled the wetness in his mouth before swallowing.

Tonight, it tasted less like the beer he liked and more like ashes.

It grew darker as clouds scrolled across the moon, cutting off its light. Quiet as a tomb, it was just him, the bugs, the sea, the beach, and ... what the— A noise coming from the beach?

He straightened. The bottle slipped from his fingers and he did not hear its thud when it hit the grass. He rose to his feet and crossed over to the beginning of the path, peering down at the darkened beach. Wait a moment. Had something blacker than the night moved in the water not far from shore? No, that must have been his imagination. Too damn dark to tell for sure anyway.

A splash, then a grunt came from the ocean.

Shit!

Not pausing to get a flashlight from inside or even his gun, he ran down to the water. Luckily, he didn't trip over anything in his path, but he stopped on the sand, right where small waves lapped hungrily at the shore. Water covered the toes of his leather tennis shoes as he inched closer, cussing the clouds for cutting off the moon beams. He heard nothing but the water. No other—

Another grunt filled the air.

What's that? That sounds close. Damn, why didn't I take a flashlight? Or my rifle!

He stuck his hands in the pockets of his jeans and realized that he didn't have his cell phone on him.

Dumb ass.

Nervous, he remembered stories his fisherman stepfather told him and his sister about how more than fish lurked beneath the murky waters of the Pacific. Things not of the natural world. Things man had forgotten except in legends. Things he thought of as made up crap spun by fishermen and sailors after several beers.

I only had one beer...

A roar rent the air. He whipped his head around, heart pounding. His stomach cramped.

WTF! What the hell made that noise?

Sea lions? No, that didn't sound like a sea lion. If that was a sea lion it had to be the size of a killer whale. Anyway, killer whales didn't roar, he remembered learning that they stayed silent when hunting and when not on a hunt, communicated by clicks and calls. As for sea lions, he heard the beasts roaring before, and that did not sound like one.

Whatever it was, he didn't want to meet it.

He bolted back to the motorhome. Loud splashes through the water, followed by the thuds of something heavy on the sand and moving through the thick grass dogged his footsteps. He prayed he didn't trip over a rock.

Oh God, oh, God, where is our motorhome...? His breathing grew ragged in his lungs and his legs protested at the running.

He reached the end of the path and saw the darkened motorhome. The lights inside came on. His breath blew out in agonizing puffs, but he still managed to scream.

"Desiree! God, Desiree, get the door open!"

The door swung open and light spilled out, his wife standing in it, a loose robe over her thin nightgown the only defense against the cool night. "What's wrong?"

He scrambled up the steps and pushed her inside. "Get in, before it gets us."

He slammed the door shut and locked it. Fighting for each breath he took and trying to slow his heart rate—unsuccessfully—he lifted a corner of the blind at the window and peered out. The darkness made it impossible to see anything.

Of course, you idiot, turn the outdoor lights on.

He hit the switch on the wall beside the door and the yellow bug light flared to life, showering a sickly light over the lawn chair and the picnic table, but nothing else. *Damn, he should have bought those LED lightbulbs he saw in the store.*

The beer bottle. Where is it? I don't remember throwing it away before heading down to the beach.

Something tapped his shoulder and he flinched. He turned and when he saw his wife, he settled down. Her eyebrows wiggled like pencil-thin caterpillars as lines grooved her forehead.

"John, tell me what's going on."

"I'm not sure."

"Not sure?"

He listened for a second and took another peek through the window, still seeing zilch. "There was something in the water, close to the beach. I didn't stop to think or grab a flashlight or my gun, I just hustled down there. It was dark and the only noise came from the waves. That's when I heard a couple of grunts, plus a roar. I ran back here, and I swear, something chased me. Whatever the hell it was, it sounded big, really big. Like a grizzly bear."

Her eyes flashed disbelief. "I don't think you'll find grizzly bears, not this close to Solana Beach."

"Really, honey. There's something out there."

"Aha. Right." She unlocked the door.

"What are you doing?" asked John, panicked.

"Proving there's nothing out here." She lifted a flashlight from a table nearby and clicked it on. The light blinded him for a moment before she shut it off. "I'll flash the light beyond the reach of the motorhome's light. I promise there will be nothing other than what your own imagination dreamt up."

He clawed for her. "No, no, no..."

Too late, she opened the door and stepped outside. He stared at the doorway, barely acknowledging the cool air seeping in. Scared shitless, but more worried about Desiree, he slipped out after her.

She stood a few inches away, swinging the light from left to right. The beam fought the darkness and won. The illumination showed nothing. Just grass so tall that it needed to be cut and a couple of trees. The light didn't reach all the way to the water, but in the immediate area, no bear or any other animal waited. Not even another human being.

He laid a hand on her shoulder. Not looking at him, she flashed the light for a second time. "See. Nothing. Maybe you fell asleep in the chair and had a dream."

"Maybe." Uneasiness filled him. "Come on inside, hun. Maybe you're right. I'm probably tired from everything we've been through since Jo-" Acid ate at his belly as he realized he almost said Johnny's name.

Either she hadn't noticed or pretended not to, for she took his hand. "Good idea. I only got up for a glass of milk. I couldn't sleep, but now I do feel tired. Let's go to bed."

He let her lead him back inside and to bed.

Once they both snuggled beneath the covers, he fell asleep. At some point that night, he dreamed.

In the nightmare, he dashed from the beach, struggling through the grass. Something snarled as it chased him. His heart beat in time with his pursuer's growls like a macabre melody.

Oh God, the motorhome! The door! Safety. His fingertips wiggled within inches of the knob. Suddenly, something hooked him by his sides and flipped him over like a pancake, laying him flat on his back. Twin red orbs reflecting the light hung in the darkness, drawing nearer and nearer. An awful smell of decay rammed up his nostrils ...

He awoke with a gasp and sat up, his hand to his chest. His heart hammered hard and fast. A revenant of that scent teased his nose. Desiree slept beside him, undisturbed. She lay on her stomach with her right cheek pressed to her pillow, snoring. Obviously, her dreams held nothing scary. At least one of them found some peace from being here.

God, I haven't had nightmares since I was a kid. Not even after Johnny's death.

Desiree rolled over and opened her eyes. "What's the matter John?"

He was taken back. For a moment, her eyes seemed to glow red. But when he looked again, her normal brown ones stared back at him.

"Nothing. Just a nightmare. Go back to sleep."

A yawn escaped her mouth as she sat up. She closed her mouth and smiled. His fear evaporated as his breath hitched in his chest. He hadn't seen that smile for months. It was her come hither smile. The smile that said, "Take me now." Her arms wrapped around him as she plastered her breasts against his torso.

Her mouth by his ear, she whispered, "I can make you forget that nightmare."

He let her push him onto his back as her lips found his. They trailed down to his chin, ducked below to brush feather light against his neck, and continued down his upper body, passing his belly button, lower and lower. She was right. The nightmare vanished from his mind as the heat of desire replaced it.

The next morning, he discovered his wife's spot beside him empty. A smile on his lips, he got up and whistled a tune as he grabbed jeans and a sweatshirt out of the closet, then went to use the shower. An hour later, dressed, but barefoot, he wandered to the front of the motorhome.

He didn't find Desiree.

She must have gone outdoors. Slipping on his tennis shoes, minus socks, he opened the door and stepped down to the ground. She wasn't anywhere near the campsite.

Maybe she's down at the beach?

Worried, as he still believed what happened last night was not a dream, he took the path. He didn't find any footprints but continued to follow the path down to the water's edge, calling out her name every once in a while. Still too early, no boat motors or voices filled the air.

"My love is down in the water, deep, deep, deep. Oh, my bonny love is waiting for me, down deep in the river."

It sounded like Desiree, but he didn't recognize the song. "Desiree?"

The singing grew louder as he began to jog. A nasty odor wafted to his nostrils, growing more repugnant as the singing resonated louder. For a minute the scent reminded him of that stink from last night. God, it smelled like dead fish combined with something else he couldn't figure out.

He froze. His wife stood naked as she stared down at the calm salt water with fascination. She had a funny grin on her face as she sang and rubbed her belly.

"Desiree?"

She stopped the chant and turned. Lines furrowed her forehead and her brows met together, no recognition in her eyes. He closed the distance between them. Wrinkling his nose, he realized that the pungent smell came from her. Had she rolled in something? Water droplets beaded all over her skin. Had she taken a dip in the sea? He would ponder about it after he got her back to the motorhome.

He snapped his fingers at her face. "Hey, Desiree. It's me, your husband."

"Ah yes, my husband. John." She stood up on tiptoe and kissed him. "Is it not a wonderful morning? I could just dance."

Not naked, you won't. He hoped no one had seen her.

He grabbed her arm. "Well, yeah, but hun, let's get back inside. I'm not sure flaunting your nudity to the world is a smart thing to do."

"Whatever you say."

He took her back to the motorhome and once inside, he urged her to take a shower. While she did, he poured cereal into two bowls, drowning the granola with low fat milk afterward. He grabbed two plastic bottles of orange juice from the fridge. Coffee would be great, but he didn't want to take time to make it. It was easier to keep breakfast simple.

"Hello, John. I am done showering."

She stood there, still naked and soaking wet. Water dripped off her, wetting the floor.

"Damn, Desiree, didn't you dry off with a towel?"

Confusion flickered in her eyes.

"Never mind." He led her back to the bedroom and dug a towel out of a tote, handing it to her. She stared down at the cloth in her hands as if she'd never seen it before.

"Desiree, go ahead. Dry yourself. The cereal's getting soggy, so quit playing around."

Finally, she used it to rub her body dry. He took the towel from her and hung it up. Biting his lower lip, he snatched a pair of her sweat pants and a T-shirt from the closet and thrust them at her. The woman frowned at the clothing. With an oath, he yanked the shirt over her head. She shoved him away and finished dressing herself.

What was wrong with her? You'd think it wasn't really his wife, but some stranger in his bedroom. Someone who didn't know how to use a towel or put on clothes.

He snorted. *Looks like my wife to me. Hope this isn't a relapse like she had when Johnny died, just in a bizarre way? This week staying in Solana Beach was supposed to help, not make her worse.*

They sat down to eat. Her nose wrinkled as she picked up the spoon. Watching him as he scooped up a bit of milk-soaked granola from his bowl, she dipped hers and did the same with no problem. She ate every bit of it, but with distaste evident on her face as she did so.

He was puzzled by this, as he knew his wife had picked the cereal, because she liked it.

After breakfast, the weird Desiree left and the one he knew returned. They rode his motorcycle to the Belly Up Tavern for lunch and afterwards, went to Fletcher Cove Park where they both drank Starbucks lattes and watched the people. A couple of times, he thought he saw a hint of hunger in her crimson eyes. When he did a double take, he saw only brown eyes, not red, as she looked around with friendly interest.

It was late afternoon when they got back. John grilled fresh fish they'd picked up at a grocery store for dinner. Afterwards, full and happy, they relaxed in lawn chairs and watched the sun make its way down below the horizon as they drank beer. Well, he chugged a beer. Desiree had a bottle of water, as that was all she wanted.

As dusk darkened the sky, he said, "Go on in, hun. I'll throw away the trash, then I'll be in after that."

She left him alone. He tossed the bottles in the trash can, and being cautious, he looked for suspicious signs like tracks or anything out of the ordinary.

Nothing. Maybe whatever it was had swam farther out to sea. He entered the motorhome. Before he closed the door to lock it, he clicked the light switch to turn on the outside light and double-checked that the windows were secured. He even put his loaded rifle next to his side of the bed.

Before he hit the sheets, Desiree climbed onto him, initiating a wild lovemaking like he never had from her before in all their years of marriage. Not even what happened last night could match it. When the both of them settled down to sleep, the dream overcame him.

He stood at the edge of the beach and heard a noise. Nervous and trying to be silent, he shuffled on bare feet through the sand to a thick bush. Dropping down behind it, he peered through a hole created by the branches. At first, he couldn't see anything due to the darkness. Suddenly, moonlight lit up where the ocean kissed the sand.

Something large and dark lay in the water and a smaller figure sat on top. John leaned as close as he could without jabbing branches in his eyes and focused. He wished he had binoculars.

The light washed over the figures. What he saw freaked him out. The bottom creature appeared human-like, except dark green scales shimmered over its form. It raised its massive head to nuzzle at the neck of the figure on top. The female (for it had breasts that gleamed pale in the light) arched her back and cried out in ecstasy. Scales outlined in silver covered her body.

Oh, God, I think they're mating!

The female flopped forward, and long strands of golden hair fell over her head and shoulders. John fell back on his buttocks.

That looks like Desiree having a go at that thing. But she's covered in fish scales! She is as bizarre as the monster she's fucking.

He stumbled to his feet. A snap of a twig under his foot and everything grew quiet as a cemetery. The throbbing of his pulse loud in his ears, he stepped away from the bush and saw Desiree tumble off the creature into the water. With a roar, the beast rose to its feet and stepped out of the water and onto the land. It was gargantuan, hell of a lot taller than John's friend, Big Boy, who stood at six foot, six.

Desiree joined the monster. "Isn't he perfect, John?"

What the hell is wrong with Desiree? The creature charged John. Not staying around to fight it, he ran. Heavy crashes through sand and grass told him that the beast was in hot pursuit. He didn't care that he'd caught his wife screwing someone else. Not when that someone else appeared like something out of a horror film. No, he felt concerned about his own survival.

But this was a nightmare, right? Then why the hell didn't he wake up?

God, where's the damn motorhome?

A roar pierced the air.

Damn it, that's close. Too close. He could smell his own sweat. God, he didn't remember smelling in any of his dreams before!

Breath rammed his lungs, and his body cried out at its misuse, but he arrived at the motorhome. His hand on the knob, he twisted.

Something seized him before he could throw open the door. He slammed onto the ground hard and like a fish on a hook, felt himself being dragged backward. Tiny rocks in the grass bit into his flesh.

God, oh God. He realized he hadn't thought the words, but actually screamed them. "Oh, God, help!"

Gritty sand filled his mouth, and he almost choked, when suddenly, he hit water with a heavy splash. Salty water surged down his throat. No time to drown, as something sharp dug into his sides and flipped him over onto his back. The creature bent over him; its unholy face lowered to his. An unclean stink whooshed at him as it opened its maw. He'd never seen so many sharp fangs.

He screamed.

No longer dark, he noticed the sun above.

He struggled to sit up, but he couldn't move a muscle. That's when he realized he was lying in water. Unable to lift his head, he cut his gaze to his feet and saw his toes grazing the shore.

I'm in the ocean? He must be dreaming. Otherwise—

John looked up and saw a man and a woman standing over him. He blinked, not sure what he was seeing. The man looked exactly like him. Further discernment revealed that both his twin and the false Desiree didn't wear a stitch of clothing. He wanted to yell for help, but he couldn't open his mouth

I have to be dreaming. Right?

Desiree chuckled. "Oh no, you are not dreaming, John. This is real."

How did she...

She laughed. "Mermaids can read the minds of humans."

Mermaids? Crazy, right? Yet, how could she look exactly like Desiree? Or that man looked like him?

She continued. "My kind made sure that humankind kept believing that mermaids and mermen only existed in fairytales. Unlike others of our kind who were happy to subsist on fish and the occasional foolish sailor that fell overboard from a ship, my mate and I wanted more. Human flesh is such a delicacy." She licked her lips. "We will enjoy your flesh like we did your air-breather female."

She caressed his lookalike. "See how easy it was to exchange places with the foolish humans, my beloved. Since they own this land by Mother Sea, becoming them, we can stay here always. Be near the salt water so we can always return to it. And with so many human lives in this city, there's plenty for us to feast on for a long time before they figure out about us." She flashed a knife sharp grin at John. "If they ever do."

His twin growled and leaned over to lick at her neck. "Hungry."

She arched her neck into his lick. "Get our meal out of the water so we can feast. I always said California has the best food; healthier and leaner. But the occasional Southern dish won't harm us."

Whatever spell held John immobile and kept him from crying out, broke as his lookalike lifted him out of the water. He yelled and thrashed, but no one heard him. Not even when his shrieks rose as both beings shifted back to their real shapes and sank their fangs into him, bloodying the incoming tide.

Pamela K. Kinney

Pamela K. Kinney gave up long ago ignoring the voices in her head and has written horror, fantasy. science fiction, poetry, plus nonfiction ghost and cryptid books ever since. Her horror short story, "Bottled Spirits," was runner-up for the 2013 WSFA Small Press Award and considered one of the seven best genre short fiction for that year. Her poem, "Dementia," in the *HWA Poetry Showcase Vol VII*, got her a mention in Best Horror of the Year, Vol 13. Three books of hers won in The Book Fest Awards in 2024 and 2025. Her latest horror novel is Nowhere Land. Along with writing,

Pamela has acted on stage and film, and does paranormal investigating with the Paranormal World Seekers. She is a member of both Virginia Writers Club, James River Writers, and Horror Writers Association. https://PamelaKKinney.com

2020s

LIVING IN A COVID WORLD

Sheri White

Hannah stood on a red circle, shivering in her light jacket. She hadn't thought about needing to wait in line to enter the grocery store, so she didn't dress warmly enough. She had her foldable cart with her, so she couldn't even put her hands in her pockets.

She stepped on the next circle in front of her as another person was let in. She mentally counted the number of people ahead and groaned as she realized she would have a good 15- to 20-minute wait in the chilly air.

Hannah usually ordered her groceries online and had them delivered, but today she needed to get out of the apartment for a while. Life was so hectic since lockdown and having her 12-year-old Gracie home all the time now added to the chaos.

She was glad she didn't have to worry about her daughter getting sick at school or bringing the virus home, but Hannah still worried with every sneeze and cough she heard from Gracie's room.

Zoom school every morning was a relief; it gave Hannah the time she needed to get her projects done. Afternoons were spent watching TV together or baking or playing games. Anything to distract Gracie from the monotony of lockdown. She also gave in, more often than not, to letting Gracie go online to hang out with her friends. Hannah enjoyed hearing the laughter from her daughter's bedroom.

"Hey, move up," an irritated voice said from behind her. Hannah realized she'd been daydreaming and moved up two circles.

Once inside, she grabbed a disinfecting wipe from the attendant—the look in his eyes behind his mask made it obvious this wasn't optional—and wiped down the handle of the grocery cart.

Hannah made sure she followed the direction the dotted lines took her, stopping when the person in front of her stopped. *Social distancing keeps us all safe!* The irritating little jingle that played before the evening news popped into her brain.

As Hannah tossed various items into her cart, she realized that although there were barely any customers, she felt claustrophobic. She wasn't used to being around other people lately, and hearing people coughing throughout the store stressed her out. Her mask seemed tight against her face, making her feel as if she couldn't breathe. She gripped the shopping cart handle and tried to take deep breaths but only pulled the mask into her mouth. She coughed hard into her arm with her head down, trying to ignore the scared and angry glances thrown her way.

"Hey!"

Hannah looked up to see the woman in front of her looking at her. The woman's arms were crossed; her eyebrows pulled together in anger.

"Maybe you should go home instead of spreading your disgusting germs to everyone!"

Hannah watched the woman speak, fascinated by her lips moving under the mask.

"Did you hear me?"

The others in the soup aisle had stopped their own shopping to watch the drama play out. Hannah felt her face get red and hot.

"I'm sorry. I'm not sick! I tried to take a deep breath, but it made me cough. I swear!"

The customers grumbled but returned to their shopping. Hannah reached out with a shaking hand and grabbed a four-pack of chicken noodle soup. The rest of the shopping trip was uneventful until she got to the checkout.

After putting her items on the conveyor, she was confronted by a huge square of plexiglass between her and the cashier. Only a small slot at the bottom allowed for contact. Unsure what to do, Hannah bent down to the opening.

"Hello! How are you today?"

"Ma'am, step back from the window. Please remember social distancing."

"I'm sorry." Chastised, and blushing once again, Hannah swiped her card. She attempted to put in her PIN, but the rubbery-feeling cover over the numbers made it difficult to push the keys all the way down.

Card declined; try again.

Hannah's heartbeat quickened and rivulets of sweat ran down her face. "Don't worry, I do have the money!" she told the cashier in a high squeaky voice.

The cashier just looked at her. A customer waiting behind her grumbled behind his mask.

Finally, Hannah was able to complete her PIN and leave with her groceries.

The chilly air was a relief while Hannah walked home, pulling her cart behind her.

How am I going to make it through this? Everything is different, scary. People are different and scary. How long is this going to last?

Tears welled in her eyes.

I don't want this life for Gracie. Stuck at home, not playing outside or with friends.

Not for the first time she thought, *life would be so much easier if I were alone.*

Hannah squeezed her eyes shut and dug her fingernails into her free hand, hating the voice that whispered such a sinful thought in her ear.

She unlocked the door and pulled the wagon in. She called down the long hallway, "Gracie, I'm home," and walked to the kitchen.

She didn't get a response but heard voices in her daughter's bedroom. Figuring Gracie was chatting with friends, Hannah put the groceries away. She stumbled a bit, her legs suddenly weak, as a wave of exhaustion washed over her.

She left the kitchen and knocked on Gracie's door. "Hey, I'm going to take a nap. There is pizza in the freezer you can make after you're done with your homework. And don't forget, I will check to make sure you did it! Love you."

She crawled under her covers and turned out the light. In seconds she was sound asleep.

Hannah jolted awake, disoriented, her heart beating fast. Her room was dark, and the apartment was completely silent.

She groaned and held her head in her hands.

How long did I sleep? She grabbed her phone to check the time. *8:5? Oh my God, I've been asleep for almost five hours!*

Hannah threw the blanket off and stood up fast. A wave of vertigo hit her, and she fell back on the bed. She touched her forehead and knew she had a fever. She swallowed and grimaced in pain.

It's just a cold, that's all. It's not what you're thinking.

Hannah stood up and put her hand on the wall for balance. She slowly made her way out of her bedroom and down the hall to knock on Gracie's door.

"Gracie, did you finish your homework?" Hannah asked in a raw, gravelly voice. She tried to clear her throat. "Do you want pizza?"

She opened the door, expecting her daughter to be asleep or wearing headphones, but Gracie wasn't in the room. She went to the living room, but Gracie wasn't there either. Nor the bathroom or kitchen.

Hannah stumbled back to her bedroom and sat on the bed. She grabbed her phone from the nightstand, and thumbed through her contacts, looking for Gracie's best friend's mom, figuring Gracie had gone over there, even though she had strict instructions to stay home.

She would've left a note, though, Hannah thought.

She looked through her phone, scrolling faster as she began to panic, not finding Emma's mom's number.

"I know I added it. It was the first time Gracie slept over there. Where is it?"

Hannah's vision began to blur as her fever rose. She stood in her doorway and called out her daughter's name.

"Gracie, please! Where are you?" Hannah sobbed as she left her apartment. She clung to the wall and made her way to the apartment down the hallway. She weakly slapped her palm on the door.

"Please! Help me find my little girl!"

She kept slapping the door and crying as she fell to her knees. Her neighbor finally opened the door.

"Hannah? Are you all right?"

"My daughter ... help me find ..."

Then everything went dark.

The nurse watched the patient through a monitor. She was unconscious and hooked up to a respirator. Another nurse approached her.

"How's your new patient doing?"

"Hannah? Not good. I don't think she's going to make it. She was delirious when they brought her in. It looks like she's had Covid for a while now. Her neighbor heard her moaning in her apartment and found her in her room. While she waited for the paramedics to get there, Hannah kept begging the neighbor to find her daughter."

"Is someone looking for her daughter right now? Do you think she can be found before her mom passes? She could at least say good-bye through the monitor, even though she won't be able to go in."

Hannah's nurse shook her head.

"What about the father? Is he around?"

"One of the paramedics questioned the neighbor while the others prepared her to go to the hospital. Asked if she had any close relatives. The neighbor said she moved in about a year ago—alone.

"When the neighbor asked her about family, she said Hannah got this look of deep sorrow and said she didn't want to talk about it.

"The neighbor also told the paramedic she hadn't left her apartment in weeks. Poor thing had hardly any food, not that she'd be able to fix herself anything. She was just too sick. The neighbor felt terrible for not checking on her sooner."

Hannah began to drift. It was a pleasant feeling, like flying high on a swing as a child.

In the distance, she saw her husband and daughter waving to her and shouting her name. She smiled with joy and ran to them.

Hannah's cardiac monitor emitted a long beep, indicating she was flatlining.

Doctors rushed in and the nurses followed.

"If she passes now, we'll never know. I feel so bad for her, dying alone," Hannah's nurse said, shaking her head.

"Time of death: 4:34 pm." The doctor sighed and left the room.

Hannah hugged her daughter tightly, as if she'd never let go of her again.

Sheri White

Sheri White's stories have been published in many anthologies and zines. Recent publications include *The Horror Collection: Amber Edition* (edited by Kevin J. Kennedy) and *Push: An Anthology of Childbirth Horror* (edited by Ruth Anna Evans). https://www.facebook.com/sheriw1965

2030s

ANIMALS

B.C. Lienesch

U ltimately, the end of the world was a lot less exciting than most
envisioned.

There were no zombies or giant meteors or self-aware robots; just what
the scientists told us it would be all along. The glaciers and sea ice melted,
the oceans rose, and by 2035 a billion people globally were refugees to a
whole new breed of natural disaster. Stateside, entire cities like New York,
Miami, and New Orleans became asphalt archipelagos. The government
itself splintered into a half-dozen different factions. And when the 2036
election ended with no clear winner, the nation as a whole descended into
chaos.

Then there was me, Chase Myers, experiencing the apocalypse first
hand from the back row of my parents' Chrysler Voyager. We'd been on the

road for a week, our home in coastal North Carolina just a memory, having finally decided the refugee camp in Raleigh was more violence and disorder than we could endure. Our plan was to head west, but we only made it as far as Knoxville before the governor of Tennessee declared martial law and ordered all non-Tennessee citizens to leave the state, or be detained by the national guard. With fires raging out of control in the remaining parts of the Southeast that weren't underwater, we decided to head north.

"God, that looks bad," my dad said as he craned over the wheel and studied the sky overhead.

I played with the ends of my long, coffee brown hair as I shifted my knees to the side and dropped my head down to see what he was looking at. The sky ahead was even darker than the interstate we were driving on.

"Maybe we should turn back for Columbus. There was another camp there," Mom said.

Dad shook his head. "We left those camps for good reason."

I shifted my knees back, struggling with being five-eight in the third row of a minivan. Dad wasn't wrong. The refugee camps had been awful. It'd been like *Lord of the Flies* thinly veiled as civilization under emergency tents. When we saw a man stabbed in front of us over bottled water, we'd finally had enough.

I looked over at my little brother, Tate. He was staring out his own window, trying to see the coming storm. He brushed his long, raven bangs out of his green eyes, rubbing at them.

"Mommy, I'm scared," he said.

Before my mom could ease his worries, my older sister, Addie, whipped around in her middle-row seat and reached for his hand, her loose ponytail of auburn hair bouncing as she did. Her heart-shaped face cradled her easy smile.

"It's okay, bub," she said. "It's just a little thunderstorm."

Addie turned and met my gaze. We both weren't so sure. The sky was onyx up ahead. The hot and humid summer months had become ever increasingly plagued with these powerful thunderstorms. Tate was seven; barely old enough to notice. But Addie and I, nineteen and eighteen, respectively, had noticed their increasing ferocity. So had my parents. Derechos, the weathermen called them, on what TV outlets still broadcast.

"We should at least get off the highway," Mom offered. "We don't want to get stuck like we did outside Bristol."

Dad didn't say anything, but signaled and took the next exit. It dumped us onto a long, straight road that cut through open farmland but still had us heading into the storm. We drove on in silence, and some ten minutes later, we hit it.

A tempestuous deluge rained down on our car as fierce winds jostled us side to side. Dad had the windshield wipers working so fast, they looked as though they might snap off, and still, their efforts were in vain.

"Robert, pull over!" Mom begged.

"Carol, it's fine!" Dad assured her. "We just have to get through this cell and it'll clear up."

The downpour was deafening as it engulfed our car, like a hundred drummers playing rudiments on its aluminum body. A loud clap of thunder rocked the earth beneath us.

Tate leaned forward and reached out for Addie. "I'm scared!" he cried.

Addie tried to turn around but Tate had gripped a tiny handful of her hair in his fist. I leaned over and put my arm around him, ushering his head into my chest.

"It's okay, bub," I said. "Remember? Thunder is just the angels bowl—"

Before I could finish the sentence, I felt us lose control. The back of the van slid sideways as the wheels hydroplaned. Dad tried to come out of the skid, but water glossed the roadway, turning it into a skating rink in July. The nose of our van shimmied one way, then the other, before leaving the road altogether.

I barely caught a glimpse of the utility pole before we hit it.

All my senses were dulled as if I were enshrouded in some sort of fog. I opened my eyes, but my vision was blurry. There was a blinding flash followed almost immediately by a clap of thunder. Somewhere up front, Mom groaned.

"Mom? You okay?" Addie asked.

Another groan vaguely resembling a "yes" came in reply.

Addie turned around. "Chance? Tate? What about you?"

We said yes more clearly.

I heard my father try the ignition, but the engine did nothing.

"Computer code P0300," said our car's AI. "Multiple cylinder misfire."

A sudden gust of wind broadsided us, and for a moment, it felt like the van might roll onto its side.

"We have to get out of here," Mom said.

"I'm trying," Dad replied.

"No, out of *here*. Out of the car, somewhere safer."

"We're in the middle of nowhere!"

Addie looked down at her lap before turning back to us. "Check your phones; any of them working? Anyone have service?"

I checked even though I knew there was no point. Who were we going to call? Friendly police and roadside assistance stopped being a thing here in the end times.

"There," Dad said.

I looked up. He was pointing past my mother at the passenger window.

"It looks like there's a house," he said, "or multiple houses there. In between those trees."

"We can't just walk up to it," Mom countered. "They'll figure us for looters. We'll be lucky if they don't shoot us immediately."

"You said it yourself. We have to get somewhere safer. We have no choice." He paused, thinking. "I'll go. One person running in the rain will be a lot less threatening to anyone inside. I'll see if they don't mind taking us in just until the storm passes."

Mom's voice quivered. "Be careful."

Dad looked back into the van at the rest of us. "I'll be right back."

He kicked his door open, climbed out, and disappeared. Minutes ticked by and we waited in silence, terrified that he might not return. Or worse, return with a band of murderous farmers. I watched the time on my smart ring. Seventeen minutes later, we saw his lanky figure jog back to the car. He opened his door once more and poked his head back in.

"No one's there," he said.

Drenched, his salt-and-pepper hair was matted from the rain and his browline glasses fogged from the sudden change in humidity.

"Are you sure?" Mom asked.

Dad nodded. "I knocked loudly three times, then tried the door. It was unlocked, and I went in and checked it out. It's empty. We can at least wait out the storm inside."

I still wasn't sure, but anywhere had to be safer than here. I grabbed Tate and ushered him into the middle seats. Addie opened her door and helped us both climb out. The rain had let up a little but not much. Together we came around the van, joined my mom and dad, and ran for the house. The drive up to it was a pair of dirt tracks bisected by a median of weeds. In the downpour, it had all become muddy and our shoes made loud squishing sounds as we hurried for cover.

Dad got to the door first and threw it open, allowing the rest of us to hurry inside. We stood in the kitchen. It was completely dark, save for a blue glowing halo coming from a white console on the wall. Whoever's house this was, they had a Google Abode—an integrated AI home system, like central air conditioning, but for all your home's tasks. It required power, which meant the house still had electricity, and was dark by choice. Mom, seeing this, felt around for a light switch. A moment later, the kitchen flooded with harsh fluorescent light.

Mom turned to Dad. "What do we do?"

Dad leaned against one of the counters. "We ride out the storm here and then figure out our next move."

My mom held her hands out. "How? Where?"

"There's got to be a town or something nearby." My father turned and looked at the Abode console. "Abode, where is the nearest food or gas near me?"

The halo on the Abode turned red. "I'm sorry, I am not connected to the internet right now."

Dad huffed. "Of course."

I pulled out my phone and looked at it. "I don't have service, either."

Dad put his hands on his hips. "It doesn't change anything. The safest place for us right now is here."

None of us said anything. We knew venturing out carried a ton of risks.

"We might as well try to get some rest," Dad said. "We don't know how long the storm will last." He strode over to a doorway on the other side of the kitchen. "There's a living room here with some couches and a recliner. Why don't you guys lay down."

We did as he suggested. I went in and plopped down on one couch and Addie did the same on the other. Tate came trotting in and threw himself into my arms. I pulled him into me and squeezed him tight, snuggling with him on the couch. I was sure I was far too anxious for sleep to come, but as I listened to the storm outside, my eyes grew heavy. I closed them and drifted off.

I woke to the snapping of venetian blinds. I opened my eyes and turned to see Dad standing at a window beside the sofa I'd drifted off on. His gaze was fixed on something outside.

"What is it, Dad?" I asked.

"There are people at our car," he said softly.

I pushed myself up as quickly as I could without disturbing Tate, and crawled down to the far side of the couch. The storm had passed and there was a pickup truck out on the road, stopped just behind our minivan. I counted three people taking in our wrecked car.

Mom stepped in quietly from the kitchen and joined us at the window. "Are they looters?"

"I don't know," Dad replied.

Mom folded her arms. "What do you think they want?"

Dad didn't say anything

"Maybe it's the people that live here," I offered.

Dad shook his head. "If it is, we'll have to explain ourselves. Even if they don't live here, they're clearly curious. It's only a matter of time before they check out the house."

As if they could hear him out on the road, two of the men turned and looked at the house. Instinctively, all three of us backed away from the window. Our commotion awoke Addie.

She rubbed her face. "What's going on?"

Her question returned Tate to the world of the conscious, as well.

"There are people out by our minivan," Dad said. "I'm going to go talk to them."

"Robert, I don't think that's a good idea," Mom cautioned.

Dad looked at her. "What choice do we have? Better to go to them then let them find us hiding in here like a bunch of squatters."

"At least let us come with you," Addie said. "If they're looters or something, there being more of us than them might make them think twice about trying anything."

Dad looked around the room at us. No one seemed particularly euphoric about the idea but no one made any objections, either.

Single file, we went to the door in the kitchen and headed outside. We followed the drive back to where it turned onto the road and headed down it. The men at our minivan saw us approaching. When one of them came around from behind the minivan, we could see he had some sort of rifle in his hand.

Dad extended an arm toward us. "You guys stay right here," he said.

"But Dad ... numbers," I said.

"They can count you all from there."

He extended his other arm out and walked like that, hands open, until he got to where the driveway met the road. The man with the gun motioned for him to drop his hands and come over to them.

They talked for what seemed like an hour, but in truth couldn't have been more than several minutes. I waited for the man to suddenly raise his gun and shoot my dad, but he never did. And after a while, Dad waved us over.

We came down the drive and joined him. Up close, I could see now that the man with the rifle was significantly older than the other two. He had a paunch belly and graying hair that ran down to his neck. The scruff on his face said he hadn't shaved in probably a week.

"Guys, this is Latimer," Dad said. "And these are his boys, Bradford and Rowan." He gestured to each of them as he introduced them.

They nodded at us. If they weren't twins, they were close in age. I took them to be in their thirties. They were stocky with sunkissed complexions and brown hair cut short, but Bradford's was sandier and Rowan's was more reddish.

"I explained what happened," Dad continued. "They've offered to tow the van to their farmhouse and take a look at it."

Latimer shrugged. "None of us are mechanics by trade, but you don't make a go of it running a farm without knowing how to fix a thing or two. Especially these days."

"Tow?" I asked.

"Sure, with the tractor at the farm," Latimer said. "I reckon if we can get some straps and chains around that front axle, we can take it on down the road to our place."

"How far is it?" Addie asked.

Latimer shrugged again. "Just a mile or so. Easy job."

My mom flashed a forced smile at the men. "Can I talk to my husband for just a second, please?"

Latimer grinned. "It's a free country, innit?"

Mom took Dad by the arm and pulled him several feet away. In hushed tones, they began to argue. I didn't have to be a part of it to know what it was about. Mom was worried about trusting strangers. Dad was saying we didn't have a choice.

"If they wanted to rob us or hurt us, they already could have," I heard my father say.

I felt my face flush. If I heard it, Latimer and his boys must've too. Latimer just chuckled as he kicked at the asphalt as though Dad had said something amusing.

After another minute of debate, Dad turned back to everyone.

"We'd be grateful for your help," he said. "Assuming it's not too much trouble."

Latimer shook his head. "Course not. We're just lucky we ran into y'all on the way back from picking up feed." He turned to Bradford and Rowan. "You boys take the truck and come back with the tractor."

It took almost an hour to get our wrecked minivan hooked up and taken to Latimer's farm, all of us following behind packed into Latimer's pickup truck. As we rolled in, the last rays of sunlight were retreating behind the trees to the west, leaving only enough light to paint the farm in silhouettes. There was a two-story house with a wraparound Victorian-style porch nestled atop a sloping hill. Behind it and to the right was a barn almost twice as big as the house, with a raised peak in the center of the roof. Next to it was a silo a bit taller than the barn.

Bradford and Rowan, ahead of us on the tractor, turned right and took our minivan past the farmhouse and toward the barn. Latimer turned left and eased into a parking space directly in front of the farmhouse's porch. He killed the engine and tossed the keys onto the dashboard. As we all climbed out, I watched Bradford and Rowan as they disappeared around the side of the house.

"They'll take a look at it straight away," said Latimer.

I turned and found him watching me. I smiled shyly.

A screen door on the front of the farmhouse whined open and out stepped a petite woman with long, dark hair. "Not before you all eat," she countered. "It's nearly two hours past when you were supposed to be home for supper and the stew meat's only gonna get dry and tough from here on."

"We found these folks stranded a mile or so up the road," Latimer said. "We couldn't very well leave them."

Mom took the first step up onto the farmhouse porch. "We're sorry, ma'am," she said. "We didn't mean to ruin your dinner."

"You all didn't ruin nothing, honey," the woman replied. "Latimer was running late as usual and he knows it. Now, you all come up here and join us for dinner. There's plenty of food. Can't say the same for space around the table, but we'll all just get comfy."

Dad joined Mom on the first step. "Really, ma'am, Latimer was already very generous in helping us out, we don't want to be a burden."

"Then I suggest you all hurry on up here because me holding this door open's letting the bugs in. And stop with that 'ma'am' business; I'm Millie."

We all looked at one another for a moment before Latimer stepped around us and started inside. Dad turned and watched him, then followed. The rest of us filed in behind him. One by one, we ascended to the porch and made our way to the door Millie held open for us.

As I stepped past her, I nodded in thanks. With the porchlight illuminating her face I could see she had protruding gray eyes. Her hair was indeed dark— chestnut brown—but also had strands of silver in it.

"Thank you," I said.

She grinned and nodded into the house, "Go on and wash up."

I did as Millie asked. I caught a glimpse of the dining room straight ahead, and moved down the hallway. The kitchen was to the left of the dining table, separated by a large counter. My parents were huddled over the counter, talking to one another. Addie was already at a large sink helping Tate wash his hands. I joined them and when we were all done, we looked at the wooden dining table with place settings all around it.

"Go on," Latimer said as he stepped past us and opened the refrigerator. "Don't be shy, pick a seat."

Addie, Tate, and I slid onto the bench against the back wall. My parents finished their conversation and Mom joined us on the bench. Dad took the chair at the end of the table. Latimer came over to the table with a dark glass jug and took the seat opposite Dad.

"Mead," Latimer explained, raising the jug before putting it on the table. "We make it with honey from the bees we've got out back. Would you all like some?"

We shook our heads.

Latimer shrugged. "Suit yourselves." He took a glass in front of him and filled it.

Bradford and Rowan entered the room, plopping heavily into seats at the table. Rowan grunted a little as he reached for the pitcher. I turned as footsteps echoed down the stairs. A boy, probably a few years younger than me, burst into the room, eyeing us through thick-framed glasses. The chair scraped against the floor as he joined us.

"You all, this is Titus, our youngest," Millie said as she came down the hall and joined us in the dining room.

I reached my hand over the table and extended it toward Titus. "Hi," I said. "I'm Chance."

Titus flinched at my movement and shrieked. Startled, I pulled my hand away.

"Oh, Titus, stop," Millie said, sounding annoyed. "I'm sorry. Titus is a little more … *special* than our other two sons."

"There's nothing to apologize for," my mother said politely. She smiled at Titus.

Titus stared back at her with a blank look on his face.

Millie went into the kitchen and brought one large stock pot over before going back and bringing in a slightly smaller one. "I didn't know we'd be having guests when I started the stew this morning," she said. "Luckily, I had some vegetable soup in the freezer I was able to get going when Bradford and Rowan told me you all would be joining us. I hope that's okay."

"More than okay," Dad said. "You all are far too kind for doing this."

"It seemed like fate that the boys ran into you out there. Couldn't let a gift from God like that go to waste."

Millie began ladling vegetable soup into the bowls in front of us, but as she filled my dad's bowl, Titus pointed at it and began screaming again. His eyes darted back and forth between the bowl and my dad.

Rowan reached over and restrained Titus' arm. "Stop it! That's enough!"

When Millie had filled my dad's bowl, she put the pot down and stroked Titus' head. "That's not for you, Titus. That's our guest's supper."

My dad took the bowl and offered it to Titus. "No, please. By all means."

Titus jerked his arm away from Rowan and slapped the bowl out of my dad's hand. He screamed even louder.

"Titus, if you're going to be that way, you can go to bed without supper," Latimer said sternly. He nodded at the hallway over his shoulder. "Go on and take him up to bed, Millie."

"It's really, okay," Mom interjected. "He's not bothering ..."

Latimer slapped the table. "He's my boy and he'll mind his damn manners!"

A quiet fell over the room. Addie and I exchanged glances. Tate looked back and forth between us.

Latimer cleared his throat and composed himself. "Millie, please take Titus up to his room. Everyone, else, let's just get on with supper. Rowan, finish serving our guests."

Millie and Rowan each did what Latimer asked of them and before long Millie and Titus were upstairs and each of us had a full bowl of soup in front of us. I took a spoonful and tried it. Someone had used a heavy hand seasoning it, but it was far better than anything I'd had in months. My appetite overtook me and I found myself taking spoonfuls of soup as fast as I could put them down. Millie returned and brought a pitcher of water to the table before sitting down and starting to eat herself. I took the pitcher and poured myself a glass. As I took a sip, I noticed the rest of my family was eating just as quickly. Each member of Latimer's family seemed to be studying us in between much slower bites.

"I'm sorry if we're being rude," I offered. "We're just hungry and it's so good."

Latimer looked at me, expressionless.

"That's nice, honey," Millie said across the table. "Would you like some more?"

"Please!" I offered my bowl up.

Millie took it and refilled it, then handed it back to me. I went to work on my second bowl almost as fast as I'd devoured the first. When I was done, I wiped my mouth with the napkin that'd been set in front of me.

"More, dear?" Millie asked.

I shook my head. "No, thank you. I'm going to go into a food coma if I have any more."

"We have a spare bedroom just down the hall. Would you like to rest?"

I felt like it would be rude to do so, but truthfully lying down felt like it'd be really nice right then. I nodded with a smile and my mom and dad stood to let me out. I made my way into the bedroom down the hall. As I entered the room, though, I suddenly felt funny. I was lightheaded and my vision became blurry. I tried to say something, but my mouth couldn't find the words. I heard a loud bang somewhere far off behind me followed by my mom shrieking, but it too was impossibly distant. I tried to turn, but my knees became weak underneath me.

The last thing I remembered before everything went dark was the floor rapidly rushing toward my face.

The first sensation I had when I awoke was the smell of urine and feces. The second was feeling itchy. My eyelids felt like lead weights but my other senses came back to me one by one. I heard a low hum and the murmuring of people. My mouth tasted bitter and metallic. Finally, my eyes opened.

I was laying on a pile of hay with no memory of how I'd gotten here. I took stock of myself. My clothes were gone and instead I was wearing some sort of long housecoat. I ran my hands across it, feeling the scratchy wool. But there was also something cold around my neck. I slid my hands up to it and felt a steel collar. On instinct, I started to tug at it.

"I wouldn't do that," said a voice next to me.

I turned and looked and for the first time noticed my surroundings. I was inside a cavernous wood building. Something told me it was the barn I'd seen as we pulled up to Latimer's farm. Livestock fencing ran the length of the interior, creating a long, narrow enclosure that I was trapped in. I looked further down it and found several people staring at me.

"They catch you messing with that, they'll zap you," said a young blonde woman. She'd been the voice I'd heard.

"What is it?" I asked. "What is ... all this? Where am I?"

"Let me guess," a woman with curly black hair said, standing next to the blond. "Latimer or his boys offered to help you out. You ended up back here, at their farm."

My jaw hung slack, so I just nodded.

"Welcome," the woman said, her tone icy.

"Why are we here?" I asked.

"Chance!" my mom screamed.

I turned and looked in the direction her cry came from. She and my dad were in a matching type of enclosure on the other side of the barn. My dad stood next to her, an arm wrapped around her. They too were in the housecoats.

"Mom!" I said. "Why are you guys over there?"

"I don't know, honey," she said, tears forming in her eyes. "Is Addie okay?"

"I don't know..."

My mom pointed to the opposite end of our pen and there, laying on a mat of hay like I had been, was Addie. I hurried over to her, knelt down, and rocked her gently.

"Addie! Addie, are you okay?" I asked.

Addie groaned and began to stir.

"Is Tate over there with you?" my mom called out.

I looked up and down the enclosure we were in but didn't see Tate anywhere. Just young men and women around Addie and I's age.

"No, he's not here," I shouted back.

"How old is he?" the young blonde, still standing and watching me, asked.

"Seven," I answered.

"He's most likely with the other children then in the silo. The piglets, as they call them."

I squinted my eyes, confused. "Who calls them?"

"Latimer and his family."

I didn't understand. I looked around the barn once more trying to. "What is all this? How did we end up here?"

The woman with curly black hair stepped around the blonde. "You had the vegetable soup, didn't you? You ended up back at the farmhouse and they offered you the soup."

A chill roiled through me. "How did you ..."

"Because we all did. The soup was drugged. Now, you're here with us."

"What do they want with us?"

Before she could answer, large barn doors swung open. In stepped Latimer, Bradford, and Rowan, the latter two each with a shotgun in hand.

They studied the enclosures on both sides of the barn. When Latimer's eyes met mine, he winked.

"Good, you're awake," he said.

"Why are we in here?" I asked. "What do you want with us?"

Latimer chuckled. "Isn't it obvious? We aim to farm you."

I saw now he had a large knife in a sheath on his belt. I felt my legs go weak again and wondered if whatever they'd drugged me with hadn't completely worn off. I dropped to my knees and uttered the only word still pinballing around my head. "Why?"

"You've seen the world out there. It's gone to hell. Now, it's everybody for themselves. Markets have closed up, people have hunted whatever's around them to damn near extinction. There's only one type of meat still in abundance: people."

I gagged. I was going to be sick.

"Just be thankful you're over there in the husbandry pen. A lifetime of eating and fucking doesn't seem so bad with everything going on." Latimer moved toward the enclosure with my parents in it. "You all, on the other hand..."

He came to a section of fencing in the middle of the enclosure hinged on one end with a padlock around a latch on the other. Bradford and Rowan flanked their father as he undid the padlock. When it was off, he slid the latch back and opened the fence section. Bradford and Rowan leveled their guns.

Latimer stepped in. "Which one you boys want to take?"

Their backs to us, I heard one of them laugh.

"Let's play a game for it," Bradford said. "See who wants it more."

"Yeah," Rowan agreed. "Starting with the fresh meat."

Latimer rolled up his sleeve to reveal a device strapped to his forearm. He brought it up in front of him and punched at it with his finger. A moment later, my mom, dad, and one other person in the pen fell to the ground as the eerie hum of electricity reverberated through the barn. All of them cried out in pain.

Everyone else in the enclosure retreated to the polar ends of it. Rowan, and Bradford stepped through into the space and picked my mom and dad up as Latimer grabbed the other person. They dragged them into the center of the barn, stopping only to relock the padlock behind them, and took the three of them to the far back wall of the barn. Leaving them there, they crossed the barn and stood just outside its open doors.

"You heard my boy," Latimer said. "We're going to play a little game. You all have been caught out of your pen and we don't have patience for misbehaving livestock. But we only need one of you right now, which means you all have a chance to redeem yourselves." He took the key for the padlock and dropped it on the ground in front of him. "The first two of you to get back in the pen with it closed get a second chance. The third?" He shook his head. "Well, your troubles will be over soon enough."

I began to weep as I looked at my mom and dad. They exchanged looks with one another. Mom, too, was crying. Dad, though, had a look I'd never seen from him before. A kind of steely determination.

"We can do this," he said.

I looked over at the third person with them. She was a woman, middle-aged, with short, gray hair. Her eyes were locked onto someone in our pen. I followed her gaze to the young woman with black hair. My gut told me they were mother and daughter.

Bradford pointed his shotgun into the air and fired it.

"Go!" Latimer shouted.

My dad and the woman hopped to their feet and sprinted for the key. A beat later, my mom followed. It was a mad dash, but my dad threw himself the final five feet, diving and landing with the key in arm's reach.

The woman tried to kick it away, but my dad got it, turned, and threw it to my mom who was ten feet behind them.

"Unlock it!" he shouted.

My mother caught it and ran for the padlock. The woman tried to follow her but my dad grabbed her ankle. She fell. He then scurried to his feet and sprinted for my mom, getting to her just as she'd gotten the padlock off and the fence open. The woman had recovered and was gaining on my dad. She was just feet away, but still too far. My dad shoved my mom into the enclosure, stepped in, and pulled the fence closed behind him. A half second later, the woman slammed against the fence

Realizing what this meant, she started to back up deeper into the barn. Latimer, Bradford, and Rowan approached her, spread in a line.

"Please, no!" the woman cried.

"It is what it is, lady," Latimer said.

Cornered, the woman charged at Latimer and his boys, but Latimer brought up the device on his forearm and hit a button. The woman collapsed to the ground, convulsing. Under the screams of people in each enclosure, I could hear the electric current thrumming.

Latimer shocked her several seconds longer, until Bradford was standing over her. He pulled out a pair of ties from his back pocket and bound her wrists behind her followed by her ankles. Rowan went to the front of the barn and pressed a button on a console just inside the door. A thick, metal hook and chain began to clank as it descended from the barn's rafters above. It kept dropping until it hit the barn floor near the woman's head.

Bradford took the hook and secured it around the ties on the woman's ankles, then signaled for Rowan to raise it back up. Rowan hit a different button and the chain retracted. It lifted the woman, hanging upside down, until her head hung just a couple feet off the barn floor. She was sobbing uncontrollably.

"Back in the day, we'd just brain the livestock and be done with it," Latimer said. "But me personally? I think the meat is extra tender when you let them bleed."

"You're fucking animals!" the woman cried between tears.

"No, lady," Latimer hissed. "You are."

He grabbed a handful of the woman's hair, unsheathed his knife, and sliced clean through the front of her neck. The woman's daughter let out a guttural wail. I closed my eyes, but it didn't do anything for my ears, hearing the woman cough and gag, the chains rattling as her body jerked around. Finally, after what seemed like forever, it all stopped.

I opened my eyes but didn't dare look out at the dead woman. I focused on her daughter, caterwauling in the corner of our enclosure. My body was numb. I had reached my breaking point. I went limp and collapsed onto the ground. Addie crawled over to me and took me in her arms. In my periphery, I could see the woman being dragged away. Rowan had taken her out of the barn, but Bradford and Latimer remained. I dared a look at them out of the corner of my eye. They were looking at Addie and I. In my semi-fugue state, their voices sounded distant and muffled, but I could still understand them.

"Go on and help your brother with the butchering," Latimer said.

"I will in a bit," Bradford said. "First, I want to play with one of the new breeding stock."

Now, everyone in our enclosure turned their eyes to Addie and I. Latimer chuckled and slapped Bradford on the back before stepping to the fence section directly in front of us. I looked at either end of it and saw it had the same set up as the one on my mom and dad's, hinged with the padlock and latch.

"No!" I screamed. "Stay away from us!"

"Relax," Bradford said. "I'm going to take good care of you."

My nausea returned but I suppressed it. I wasn't letting this happen. As soon as he unlatched the section of fencing, I sprung and hit it with as much force as I could muster. Catching Bradford by surprise, he fell backward, the fence section swinging open. Latimer and I were the same distance away from the open barn door. I bet my life I was faster. I ran as hard as I could for the dark night ahead. I'd nearly made it when a wave of electricity surged into my neck.

I hit the ground like wounded game. I got my feet underneath me, but Latimer shocked me again, longer. The fight left my body. I hadn't given up but my muscles, spasming, had. I felt two pairs of hands—what had to be Latimer and Bradford—pick me up under each arm and drag my limp body to a shed-sized building I hadn't seen tucked away on the other side of the barn. They opened a door and took me in. Inside, was nothing more than a dresser and a tattered mattress on a metal bed frame.

"Stop!" I groaned.

They ignored me and dropped me onto the bed. Bradford went over to the dresser, opened a drawer, and got out four metal shackles. He tossed two to Latimer and each of them began chaining my limbs to corners of the bed frame. As Latimer worked on my right arm, his face was just inches from mine.

"We didn't do anything to you," I said.

"This isn't about you," he answered. "This is about survival."

"You took us in and made us feel safe. It was all a trick."

"Sweetheart, I've been hunting and fishing all my life. It's all about the bait you use. For fish, you got your grubs and worms. For deer, you've got feed corn. But you know how you bait people?" He flashed a sinister smile. "You give them hope."

Tears streamed down my cheeks as he and Bradford finished shackling me to the bed frame. When they were done, Latimer stepped toward the door. He nodded back at Bradford.

"Don't take too long now," he said.

Bradford turned to face me when the three of us heard Rowan call out from somewhere outside.

"Hey! You all going to give me a hand with this or what?" he shouted.

Bradford grumbled and looked at Latimer. When Latimer nodded toward the door, Bradford reluctantly went and Latimer followed him out, shutting the door behind them.

I began pulling as hard as I could on all the shackles, hoping one of them would break. My body rocked around on the bed, creating all sorts of noise as I twisted in different ways, trying to get leverage.

The door swung open on squeaky hinges and I froze, terrified it was one of them coming to admonish me for making so much noise. But instead, Titus stepped inside. I didn't know what to think. He stared at me with a blank expression.

"Please, help me," I said.

He pointed to the shackle on my left ankle and grunted.

I looked down, then understood. "Yes! Yes, please help me get these off."

He stared at me again.

I looked around, then nodded at the dresser. "In there. Maybe there's a key."

Titus went over to the dresser and began opening drawers in no particular order. I was just about to beg him to hurry when he turned around with a key in his hand.

A shot of adrenaline coursed through me. "Yes! Let's try it."

But Titus just stared at me, expressionless, again. He pointed at my neck. The shock collar.

I guessed what he wanted to say. "No, not for this. For the shackles. Help me get them off. Please!"

But Titus just pointed at the collar again emphatically before dropping the key onto the floor and running out of the shed.

"Ugh, fuck!" I stammered.

I came back to the reality I was in—where I was, and what was to become of me. Latimer was right about one thing; if you want to bait people, you give them hope. Mine was now gone. Tears welled up again in the corners of my eyes and I resigned myself to whatever was about to happen to me when Titus came back into the shed and shut the door behind him. He came over to my side and showed me a tool. It looked like a screwdriver but with a weird head I'd never seen before.

"I don't think that will help," I said. "Please, try the key."

Titus came at me with the tool and I flinched. He pushed my head to the side, getting at the back of the collar. Then, with a click, the collar came free. Titus took it off my neck and placed it on the bed.

"Thank you," I cried.

Titus grunted again and pointed at the key on the floor.

"Yes," I said. "Please! Try it."

He came around, got the key and worked at the shackle on my left arm. After a moment, it came free. I took the key from him and started to work on my other arm. When it too was free, I did my legs. I kicked all the shackles off, swung my feet around to the side of the bed, and hugged Titus who immediately pushed me off, shrieking.

"I'm sorry! But thank you," I said, continuing to cry. "Oh, God! Thank you so much!"

Rowan's voice rang out from just outside the door.

"Get back here!" he said. "We're not done!"

"We can finish later," Bradford replied. "I've got other things to do."

Bradford's voice got louder. He was coming back. Titus shrieked again but I held a hand to his mouth. I pushed him up against the wall next to the door, standing beside him, holding a finger to my lips. Just before Bradford opened the door, I reached out and grabbed the bulky shock collar off the bed.

The door opened into Titus and I and Bradford stepped through, his shotgun nestled in his arm.

He huffed. "What the..."

I swung the shock collar at his head as hard as I could and connected. Bradford dropped to the ground, the shotgun tumbling out of his reach. I pounced on top of him and hit him again. And again. His skull made a sickening crack and blood began to pool on the floor. I grabbed the shotgun and hopped to my feet. Titus was looking at me expectantly.

"Run!" I said.

He did and so did I. I ran as hard as I could for the barn. I didn't know where Latimer or Rowan, or Millie, for that matter, were, but I knew there were more of us than there were them. I opened the barn door and ran inside.

"Chance!" my parents screamed in unison.

I ran to the fence section with the padlock and latch. "Step back!"

I looked the shotgun over once, doubting my ability to use it.

"The safety is off," said an older man in the enclosure with my parents. "Just point it and shoot!"

I did as he said. With a thunderous boom, the padlock was obliterated. I slid the latch back and opened the panel. Everyone hurried out of the enclosure. The older man came to me and gently took the shotgun out of my hands.

"I've got it from here," he said.

The man went over and shot the lock off the other enclosure. There were hugs and kisses as people reunited, but they were short-lived. Everyone, now-freed, spilled out of the barn and into the night, spreading across the farm like a swarm of beasts, hell bent on revenge.

I followed them out and watched as the next several moments played out like a dream I was only a spectator to. The young blonde stabbing Rowan in the midsection with a pitchfork she'd found, a swarm of others bursting into the farmhouse and dragging Millie out, savagely beating her and Latimer, as thick black smoke began billowing from the farmhouse.

"Chance!" I heard someone call out.

I snapped out of my delirium. Addie had Tate in her hands, a half dozen others behind her similarly carrying children from the silo. My mom and dad joined Addie with Tate.

"Chance, let's go!" Addie said.

The five of us made our way through the chaos, around the farmhouse, and over to the dirt driveway out front. Latimer's truck was still where he'd parked it. My dad opened the door and found the keys on the dashboard.

"Everyone in!" he said.

We all climbed inside and Dad started up the truck. It rumbled to life.

"Wait, what about our things?" Mom asked.

"Forget it," Addie said.

"Or we can come back later," I offered.

Dad nodded. "For now, let's get the hell out of here."

B.C. Lienesch

B.C. Lienesch is an award-winning suspense author hailing from the nation's capital. A former freelance writer, featured columnist, and editor for guysnation.com, he is an author-member of the International Thriller Writers and the recipient of three 2024 LitStar Book Awards including Outstanding Book Series for his Jackson Clay & Bear Beauchamp Series. Born in Washington, D.C. and raised in Northern Virginia, he now lives in the same area with his wife, Meg, and their cat, Hitchcock. He's written four novels and his fifth, *Safe Harbor*, is due out mid-2026. https://www.bclnovels.com/

About Scares That Care

Scares That Care is an IRS approved, 501(c)(3) charity built by horror fans, for families with a child affected by illness, severe burns, or people fighting breast cancer. Founded in 2006, Scares That Care unites the dark fiction community to do good in the world.

The proceeds from this anthology will be donated to Scares That Care to help them continue their mission of compassion and care. To learn more about their work, get involved, or make your own donation, visit scaresthatcare.org.

One More Thing ...

Horror survives because readers talk about it. If A *Chronicle of Horrors* entertained, disturbed, or surprised you, please consider leaving a review. It helps independent horror reach new readers and ensures more stories like these can exist.

From all the authors—thank you.

www.ingramcontent.com/pod-product-compliance
Lightning Source LLC
Chambersburg PA
CBHW070209260626
47160CB00002B/494